Oᴘᴇɴ ᴛʜᴇ ᴅᴏᴏʀ...

OF JOHN DICKSON CARR

Before Dr. Gideon Fel̶ was the suave, sardonic M. Henry Bencolin of the Sûreté, John Dickson Carr's first detective. Bencolin solves four extraordinary cases about men who are murdered in locked rooms, disappear while surrounded by witnesses, or are strangled in a locked compartment on board a moving train.

THE DOOR TO DOOM is a rich selection containing three creepy horror stories written in the mid-1930's, two marvelous parodies of Sherlock Holmes (in one Queen Victoria is alleged to have sent Prime Minister Gladstone a bottle of poisoned whisky for Christmas), and a half dozen radio scripts from the classic series *Suspense*. These include "Cabin B-13" in which a young woman boards a ship with her new husband and after depositing her suitcase, discovers not only that her cabin has disappeared, but that her husband's very existence is denied by everyone on board. (This play was later filmed as *Dangerous Crossing* and starred Jeanne Crain and Michael Rennie.)

The book concludes with an exciting discovery: the complete version of Carr's famous essay on the art of detective fiction, "The Grandest Game in the World." For many years, the last half of this essay was believed lost, but it was recently rediscovered and appears here for the first time.

First Time In Paperback

Contains Previously Unpublished Material

JOHN DICKSON CARR

THE DOOR TO DOOM

EDITED AND WITH AN INTRODUCTION BY
DOUGLAS G. GREENE

LIBRARY OF CRIME CLASSICS®

MISTER E'S™

INTERNATIONAL POLYGONICS, LTD.
NEW YORK CITY

THE DOOR TO DOOM
and Other Detections

Printed and manufactured in the United States of America.
First IPL printing October 1991
10 9 8 7 6 5 4 3 2 1

CONTENTS

STORIES OF THE SUPERNATURAL

SHERLOCKIAN PARODIES

ESSAYS

Acknowledgments

I am grateful to the following people for sharing their knowledge with me and for helping to locate material for this book: Robert C. S. Adey; Edwin Bronner, Librarian, and Diana Alten, Manuscripts Cataloguer, Haverford College; Bill Blackbeard, Director, San Francisco Academy of Comic Art; Robert E. Briney; Lloyd Busch; Margaret Edgar, Programme Planning, Independent Television, London; the late Larry L. French; Hoa L. Gartman; David L. Greene; Michael Patrick Hearn; Edward D. Hoch; Allen J. Hubin; Ben P. Indick; Margaret Manuell, British Broadcasting Corporation; Dick Martin; Jan Mitchell, Old Dominion University Library; Jeffrey M. Nelson; Francis M. Nevins, Jr.; Justin G. Schiller; Ray Stanich; Derek H. Smith; Hildegarde Tolman Teilhet; George H. Walser; and Robert Weinberg.

Special thanks are due to the staff of Harper & Row who have, as a labor of love, contributed much to make *The Door to Doom* a tribute to John Dickson Carr: William Monroe, the production editor, Robin Malkin, the designer, Marge Horvitz, the copy editor, and above all Joan Kahn and Susan Arterian.

DOUGLAS G. GREENE

Introduction—
John Dickson Carr:
The Man Who Created Miracles

"For subtlety, ingenuity and atmosphere, he was one of the three or four best detective-story writers since Poe that the English language has known." In this tribute to John Dickson Carr, Edmund Crispin summarized the accomplishments of one of the greatest of all grand masters of the detective story. For almost fifty years, from the publication of his first stories in 1926 to his final novel in 1972, Carr created stories of terrifying suspense, of hints of the supernatural, of crimes committed seemingly without human agents. "Let there be a spice of terror," Carr wrote, "of dark skies and evil things." Striding through these adventures, bringing order and reason to the world, are four towering figures of detective fiction— Henri Bencolin, Dr. Gideon Fell, Sir Henry Merrivale, and Colonel March. John Dickson Carr was not only a master of shuddery atmosphere; he was also a genius of comic scenes. Sometimes in the same book, unspeakable horrors exist side by side with uproarious comedy. Part of Carr's mastery of the detective novel was this ability to combine the terrifying atmosphere of Edgar Allan Poe with the humor of P. G. Wodehouse.

Despite the fact that Carr wrote in the mood of neo-gothic horror or high comedy, almost all his novels are formal detective stories. No detective novelist was more scrupulous in giving every clue to the reader and in presenting rational explanations of all the seeming impossibilities. Carr handled clues, suspects and motives with such dexterity that few readers are able to predict the solutions.

Carr was, moreover, the unchallenged master of ingenuity of method. His books normally ask not only "whodunit" but "howdunit." Carr's crimes are committed in rooms all of whose entrances are locked; bodies are found in buildings completely surrounded by unmarked snow or sand; people enter a house or dive into a swimming pool and utterly disappear. And for fully three quarters of the novel Carr suggests that only a vampire, a witch, a ghost or someone lighter than air could have committed the crimes.

Although locked-room crimes and other apparent miracles have occurred in real life, Carr's novels may be called "improbable." Indeed, Carr gloried in that description; in reviewing a book by another author, he remarked: "that I of all people should complain of improbable solutions would be like Satan rebuking sin or St. Vitus objecting to the Twist." The real problem, as Dr. Fell points out in *The Three Coffins,* is that some people "gull the unwary into their own belief that 'improbable' simply means 'bad.'" Carr was less interested in whether a story is probable than in whether it is entertaining and believable. Carr's books are usually based on a series of events, motives, misunderstandings and even accidents which, individually, are normal and acceptable but which, taken together, produce something as monstrously unlikely as murder in a locked room. As readers, however, we are faced with an impossible crime before we know any of the reasonable events which produced it; we can discern no explanation but the supernatural until the detective makes everything clear.

Carr also made his stories believable by a punctilious attention to detail. When he described a room, he included enough vivid points so that, for the reader, the room is real. When he talked about such things as tarot cards, a watch in the shape of a skull, strange poisons, a transatlantic voyage or swordplay, he wrote with the authority of an expert. His early stories are as completely researched as his later historical novels, so that even though the crimes *seem* humanly impossible, the settings and the other trappings of the mystery are real.

Carr has sometimes been classified within the traditionalist school of the mystery novel, perhaps because he did not write either the brass-knuckles private-eye book or the detailed analysis of a murder from the viewpoint of the criminal. Carr insisted that certain elements cannot be eliminated from the detective novel. Good storytelling and plot must be foremost ("the one unforgivable sin," Carr said, "is being dull"). The story must be built around solution of the mystery—in short, a detective story must have detection. Characters should be believable and act with sufficient motives, but all facets of their personality cannot be revealed or there is no mystery. Such actors in a detective story are, of course, not so fully developed as in a "novel of character" (nor, indeed, should they be), but that does not imply that they are unreal. They are as real as are our views of most of the people we meet in everyday life.

But within the framework that the detective story requires emphasis on plot, on clues and on detecting, Carr was probably the most innovative of all detective novelists. During the 1930s he broadened the appeal of the detective story by combining its fundamental characteristics with other forms of popular literature. With *Devil Kinsmere,* published in 1934 under the pseudonym Roger Fairbairn, Carr may have been the first to write a historical detective novel. His first two stories for the pulp magazines, both written in 1935 and reprinted in this book, are what Carr called "mysteries-cum–ghost stories," with supernatural resolutions to human crimes. *The Murder of Sir Edmund Godfrey,* published in 1937, reconstructs a genuine murder of the past as a fair-play detective novel, with all the clues presented and the criminal identified. In the same year Carr wrote *The Burning Court,* probably the only detective novel to accept both the rational and the supernatural: it begins with an impossible crime, builds suspense by implying that a supposed witch is the murderer, then like other Carr novels finds a rational explanation. But just as the reader begins breathing a sigh of relief that the supernatural horrors have been dispelled, *The Burning Court* concludes with a second solution, that the witch has indeed used black magic to commit the crime. Carr's innovations were not limited to the early years of his career. During the 1950s he wrote historical mysteries which combine detection with the fantasy of time travel.

John Dickson Carr was born on November 30, 1906, in Uniontown, Pennsylvania. His father, Wooda Nicolas Carr, was a politician and a lawyer, and it was from reading his father's lawbooks and listening to his accounts of criminal cases that Carr first gained an interest in crime and detection. He was a voracious reader, enjoying at an early age L. Frank Baum's Oz books, the historical romances of Dumas and Stevenson, and Sir Arthur Conan Doyle's Sherlock Holmes stories. By the time he had entered his teens, he was writing for the local paper (owned by his grandfather) and continuing, as he later said, to improve his mind with sensational fiction. He was drawn to detective stories that feature solutions to impossible crimes—Jacques Futrelle's chronicles of The Thinking Machine and Thomas W. Hanshew's florid romances about Hamilton Cleek, "The Man of the Forty Faces." Perhaps the most important influence on Carr's writing was G. K. Chesterton's Father Brown stories, with their emphasis on atmosphere, paradox and of course impossibilities. In his college days Carr enthusiastically wrote that a new Father Brown book contains "the best detective stories of the year, and not even Conan Doyle has ever come within a pistol-shot or a knife-throw of them. We have haunted castles, winged daggers, vanishing men . . ."

Carr entered the Hill, a preparatory school, in 1921, and went on to Haverford College four years later. He became associate editor of *The Haverfordian,* a monthly literary magazine, in April 1926, and editor in June 1926. For the next three years, stories poured from Carr's pen; most of them reflect his abiding interests in the past and in crime. Five of his tales written at Haverford are historical romances of honor, treachery, love and loss, with such titles as "The Inn of the Seven Swords" and "The Dark Banner." He also wrote an important series of detective short stories about impossible crimes solved by a prefect of the Paris police, Henri Bencolin, often with the assistance of Sir John Landervorne (whom Carr enthusiasts will recognize from his major role in Carr's 1931 novel, *The Lost Gallows*). Carr's first descriptions of Bencolin were sketchy; we know little more than that he is about thirty years old, often dresses shabbily, and has a small stooped figure, a black beard and kindly eyes. But Carr soon sharpened Bencolin's character, and in the final Bencolin short story, "The Murder in Number Four," the detective has taken on most of the characteristics that he has in the later Bencolin novels. He looks like Mephistopheles; he has become an aristocrat; and he treats a suspect with contempt.

All these early stories illustrate a belief which Carr expressed as editor of *The Haverfordian* and which he never abandoned: "The things which are closest to the heart are fancies. . . . If we lived always in reality, we should all be poor things indeed. Truth? Is there anything more true than what one in his inmost self desires? . . . Realists are the people who look in a mirror and get disgusted. They are the ones who will explode all your fine ideas. They would pull down Kenilworth Castle and substitute an efficient gas-station; they would take the Lorelei off the rocks and substitute Margaret Sangers and Carrie Chapman Catts. . . . If we assume that there is a higher thing in fiction than the realistic thump of the janitor's mop, at least we do little harm. The most dangerous trap about writing is that an author finds it so easy to be scowlingly cynical on paper that he twirls round his Byronic tie and takes a leer at romance."

About 1928, Carr's parents sent him to France to study, or so they hoped, at the Sorbonne. Carr had done well at Haverford in history, literature and foreign languages, but he had come a cropper in mathematics, including (as Dr. Fell remarked) "algebra, economics and other dismal things." But Carr never attended the Sorbonne; he preferred to try his talents as a writer. He wrote and later destroyed a historical novel, and probably his next Bencolin story, "Grand Guignol," was written in Paris. When he returned to America, he sent the manuscript to *The Haverfordian,* which published it in March and April 1929 as a short novel of some twenty-five thousand words. Carr then revised the story, increased its length to about seventy thousand words, and promoted Bencolin from prefect to *juge d'instruction* (police magistrate) of the Sûreté. In the summer of 1929 he submitted the manuscript to Eugene F. Saxton of Harper & Brothers, and it was published early the next year under the title *It Walks by Night.* When the verdict of the buying public was in, the respectable total of fifteen thousand copies of *It Walks by Night* had been sold, and Carr knew that he would make his living as a detective novelist.

It Walks by Night, like most of Carr's work, was innovative while remaining within the tradition of the formal, fair-play detective novel. A short detour to examine one type of detective story that was popular through the 1920s will indicate Carr's originality. Many books written during that decade begin with the murder and present characters who are easily recognizable types—Chief Suspect, Least Likely Person, Suspicious Servant, Ne'er-Do-Well Nephew, Greedy Cousin, Helpless Damsel, and so on. The detective interviews all the suspects for chapter after chapter, writes lengthy timetables, investigates floor plans and examines myriad bits of physical evidence. There is little tension in the plot, and indeed in some books almost nothing happens. This type of story has been called the "chess problem," or less kindly, the "humdrum." In Carr's essay "The Grandest Game in the World," which is included in this book, he refers to some of the authors of these novels as "lady waltzers." He may have been thinking primarily of Carolyn Wells, whose once popular books about Fleming Stone are now almost forgotten. (Even though his own writing was quite different, Carr always retained a nostalgic fondness for Wells's novels, and in the late 1940s he purchased a complete collection of her mysteries.) Typical of her work is *The Gold Bag:* The victim is murdered in his study; the suspects have the simplest and most transparent motives; and all of them treated the study like Grand Central Station, visiting it on the night of the murder and divesting themselves of all sorts of physical clues ranging from railway tickets to wilted flowers. Eventually Fleming Stone enters the case and finds that the clues (and most of the book) have nothing to do with the solution. This is an extreme example of the chess problem; more accomplished authors, like R. Austin Freeman and F. W. Crofts, wrote much more convincing books. Nevertheless, the limitations of even the better tales are revealed in S. S. Van Dine's "Rules for Writing Detective Stories," written in 1928, in which almost every human element is forbidden. "There must be no love interest in the story," Van Dine proclaimed. "To introduce amour is to clutter up a purely intellectual experience with irrelevant sentiment. . . . A detective novel should contain no long descriptive passages . . . no 'atmospheric' preoccupations." Not all detective novelists followed Van Dine's rules to the letter, but even such notable writers as Agatha Christie and Dorothy L. Sayers, at least in their first novels, seldom showed concern for the emotions of those enmeshed in crime and detection. By the late 1920s and the early 1930s, however, many detective stories began to be presented as novels of human conflict. Ellery Queen in his early books agreed with Van Dine that detective novels should be an "intellectual experience," but he invested physical clues with freshness and excitement. It was John Dickson Carr, however, who most perfectly combined fair-play detection with suspense and atmosphere.

It Walks by Night almost seems a direct response to Van Dine's rules, and as it has much that is characteristic of Carr's work throughout his writing career, it is worth examining in some detail. The book begins with an eerie atmosphere by references to "night monsters ... with blood-bedabbled claws." In Carr's hands even an ordinary act like opening a door can be filled with terror and suspense: "When I turned the knob of that door it opened in an oiled lock, and the hinges were oiled and soundless, so that the movement of the door had the odd dreamlike quality of an opening gulf. . . . I saw, too, faint gleams from a perforated lamp, threading slow smoke against the weird moving rustle of the dark." Unlike Van Dine, Carr believed that readers would be involved in the story if it includes romantic interest. The narrator, Jeff Marle, an American living in Paris, becomes involved with Sharon Grey—though she is much more anemic than women in later Carr stories. Bencolin's kindliness in the short stories is downplayed in *It Walks by Night,* and his sardonic manner and Satanic appearance are emphasized. His black hair is "parted in the middle and twirled up like horns." His eyes, earlier described as kindly, are now "dark, veiled." His smile is "inscrutable"; his face is cruel; and he has a sadistic desire to make his prey suffer. Even in the "Grand Guignol" version of the novel, Bencolin admits that "I am fond of sticking pins in my fellow-mortals to see how they will react." In the later Bencolin novels, his tendency to be theatrical is exaggerated to the extent that he varies his costume depending on how close he is to pouncing on the criminal: "When he walks in evening clothes, with the familiar cloak, top-hat, and silver-headed stick, when his smile is a trifle more suave and there is a very slight bulge under his left arm— messieurs, that means trouble. . . ."

It Walks by Night contains Carr's hallmark, an impossible crime, and it has the typical Carrian plot development. The murder, beheading in a room all of whose exits are under observation, is one of the bloodiest in detective fiction. Carr's plots were strongly influenced by Chesterton's Father Brown stories, in which physical clues play minor roles and the crime is solved by discovering the pattern which the events form. Carr improved on Chesterton in one way: although the pattern is normally revealed about three quarters of the way into a Carr novel, the criminal is not unmasked until the final scene. Most Carr novels thus have two denouements, allowing him to explain his intricate plots gradually rather than in one undigestible lump at the very end. *It Walks by Night* might easily be used as a textbook of sound plot construction in a detective novel.

Bencolin and later Carr detectives discern the pattern not by examining objects left at the scene of the crime but by interpreting the emotional responses of the characters: their tones of voice, their half-completed sentences, their glances. Carr was uninterested not only in physical clues but also in formal police investigation, which he later described disparagingly as "machinelike." It might be argued that *It Walks by Night,* even with its locked room and "night monsters," could have been solved by checking fingerprints, but that misses the point. Carr believed that straightforward police procedure, including examination of fingerprints, is usually out of place in a crime that is not at all straightforward. "When you add the evidence of the cigarette ashes . . . [and] the fingerprints on the window," Bencolin says, "you add a couple of details which never interested me." Occasionally, as in *The Third Bullet* (1937) and *Nine—and Death Makes Ten* (1940), physical clues are introduced, but only to emphasize the impossible nature of the crimes, which are usually solved by other, less tangible clues. Carr summed up his attitude toward police procedure in the final Bencolin novel, *The Four False Weapons* (1937). Bencolin describes a hypothetical detective novel in which the victim wears a domino mask, is found with a teaspoon in his pocket, and all the clocks are turned to the wall. The reader, Bencolin explains, would feel cheated if such a case were solved by the discovery of the murderer's fingerprints on the victim's collar: "You would strangle the author, lynch the publisher, and shoot the bookseller." In later stories, Carr developed a wide variety of methods to avoid describing normal police investigation; my favorite is a short story in which the narrator comments simply: "Of course the police came. I do not understand such things, I am afraid."

After the publication of *It Walks by Night,* Carr married an Englishwoman, Clarice Cleaves, moved to England, and began a regimen of writing three to five novels a year. His next three books also feature Bencolin, but although they are well plotted, it is clear that Carr found some of the formulas of *It Walks by Night* constraining. Sometimes, especially in *Castle Skull* (1931), the oppressive atmosphere seems synthetic. The crimes continued to be grisly, and Will Cuppy's comment that one Bencolin novel has "abundant paraphernalia of horror in every direction" may indicate that Carr was overdoing it. To explain such horrors, Carr had to assume that the criminal was mad and therefore not limited to rational behavior and motives. Since Bencolin was supposedly with the Paris police, it became more difficult to ignore police procedure. Two of Bencolin's succeeding cases thus take place in England and Germany, where he cannot use the Sûreté's laboratories, and I suspect that *Poison in Jest* (1932), which is also narrated by Jeff Marle but which features a different detective, was first planned as a way to bring Bencolin to America. Carr, moreover, came to believe that he had made Bencolin too cruel in the novels. In 1937, some years after he had invented other detectives, he revived Bencolin in *The Four False Weapons* to show that the original Bencolin of the short stories was the genuine version of the detective. In *The Four False Weapons* Bencolin is again kind-hearted, and we learn that his sadism and theatricalism were merely "careful stage-trappings, which he found useful in his business." Obviously his promotion to *juge d'instruction* had affected the facets of his personality which he allowed the public to see. Incidentally, *The Four False Weapons,* with its extraordinary coincidences, is hardly major Carr, but as a commentary on the physical clues and alibis of the "lady waltzers," it is a fascinating work.

When Carr reacted against the flamboyant Bencolin (or at least the later version of the detective), he invented detectives in the opposite extreme. Patrick Rossiter of *Poison in Jest* is nondescript. Better but still rather bland is the elderly and "slightly drunk" John Gaunt of *The Bowstring Murders* (1933), written under the pseudonym Carr (later, Carter) Dickson. Detectives must be memorable, and Rossiter and Gaunt were too easily forgotten; but no one could forget Carr's great detectives invented in 1933 and 1934, Dr. Gideon Fell and Sir Henry Merrivale. Unlike Bencolin (and perhaps again as a reaction against him), Merrivale is stout and Fell is enormously fat.

Gideon Fell, Ph.D., F.R.H.S., has none of the sadism or sardonic manner of Bencolin. He was patterned on the appearance and character of Carr's idol, G. K. Chesterton, with a liberal dash of Samuel Johnson thrown in: "Vast and beaming, wearing a box-pleated cape as big as a tent, [Dr. Fell] sat in the center of the gaudy swing with his hands folded over his crutch stick. His shovel hat almost touched the canopy overhead. His eyeglasses were set precariously on a pink nose; the black ribbon of these glasses blew wide with each vast puff of breath which rumbled up from under his three chins, and agitated his bandit's mustache. But what you noticed most was the twinkle in his eye. A huge joy of life, a piratical swagger merely to be hearing and seeing and thinking, glowed from him like steam from a furnace. It was like meeting Father Christmas or Old King Cole." Fell smokes an obese meerschaum, at which he peers cross-eyed; he consumes countless tankards of beer with the comment *"nunc bibendum est";* his favorite exclamations are "Archons of Athens" and "by thunder." He is warm-hearted, genial, childlike and scatterbrained. Like a child watching a magician, Fell is seldom fooled by the trappings of a trick. His speech is full of non sequiturs and cryptic remarks which are natural to his woolgathering mind and which, incidentally, allow Carr to mystify the reader.

In his first appearance, *Hag's Nook* (1933), Fell is described as a lexicographer, but he quickly becomes a historian and many of his cases are dominated by a sense of the past—ancient murders repeated in the present, medieval artifacts, witchcraft and vampirism. In such mysteries as *The Crooked Hinge* (1938) and *Below Suspicion* (1949), he deals with surviving witch covens. Like his creator, Fell has a wide knowledge of esoteric facts and occult practices. He resembles Bencolin in one way: he doesn't depend upon physical evidence to discover the murderer. Although Fell once asks for a magnifying glass to examine bloodstains, he adds, "I'm not sure it would be much good to me. But it makes an impressive picture, and gives the user a magnificent sense of self-importance."

When physical clues are present in Fell's adventures, they are bizarre and seldom instrumental in the solution. *The Arabian Nights Murder* (1936), for example, begins with the clues of a cookery book, two pairs of false whiskers, and a photograph of coal on the wall of an Eastern stall. The type of evidence Fell prefers is listed in the 1934 novel *The Blind Barber:* the clue of suggestion, the clue of invisibility, the clue of terse style, the clue of avoided explanations, the clue of personal taste, the clue of misunderstanding, and the like.

Sir Henry Merrivale, holder of one of the oldest baronetcies in England, is both a qualified barrister and a physician. In his first adventure, *The Plague Court Murders* (1934), he occupies a room in the War Office with a portrait of Fouché on the wall, a whiskey bottle in the safe (labeled "Important State Documents") and a secretary named Lollypop. There he grouses about the ingratitude of the world, especially as represented by "that reptile" Inspector Masters, who is always trying to "do me in the eye." Although first described as a socialist, H.M. (as he is known to his friends) eventually succumbs to Carr's dislike of the Labour party and ends up as a member of the Senior Conservatives' Club. In "The House in Goblin Wood" (1947), the only short story about H.M., the Great Man is described as follows: "Out of the portals of the Senior Conservatives' Club, in awful majesty, marched a large, stout, barrel-shaped gentleman in a white linen suit. His corporation preceded him like the figurehead of a man-of-war. His shell-rimmed spectacles were pulled down on a broad nose, all being shaded by a Panama hat. At the top of the stone steps he surveyed the street, left and right, with a lordly sneer." Unfortunately, H.M.'s regal descent was interrupted when he stepped on a banana peel: "From the pavement, where H.M. landed in a seated position, arose in H.M.'s bellowing voice such a torrent of profanity, such a flood of invective and vile obscenities, as has seldom before blasted the holy calm of Pall Mall." Calming down, H.M. explains to a young lady: "My behind's out of joint. . . . I'm probably goin' to have spinal dislocation for the rest of my life."

Sir Henry Merrivale, his own belief to the contrary, is wildly undignified. His cleanest epithets are "Burn me" and "Lord love a duck"; he addresses a jury as "my fatheads"; he describes the Prime

Minister as "Horseface," the Commissioner of Police as "old Boko" and a member of the government as "Squiffy"; when he gobbles down his favorite drink, whiskey punch, his toast is "honk, honk" or "mud in your eye." H.M. enters his cases, as Carr said in a letter, "with a rush and a crash, heels in the air." During his investigating career, he drives a train and hits a cow, launches a ship by hitting a mayor on the head with a champagne bottle, disguises himself as a Moslem holy man, causes a riot in the New York subways, dictates scurrilous memoirs, and takes singing lessons with disastrous effects on the ears of everyone in the vicinity. In short, the Sir Henry Merrivale books are probably the funniest detective novels ever written. But despite all this, H.M. is not a buffoon. Like Dr. Fell, he has a "childlike, deadly brain." While "sittin' and thinkin'," he can sort out all the facts of a case and perceive the pattern they form. The comedy of the H.M. stories is often used to conceal the clues. "Once we think an author is only skylarking," Carr said, "a whole bandwagon of clues can go past unnoticed."

Shortly after inventing Dr. Fell and Sir Henry Merrivale, Carr decided to try his hand at writing short stories for popular magazines, and in 1935 he published his first short tales since the early Bencolin stories. "Terror's Dark Tower," which is reprinted for the first time in this book, is one of his best stories about murder in a sealed room. The explanation of the seeming impossibility was so good that Carr later reused the central gimmick in a Dr. Fell story, "The Wrong Problem," but with a new plot and a setting that lacks the excellent evocation of the moors in "Terror's Dark Tower." Soon Carr was in demand as a short-story writer. Dorothy L. Sayers had increased the market for his work with a perceptive review in which she wrote: "he can create atmosphere with an adjective, alarm with an allusion; in short, he can write—in the sense that every sentence gives a thrill of positive pleasure." By the late 1930s, his stories were appearing in such major magazines as *The Strand* and *The Illustrated London News*. Most of these adventures describe miracle problems solved by Colonel March, head of Department D-3, "The Department of Queer Complaints," to which Scotland Yard sends all cases that seem to have no rational explanation. Colonel March, like Dr. Fell and H.M., can hardly be described as thin. He resembles "a stout colonel in a comic paper," with a florid complexion, bland blue eyes and a sandy mustache. Interested in puzzles of all sorts and with a large supply of useless knowledge, he investigates such cases as the murderous disembodied hands and the murder in a room which doesn't exist. Seven of his adventures were collected in a Carter Dickson book, *The Department of Queer Complaints* (1940), which Ellery Queen has called "one of the most important [books] in the modern school."

During the 1940s Carr's productivity declined to only one or two books a year. Much of his time was occupied in writing and narrating propaganda broadcasts for the British Broadcasting Corporation, with titles like "Black Gallery: Heinrich Himmler" and "Women on the Guns." He also wrote mystery dramas for the BBC and for the CBS network in the United States; some of his best are included in this volume. After the end of the war he concentrated on writing his definitive biography of Sir Arthur Conan Doyle. But although he was pulled in several different directions, Carr maintained the high quality of his novels. The Dr. Fell book, *The Case of the Constant Suicides* (1941), perfectly integrates uproarious comedy, two locked-room crimes, and a Scottish setting where "all the earth was rich and breathing with names, with songs, with traditions, with superstitions." Another Fell case, *He Who Whispers* (1946), almost has the reader believing in vampires; it is one of Carr's most satisfactory combinations of chilling atmosphere and fair-play detection. Sir Henry Merrivale was faced with ingenious impossible situations in the Carter Dickson books of the middle 1940s. *He Wouldn't Kill Patience* (1944) tells of murder within the most inaccessible locked room in fiction, with all the doors and windows sealed with tape on the inside. In *The Curse of the Bronze Lamp* (1945) the heroine disappears almost before the eyes of the onlookers. But by the later years of that decade Carr's books, though still well worth reading, were showing a few signs of becoming mechanical. Dr. Fell occasionally crossed the line dividing Johnsonian formality from meaningless posturing. H.M.'s adventures began to emphasize comedy to the extent that the mystery became insignificant. Carr was, however, not content to continue producing the same kind of books, and he began almost a second career—as author of historical novels.

To understand why Carr decided to set his mysteries in the past, we have to examine his attitude toward the world. It has been argued that the formal detective novel appeared with the growing dominance of the middle class, which valued law and order as a way to protect property and profits. A crime, therefore, threatens the structure of society, and the state must restore order by punishing the criminal. Carr's attitude was quite different; in fact, criminals in his books are often not punished at all. In *The Mad Hatter Mystery* (1933) Dr. Fell and the police allow the murderer to escape justice because they sympathize with him. Fell burns down a house in *The Man Who Could Not Shudder* (1940) to allow another murderer to go free. "You surely don't imagine," he remarks in *The Case of the Constant Suicides,* "that I mean to confide any of my beliefs to the police. . . . My present purpose (between ourselves) is to swindle the insurance companies." Even Henri Bencolin, himself a policeman, pays little attention to the law: "I can tamper with the law when, where, and how I like. I have tampered with the law when, where, and how I liked, and I will do it again." Sir Henry Merrivale is constantly disrespectful toward authority, and like Fell, he sometimes helps the criminal to fool the police. In *Behind the Crimson Blind* (1952) he blows up a ship in Tangier harbor to cover up the crime because he likes the criminal's wife: "Cor! Before I'd let 'em break that gal's heart by arresting her husband, I'd have upset the government of hell and kicked Satan off the smoky throne! Don't come any moralist nonsense over me; it won't go down. Don't try any blatter about 'law' or 'justice'; we both know they don't exist, unless we go out and get 'em for ourselves."

Why, then, must the puzzle be solved if not for law or justice? Because the mystery threatens the happiness of the protagonists and more fundamentally because it questions the rationality of the universe. The locked rooms, disappearances and other miracle crimes with their hints of black magic challenge our belief in rational cause and effect. If we don't carry the comparison too far, Carr's detectives act almost as exorcists; they dispel the devils and demonstrate that the seemingly supernatural events were created by humans for human motives. Sometimes an impossible crime occurs merely by chance—in H.M.'s words, "the blinkin' awful cussedness of things in general"—but Carr's books are detective novels, not theological tracts, and he avoided discussions of the role of chance in an ordered creation. It is enough that the devils are proved fictions and rationality is restored.

Carr did not believe in a static world in which middle-class values of law and order are protected, but rather in one in which high adventure is possible. Many of Carr's protagonists in his early novels are Americans escaping their brash moneymaking society for the traditions of England and France. The lawyers and college professors through whose eyes we often see the story long to break out of their stodgy, predictable lives. "What sort of adventures did I ever have?" asks Professor Tairlaine in *The Bowstring Murders*. His friend replies, "What do you mean by 'adventures' anyway? Do you mean in the grand manner? A slant-eyed adventuress, sables and all, who suddenly slips into this compartment, whispers, 'Six of diamonds—north tower at midnight—beware of Orloff!' " "Yes," says Tairlaine, "I suppose I did mean something like that."

Carr's stories are generally based on upper-class life—London clubs, castles, town houses, first-class accommodations on ships: "If you can't afford to travel first-class," says one of Carr's characters, "then don't travel at all." Carr praised virtues that are often considered aristocratic—honor, chivalry, fair play, generosity. Even someone who is poverty-stricken must live by those standards. Kit Farrell, a young lawyer in *The Curse of the Bronze Lamp,* is admirable because he takes someone to a ritzy restaurant which he can't afford, insists on picking up the tab, and then lives on "sardines and biscuits for the rest of the month." The criminal in the same book is nasty because he lives off others. Carr supported an individualist code in which the proper way to settle disputes is man to man. Hauling someone before a judge and jury is dishonorable. Bencolin calls dueling a "decent honourable affair, much more sane than dragging a dispute through the law courts to have one's wounded heart healed with franc notes." In some Carr books which are set in the contemporary world, "duels" are fought in the name of sportsmanship. Although Alvarez, one of the heroes of *Behind the Crimson Blind,* is badly wounded, he still agrees to box with an expert because of "sportsmanship. That's my God. That's all I ever worshipped."

After the end of World War II and the election of a Labour government in Britain, Carr found it difficult to express his values in novels taking place in modern England. To escape socialism, Carr moved back to the United States in 1948, and he decided to concentrate on writing detective novels in period settings. Some fifteen years earlier he had tried his hand at the historical mystery with *Devil Kinsmere,* but that book had not been a popular success. His historical novels of the 1950s, however, received both popular and critical acclaim. *The Bride of Newgate* (1950) is one of his best books. Set in England in 1815, it features a former fencing master, duels and swashbuckling action. The next year Carr published *The Devil in Velvet,* which sold more copies than any of his other novels and which Carr always considered his finest work of historical fiction. This book clearly reveals Carr's changing attitude about where adventure in the grand manner can be found. In Carr's novels of the 1930s an American could escape his stodgy existence by visiting England or the Continent, but by 1951 Carr believed that adventure is almost absent from the modern world. In *The Devil in Velvet* a middle-aged professor makes a bargain with Satan to carry him back to the England of King Charles II. Like many who find the twentieth century dull, he did not merely *wish* to live in the past: "How I longed for it," he exclaims. "How I writhed on a bed of nettles, as men scarify themselves for money or women for social position!" In two other Carr novels, *Fear Is the Same* (1956) and *Fire, Burn!* (1957), the hero is magically transferred from the twentieth to the late eighteenth or early nineteenth century. In other stories Carr found romance, honor and adventure in Napoleonic France, Victorian England, pre–Civil War New Orleans, and even the American South of the 1920s.

Carr's historical novels are characterized by meticulous research into the sights, the sounds and the language of the past. When Carr wrote, for example, of swordplay (as he often did), he knew what he was talking about, for he owned a collection of swords and he was himself an accomplished swordsman. His books conclude with "Notes for the Curious," which discuss the sources for the novel and carefully separate fiction from fact. And it was in such books that he could most clearly express his attitudes toward the world. In *Fear Is the Same* the Prince of Wales, as eloquently as Dr. Fell or H.M., states his belief that honor and fair play are more important than legal guilt or innocence: "Whether he is innocent I know not and at the moment I care not. But fairly he has met his enemies and fairly he has beaten them all. And now, when he is wounded and alone, shall he be pulled down by a pack of yapping curs? No! I think not." The Prince then leads the hero away from the representatives of law and order: "Drunken, untrustworthy, selfish though he might be, [the Prince] was still the first Gentleman of Europe." As long as one has a gentlemanly code of conduct, all else fades to insignificance. In effect, the Prince of Wales acts on Sir Henry Merrivale's belief that justice exists only when we go out and get it for ourselves.

Although Carr placed most of his later stories in the past, he remained a detective novelist. His historical novels seldom have a formal detective (and of course, they have no police procedure), but each has a mystery that must be solved. The solutions of his final novels are as fairly clued and as ingenious as his earliest stories. In Carr's world locked rooms and other "miracle problems" are as likely to occur two or three centuries ago as they are now, and swordsmen of the past have the ability of Fell, Merrivale and Bencolin to discern the pattern in an apparently unrelated series of events. Carr's fifteen historical novels have had great influence on many recent mystery writers. Anthony Boucher made a perceptive remark about Carr's contributions to what he called the detective-story-in-a-period-setting: "The current popularity of this form, which so attractively combines the appeals of the whodunit and the historical novel, certainly dates back . . . to Carr's *The Bride of Newgate;* and equally certainly no one is consistently so successful in this hyphenated genre as Carr."

In 1951 the Tories won the British general election, and Carr returned to England, where he remained until 1965, when he moved to Greenville, South Carolina. After 1972, because of increasing ill health, he wrote no more fiction, but he continued to contribute a lively book review column to *Ellery Queen's Mystery Magazine,* and he retained his interest in the past, writing the first in a projected series about seventeenth- and eighteenth-century criminals. Although the series was never completed, the installment about highwaymen stands well on its own, and it is included in this volume.

The Door to Doom and Other Detections is offered as a memorial and a tribute to the genius of John Dickson Carr. The best of his previously uncollected work is included to show his mastery of various types of mystery writing, from his first short stories of the 1920s and 1930s to his last essay, written in 1973, four years before his death. In this book I share the joys of those who are becoming reacquainted with the world of John Dickson Carr, and I envy those who are reading the works of this grand master for the first time.

DOUGLAS G. GREENE

Notes on the IPL Edition

The Door to Doom and Other Detections, first published eleven years ago, is now reissued as the third volume in International Polygonics's omnibus collections of John Dickson Carr's short stories. Each of these collections is centered on one or more of Carr's great detectives. The first volume, *Fell and Foul Play,* features stories about Dr. Gideon Fell, and the second, *Merrivale, March and Murder,* collects the short cases of Sir Henry Merrivale and of Colonel March, head of Scotland Yard's Department of Queer Complaints. *The Door to Doom* contains tales that, at the time of Carr's death in 1977, were unknown (or nearly so) even to his greatest fans, and its centerpiece is comprised of the four short stories of Carr's first sleuth, Henri Bencolin of the Surete.

This edition of *The Door to Doom* differs from earlier printings in including for the first time the complete version of Carr's famous essay on detective fiction, "The Grandest Game in the World." Carr wrote this essay in 1946 as an introduction to a never-published anthology of ten detective novels. When the essay was first printed in *Ellery Queen's Mystery Magazine,* March 1963, half of it—the section containing Carr's analyses of the novels he chose for the anthology—was omitted. After the publication of the shortened essay in *The Door to Doom,* a full typescript was discovered, and it appears on the following pages.

To make room for the complete "Grandest Game in the World," the Carr checklist that was published at the end of *The Door to Doom* has had to be omitted. That checklist, however, will soon be superseded with the publication of a new Carr bibliography that will, I hope, be included in my forthcoming biography of John Dickson Carr.

DOUGLAS G. GREENE
March 1991

STORIES
OF
CRIME
AND
DETECTION

" 'As DRINK THE DEAD . . .' " is John Dickson Carr's earliest known story, published in 1926, when he was not yet twenty-one years old. It is a fitting introduction to his work, for it contains many of the plot devices that would bring him to the top of his profession. Like many of his later stories, it combines mystery and historical romance and it revolves around apparently impossible events. Why do some people who drink from the Devil's Grail die of poison, yet others suffer no ill effects? Does God use the Grail to determine who shall live and who shall die? Are ancient crimes imitated in the present?

" 'As Drink the Dead . . .' " is an overture to the ingenuity of Carr's short stories about Henri Bencolin. "The Shadow of the Goat" piles impossibility on impossibility until we are certain that the murderer is in league with spirits. "The Fourth Suspect" has not only a locked-room murder but also several unexpected plot twists. "The Ends of Justice," as its title indicates, is concerned with one of Carr's major themes, the relationship between law and justice. The Bencolin short stories culminate in the brilliant miracle problem of "The Murder in Number Four." How can a man be murdered in a railway compartment with its single door bolted on the inside and two witnesses who swear that no one approached the compartment? Or is the Blue Arrow indeed a Ghost Train?

Henri Bencolin is portrayed in these stories as he was in his younger days, when he was merely one of the eighty-six prefects of police in France. By the time of the first novel about Bencolin, *It Walks by Night* (1930), he had been promoted to *juge d'instruction* and, probably as a result, he has become more elegant in his dress, less relaxed and more theatrical. Whatever guise Bencolin decides to adopt, we admire a detective who refuses to reduce "an intricate crime ... to the silly restricted rules of mathematics." Bencolin knows that the great detective, like the great criminal (or, we might add, the great detective novelist), is successful because of his imagination. Carr later remarked that "we must not be gulled into thinking that the picturesque never happens, and discourage writers from any dangerous use of their imagination."

"As Drink the Dead . . ."

"I AM DOING," said von Arnheim, "a novel about the Borgias. And that is why I have come. I should like to see your della Trebbia cup."

They sat in a deep room where there were candles on the table, so that their faces hung in a golden glow. People called von Arnheim the old German gnome; he looked more than unpleasant now, his shaggy beard drooping from an outthrust face—a beard that should have been on a heavy, spreading body, and went badly with von Arnheim's little bony one. But the other man's face softened the picture, for it stood out from the space like a saint's on a lighted church window. It was white, and white-haired, and the eyes were gentle. Merely those old faces in an Italian room, with Italy out beyond the long windows—portrait frames on a sky which showed the dark spires of poplars along whose top clung a cluster of stars.

"You, my friend," von Arnheim continued, "are an expert. You have a house crammed with the Middle Ages. There was once blood on your floors, I dare say. I know the worth of your treasures, because I also am an expert—in my line. Here I have come to write my novel, which will be a supreme effort—"

"Wait," said the older man. "You wanted to see my della Trebbia cup. Why?"

"Pardon me. There were two," von Arnheim told him, screwing up his face in folds. "Garcini della Trebbia made two such cups, each of which he called 'The Devil's Grail.' "

"Blasphemy!"

"Well, blasphemy, if you like. But a picturesque touch. He was a blasphemous man, was della Trebbia, and he said that his grail should contain blood of the devil, just as the other— Ah, then, we shan't speak of it! It deserves to be forgotten. But he made those cups, as I have reason to believe, to poison Pope Alexander VI and his son, Cesare Borgia."

"Other blasphemers!" cried the white-haired man.

"I agree! . . . The accepted story is that in 1503 these poisoning prelates were not content with all the wealth and power they had amassed through murder, and so they set about the destruction of some luckless wretch. . . . May I smoke, signore?"

It was a sharply false note to see a cigarette lighted there, among the swarthy magnificence of old Italy. But von Arnheim lighted one, and the smoke lay like incense. He went on:

"They were to feast with their victim at this very villa, signore, and they had already prepared the deadly wine. On their way here, as the story goes, they grew thirsty. By mistake, attendants brought them their own poison. . . ." He shrugged. "That would have been poetic justice, my friend, if it had occurred. If it had occurred! Of course, I am not sure that the legend is wrong. That is why I want to see your della Trebbia cup."

The tall Italian got up, white and stately.

"You are a very great man, Herr von Arnheim, and your visit flatters me. Naturally I shall let you see the cup. But these matters —these Borgias—God help them! In His mercy He removed the pope who mocked him—"

"Listen, my friend," interrupted his guest, speaking fiercely out of the shaggy beard, and with a kind of ascetic eagerness. "Do you care to hear of the affair as I have written it? You must understand my own version before you show me the cup, for they say that never in history has one drunk from it and lived. Now, I have here a bit of manuscript, which I must finish when I see the cup. What is its secret, signore? They have scoured it, and found no poison. Yet one drinks, and then one dies."

"The will of God . . ." said his host.

"The will of God," agreed von Arnheim, "if you wish it. Only listen to me awhile, and I will read you a few paragraphs. I believe they set forth the truth; perhaps I shall finish this book entirely before I leave the villa di Cornetto."

"One delights in the productions of a von Arnheim. . . . Your pardon if I sit by the window. There are voices," said the man vaguely, and went to one of the high slits in the darkness. He sat down, enthroned, and the bluish light brought out the side of his face and body.

Von Arnheim opened a portfolio at his feet. He was very eager, but there was something deeper than that in his manner. When he began to read in his thin, vigorous voice, it gathered up the scene into old Italy. Lanterns crept out of the garden in a breath of melody.

Von Arnheim read:

> Now Mistress Lucrezia Borgia was very fair to look upon, for her eyes were calm, and her hair was bright yellow as candle shine, and there was red beauty in her lips. About her was the lure of dim rooms, warm with kisses. Yet Mistress Lucrezia had been made all ice and fire, with hatred in her heart as a gift from her father, His Holiness Pope Alexander VI. Many husbands had she been given also, but only with Alonzo of Aragon, fierce as the Sahara, had she been even friendly. And there are those who whisper that she loved, once, the youth Garcini della Trebbia.
>
> You must remember that Mistress Lucrezia was then in the most serene republic of Venice, and that it was summer of the year 1503. Strange dragons of boats swam the canals, which by night were a far shimmer of torches on water. But in distant avenues, where came no swish of singing oar, lived Mistress Lucrezia, and only the moon sought her. Only the moon sought her, until up over a balcony reached by gondola would come young Garcini della Trebbia. And he would lounge before her, with his dark handsome head flung back and the moonlight shining on the strings of his guitar. Stars were flung up against the sky, with his body silhouetted stark and black against them. She would rest on cushioned dimness with her long cloak lying loose about her, so that the gleam of her white body showed through it. . . .
>
> They say that this Garcini della Trebbia was a student, working far into the night with books and metals. They say that in the yellow dawn he held up tubes of chemistry, where bright liquids seethed like his eyes. He loved Lucrezia as one loves in Venice.
>
> And while he played she would tell him wondrous tales of her father's cruelty; of how his unyielding will held her prisoner from the

arms of men. Then would the guitar sing and tremble with a wilder note as the dark melody throbbed in hatred. . . .

Von Arnheim had paused, but the enchantment clung like an echo of laughter. The German leafed through his manuscript; he went on:

There was a smash and roar of trumpet blasts, like a world of sound to rock Rome. And the long shout was taken up and flung in a clashing of hoofs through the Piazzi di Rusticucci to the square of St. Peter's, for Cesare Borgia rode to the Vatican. All black-clad he sat among the swaying spears, all black-clad amid the rich hues of his retinue. This man could swagger in the saddle. You saw first of all the gleam of teeth through the brown beard. . . .

It was an opportune homecoming for the Duke of Romagna. Now might he share the estate of a cardinal, whom his father had recently done away with. Besides, there were plans with His Holiness for making new cardinals, who paid well for the post and who could afterwards be quietly poisoned to make fresh ones. Ah, this Duke of Romagna was clever!

The lance butts thumped and jangled, and rows of steel came flaring back the sunlight, and a great square opened as Cesare dismounted. They were cheering him in hoarse masses; in he strode for the audience with his father, where the white wolf-faced pope blessed him when he knelt. Then they walked in sun-flecked halls while His Holiness told how soon they should set out for the villa di Cornetto, where another cardinal was to be done to death. Even as he spoke, the lines of halberds flashed beneath their windows, and trumpets sang a mighty tune for the beginning of the journey.

Through the whole of the reading the poplars wore dark cloaks, and mourned the dying stars. Von Arnheim's voice kept the same level tone. It was a Borgia room now, and even the German felt it as he continued:

Being of excessive thirst, His Holiness and Cesare, when they arrived at the villa di Cornetto, called for wine. On the terrace above a shallow fountain, blacked with water, they stood among hawkish peering faces and men clothed in doublets which were poisonous with jewels. Cesare's doublet was sable, and his father's long robe white, but the pope's face, pinched with craving, seemed to belong upon the other man's body, and Cesare's silken beard upon His Holiness. One would have been startled, as though by something devilish they wore wrong heads. . . .

Goblets were handed them upon a salver, twin silver goblets wondrously wrought, with wide chalices and small stems curving into handles. And in the background lounged Garcini della Trebbia, watching them, stroking a guitar.

Lifting these cups, the two Borgias drank to some better future. They did not finish the wine, but set the goblets upon the balustrade. Then into the villa through the long windows went the entire company, for it was growing dark.

On the terrace the light was fading, and the poplars were black as sorrowing ghosts, but atop that crumbled balustrade the twin goblets flashed fiery. A light shape beside them, a shadow on the sky with eyes of poetry, sat Garcini della Trebbia, flicking the guitar. They tell that as the last glow died on the cups, before the candle shine from the rooms had crept to the feet of Garcini, there came a cry. . . .

It was moments later that the glaring cardinal rushed to the terrace, sword in hand. Pope Alexander VI, inside, was still screaming, and Cesare was choking ugly words.

Through the half-opened doors in the candlelight, Garcini thought he could see the pope writhing on the floor, with oyster eyeballs that stared horribly. But he thought also that the room was filled with a vast throng of people who had not been there before. He thought that all these people were dead, and that Alexander saw them beckoning, smiling, stroking him with hands whose veins were poison-puffed. . . .

"They are dying!" the cardinal cried. "They are dying—and they have taken nothing but the wine in the cups you prepared, della Trebbia!" He snarled at Garcini, who only smiled. Then he put the point of his sword against the young man's breast.

"There is wine still in them. Drink!"

"It was the hand of God," Garcini made answer. "I will show you," and he took up one of the cups by its edges and drained it. The sword point did not waver even after he had emptied the second.

The tale runs that the terrace faded into darkness, but still those two were motionless beyond the clamor of the villa, and the long blade did not waver at Garcini's breast. Finally the doors behind were crowded with faces, so that a burst of candlelight fell upon the black statues of the two men.

"It is God's way," Garcini said. "Behold that it is God's way! I live, though he hath struck down the mockers. I live, because there is no poison in the cups!"

The cardinal's sword fell ringing at his feet.

Von Arnheim got up and shrugged. He laughed, throwing off the spell.

"Now, signore," he said, "the answer! What is the answer?"

"It is in your own irony, Herr von Arnheim," the Italian answered.

"Be fair with me: were you sincere in what you wrote about God's way?"

His guest made a gesture of disgust, and the bony face fumed under his beard.

"Ach, the surest test of bad writing! . . . Signore, I have lost it!" he exclaimed. "My touch . . . yes, it has gone, as I feared! How does an outsider react to this?" He tapped the sheets. "Why, coldly, as you have done, and analytically. Well, well, we shall try to improve it!"

He looked acutely miserable as he gathered up the manuscript. But his companion knew that he was afraid, because he kept opening and closing one hand, staring at it as though some lost magic had been there.

"Wait!" the former protested, rising. "You misunderstand, my friend. See, I am affected! Look at me, von Arnheim, and see my eyes. You see my eyes?"

Von Arnheim studied him.

"Savonarola might have looked as you look. . . ."

"That is idle. It is yourself again; you, who are so great a cynic that you can afford to pose as a true believer. In your irony you indicate some secret means, some hidden poison by which these men were killed. . . . Are there not pages you refused to read me? But," said the white-haired man, "you have overstepped so far that you were right in your irony. Whose hand killed the Borgias—thieves, blasphemers, despoilers of the sacred office? I say, God's."

"I respect you, signore. Well?"

"You intimate that some preparation—"

"I wish only to see the cup. Seeing it, conceiving of an explanation for my final chapters . . . ah, that might help me. I tell you I have no longer my touch!"

There was nothing more helpless and baffled than his mood. He kept clenching his hands wearily.

"Come!" said the Italian. "I will show you." He struck on a bell, while von Arnheim lay back in his chair, eyes closed.

There were ghostly steps in the house, moving along the passages, passing through the door of the room where old days were present. When the servitor appeared, it was well that only his face was visible, showing monklike and pale, for the man might have been trembling. He was frightened.

"Monsignore . . . rang? It was you?"

The older Italian did not notice it. But von Arnheim did. His eyes flashed open as the servitor asked insistently:

"Has monsignore been upstairs?"

"No, no . . . I have not stirred from the room. Go quickly, if you please, and bring me that della Trebbia cup."

"It was not you I saw. . . . lying on the bed in your room? Please, monsignore, it was not you, a few moments ago? Very white, with four candles burning around you . . . sleeping?"

His employer's eyes were on distant things, and so there was only a shake of the head in reply. But the servant bumped against the door in leaving the room.

"Oh, the devil!" muttered von Arnheim. . . .

It was only a few moments until the door opened again, but they were moments of uneasiness. The two men waited on either side of the table—a vast, narrow oblong with four candles burning at its corners. Returning, the servant noted von Arnheim leaning forward, chin in hand, with his eyes fixed on the light. Upon the table he placed a dull twisted cup, struck with bright flecks from all the candles, but old with ugliness.

"Go," said monsignore.

Again came the steps, with the turn of scared face over shoulder.

"There was," the servitor stammered, "an indentation of a head on the pillow. . . ."

Alone again, von Arnheim put out his hand to the cup. But monsignore restrained him, crying in a sudden harsh voice:

"Look, my friend! It is the same as when they drank from it that day! Its mate has been lost, but a Borgia drank from this one. Monster! . . . No alchemy kills men in the way you indicate, and spares others. Only God does that. . . ."

He did not realize that to the German he was very theatrical, and would have been absurd but for his eyes. The blood of Dominican friars was beating in his temples, transforming his face to a living crucifix.

And then it was that he took a decanter of wine from a table and poured some of it into the cup.

"See! I can drink from this devil's grail of yours, Meinherr! There are no chemist's tricks to it for me!"

Von Arnheim did not move, held by the instinctive drama of the Italian. He saw the long hands curve over the handle of the cup, and its dull gleam swept up to hide the eyes. In mockery now the old man set it down.

"You are a fanatic," von Arnheim said quite suddenly, "but so am I."

"Can you write your conclusion now?" asked monsignore, growing calmer. "Can you say that whatever the story may be, accidental or intended killing—"

"Yes," said von Arnheim thoughtfully, "yes. Your emotions are a stimulant, whether they convince me of God or not. . . ."

The bearded face was ugly now, but brilliant with thought. He ran his fingers lightly over the cup; they trembled.

"Yes," he continued, "and I am going to do a strange thing. I am going to write one scene here—now—and I shall read it to you, because I think I have the explanation. Listen, signore; your Italian emotionalism has made me . . . upset, but I can write. Ah, I can write!"

The other man sank into a chair. His splendor was gone now, and only the ruined tomb of it remained.

"Yes," he responded, "we are both fanatics. . . ."

Von Arnheim was smiling with the set vacant smile of the creator. He reversed a sheet of his manuscript and drew out a pen. There was a recklessness about him when he began to set down phrases, a dash and verve that are tokens of something beheld for the first time.

"Listen! . . . It is night in Venice, you see; it is night, jeweled with fire, caressed in star shine. A night to stir drowsy blood and set questionings in breathless eyes. . . .

Up over the white balustrade he swung, with a whirl of cloak like wings against the sky. Beside the lounge, under soaring arches, he dropped on his knees. There was a white arm about his neck now, and a breath stirred in the shadows where Mistress Lucrezia waited. His lips trembled with fear when they found hers, but hers did not tremble with fear alone.

Night in Venice under the moon . . .

"I rode by swiftest horse," he muttered, "to tell you—ah, it is done!"

Von Arnheim did not look up, but he felt monsignore's shadow cross him, for the man had risen. It may have been that he tried to speak. Wrote the German:

> . . . and her voice was drowsy when she spoke.
> "Done, my Garcini? Riddles . . . What mean you?"
> "They are dead! I tell you your father at least is dead!"
> Horror now, seeping through dulled brain, more sickening in physical languor than among judges. For Mistress Lucrezia had reckoned only to dallying with this madcap boy. . . .

Monsignore did not cry out. He was incapable of it. He dropped limply over the table. The white back of his head shone in the light of the four candles, and the tablewood reflected part of his face. Von Arnheim swept on:

> "Yes, it was the cups, Lucrezia—was it not clever?" he cried. "It was in the handles of the cups! They are heavy. To drink, one is led to take them up by the handles, unless one knows. They are sharp metal, they are ponderous—one does not realize that hidden there is a spring. Pressure on the handles releases it. . . . One tiny flick in the fleshy part of the palm by the fingers . . . that is not felt! But in a few moments, Lucrezia, a very few moments, one feels the dull dizziness of a poison that is eternal. . . ."

The cluster of stars over monsignore's head had faded, and the room grew wan, but the man across the table did not stir. Nor did von Arnheim move, even though his voice droned on, fashioning the syllables as he wrote. Hysteria and power were now in his pen. Pages followed the paling stars into immortality. At length the German threw down his pen. He rose, shaking his head.

"I have regained it," he said, glancing at his watch. "Yes, I have regained the old touch. . . ."

Then his face was expressionless as he strode forward and struck the bell.

"Down here, fools! Down here! The last of the Borgias may be dying! Will someone fetch a doctor? The signore has poisoned himself!"

The Haverfordian, March 1926

The Shadow of the Goat

IT WAS a thoughtful room, and tobacco smoke clung round the edges of the lamp. The two men who sat there were thoughtful, but that was not the only point of similarity between them. They had the same worried look of persons too much interested in other men's affairs. Sir John Landervorne had once come from that vague section of London known as Whitehall, and he had been possibly the only man in the city who might have given police orders to Scotland Yard. If M. Henri Bencolin was only one of France's eighty-six prefects of police, he was not the least important of them.

Fog had made London medieval again, a place of towers and footsteps and dim figures. It blurred the windows of the room in Fontain Court, the backwater of Fleet Street where the barristers sometimes walk in their ghostly wigs, swinging canes like swords. In the room the two men, sitting opposite each other with white shirt fronts bulging exactly alike, smoked similar cigars—Bencolin with his black beard, Landervorne's beard gray as the cigar ash. It gave one a weird feeling: picture of a detective at thirty, then a picture of him at sixty. Their eyes were somber.

"If you tell me your story," said Sir John, "you will have to tell it to Billy Garrick, because these are his rooms, and he will be in presently. But it will be safe; he was there last night too."

Bencolin nodded. He spoke rather wearily.

"I know it, my friend. Of course, I did not telephone you officially —I am not connected officially with the matter. Well! Last night near Worksop, in Nottinghamshire, M. Jules Fragneau was murdered. That is why I wanted to see you."

"Then," said the Englishman, "I shall have to tell you a story which will not interest you, unless you believe in sorcery. Because, you see, the only man who might have killed Fragneau walked through a pair of locked shutters at ten o'clock last night."

"The report is true, then. Oh, the devil!" Bencolin fretted.

"The report is fantastic, and true. I saw Cyril Merton go into a room that had only one door, which was bolted and which I was watching. The room had only one window, barred, with locked shutters. There was no fireplace, nor was there any secret means of egress; the walls were stone. Exactly that. It was a stone box. But I tell you Merton went into the place—and vanished. Lord Brandon and Garrick, who were with me when we searched it both before and after the disappearance, will verify what I say. Afterwards an even stranger thing occurred. For surely Merton killed Fragneau, and then he very nearly committed another murder, at which time I saw him evaporate before my eyes. That, my dear sir, is witchcraft, and," he added thoughtfully, "I am a sane man. At least, I think I am a sane man."

M. Bencolin got up. Fog had crept in and mingled with the tobacco smoke; the Frenchman shivered. He looked small and shrunken, and very tired. With the cigar protruding ludicrously from his mouth, he began to wander about the room.

"My friend, I am beaten. Name of God!" he said fiercely. "I am beaten! I thought that I had enough impossible riddles in my case. But unless we can prove he made a phantom of himself a third time, and got into a locked house, a poor stupid fellow named Fulke will be indicted for murder. Of course these events are connected! Tell me the whole story, please."

Sir John sat back in his chair. His face was pinched with thought.

"Very well. There's a preface, you see, about Cyril Merton. Give Merton a wig and a sword, and he would be your seventeenth-century swashbuckler—but you must grant him a wig. For though he was tall, and rather strangely handsome with a thin luminous face in which you saw every emotion as through glass, the man's head was shaven. He had studied in Germany before he became an actor, and his ugly nature got him into duels with the saber, which left scars on his head. The scars were so hideous that hair only made them worse. So he kept his head shaven, criss-crossed white. But the beauty of his face, with the short dark beard, kept him from being ridiculous.

"He was our greatest actor. If you saw him in any of the old romantic plays you know the medieval soul of the man. He could turn himself into any sort of character; that was his genius. The man's hobby was sorcery and the deadly arts, in pursuit of which he had a library stuffed with forgotten books—the works of Hermes the Egyptian, Lillius, Geber, James Stuart, Cotton Mather, all of them. He belonged in a day when they burned such men.

"That was why he bought the place. Bell House is on a tract of ground that was once a part of Sherwood Forest, about thirty miles from where Fragneau lived. Bell House! You can see the tower of the bell lifted over the trees, with a hill of silver birches white in the moonlight, and the wind moving them. It was built when William the Norman darkened England with a hurricane of swords, and there are clanking ghosts in its halls. That was a dirty, snarling age—church and the devil frightening the soul out of people, big men in armor, faces caked with blood, butchering in nameless filth —the very bogey house of history. Why, the moat around Bell House is twenty feet deep.

"I have to tell you about a dinner Cyril Merton gave. There was the banquet hall, with pointed windows of painted glass, and the candles shining on them; I remember the white shirt fronts, the cigar smoke, the flashing teeth when people laughed. One gets a series of impressions in a shadowy place like that. For example, I remember the picture of Billy Garrick with Madeline—maybe because Madeline is my daughter—on the staircase after dinner; on the staircase under the dark portraits, and the candles. They are both yellow-haired, handsome as old Saxons. It was an absurd gesture on his part, but the place for it: he kissed her hand.

"They are in love, and I have an especial interest in Garrick for that reason. I was worried about him that evening. Billy is a nephew of Jules Fragneau. Because the old man had been rather more than his father, and made him his heir, Fragneau's enemies were Billy's enemies. Which was the reason why Merton, who hated Fragneau almost to the point of idiocy, never got along with the lad. He had been forced to invite him because Billy was my guest, and I was too close a neighbor to be omitted. For the same reason Billy had been forced to accept. All through the evening I felt uneasy.

"It all culminated in a foolish argument in the smoking room. The men had assembled there by a big blazing fireplace, with stags' heads, and all that. Having just come away from Madeline, Billy was in an exultant, swaggering mood. He smoked cigarettes and laughed at Merton, who was holding forth on his hobby of medieval magic against Lord Brandon and Mr. Julian Arbor. He was standing against the mantelpiece, black beard, shaven head, using that smile with which he argues.

" 'I was telling you,' said Merton, 'about the book of Gersault de Brilliers, published by Meroit, Paris, in 1697: 'Contes du Diable,' with a subhead: 'Avec L'Histoire de L'Homme Qui Savait S'Eva-nouir.' One of the accounts deals with a man who walked into a locked room and vanished utterly. De Brilliers put it down to sorcery, which is possible. But a perfectly practicable kind of sorcery.'

"Mr. Julian Arbor protested. Arbor is a strange sort of English gentleman; doesn't at all object to helping out people who are financially in a hole—at tremendous interest. Just a polished form of moneylender. The man looks kindly, but he has a hard glaze on him like a tombstone. He protested gently: 'My dear fellow—'

" 'Bosh!' struck in Billy Garrick. 'Bosh, Merton!'

"It was a typical gathering, with a mass of stuffy landed proprietors who always have the look of just having eaten too much. Bald and florid and oratorical as the elder Pitt. Lord Brandon is one of these.

" 'This, sir,' observed Lord Brandon, 'strikes me as being a great deal of foolishness.' He waddled to the fire, waving his hands.

" 'Nevertheless, it happened,' the actor replied. 'It can happen again.'

"Billy was just a bit drunk. He protested furiously:

" 'Look here, Merton, you're usually so aloof that nobody contradicts you. And this grand superiority complex of yours is making me tired! If you can stand there and talk solemn stuff like that—'

" 'It can be done,' said Merton quietly. 'I can do it myself.'

"He was always one to play to an audience, and he enjoyed the consternation he created among that group of squires, smiling at his cigar.

" 'You mean, Merton, that you can walk into a locked room—a real locked room—and disappear?' asked Julian Arbor.

" 'Trap doors!' snapped Billy instantly.

" 'There are no trap doors. I say that I can go into a stone room here at the castle, have you lock doors and windows, and I can vanish. Just that.'

" 'Bosh!' repeated Billy.

" 'See here,' said Merton, 'if you want my opinion, even a host's opinion, your talk is damned impertinence.'

" 'And if you want mine,' said Billy, 'yours is damned nonsense.'

"Merton was furious; the glass face lit like fire.

" 'We'll drop your gutter behavior for the present; it can be argued later. Garrick, do you want to wager me a thousand pounds that I can't do what I say, eh?'

" 'Oh, I say!' cried Julian Arbor. 'Don't be a fool!' He turned to Billy in alarm. 'Surely you won't—Merton, I refuse to allow—'

" 'What have you got to do with it?' demanded Billy, who was angry too. 'Keep out of this, sir! Merton, I shall be glad to see you make an ass of yourself. I accept your wager.'

" 'If Mr. Merton will allow me, I accept it too,' Lord Brandon interposed.

"Merton laughed.

" 'Are there any other takers, gentlemen?' he said casually."

Sir John paused. Bencolin had sat down, and was staring at him. The Englishman lighted another cigar before he resumed.

"Well, the thing was fantastic, but it was done. Only Mr. Julian Arbor would not remain to see the wager carried out. He said he had to catch a night train for London, departing with somewhat jarring abruptness—"

"For *London?*" demanded Bencolin. "London? Pardon me; go on."

The words had been rather like a yelp. Sir John smiled.

"I was surprised, I must confess, but there were other matters on my mind. Merton was carrying off the affair with theatrical grace. We had to tell the ladies, who suspected some sort of joke, but insisted on following us. And yet the big halls, the weird unnatural-ness of the place, got their nerves on edge; Madeline enjoyed it. The others began a shrill rush of talk, which gradually slowed and stopped like a run-down gramophone. Anything was better than the unnatural sound of those voices.

"Merton took us upstairs. We were a solemn company, parading the halls with candles. That castle was too big for us, and the moon was too far—it followed us along every hall, peering through the windows. Once Merton paused by a window, the silhouette of him with the moon behind his head; his face jumped suddenly out of the dark as he lighted a cigarette by the candleflame, and then it vanished. The silhouette contorted as though the man were dancing.

"He led us to an immense room, quite bare, so that you could see only the aimless candles moving under people's faces. At its far end was a door, which Merton threw open. It communicated with a flight of steps, walled with stone and having at the top another door. On the threshold Merton paused, with a kind of bluish glow behind him.

" 'This,' he said, 'is the room itself. I should prefer that the ladies did not enter. Come along, Lord Brandon, Sir John, Garrick too—examine it. I shall go in here. You will bolt the door at the bottom of the steps on the outside, and watch it. First go over this staircase to be sure there is no other exit.'

"Somebody laughed a bit nervously. Merton finished his cigarette while we moved around the flight of steps. Then—"

"Wait!" Bencolin interrupted. "Please don't describe it; don't describe the room. I am going to see it, and I want to form my own impressions. It might lead me astray if I heard too many details. But one thing: was there a washstand in the place?"

Sir John's heavy eyes flashed open.

"Yes! Why do you ask? That washstand was a curious thing to see there. . . ."

"Go on, my friend."

"We will say, then, that the room was large and odd. Garrick, Lord Brandon and I went over every foot of it. Intact! A window in a big stone embrasure was firmly barred. We closed and locked the shutters. Then we pronounced ourselves satisfied, Lord Brandon red and puzzled. As we were going out, Merton stopped us. He stood by the table in the light of a lamp of blue glass, but only his absolutely pallid hand protruded from the shadow, toying with a little ebony figure of . . . a goat. Garrick, as tall and threatening as he, said: 'Anything more?'

" 'Lord Brandon,' Merton answered, ignoring him, 'I am doing a dangerous thing. If I make a mistake, if you have any cause to think that such is the case, at the end of fifteen minutes come up here instantly! You promise me that?'

"Brandon promised—"

"One moment," said the Frenchman. "Did you look in all the table drawers?"

"My dear fellow," Sir John returned petulantly, "a man can't hide in a table drawer, or escape through it."

"Of course not. Well?"

"The last thing I remember was Merton standing by the table, playing with the tiny goat's figure. It was as though he were deliberately trying to call our attention to that image."

"He was. He may have been trying to give you a clue."

"Oh, come! What do you mean by that?"

"I don't know; it merely struck me as curious. You went downstairs?"

"We went downstairs, yes. I bolted the lower door on the outside. Then it began. We found that we had left all but two of the candles in Merton's room. There we were, a blundering, half-frightened crowd in a gulf of a place, candles tossing. Nervous laughter, figures moving about us. I had one of the lights, and kept it on my watch. Fifteen minutes—dragging. And women talking, and talking. But I never lost sight of the door, nor did Lord Brandon, who was standing in front of it. Somewhere in the house I thought I heard hurrying footsteps, and once the sound of water running. Finally there occurred the thing that broke our nerves like somebody jumping on you in the dark.

"It was an explosion, the terrific noise a pistol makes when it is fired indoors. Brandon and his following would have rushed the door even had not somebody shouted, 'Time's up!' The cry ripped into a screech of the bolt and a rush of feet up the stairs, but I remained in the background to make sure nobody slipped past those who entered. Nobody did! I went up slowly, examining the stairs, and joined the group at the door when I was certain of it—"

Suddenly Sir John crashed his fist down on the chair arm.

"Merton was gone! No one left the top door; the others stood guard while Brandon, Garrick and I searched the whole apartment. We were in a kind of frenzy. Shutters fastened, bars untouched; as a matter of fact, there was dust on the bars. No Merton, no hidden door. Some sort of weapon had been fired there, for a faint tang of powder was in the air, but we found no weapon. The blue glass lamp burned dully, fixing our eyes like a crucible, and a bit of smoke hovered over it like waving hands. . . . But in spite of it all, I know that before we came nobody had either entered or left that door!"

And, as later events proved, Sir John spoke the absolute truth.

II

Lamplight had made the thickening smoke in the room a yellow haze. Both Bencolin and Sir John Landervorne looked weirdly unnatural. Bencolin said:

"That statement, my friend, would be ridiculed in a court of law. We can prove nothing on the man now—don't you see? Under the circumstances of Fragneau's death, either the man Fulke or myself, the only other occupants of his house, must have killed him. Fragneau was stabbed about twelve o'clock last night. Merton disappeared at ten, easily in time for him to have gone thirty miles by motor. There is nothing more inconspicuous than the driver of an automobile at night. Now, then, at twelve-fifteen, or thereabouts, I telephoned you at your home, because I knew that you lived close to Merton. It was no burglar's work, because nothing had been stolen at Fragneau's home; the only person who might have killed Fragneau was Merton, and I wanted to check up on his whereabouts instantly. There would be no possibility of his servants lying as to his movements if I communicated with *you*. Your butler told me that you were at Merton's, and had not returned. I left a message for you to call—"

"At twelve-fifteen," interrupted the Englishman, "Madeline, Garrick and I were returning to my home. In that interval Merton had not appeared. The question being: if he was perpetrating a joke, why did he not return? We waited two hours before we reassured

the servants and left. But in the vicinity of one-thirty, Merton *did*
come back. We will connect that up with the story later. Tell me
about Fragneau."

"The very devilish simplicity of it, my friend, is that I have no
story. You know Fragneau. His hobby was astronomy; I will not say
astrology, because it was there that the Merton-Fragneau feud
began. Every time I have visited his house he has shown me some
new device to keep out burglars. He had a big glass dome of an
observatory on the roof, an open place, so that in this fanatical fear
of intruders there was an iron fence, ten feet high and electrically
charged, around the entire roof. The house being small, every window had its own protective fastening. On each of the two doors was
a lock for which no duplicate key could be made! Imagine it—the
place was a fortress. Fulke, a big, awkward, red-haired fellow, was
his new servant. I remember his wooden face at the door when I
arrived, hair tilted over its side like a vivid wig—and the white-lit
dome uncanny up against the night sky, with Fragneau's shadow
flickering over it.

"Facts, these. At eleven o'clock Fragneau went over the place,
adjusted all his devices, locked his doors. We had been talking,
but he insisted on working in his laboratory as a nightly ritual.
I was not interested, and went to my room to read. It overlooked the front stairs. At twelve I grew tired of reading, at which
time I started for the observatory to bring him down for a final
cigar. . . .

"Fragneau sat before the telescope with a stupid grin on his face.
His chest was heavy with blood where he had been stabbed with a
bone-handled knife a very few minutes before. The glare of light,
the white-pointed face like a goat's, the yellow shaft protruding
from his chest, all calm as sleep.

"I summoned Fulke; the house was searched, the doors and
windows found locked. Neither of us had heard an intruder. We
calmly went about questioning each other; then I put in two telephone messages, to you and to the local police. That is all, except for one point. At twelve-thirty a man rang the doorbell and
asked to see Fragneau. . . . Once," added the Frenchman
abruptly, "when I learned that Fulke was a new servant, I con-
ceived a theory as to the assassination. Now it is all dark, con-

sidering what you say, unless . . ." He paused, and smiled.

"Unless what?"

"Unless, in a manner of speaking, Cyril Merton washed himself down the drain. To give you more than an indication—"

"Bencolin," demanded the Englishman, "are you insane? Great God!"

"Wait! Please wait! You would be insulted if I continued. My friend, I think the motive in this affair is money. Do you know who rang the doorbell half an hour after the murder? It was Mr. Julian Arbor."

III

A gust of colder air blew in from the foggy corridor as the door opened. Bencolin was still straining forward, elbow on the table, the fingers of his hand crooked toward Sir John. And as a third figure, lean and tall in its greatcoat, came toward them, they had the appearance of people in a storm. The newcomer took off his hat, displaying eyes of a rather brilliant vivid blue in a face glistening like wax. The eyes struck Bencolin with the suddenness of rifle shots; they had a wretched, terrible appeal.

"Hello, Sir John," he said hoarsely, croaking with a cold. "This the M. Bencolin you came to see? My name's Garrick, sir. Well, every dragnet in England is out for that damned murdering— Start a fire, will you?"

He sat down, shivering, and threw off his coat. His arm was in a sling.

"I—I just left Madeline. She was crying. . . ."

There was an odd strained silence. Then Sir John got up blunderingly and began to heap wood in the fireplace.

"He didn't suffer," said Bencolin. "I mean . . ."

"I am glad to hear it," replied the young man. They did not see his face.

"My friend," the Frenchman began, "God willing, we will find Merton."

He paused, but the words had something like the ring of an oath. Then he looked at Garrick's arm. "The second victim! When did he attack?"

"It was about one-thirty. Sir, the thing is too incredible! Are you sure Merton is a *man?"*

"Steady!" warned Sir John.

"Well . . . I had gone to bed. It was bright moonlight in the room, hard and clear as glass. I was fuming about Merton, just drifting to sleep, when I heard someone cry out."

Sir John paused with a lighted match in his hand.

"I was at one window across the quadrangle," he interposed. "My room. I could not sleep. Then I saw a shadow move. The moon shone on a head that was perfectly white. Something began climbing the ivy toward a window on the second floor, and when I realized whose window, I knew who that person was. I could not help screaming to warn Garrick—"

"It saved my life," the other said calmly. "When I sat up in bed, a silhouette reared up over the windowsill, but I saw the white head. And then," he rushed on, "it came at a kind of bound, like a goat. The light from the open window was blocked as it got me; I felt the tangle of the bedclothes, the rip into my arm of a pain, blinding and sickish like ether. My arm began to grow hot, but I fought him. Somehow he tore away— Sir John, are you *sure* nobody left by the door?"

"I would swear to it. Listen, Bencolin, for your final riddle. After I cried out, I ran out of my room. In the central hallway I met Dorset, the butler who took your message. I didn't explain, but I told him to hurry outside and stop anybody who came out by a window. Don't you see? If we were in time, we had Merton trapped! Doors were banging open in the house, lights flashing on. When I reached Garrick's door the lights in the corridor were blazing. Behind the door was the furious wheezing and thudding of a fight; a chair clattered over; somebody began to run. The door was bolted, but it was flimsy wood. I battered it until the bolt ripped out. Billy almost ran into me —and before him there was a shadow. I switched on the lights, standing in the door, and for one instant the picture was hideous and sharp and motionless as waxworks. Billy, full white on the square of gray moonlight, with a sheet trailing him, his arm running red as though it were alive. The intruder was gone! We hunted the room over, after which I called to Dorset. He answered that nobody had left by the window."

"He was going for the door!" Garrick cried excitedly. "Then you opened it in my face. And yet I touched him a moment before!"

Bencolin sat with his head between his hands; Sir John was standing by the fireplace without moving, and held the charred curl of a match. Fog had seeped into the room until the lamplight was all but obscured.

IV

Bencolin had not slept for twenty-four hours. If the man who had listened to the amazing recitals of Sir John Landervorne and Billy Garrick the night before had been neat, correct as a picture, then it was somewhat of an apparition which went stamping about Bell House the next day. Unshaven, with a battered hat stuck on his head like a helmet, the man resembled a conception of an early Goth. He had been seen early in the morning standing against a red tattered sky among the mists at the edge of the moat, and he was poking in the water with a walking stick.

This was no England of the sort called merrie, of Robin Hood and warm leaves and gray goose feather. It was stern as the Norman. And the work which presently occupied the constables under Bencolin's direction was sterner still. Through the November morning they were wading in the moat.

When, after a while, he entered the big silent house, there were only a few servants for him to question. Their employer had not returned, and yet they were fearful to leave. While he explored every dusty corner, he could hear the solemn tramp of feet. Finally he went upstairs to the tower room. It was there, in the afternoon, that those he had summoned found him.

The afternoon sun, an ugly rose color, shot across the room like a spotlight from the window embrasure. It rested on the closed door of a closet, which Bencolin had earlier in the day explored and found empty. In the middle of the apartment stood the table with its tiny goat's statue, so that the sun outlined on the closet door a monstrous figure of a goat. When Sir John Landervorne opened the door to the room, he saw only that shaft of light in shadows, beyond which was the glow of Bencolin's eternal cigar. The Englishman shuddered, fumbling at his beard.

"That you, Bencolin?" he asked. "Ugh! What a place! Shall we come in?"

"I see no reason," protested a voice behind him, "for dragging us up here from London! I told you everything you wanted to know last night." It was Julian Arbor, who pushed past Sir John; though he seemed angry, not a muscle in his big white face moved.

"The matter is serious," Bencolin responded. "Will the rest of you come in? Lord Brandon? Thank you. And Mr. Garrick. Who's that?" His nerves were jumpy, and he leaned suddenly out into the light at the sound of another voice.

"Madeline insisted—" said Sir John.

"I did!" a little voice confirmed him, laughing. The girl looked light as though she might be blown by a wind, with a sort of half beauty in her face that was rather better than loveliness. White-clad, she moved forward. "Mayn't I stay? You've promised us a solution, and I want to hear it."

"Sir John, this is impossible!" the Frenchman snapped.

"I won't go," said the girl. "I have as much right to be here as anyone."

Bencolin stared at her; at the sight of his face a movement went through the watchers. They knew why. In that room was terror.

"Merton is here!" said Bencolin.

That was it—terror. Sir John began thickly, nervously:

"Go out, Madeline; please go out. My God, what are you saying?"

"He is here," went on the Frenchman, "he is in this room. Lord Brandon, stand in front of that door. The rest of you sit down, and whatever happens, do not move."

In the half darkness somebody stumbled a little. Bencolin had stepped in front of the window. Against the reddish light they saw his profile with the high hooked nose and bearded jaw. The energy had gone out of him; his shoulders were stooped, and he stared out thoughtfully into the sky.

"It's an odd case," he said. "It's the only case on record in which a man proves an alibi for his murderer. And it shows many curious things. For example, there is that appearance of Mr. Julian Arbor at Fragneau's house after the murder—"

"Look here," snapped Arbor, and he came into the light with his big white face intent. "I told you I was there, I admitted it. But what does that mean? It doesn't show that I killed Fragneau, if that's what you think! It doesn't show that I had any criminal intent—"

"Of course not," said the Frenchman, "but what does it show? I mean, you have been telling me what it doesn't show; now I ask you what it does show." He did not turn from the window, but he went on rapidly: "And what does the white head of this midnight prowler show?"

"Why, that it was Merton." Sir John stared at him oddly.

"You are wrong. The white head shows that it was *not* Merton."

"Then you say," Sir John cried, "that Merton did not stab Garrick?"

"Not at all. Merton did stab Garrick."

"Well, why didn't Merton come in the window, then?"

"Because he was dead," said Bencolin quietly.

There was a sudden silence like the stroke of a gong. They all looked at Bencolin as though he had gone mad and were gabbling calm nonsense.

"You will find Merton's body in the closet behind you, Sir John," continued the Frenchman. He turned full about, and he did not raise his voice when he spoke again, but it had a horrible sound of finality:

"Open the closet, Garrick. One of your victims is inside."

V

Garrick stood looking stupidly before him, his hand moving in a tiny futile gesture. The others were perfectly motionless.

"We got his body out of the moat this morning," Bencolin said with dull flat monotony, "where you threw it. Open the door!"

A tiny space separated Garrick from collapse. He looked down at his feet. There was a trickle of water crawling from under the door.

"I—can't," muttered Billy Garrick.

"Listen! You killed Fragneau."

"Yes. I killed Fragneau." The reply was mechanical. Sir John suddenly sat down, with his head between his hands.

"Shall I tell them how it happened?"

"No!"

"But I will, Garrick. You and Merton were in debt to Julian Arbor.

You arranged this impersonation, you and Merton, so that by following your own example, Lord Brandon and others would wager five thousand pounds. Really, some sort of plot was obvious when I knew that no such book as 'Contes du Diable' exists! Julian Arbor did not know, which was why he protested against a wager in which either of you two must lose. You are exactly the same height as Merton—Sir John said so—and of his build. When he went to his room he put into effect the genius at impersonation that Sir John has mentioned. He shaved off his beard, he wore a wig which he had prepared in that table drawer, and cosmetic touches under the lights completed the effect. It was his genius! Remember: candle-light! Nobody could detect it. There might have been a slip only in the *voice,* but you had a cold, the same cold you have now, and hence it was easy. After the door had been bolted on the outside and Merton had completed his preparations, he went to the stairs and waited, flat against the wall by the lower door. On his way down he fired a blank cartridge, which was the one thing that would send the watchers flying pell-mell through the door. It was dark; Brandon had no candle, and could see nothing before or behind him except the lighted door at the top of the stairs. Those who came through the door felt only jostling bodies—Merton mingled with them and went upstairs again *as you.* You had already slipped down into the house and out of it; remember that Sir John did not see you from the time he left the tower room until after he had entered it again in search of Merton, and that he heard footsteps in the house. Nobody was watching any door except the one behind which Merton had locked himself. Nobody saw you go out. For the space of the next three hours *Merton was yourself.*

"But you had a deeper motive when you connived with Merton for this impersonation. Ostensibly it was a mere matter of winning the money bet by Lord Brandon and dividing it; that was how you obtained Merton's assistance. Your real motive was murder. Your real motive was in establishing an alibi for your presence at Bell House while you motored to Fragneau's home. Diabolical cleverness of it! You could not conceivably be accused of the crime when all unknowingly Merton had proved you to be at Bell House while Fragneau was being killed. And you meant Merton to be accused of the deed instead!" He turned to Sir John. "Think, my friend! Who would be the only person in the world who would have a key to that Fragneau house? Why, the man Fragneau trusted, the man who was his heir! Did that never strike you as logical? Fulke did not know, because Fulke was a new servant, and I nearly overlooked the possibility because you, Sir John, had sworn Garrick was at Bell House the entire evening. Garrick needed money; therefore Fragneau, he reasoned, must die. The winning of a fortune, and Merton punished for the act. But because Merton had established his alibi, Merton too must die, or otherwise the plan would be revealed.

"What does he do? He lets himself into Fragneau's house, kills him, and returns. Meanwhile Merton, masquerading as Garrick, has been forced to go home with Sir John. He retires immediately, lets himself out of the window, and goes back to Bell House, where he has arranged to meet Garrick that they may change identities again before daylight destroys the complete reality of the make-up. At the edge of the moat Garrick meets him. Ah, don't you see it? The struggle by the water, where Merton, almost wresting the knife from Garrick before the latter stabs him, wounds Garrick in the arm. Then Merton's death, the sack filled with stones into which the body is stuffed, the disappearance into the water. It is done! For though police authorities might search Bell House for a living Merton, they would never search the moat for a dead one.

"Garrick, wounded, returns from Bell House to Sir John's residence. As he crosses the lawn Sir John sees him, but imagines very naturally that it is Merton, whom he has no grounds to suspect dead. Yellow hair in the moonlight makes an excellent 'white head'; try the effect of it for yourself. Garrick hears Sir John's warning cry; he knows that he is trapped unless . . .

"Then," cried the Frenchman, "what occurs to this master sorcerer? Why, Sir John has fancied that Merton is attacking him; why not pretend that such was the case, else otherwise Garrick could never explain the wound in his arm? It dovetailed perfectly! Garrick strips off his clothing, dons pajamas, and tears the bandage from his arm, allowing the blood to flow. Something like four minutes elapsed before Sir John came to the room. Garrick scuffles with himself in the dark, invents an ingenious story which is the only thing that will save him from discovery. Out of near catastrophe he has produced another attack that will be ascribed to Merton!"

VI

The tensity had gone out of them all, and there remained only the ruin of tragedy. False emotional stimulant left a sickish after-feeling. Arbor and Sir John had moved away from Garrick. All the elaborate mummery that had been gone into seemed cheap and tawdry as a music hall illusion. Here was simply a felon.

Bencolin made a little gesture of weariness.

"Eh, bien!" he murmured. "You do not find it pleasant, you do not find it even clever. It upsets every beautiful tradition of a story; not only have we shattered our hero, but there is not enough of the theatrical in him to follow a story formula and kill himself. Because reality is infinitely more childish than the stories about it. Messieurs, you have lived an allegory. What do you make of it? And how do you explain the chance that made Mr. Arbor, irritated by this blind wager of those who could not afford it, leave Bell House and go to Fragneau's to demand recompense for his nephew's debts?"

Rather absently Sir John put on his hat.

"Well . . ." he said without looking at Garrick. Lord Brandon opened the door. He had not spoken. There was nothing in his face but contempt.

Julian Arbor muttered, "You gutter rat!" somewhat incredulously. A constable had come into the darkling room and was going toward Garrick. The latter's nerves were entirely gone; he had slid down to the floor, and Bencolin thought he heard him moan just once. The Frenchman was speaking softly:

"We should none of us fancy that we are devils. Merton did, because he could take any form at will, like Satan, who appeared at the witches' sabbath in the form of a goat (that was why he kept calling your attention to the goat). . . . Somewhere we people of the old school thought that there was faith, and honor, and loyalty. We do not believe it now, Sir John. We have seen the other side of youth. . . . It is our last illusion, as the impersonation was Merton's. . . . We do not think it now, Sir John. . . ."

It was almost dark in the room now. The others were all at the door, except Madeline Landervorne. She had come up steadily, and she was bending over the man on the floor, and as she knelt, her eyes glittered with tears.

"Billy," she said, "I don't believe them. I don't believe them!"

The Haverfordian, November, December 1926

The Fourth Suspect
Another Adventure of M. Henri Bencolin

IT HAS always been a matter for wonder to the Paris newspapers, which adore the spectacular, that M. Henri Bencolin did not rise to higher rank in his profession, and that he was not head of every detective bureau in France. The sober ones shook their heads, opining that it was because he had far too much imagination, so that he worked out his cases with an eye to the dramatic rather than to the truth. They cited, for example, the murder of his countryman Jules Fragneau, which had caused so much of a stir in England. True, the little Frenchman had solved a problem which baffled the best heads in Europe, but he introduced so much unnecessary theatricality that his man almost escaped. On the other hand, more knowing people decided that the innate sentimentality of the man worked against him; at odd moments he might be found dreaming at the opera, or buying wine for Bohemian friends on the left bank, or consorting with beggars whose obviously false tales drew large sums of money from him. He, whose business was truth, never seemed able to detect a falsehood which was practiced on himself. Nevertheless, when a member high in the War Office wired for help in a matter which had kept the lights burning late in the departments of government, there came the reply: "WE ARE SENDING YOU THE BEST IN THE BUSINESS."

High up burned the lamps that night on the Quai d'Orsay, over the black Seine and the tracery of lights, the singing lights of Paris, as murmurous as an old waltz. Like all good Frenchmen, Bencolin loved his Paris. He loved the pink-and-white-flowered trees, the hurdy-gurdies, the gaiety that is almost sadness. And something of it all touched him when he entered Villon's office in response to his superior's order.

In the big oaken room sat Villon behind a great plateau of a desk. He claimed descent from that other Villon who had once grinned over Paris like a gargoyle, and he had an odd intent expression now on his face—large and bald, with a loose underlip. His eyes were all pupil points. The capacious head was said to contain more information than that of any four men in France, and it was likewise said that he never forgot a fact. He merely sat and stared at the door until Bencolin's knock roused him. Then he rose.

The little detective came shambling in with his rather apologetic air. Bencolin's eyes were kindly and squinting; Villon could picture the stooped figure, black beard, high nose, all redolent of cigar smoke, even with closed eyes. Bencolin had a top hat stuck rather rakishly on his head; his cloak sagged after him when he advanced to the desk.

"M. le Comte," he said, "my greetings. Your agents found me listening to Mme. St. Marie's singing. I gathered that the message was urgent."

"Sit down, monsieur. A cigar? My dear Bencolin, I sent for you for obvious reasons. We have not forgotten your work on the 'newspaper' murder of the Rue des Marchands, nor your more recent adventure in England (though we were forced to deprecate your assumption of authority there, monsieur)." Villon nodded his big head slowly, like a wooden mandarin. Then he said abruptly: "You did well to listen to Mme. St. Marie, my friend."

Bencolin sat down and lighted a cigar. The office was silent awhile, almost as though it were empty under the brilliant light.

"She sings divinely," Bencolin remarked, blowing a cloud of smoke.

"Bah! I must correct you there. She has no great voice; she will never appear in the opera. She is only a gypsy, a winking red-haired gypsy whom men want to kiss because the sight of her affects one like the touch of her. And yet, my friend, last night I thought that she was guilty of murder."

He spoke unemotionally. Bencolin shrugged, and waited. His companion looked faintly disappointed, the pinpoint eyes blinked, but he went on:

"In these days after a great world war, it is almost ridiculous to speak of spies or espionage. Yet there is such a man near Paris. He is a spy exactly as von Stumann was a spy ten years ago. For what reason, or in the employ of what nation, we do not know; that is the worst feature. Why does one have spies in peacetime? Who should be interested in knowing what goes on in our councils? What of our finances, our battleships, our code signals? We do not publish such information broadcast, yet this man has it, because we have detected him. And we cannot punish him, monsieur, because the world is at peace. Such information may be even more deadly to us now than ten years ago. Italy, England, America, Germany . . . You have often been called upon to investigate the spy of war, my friend. Now you are called on to investigate the spy of peace."

"And you want me to discover who he is?"

"No!" Villon said triumphantly. "We know the man. But you have been summoned because he was shot through the head last night. Listen to me, Bencolin. The person who called himself LaGarde had a brilliant mind, a mind handsome as his face was handsome, but he was indiscreet. He carried with him constantly some paper whereon was written his commission, *and the name of the government which commissioned him.* We know it because we have a letter, in a very childish cipher, boasting of its possession. Some say he had an accomplice, a woman, but we do not know. Don't you see? Living, LaGarde with this commission was a danger. But dead, he may be fatal. That commission has not been found. If it chances to be found, and published"—he was growing excited, so that the big form underwent an odd alchemy, like jelly into stone—"published, it might mean war. There is an international etiquette; publicly, France could not overlook such a breach of it. And France does not want war. Let us suppose, M. Bencolin, that a nation, which we shall call X, were for some reason prying into our secrets, and that every newspaper in France carried news of it—or that it even got outside the proper channels. Ah, you see the consequences?"

For a long time Bencolin looked at his cigar.

"M. le Comte flatters me with his confidence," he said.

"For an evident reason! You must find that slip of paper—identification card, if you will—and bring it to us. And when you do that, monsieur, you may be able to discover who killed LaGarde. This time, as in the Fragneau case, you will be dealing with a vanishing assassin. Your department boasts that you have never been beaten. But here I think that you will be beaten at last. . . . Because, my friend, it is all as simple and baffling as life. We have seen this incredible thing occur, yet we cannot conceive of an explanation. Someone shot LaGarde, after which the murderer disappeared. There was no trickery, no stealing away in half light or any such mummery as the Englishman Garrick perpetrated. He merely vanished. . . . Let me tell you the story."

Villon rose heavily and lumbered to the wall. He turned off all the lights except the desk lamp; when he returned to his seat Bencolin was in shadow. But the official sat there motionless as a monstrous bald idol while his lips fashioned the words slowly and clearly, and the pinpoint eyes did not waver in their stare.

II

If you know Mme. St. Marie (said Villon) you may possibly know M. Patrick O'Riordan, the drunken Irishman who is her husband. Sometime we shall be forced to give O'Riordan his dismissal from the secret service bureau; when he is sober, there are few better men in the department, but his erratic conduct cannot be pardoned by that. He saw three years of the most horrible blinding fighting on the western front; after a series of insane stunts he was railroaded to Paris, full of gas and shrapnel. He had the Cross of Honor, but he had no right arm. . . .

I saw him once in the Bois, quite thin, with eyes wretched because he who was so handsome had his right sleeve pinned across his chest. He was riding on a fine black horse, and beside him rode a girl with blood-red hair bound around the white of her face. It was Mme. St. Marie. I said she had no great voice, but ah, my friend, who can forget the night war was declared, when she, very young, sang "La Marseillaise"—with her wild hair streaming and every beautiful vibrant thrill in her body! That night, monsieur, one heard again the drums of Jena and Sedan.

O'Riordan met her on one of his rambles about Paris, as I have said. They were crazily in love, but they did not marry for a while, because he volunteered for intelligence work. He wandered all through the Balkans, the great tall Irishman with his drunken grin; he got through the German lines on sheer nerve, and once he was seen in Constantinople, riding like a lord in a German general's motorcar. When the armistice was signed, he came up from the East, singing, and married Mme. St. Marie.

Now I must gather up the narrative. I suppose you have heard enough of the man LaGarde to consider it natural that since he has been in France he should have paid attentions to Mme. St. Marie. Handsome man—hands like a musician and eyes like a poet, but slightly fat. Women used to rave over his beautiful hair; yes, and I did not know that it was a wig until I saw it slipped partly off, while he had a bullet hole through his head. He had an establishment some few miles up the Avenue de la Défense; literally, the house used to be full of women. Last night he gave a masked ball.

I warn you that you are going to meet odd characters in this affair. Had it not been for one of Patrick O'Riordan's two guardian angels, O'Riordan and I might not have gone out to LaGarde's house. At least, we should probably not have gone that night. Of these two guardian angels, one is a little Turk named Gomboul, whom O'Riordan brought back from the Balkans—a chocolate-colored fellow with shiny eyes and teeth like a tame tiger. O'Riordan frisked him out from under somebody's sword, so that Gomboul is annoying in his constant attention on his master. He waddles around after him, fanatically fearful that somebody is going to hurt him, all daggers or smiles, mumbling, "Yus, master." He will throw back his head and intone long passages from the Koran like a dog crying to the moon.... Then the other person is even more of a religious fanatic, in a way. It is a dried-up woman, a crooning soul who has been housekeeper for O'Riordan. Her name, to be exact, is Celeste Gratin; she has the air of a stone virgin, with a slight mustache like such women, and eyes that follow one around in the manner of a picture. She is religion-crazy. Sometimes, O'Riordan has told me, you will see a wild ridiculous scene, with her shrieking the Ten Commandments at the heathen, and he bawling out his Koran with head back, while O'Riordan sits in a corner applauding and drinking brandy.

Well, then! For nearly a month O'Riordan has been away on a government mission. It had to do with LaGarde; specifically, he has been attempting to discover what government sent him. No success, my friend! And in the meantime, all very cleverly, LaGarde has been doing his own secret service work. He has hunted the hunter, and he has stalked the hunter's wife. You see the trend of affairs?

I met O'Riordan at the Place de l'Etoile; he was flushed and despondent, but he talked with eagerness about seeing his wife again. He had returned unexpectedly, with only a wire to me, and he planned on surprising his wife. . . .

I shan't soon forget his expression when we arrived at his apartment on the Avenue du Bois du Boulogne. In the dusk it was quite empty, but shadowed with blowing branches and filled with the scent of flowers from the trees outside. You could almost feel someone stepping lightly over the carpets. But she was not there. Instead this mustached, grim-eyed woman sat in the middle of the drawing room, telling her beads.

"She is gone," said Celeste Gratin, rising and clenching her mannish hands. "May the good God have mercy upon her soul for hurting you! She has gone with M. LaGarde, to his house, and she has taken a valise."

III

Subsequent events (continued Villon) are confused in my mind. I remember that O'Riordan sat down to wait; he steadfastly refused to believe that Mlle. Gratin spoke the truth. He said, trying to smile, "She'll be in, Villon; she'll come in from shopping— There! Isn't that her laugh in the hall? Of course!" But she never came. Celeste Gratin went out, mumbling; I heard her rifling among drawers in the next room, and presently she stalked out of the apartment.

It grew later and later, until O'Riordan's talk of shopping tours became a rather ghastly farce. He paced up and down, smoking cigarettes. Nor had he bothered to turn on any lights, so that I could hear his steps go padding about in darkness, or see his spectral figure move across the moonlight in the windows. I must have fallen into a doze. When I awoke he was shaking me by the shoulder. He had turned on every light in the room, and was standing with a big black cloak billowing around him, a weird and lofty form with white, staring face.

"Get up, Villon!" he muttered. "Get up. We're going to LaGarde's place. By God, I can have it out with him in more ways than one! I'm going to get to the bottom of this thing if I have to kill him, and I'm going to find out about Sylvie. . . . Is your car still downstairs?"

That drive was a stormy, roaring race. O'Riordan was at the wheel of the roadster; I can remember only a stream of lights, the screech when he jumped on the brakes, the people scuttling past us like chickens—black silhouettes on the windshield. We turned right at the Boulevard des Lannes, then left up the Avenue de la Défense. I was wide enough awake when we got out on the open road. White road, rushing in the car lamps, and the scarlet A's on the stop signs reeling and falling behind, with the call of the horn screaming before us like a battle cry.

Presently we smashed in through a tapestry of trees, eerie and ghostly like flying clouds. The wet perfume of gardens, the swish of leaves, the gleam of a statue—we mounted past them and stopped lone as on some deserted windy height. There it stood, forlorn under the stars: the house and the gardens, which were strung with vague lights. Yes, I tell you the gardens glowed all naked, but the house was black except for one illuminated window. And the rustling branches, and the gravel drive rutted with car tracks, all looked uncanny, as though an army had passed. It was then that I remembered: LaGarde had given a masked ball that night. It must be near dawn, I decided, for the guests had gone. Nothing moved in those lighted gardens.

We got out of the car; we moved over the lawn rather breathlessly. Then, close to the house, we saw it, full black on the yellow oblong of the window. It was a shadow, rearing up like smoke, and it was the shadow of a woman. O'Riordan muttered something. . . .

We were almost at the steps when we heard the sound of the shot. It was unmistakably that, and it had come from the room of the lighted window. O'Riordan broke into a run. He leaped the porch stairs, he had knocked open the door of the house before my wits were aroused. When I reached the front door I saw him in the hallway, terrifying as a cloaked god, and he was surging his shoulder at one of the doors. When I heard it tear open, and saw him half fall inside, I noticed another thing in that blank corridor, where a single lamp beamed high. It was a little brown figure, gibbering like a monkey under the lamp: it was Gomboul, the Turk.

I went quietly to the shattered door. O'Riordan was leaning against the jamb, and his head was bowed.

"I thank God," he said, "that we are too late, monsieur."

In the middle of the room, partly facing the door, a man sat throned in state, except that his legs had a curiously sprawled look. He was in velvet and satins, white wig of the eighteenth century, all white in the somber furnishings of the room. Incongruously, one hand lying on the table beside him held a lighted cigarette, from which the smoke went up very straight. Just that lonely figure, head on one side, looking at us through the eyeholes of a white mask. But in the center of the forehead, like another eyehole in the mask, there was the round red blot of a bullet mark. Then, as we looked, a little streak of red shot down from it across the white mask.

From the doorway O'Riordan suddenly asked, *"Where is she?"*

That was a last bitter tangling of strings. There was nobody else in the room except that grotesque dead man—nobody else. I examined it with care. No one hiding. There was one full-length window, fastened on the inside with sliding bolts and a catch. Obviously it would have been impossible to step outside and lock that window from the inside. And as for LaGarde locking it after he had been shot, that was just as impossible; death was instantaneous. We had both been watching the door of the room, and we had seen nobody leave. Certainly the person who killed LaGarde could not have left, *yet that person was not in the room.* Secret entrances? Quite out of the question, as we discovered; besides, my friend, that is a sheer wild device of melodrama, and one does not find such things in prosaic country houses. Suicide, then? Again out of the question, because there was no weapon.

Name of a name! The whole matter was appalling. And it was so aimless. I remember what a horrible significance small details had: O'Riordan, in a sort of daze, meticulously taking the cigarette from the flabby hand and squashing it out on an ashtray—it was a homemade cigarette, and it crumbled; then Gomboul, sidling in with a scared look. In the doorway behind him a lot of faces had begun to peek in like curious chickens—servants. The insanest gabble went up, and when we took the mask off LaGarde's face, so that the eyes peered out, Gomboul began singing out his religious chants. O'Riordan cursed him into silence, after which he demanded in English, what the hell Gomboul was doing there.

"Master say, 'Take care Sylvie,' " the Turk answered. "I haf followed. Master, she go in this room, after she dance. Master, she not here now."

O'Riordan's slow eyes moved as though they alone were alive in his face, from Gomboul to me, and then to the dead man. Then he made a little sniffing, shrugging motion, after which he turned his big back and went toward the door.

When I followed him to the porch, the dawn was brushing out over the trees, drowsy on the eyelids. The garden lights glowed on the gray. There was a faint rustle of birds. And in the middle of the lawn, like a figure in mist, stood a lone woman, looking at the house. It was Celeste Gratin. . . . O'Riordan sat down on the steps.

"I'm tired, Villon," he said. "I'm so tired. . . ."

IV

Quite suddenly M. Bencolin realized that the quiet voice had stopped speaking. The little detective had sunk so far down in his chair that his elbows over its arms looked like wings. His cigar had gone out.

"Well!" grunted Villon, drawing a long breath. "What do you make of it now?"

Bencolin accepted another cigar. He got up and went wandering about the room, his head forward and bobbing on his shoulders. Then he paused.

"With all this evidence," he remarked, "why has not Mme. St. Marie been arrested?"

"Because, my friend, she has a perfect alibi!"

Bencolin struck the desk. "Monsieur," he said wildly, and he flourished the cigar, "are you now so blind as to doubt the existence of a God? It was the one chance for which I had been hoping. Ah, yes; you are going to tell me, are you not, that she was seen outside the house before the shot was fired?"

"If I doubt the existence of a God," replied Villon politely, "at least I cannot doubt the existence of a devil. How does monsieur know? Yes, she was seen getting into a motorcar on the other side of the house just as we approached. She must even have seen *us*. We have witnesses in the form of a couple who were coming over the hill behind LaGarde's house, and who met her face to face. We shall not pry into the reason why they were abroad at that hour, this man and woman; they are lovers, and their business was at least honest. We are withholding their names; monsieur sees? But they are well-known peasants. Mme. St. Marie has bought milk from one; she recognized her, and called on her today for identification. Yet," said Villon, "I think that all three are lying. The thing is incredible! How did she leave the room, if she did not shoot LaGarde, with the Turk guarding a bolted door, and the windows locked? And who *was* the woman in LaGarde's room, if not she?"

"Ah! Well, M. le Comte, how did she leave the room even if she did shoot LaGarde? As for the second question—stay a moment! This matter of the paper with LaGarde's commission: you searched for it?"

"We searched the house from cellar to attic; we have been through all LaGarde's effects very carefully. No, monsieur, we have not found it. The paper *must* exist—"

Bencolin laughed. He seemed very lively now.

"Yes, of course... My friend, a great American once wrote a story. ... No matter! Now tell me, if you will, where was the window of this room?"

"It faced the lawn, opening on the porch. As one entered the room, it was on the left-hand side, at right angles to the door."

"You see the significance of that?"

"No."

"And the cigarette? Monsieur does not see the significance of that? Of course not; being on the scene, you were blinded." Bencolin put on his hat thoughtfully, hunching his shoulders under the cape. Then he went to the door.

"M. le Comte," he said, "I have a theory. I do not know whether it is true, and there are parts of it which are as puzzling to me as to you. I shall want time. And now may I bid you good evening? I shall want to walk the streets a long time to think. Paris at night-time! Is it not fit subject for a dark romancer, another Villon with singing heart and swinging tankard?"

Villon was annoyed. He blinked his eyes slowly. "No," he admitted, "I have no theory, because I am a man of facts. I can conceive of none whatever to fit this business. Can monsieur suggest any?"

"There are many, many theories," responded Bencolin, with his hand on the door. "Consider! There is the theory that while O'Riordan was rushing into the hallway ahead, M. Villon himself went along the porch and fired through the window, using, let us say, a Maxim silencer, and that afterwards he locked the window on the inside, unnoticed."

"Ridiculous! What of the shot we heard? What of the woman in the room? You do not imply that I am telling an untruth. . . ."

"Naturally not. The idea is, of course, ridiculous. But M. le Comte de Villon has said that there could be no theory. I know that it is not the true one; nevertheless, it is a theory."

"But who," cried Villon, rising up like a mountain behind the desk, "was the woman in the room?"

"I may be wrong," answered the little detective, "yet I think that it was Celeste Gratin."

"It means, then, that she is guilty?"

"No, my friend, nothing of the kind," said Bencolin. "It means that she is innocent."

And he bowed politely as he backed from the room.

V

In the springtime of Paris, which is a blue dawn over a city of old ghosts, there was a window in the Avenue des Bois beyond which white trees moved. And framed in the window sat a girl all in white, except for her unbound red hair. Hers was a paleness like ivory, with drooping eyelids and a slow curving smile. But something of the lift and defiance of the falcon's poise was in her profile, the falcon as well as a frightened bird, so that her blue eyes were truly as those of one who explores the sky. Beside her there knelt a tall quiet man, with his dark head bowed, so that in the peace of it all there was something closely akin to a shrine.

When M. Henri Bencolin entered through the portieres, a trailing apologetic figure, the man rose.

"Come on in, old top!" he said, and the voice had a thrill that woke the picture to life, as though tapestries assumed vital form. "I was expecting you, after our conversation this morning."

He stood there, vibrant with his laugh, and the empty sleeve was almost unnoticed in that warm light. Sylvie St. Marie smiled too.

"M. Bencolin? Of course I know you! Who does not?" she added, shrugging. "Please sit down! I should hate to consider you a police officer." (The falcon, head back, gay, defiant, poised.)

"Do not inconvenience yourselves," said Bencolin rather fumblingly. He glanced round at the maid in the doorway, who was retiring. Then he sat down. Patrick O'Riordan seated himself beside his wife.

"I bring bad news," Bencolin continued, "but I bring you news that will set you free. I know the truth about LaGarde's death."

He said it simply and quietly, blinking at them. Sylvie St. Marie looked at him with unmoving eyes. (The frightened bird, steadying for flight.)

"When I left you this morning, M. O'Riordan, I discovered something. . . . I learned that the woman Celeste Gratin has killed herself. Let me finish, please. She drowned herself in the Seine. They got the body out this morning, with a little silver crucifix twined about the neck. She had already written a note which she just addressed 'To the Police Department,' confessing that she had shot LaGarde. She confessed to a crime she did not commit."

Bencolin was leaning forward, speaking in a low voice which held the others motionless. The wind-touched bright room, the shadows of white blossoms, the little black figure who addressed them very gently.

"She thought that she had killed LaGarde. Listen, she meant to kill him. She loved both of you, but she loved M. O'Riordan best, for she could not see him suffer, and she could not let go unavenged this thing which she considered so blasphemous. When M. O'Riordan returned, she got a pistol from the next room. By hired car she went to LaGarde's house. The guests were departing. Through the window she saw LaGarde and Mme. St. Marie in that room. . . .

"You perceive it? She waits, praying there with the pistol in her hand, driven to a frenzy, moving in the moonlight. LaGarde is talking, at his ease with mask up and lolling over a chair in his white-stockinged finery. The last car has gone. She raps on the window!

"No," cried Bencolin, "she does not know that a wife, playing alone against LaGarde, has been attempting to find out from him what she knows her husband is attempting to find out in another country. She enters the room, this maniacal woman, and at pistol point she orders Mme. St. Marie out. There she stands, and when madame has gone she pours out every cold, taunting fact she knows. M. O'Riordan is back! He has discovered the whereabouts of his wife! He will kill M. LaGarde. . . . There, it is the humming of an auto in the drive. LaGarde, furious, rushes forward in the dim light. She fires.

"Then she goes out by the window, unseen as Villon and O'Riordan pass the corner of the house. *But she has missed her aim.* She has lodged the bullet in the dark paneling, where only a search with a glass will reveal it. LaGarde knows that he is trapped, unless he can be his calm, debonair self and insist that nobody was in the room. He locks the window, pulls down his mask, and attempting calmness, lights a cigarette when he sits down in a chair facing the door. . . .

"You, M. O'Riordan, breaking open the door, face to face with LaGarde and seeing no one else in the room, conceive that he has shot her. You fired through the folds of your long cloak, and using a Maxim silencer on the pistol you had prepared for this event, you killed LaGarde in his chair."

VI

It seemed incredible—not these amazing statements of M. Bencolin, because they had about them the quiet clarity of truth, but that in so short a space of time Sylvie St. Marie should have undergone such a transformation. The falcon tossed its head, the body became stiff, the hardening lips suddenly grew rather horrible. You thought of no childish simplicity now. She shook back her red hair.

"You killed him!" she said.

O'Riordan shrugged; he tried a little laugh.

"That's it," he replied, blinking his eyes. "You've guessed it neatly. I was going to confess there, because I thought they would accuse you, but when I discovered you were out of the house... Now I suppose I'm arrested, eh, old top? Well ..." He stood there, tall and dark, playing aimlessly with the empty sleeve. Then he said, "Oh, my God!" in such a voice that it gave away his self-control, and he shuddered.

There were no lamps at the shrine now. Vaguely M. Bencolin recalled that the Furies were supposed to have red hair. Sylvie, whose face was a weird thing between tears and hate, went to her husband and began tugging grotesquely at his sleeve. Her eyes were wide open in their stare.

"You killed François! You killed LaGarde! May God blast your soul!" she cried, striking at him. "I loved him! I never loved anybody else, do you hear that? I never loved anybody else. . . ." Then she turned round, with the tears on her face. But she began to smile.

"Well, monsieur le gendarme," she added, triumphantly, "now that you have been so good as to tell me, will you go and report the matter to the authorities, or shall I?"

Bencolin had risen. He looked as though he could not believe what he had heard.

"Madame means," he muttered, "that she would betray her husband?"

"There is a telephone here," the woman answered. "Yes, there is a telephone here—by your arm, M. Bencolin! My husband! I knew LaGarde before I knew him. I loved LaGarde. Well, you simpering idiot, will you get me the police department, or whoever it is? You know the number."

"To hell with you!" O'Riordan suddenly shouted, and he laughed. "I'll call them myself. Here, give me the phone!"

Bencolin was angry too, but the little figure was clothed almost with dignity in it. "I have a commission to execute for madame," he said, and he bowed and took up the instrument. Then he stood looking at them over it with eyes that had become glittery.

"We shall give them the information, yes," he went on. "Yes, and because I was mistaken in madame, we shall give them other information too, which I suppressed because I thought you loved the man who will be guillotined for you. We shall tell them, madame, who was the accomplice of LaGarde in the employ of another government—who was the spy who, because she was married to a French official, could obtain the information LaGarde wanted. We shall tell them whose name besides LaGarde's is written on that identification card"—he gave a number into the telephone—"and finally, we shall tell them where that damning identification card may be found. I should have been fool enough to have concealed all this for the sake of a man who loved France only less than he loved you. Take part of your information or all of mine—but in the name of God, let there be an equal falsehood or an equal truth! . . . Madame," said M. Bencolin, extending the telephone, "here is your party."

The telephone buzzed and tinkled with a tiny voice. Bencolin was still holding it out to the motionless woman when O'Riordan burst out laughing.

"Right again!" he cried. "I knew it all when I came back, but I was going to be treacherous enough to conceal it because of . . . Sylvie. I had discovered where the piece of paper was that contained the names, and when I saw that self-rolled cigarette in LaGarde's hand after the murder, I even squashed it out to preserve it intact. . . . But how did you know all this?"

"A man of such fastidious tastes, smoking a rolled cigarette when he had on him a full case of manufactured ones?" queried Bencolin. "What does it suggest, especially as we have the police hunting for a missing paper which they will swear is nowhere about the house? Does it not at least require an examination? Then, when one finds Mme. St. Marie's name on the cigarette paper also, it will explain that her husband knew, because for no reason at all he attempted to put it out—that in itself would first have drawn my attention to the cigarette. In LaGarde's haste he took out of his case the one cigarette he had always intended to save. Why, how obvious it is! The murder in particular, as linked with it. Could LaGarde have been holding that newly lighted cigarette if he had been shot at the time we saw the shadow on the blind? He died instantly. Could he have been sitting *facing* the door, at right angles to the window, and be shot through the middle of the forehead by someone at the window? And above all, could there have been a bullet hole in the paneling if Mlle. Gratin's bullet had taken effect? No! Or consider this: LaGarde was wearing his mask down when he was murdered.

Can one expect that during his tête-à-tête with Mme. St. Marie he wore it down? Or does one rather infer that he pulled it down after both women had gone? Only one person could have shot him, from his position, and that was a man in the doorway. Who alone had stood in the doorway before the murder? O'Riordan. Who alone wore a costume that would enable him to conceal, say, a silencer—"

"Put down the telephone, M. Bencolin," interrupted the woman. She looked at him defiantly. "You have won, I suppose. What do you intend to do?"

"Nothing, madame. Have there not been tragedies enough in this ghastly affair? And would not exposure interfere seriously with ... madame's career?" the detective said. "Because of her husband, I shall not make these revelations, but I shall be watching her henceforth. And monsieur? Look out the window: you see the Arc de Triomphe? Once I saw him ride under that. . . ." Shamblingly, apologetically, Bencolin gathered up his hat and stick. "You flatter me, madame, you flatter a poor simpering idiot of a gendarme. I have lost."

VII

M. le Comte de Villon was exultant when Bencolin came to call on him that night. They sat as they had sat two evenings before, in the big lighted office; but now Villon regarded his companion mockingly.

"I have often wondered, my friend, where you get your reputation," Villon observed. "I understand now. Monsieur has been reading too much fiction. He loves to puzzle, he loves to hint. And yet without phenomenal luck, he can do nothing." He smiled in his expansive fashion. "Did not monsieur assure me that Mlle. Gratin was innocent?"

"I fear so," Bencolin admitted, and he sighed.

"Yet we have her confession. You see," went on Villon airily, "it is all very simple at bottom. Now that we have it explained, I could not swear that the window was locked on the inside. I do not doubt that I was merely mistaken about the window. You know, of course, that I suspected Mlle. Gratin from the first. I have given my explanation to my own superiors, and they agree. Ah, it is splendid!"

"M. le Comte is to be congratulated," murmured Bencolin.

"It is nothing. Again, my friend, you failed signally to locate the paper. *I* have done that! Stop, monsieur; let me explain. Is it not odd that the great Bencolin should have been beaten by a woman?" asked Villon merrily. "This afternoon Mme. Sylvie St. Marie came to me. She explained why she had been in the room that night. She had been aiding her husband, trying to find the paper herself! From him she stole the paper, and as LaGarde sought to take it from her, she destroyed it before she could read it. It is a pity that we do not know who employed LaGarde, but at least the paper is done away with. *Madame St. Marie told me to search no further for it.* Ah, there is a woman, Bencolin! I admit that I was mistaken in her."

Bencolin smiled very faintly.

"And all your brave mysterious talk," continued Villon, "was a rather amusing fraud. Bencolin, Bencolin, will you never learn that the true brain scoffs at theories? And monsieur had the temerity to suggest to me some weird tale of a Maxim silencer!"

"Yes," returned Bencolin, smiling again, "I fear I had the temerity to suggest that also. . . . Parbleu!" he added, searching in his pockets. "I have no cigars! Well, here are some vile cigarettes. I have been forced to adopt LaGarde's method of rolling them myself. Will M. le Comte honor me by accepting one?"

"In your honor, Bencolin—thank you. It gives me great pleasure to smoke this way, as LaGarde smoked, and smile at you as he must have smiled could he have known the strange theories you would build up. . . ." Whimsically Villon took the cigarette. "You are a bad manufacturer, my friend. This has a wilted appearance. You must have tried several times before you rolled it correctly."

They both lighted their cigarettes. Villon kept talking, pointing out one fact after another. He was in high spirits when Bencolin finally rose to go.

"Well, good-bye, my friend," said Villon, nodding his big head. "Perhaps we shall have need of your romancing another time." He flipped his cigarette out the window.

"Did madame by chance tell you where the paper was hidden?" Bencolin asked, his hand on the knob, his old top hat askew.

"Alas, no! Except that he carried it with him. I did not pry into these secrets of hers," replied Villon, winking. "And yet I confess it irritates me that I did not find it. Apparently the whole thing was right under my nose the whole time!"

"M. le Comte," said Bencolin, making a flourishing salute with his stick, "speaks more truly than he knows!"

The Haverfordian, January 1927

The Ends of Justice

It HAS often been remarked that in M. Henri Bencolin's most baffling case he did not interfere until it was too late. The convicted murderer of Roger Darworth was sentenced to be executed at Blackfriars on May fourth. On May third, on one of those drowsy evenings when the English countryside is in full bloom, Bencolin was taking tea with his old friend Sir John Landervorne. They sat among the purple lilacs, shaded by a rustic arbor, and a bright singing stream ran past them. Up over the terrace were the gray gables of Sir John's house, stark against the last fire of the sun; a sleepy twilight hovered over them.

The gaunt baronet stood by the tea table, lighting his pipe. Bencolin sat watching the rippling water. He wore careless gray tweeds, and needed a shave, for his black beard was scraggly and his hair rather wild. Beyond him, dark against the lilacs, sat Bishop Wolfe, with his narrow face and slow-blinking eyes, blond hair parted carefully in the middle. It was a devout face, an earnest face, but the eyes were a bit palely blue, and rimmed with red. His clerical garb was neat, and his nails polished.

"It was opportune," Sir John was remarking, "that you should come here at this time, Bencolin. I wanted you to meet Bishop Wolfe. You said that you had been away some time, I think?"

Bencolin lifted eyes that were very tired.

"Six months," he said, and smiled. "In the south of France."

"You succeeded?"

"I got my man," the Frenchman said. "Come, come, this is in the nature of a vacation, my friend. You don't want me to talk shop, surely?"

"Well, I know you. You would be interested, wouldn't you, in hearing of a churchman turned detective?"

"From what I have heard," Bishop Wolfe put in, raising his colorless eyebrows, "I personally should be much more interested in a detective turned churchman."

"Are you referring to my religious ideas?" asked Bencolin. "Well, well, one sinner more or less doesn't matter, does he?" He smiled at the stream. "Am I to gather that Bishop Wolfe did detective work?"

While the bishop made a protesting motion, Sir John went on enthusiastically: "Well, rather! He solved the most perplexing case *I* ever racked my wits over! . . . Did you ever hear of Roger Darworth?"

"The spiritualist?"

"Call him that if you like." The baronet shrugged. "He always impressed me as a stagy fake, you know. And I suppose you know Tom Fellowes?"

Bencolin slapped the table.

"Know him? I'm proud to know him! I always admire these crazy young hellions; they do all the things I should like to do. . . ." Bencolin scratched his head, and looked apologetically at the bishop.

"Your instance is bad for your case, M. Bencolin," said Bishop Wolfe with sudden harshness. "Would you like to commit murder? Fellowes did."

Startled, Bencolin leaned back and stared at him with his wrinkly black eyes.

"My friend," he replied quietly, "I do not doubt your word, of course, but when you tell me that Tom Fellowes committed murder, I find it hard to believe. No, no, I tell you! Ah, monsieur, I who know the wickedness of the many know also the goodness of the few. Were it not for Tom Fellowes' money, thousands of children in London would die every year. It is he who feeds them. Were it not for Tom Fellowes' money, hundreds of maimed soldiers in France would die. It is Tom Fellowes who supports them. Does not your church take cognizance of that?"

"I am not sentimental like you, M. Bencolin," said the bishop, stroking his colorless hair. "I judge a man by his fruits. Fellowes killed Roger Darworth; I am surprised that you have not heard of the case."

"It *is* strange, old top," put in Sir John. "It was a sensation. Fellowes is to be executed tomorrow. I'm sorry about it, naturally, for he seemed to me a splendid fellow. But the evidence was conclusive."

"Then," said Bencolin, "will you be so good as to tell me about it? Fellowes to be executed . . . It's unbelievable!" He passed his hand over his forehead. "I count myself a good judge of men, but if Fellowes is a murderer, I shall acknowledge myself an utter idiot."

"The English law courts—" said the bishop.

Bencolin made an impatient gesture.

"Damn the English law courts! . . . I'm sorry," he apologized, catching himself up and looking at Sir John with a wry smile, "but I don't understand just yet. Will you tell me about it?"

"I will give you the facts," responded the churchman with precision. "You shall then make whatever judgment you like on your ability to size up men, M. Bencolin. Sit down, please, Sir John. . . . No, thanks; I don't smoke."

He waited until Bencolin had lighted a cigar and whirled a wreath of smoke around his head. Then, in the fading twilight, Bishop Wolfe, with his hands folded in his lap, began his story.

II

I had known Roger Darworth a long time. He was a devout man, for all he meddled with spiritism, and his belief in communication with the dead was sincere. He sought to establish it with the zeal of a scientist. I have seen him give demonstrations in which the most extraordinary things occurred; Darworth bound and roped in a chair at one end of a darkened room while bells were rung, tables moved, spirit hands materialized. Of course, my religion did not permit me to sympathize with him; but I respect any man's beliefs, except atheism.

The personality of the man was vibrant. His eyes had an uncanny penetrating look, and would change from blue almost to black; he had a great skull, with plumes of reddish hair, and a loose-jointed, powerful figure. He used to walk the streets of Bayswater at night, under the moon, head sunk forward and hands clasped behind his coattails, mumbling to himself. Well, of course, he had a violent temper, and used to play practical jokes on children (loved to scare them a little), but it was just his own particular humor. He gave a great deal to the church. Then, too, for some reason he always had a doctor about his house—a Dr. Joseph McShane, of whom you'll hear later.

I suppose you know of his relationship to Tom Fellowes. He was a cousin, and had inherited a great deal of money from his grandfather. Half of this money (it amounted to about a million pounds) was to go to Tom Fellowes on Darworth's death. Now, it has been proved that for all Fellowes' charity work, he was almost out of money; he had been begging loans from Darworth. It was just a part of Roger's whimsical humor that he would half promise a loan, and then laugh at Fellowes when Fellowes came for the check; the young scapegrace needed a lesson. Then there was the girl. You very rarely hear of an actual case in which two cousins, utterly unlike, are after the same lady, but it happened in this instance. For Roger's sake I am glad that this Cynthia Melford preferred Fellowes; she is an utterly frivolous chit, one of the type called "saucy" (ugly appellation!), with bobbed hair and what is known as "make-up." I am sorry that Roger took it hard when she became engaged to Fellowes. She was unworthy of him, of his co-lossal mind. She actually grew hysterical once when Roger, purely as a joke, sent her a dried arm from a dissecting room in a flower box.

Roger, as you probably know, lived in a big house in Bayswater, furnished in accordance with his somber, studious type of mind. It was a model of neatness; Roger neither smoked nor was untidy, and to his orderly trend of life the slightest thing out of place was a horror. I often wish, in these careless, untidy days, there were more like him. He often had a group in to a séance, however, which he held in his vast library, shadowed with gloomy hangings and books, and with a red lamp burning on the center table. Some of the most renowned scientists in the world have sat there, shivering (for the house was healthfully cold), and marveled at the effects he produced. I can see him yet, sitting behind the glow of the red lamp, with his long white face and weird, changing dark eyes under the straggle of reddish hair. Then the solemn circle ... the dark ... the sudden clash of a tambourine, or ghastly spectral hands moving in the air, while, mind you, Roger sat bound and handcuffed in his chair.

One night last January (it was blustery, and driving with snow) Roger invited me around to his house. I remember the dully lighted hall when I was admitted, and the Chinaman, Mock Yen, who was Roger's housekeeper and whom he always kept in Oriental costume. Mock Yen was an absurdity—a Chinaman with a glass eye, which lolled grotesquely and made his yellow, slant-eyed face a thing at which Roger laughed constantly. Well, the door to Roger's library was closed, but as I approached I heard voices. I heard Dr. McShane's voice say:

"You realize, then, your own grave danger?"

And Roger answered:

"Oh, Fellowes has made his threats to kill me, right enough. I don't doubt I shall be dead within a week. But he'll hang for it!"

Then I knocked on the door, and they both seemed embarrassed. They stood by an old-fashioned grate with a gas fire, which sputtered blue flame over the hangings and the rows of books. McShane, a little fat man with eyeglasses and a bald head, stammered:

"Come in, come in, sir. I didn't expect you so early."

"Look here, Bishop," Roger burst out, kneading his big white hands over the fire and peering at me from around his shoulder. "I don't see any reason why you shouldn't know. That damned cad Fellowes has been after me again. I can't express to you," he cried suddenly, and I was actually frightened at the expression on his face, "the way I hate that bounder! He means to kill me. Why shouldn't he? He's got money coming to him. Five hundred thousand quid if I die. Why, it's enough to tempt your cloth, Bishop—but you needn't worry. I've put ten thousand pounds church money in my will."

I must confess that there are times when Roger's jokes were a bit hard to bear, though he meant nothing by them. He laughed and said:

"Listen, I'll tell you how it is. He wants to get married. If he'd kept his fortune and not thrown it about trying to help sniveling soldiers, he'd be a rich man today. He, who keeps up a fine brave pretense of money, with his Vauxhall roadster (and not a sixpence for petrol!) and his grand fur coat! ... Well, he's coming here tonight. He was desperate. Said he'd got to have money, and I told him there might be a chance if he came around. But I'm afraid of him."

"Whiskey and soda?" said the doctor, reaching for the siphon.

"No ... Now listen. I am going up to my study to finish up some work. You two remain down here. When you hear him come up on the porch, go upstairs quickly, and don't let him see you, above all! I'm supposed to be alone in the house. You know where my study is: at the back, at the end of a long hall. Well, the hall is brightly lit. At the other end, directly opposite my study, is another room. I've laid a fire there, and it's comfortable. You two go in there, and watch my study door after he has gone in. Guard me! If you hear the slightest sign of violence, come in. I tell you I'm afraid of him!"

"But hadn't you better see the police, if it's as serious as all that?" I asked. The man was actually in a chattering state of fear.

"And have them messing it up and creating a scandal?" he demanded. "No, no, I've done the next best thing. I've invited Sir John Landervorne here; he's enough in touch with the police to be effective, and enough out of touch to keep his mouth shut. He'll be here any minute. See that he follows the instructions; make him go upstairs and watch the door with you. Do you understand?"

"I don't like this, Mr. Darworth," said McShane, shaking his head. "See here, it's outlandish! This is a civilized world. You aren't a mile from Trafal—"

"Do as I tell you!" Roger ordered. "You understand, don't you; wait for Sir John, don't let Fellowes see you, and above all get to me in case anything should happen. I promised to see him alone."

His big loose figure went surging to the door in its black clothes that hung all baggily around him; the great mop of hair was flung back, streaming out as he went through the curtains. It was the last time I ever saw him alive.

III

Bishop Wolfe paused, and looked round at his companions, smoothing his hair. It had grown darker; the arbor hung in vague perfumed shadow, but with a sort of moving light about the water. In the silence Sir John stood up, a black silhouette against the pale sky. The action was unconscious; it seemed like an emotional upheaval.

"I am weary," said the bishop, and cleared his throat. "If M. Bencolin is interested, perhaps you will continue the story, Sir John. You have a minute attention to detail."

The silhouette nodded without speaking. Sir John had leaned against a post covered with trailing vines, supporting his chin in his hand, and was staring straight before him, still outlined on the pale sky.

"Yes, I am very much interested," Bencolin observed, talking in a voice that was low and extraordinarily tense. "I am very much interested in that conversation you overheard outside the library door, Monsieur l'Évêque. Go on, go on!"

Abruptly Sir John began to speak.

IV

I remember distinctly the time I arrived at the house, because the snow was beginning to thin out, and I could see my wrist watch. It was ten minutes after nine. The glass-eyed butler admitted me. When I went to the library, Darworth had just gone out, and Bishop Wolfe and the doctor were talking beside the fire. I was almost chilled by that house; not physically, but with a form of brooding repulsion that made me almost afraid to touch the hangings, as though I might get leprosy. . . .

And the doctor impressed me unpleasantly, not like the genial bald-headed man Bishop Wolfe has described. He seemed always on the alert—sly, if you can understand, with pale blue eyes behind his glasses and one strand of hair sticking over his big forehead. He kept going over and looking out the windows, and for some reason asking, "Is it still snowing?"

I learned of the grotesque situation, after which the doctor turned to me.

"It's nearly nine-thirty," he said. "That's the time young Fellowes is due to arrive. You'd better go to the room opposite the study. I'll stay here. Now, don't argue! I can see what sort of mood he's in."

We left him waving his arms by the fire. I confess the thing was so absurd that it seemed we had all gone out of our wits. Somehow we *expected* a tragedy. You would have thought that we might just have stayed with Darworth, but we didn't. Just as the bishop and I got out into the hall, we heard footsteps on the porch. Like a couple of children, we hurried back, blundering through a dark hall, around a turn or so, falling over furniture, until we emerged in the hall Darworth had mentioned. It ran along the back of the house, fairly well lighted—just a narrow corridor with a door at each end. One door was closed. The other, opening into the room where we were to remain, was ajar. We went inside: a gloomy place, with heavy Victorian furniture and ghastly flowered wallpaper. A gas jet was burning over the fireplace. We stood behind the door, looking out through the crack and down at that blank door opposite: we could see it plainly, because another gas jet beside it threw a dull yellow light directly on the panels. The door was ugly, sinister: its brown boards and white knob stood out with terrible distinctness. . . . Then, outside, we heard the front door slam, and voices in the hall. One voice was high and agitated; the other, which apparently belonged to Mock Yen, was low and baffling. I felt foolish, like a child looking through a board fence, but Bishop Wolfe was gripping my arm.

Suddenly the light was blocked. A man had come into the hall, swung with his back to us, and he was going down toward the brown door. He was tall; he wore a bowler hat and a great fur coat, and a trail of shadow slanted out after him. Gad, I can see him yet, striding down that faded carpet under the yellow light, pausing at the door, where the gas jet made a shining bowl of his hat and slid down over the sleek fur coat. As he lifted his hand to knock on the door, I could see a diamond gleaming on one finger. It was Fellowes, all right; the fur coat he always wore, and the diamond ring. A voice from behind the door said, "Come in."

As he went in, and the door closed after him, I heard Bishop Wolfe gasp. It was horrible: as though one saw a dead man, whose face was invisible, come in out of the snow like an avenger. Then silence.

We waited. God knows how long we waited, in a strained posture, with our eyes on the door, which fixed one's gaze like a bright lamp. There was utter silence in the hall, except for the singing of the gas jet and the occasional sound of voices from Darworth's study. Then it came out, with the sound of ripping cloth, like a ghost voice. It cried:

"Don't! Don't!" Darworth's voice!

Down the hall we went pell-mell. Nobody had come out. I turned the knob and threw the door open, at the same instant that I heard running footsteps behind me, and the doctor's voice crying from the hall:

"What is it?"

That cold study was before us, like a stage tableau. The dirty paper, the rows of books, a spirit cabinet, a mass of musical instruments all lying in a heap. The one window was wide open, and a wind whirled through it, tossing the curtains. An oil lamp with a green shade burned on the table. In a chair in the middle of the room sat Darworth, his head back, so that we saw only the long neck and a part of his face. His hands and legs were handcuffed to the chair, in which he was still writhing spasmodically, and in his chest was stuck a long knife.

While we stood there motionless we could hear the jingle of the handcuffs as he twisted his hands. But I swear nobody was in the room; there wasn't any place to hide. While Dr. McShane ran toward him, the bishop turned to me.

"He's gone out by the window!" Wolfe said. "Hurry—look!"

I ran over to the window. When I put my head out, it was bright moonlight; the storm had cleared some time since, and the snow lay unbroken all over the tiny yard, which was fenced with a high wall. That was it! The snow had absolutely no footprint, or any sort of mark. I looked up, I looked along the wall. It was a perfectly smooth expanse of close-set brick for twenty yards around, at the sides and up; there were no windows—a fly could not have clung on that wall. Yet nobody had walked over the snow! I stood there gaping in the moonlight at the impossible nature of it. We had watched the only door, and it was impossible to leave the room by the only window. Neither had been locked, yet the murderer could not have left the room. He could not have left, but he was not there.

When I came back into the room Darworth had stopped writhing. He had been trying to speak, but that ceased also. He sat back, with his red hair hanging down toward the floor, the manacles shining on his wrists and legs, and his mouth wide open. That was all.

"Where is Fellowes?" I heard Bishop Wolfe say. "He *couldn't* have left here so quickly."

"Dead," the doctor was muttering and chuckling. "Dead! Got him just in the heart. . . . Put that window down, will you, Sir John Landervorne? It's cold in here."

The bishop, who looked white and shaken, leaned against the table.

"Better get the police . . ." he faltered.

"Well, well," the doctor was saying to himself in a surprised tone. "It's not ten o'clock—it's not ten o'clock."

V

None of the three had noticed that the arbor was quite dark. Bencolin tossed his cigar in a glowing arc into the stream. They could feel him leaning forward as he spoke tensely; they could almost feel that he was seizing the sides of his chair.

"Go on, go on!" he ordered. "They piled up the evidence, I suppose? Tell me about it."

"The steps," went on Sir John, "were easy. Mock Yen testified to having seen Fellowes come in the front door just before we saw him in the hall. He said that Fellowes seemed agitated. Well, we searched the room. There was no secret way for him to have left. Dr. McShane did not see him when he came in the front door, but he heard his voice; unmistakably that of Fellowes. The crude details of the affair were as bad as those of an American thriller: Fellowes had stabbed Darworth with a carving knife. The knife was identified by Fellowes' manservant at the trial as coming from a dinner set in Fellowes' apartment. He had evidently handcuffed Darworth and stabbed him with premeditated care. But the devil of it lay in how Fellowes had left the room!"

"Did he confess?"

"No! Again a strange thing. He was arrested the next day, and swore that he had been nowhere near Darworth's house all evening. The night of the murder, he said, he had been in his rooms in Half-Moon Street until eight-thirty. At that time, according to his testimony, he received a phone call from Miss Cynthia Melford, the lady to whom he is engaged, asking him to come to her apartment, which is some distance away—that he would find the door open, and to go in and make himself at home until she returned. She would not be absent long, the alleged message ran, and she had something important to tell him. Fellowes says he went there, though he admits that neither hallboy nor doorman saw him go in. He says he stayed there until eleven-fifteen, when Miss Melford returned.

"Well, she was questioned before she knew what was wrong, and told the investigator she had sent no message, being surprised to see Fellowes when she returned from the theater. Then, when she heard of the crime, she recalled her statement and said that she certainly had sent the message . . . but the puzzling thing was why, in the face of so much evidence, Fellowes insisted that his story was true."

"What about his appointment with Darworth?"

"Fellowes said he had none. You can see that the evidence against him was overwhelming."

"Well," temporized Bencolin, "how did he get out of the room?"

"If he stuck to his story of innocence," said Bishop Wolfe coldly, "he could hardly be expected to explain *that.*"

Sir John hurried on: "But the most conclusive proof against him was unearthed by Bishop Wolfe. It was Bishop Wolfe who produced a witness who had seen Fellowes leaving Darworth's house."

"What?" cried Bencolin.

"Quite so. You remember my telling you of the little walled yard that encloses the window of Darworth's study? There is a gate in that. A Mr. John Simpson, who is a banker's clerk, was passing by outside—on the street that runs past the wall. Through the merest chance Bishop Wolfe unearthed him. As Mr. Simpson was crossing the street the night of the murder, he saw a man come out of that gate. There is an arc lamp near, and by its light he could see a man in a fur coat and bowler hat slip out and go running down beside the wall. So somehow Fellowes *did* get out the window."

Bencolin gave a sudden exclamation, like a shout of triumph. They heard him strike the table and cry:

"Of course! Of course! I might have known it! . . . What time was this?"

"Mr. Simpson didn't remember. One doesn't, ordinarily, but it was around the time of the murder."

"At least," said the bishop complacently, "it proved him guilty, however he left the room."

"You fools! You fools!" Bencolin snarled, with more excitement than Sir John had ever seen him show. "Don't you see? Don't you see that it proves him innocent?"

There was a queer crushing silence, after which Sir John began to grope around blindly and mutter:

"Strike a light! I've got to *see* you, Bencolin! What are you talking about?"

"Listen: one question about this thing," the detective said rapidly. "Do you remember anything about Darworth's will? He made one, didn't he?"

"It was an odd kind of will," said the baronet. "Darworth's would be. He left his house and a life annuity to Dr. McShane; a thousand pounds to the Chinaman; and some other charities—the church too, I believe. . . . For God's sake, you don't really doubt that Fellowes killed him, do you?"

Darkness lent a tinge of unreality to the conversation. It was like a ghost conclave, except that the little Frenchman's voice was much too vibrant. He snapped:

"You have your car here, haven't you, Sir John?"

"The Daimler."

"How long would it take you to drive to London?"

"Starting when?"

"Now!"

"By fast driving, I could do it in six or seven hours."

"Then get the car out! Get it out, I tell you! We're going to London tonight. You have influence; telegraph Blackfriars to stay that execution as long as they can—get in touch with the board of aldermen. Use my name! Quick, for the love of God! If I can see McShane before tomorrow morning, we may save Fellowes!"

"You're insane!" the bishop said. "I refuse to be party—"

They stood up, opposite each other, clergyman and detective, each vaguely visible, but the hatred that sprang between them lit each face like fire.

"Bishop Wolfe," Bencolin said quietly, "Pilate was more merciful than *you.*"

Then he went out into the blue-shadowed lawn, striding up the terrace with Sir John after him.

VI

For three hours Dr. McShane had been sitting in the library listening to the clock strike. It was Roger Darworth's library, and he was master of it. In the great gloomy place, with lines of books and horsehair furniture, he sat at a table, playing with a child's toy Humpty Dumpty circus. The bright-colored dolls of clowns, the wooden animals, the bandmen, the ladders and barrels, were all arranged before him under the light of a gas lamp. He had bought them this afternoon, on an impulse, and he was childishly chuckling now. The lamplight shone on his glistening face, with the eyeglasses stuck on a round nose, the startled eyes, the wisp of hair straggling down over his bald head. Dr. McShane did not understand why he should grow afraid every night. He never wanted to go upstairs, nor did he want to go into the back of the house, for he might have to pass the brown door of Roger Darworth's study. There, the clock was striking again. Four. The windows were wide open, so that occasional noises from the street were startlingly distinct in the night stillness: the clop-clop of hoofs swinging past, the rattle of a cart, the brawling voice of a huckster. Once the doctor thought he heard a motorcar stop.

If McShane was very nervous, it may have been due to the fact that he was steadily drinking himself into a stupor. Brandy at intervals had unstrung him; one of the toy clowns plopped off a ladder, and the clack as it landed on the table made the doctor jump. . . . He kept imagining that people were moving around in the house, or fancied the click of the door latch, though he knew that Mock Yen, the Chinaman, must be in bed. Vaguely McShane wondered whether his glass eye stayed open while he slept. It might be disconcerting to find him asleep sometime, with one stary eye looking up at you while he breathed deeply in slumber.

He had pots of money now. There was no need to practice. He could get drunk all he wanted, thought McShane, and reached for the decanter. Dark in here; almost the way it had been when Roger Darworth gave his séances. It would be terrible to look up from the table sometime, and find Roger Darworth staring at him over the red lamp, the way he used to do. . . .

McShane looked up then, suddenly and unaccountably. He sat with a toy elephant in his hands, motionless, with his eyes getting wider. There was a man standing by the library door.

He was only duskily visible; he wore a fur coat, and a bowler hat, and had one hand on the portieres of the door. A diamond ring glittered on the middle finger.

McShane did not move, or cry out. He felt the rumblings of the brandy in his stomach, his sight swam a little, and he felt nauseated. The toy elephant fell with a thump on the table.

"Darworth!" said McShane. "Darworth."

The stranger came forward. As he moved more into the light, McShane saw that it was not Darworth's face. It was a lean, tired face, with steady black eyes, black mustache and beard, and a hooked nose.

"I am not Darworth," the newcomer said, "but you recognize the costume, Dr. McShane. The police will be here to take you soon."

Behind the portieres of the door were two other figures, peering in the gloom. Over the shoulder of the man in the fur coat they saw McShane totter up behind the grotesque pageant of the toy circus. They heard him say:

"I didn't kill Darworth. . . ."

"I know you didn't," said the man in the fur coat.

Abruptly the doctor pointed.

"Why are you wearing those things?" he cried. "It's . . . summer!"

"Because I found them in Darworth's study, doctor." The watchers saw the man in the fur coat lean on the table, over toward McShane, who was backing away. "You know about it. I found them in the chest where he had hidden them. Listen!"

"I won't! I didn't kill anybody!"

"Listen! What was the disease with which Darworth was dying? What was the disease that would have killed him within a month if he hadn't been stabbed?"

"There wasn't any. . . . Oh, my God, get away."

"Yes, there was, doctor. You warned him against it. You warned him the night Bishop Wolfe came here. You knew Darworth's spiritualism was a fake, only another of his ghastly jokes. You knew he was a ventriloquist and a handcuff king. You knew that he had summoned reliable witnesses here to see a fake murder. You knew that when he left this room the night he died, and told you to wait, that he went to his room and put on these imitations of Fellowes' clothing; that he went out his own window, and came around to the front door to impersonate Fellowes. You knew he went down the hall, where Bishop Wolfe and Sir John Landervorne were watching, used his ventriloquism to throw his own voice into an empty room and say, 'Come in.' You knew he entered the room, stabbed himself with a stolen knife, and just as he was able to get out of handcuffs, so he was able to get into them after the knife was in his chest. You knew he bribed Mock Yen to swear Fellowes had really come in. You knew the whole thing was a plot to convict Fellowes of murder, since Darworth was dying of disease!" His voice went into a shout: *"You knew that, didn't you?"*

The strain of the battle could not last much longer. It was as though every nerve force of the two men was locked over the table with the circus, weakening with the faint gray light of morning. McShane's eyes closed; he choked, as though with sickness, and he sat down drowsily.

"All right, all right," he said.

Bencolin turned away from the table. He went trailing over to the window in his absurd fur coat, and put his forehead against the cool glass.

"Sir John!" he called in a dull voice. "Bishop Wolfe! Get me some water, will you? I'm sicker than he is."

VII

Sir John Landervorne came running into the room. The old baronet looked haggard after a night of driving.

"Where's the telephone? McShane!" he demanded. "Where's the telephone? If we can get the prison . . . Quick, where is it?"

McShane looked up with a lopsided grin, and cackled:

"I won't tell you!"

"Are you insane? Look here, wake up! A man is to be executed this morning—don't you understand that?"

"I won't tell you!"

Bencolin was still standing motionless, with his head against the glass. Sir John looked around helplessly, at the drunken smile in the chair and the grinning clowns on the table.

"Here it is!" clamored Bishop Wolfe with eagerness, putting his head in at the door. "I found it in the hall. You can call them, can't you?"

When Sir John had gone hurrying out, Bishop Wolfe went over to Bencolin. McShane was pouring out another drink. The cleric, lit by the gray dawn and the dull gaslight, blinked his red-rimmed eyes, stroked his light hair, and said apologetically:

"I—I really don't see how you knew all this, sir."

Bencolin put up the window, breathing the warm wind that blew in. He turned his old tired mocking eyes.

"Why, you didn't recognize that the man who was seen leaving by the gate was not Fellowes at all, but Darworth in his costume," he said. "The witness said it was still snowing, didn't he? And at the time of the murder it wasn't snowing, so it was before the murder —it was the time when Darworth left his house, to return in the character of Fellowes. Please go away. . . ."

"I know, I know you're tired," prompted the bishop in a flurry, "but Darworth must have known there would be no snowstorm to efface the footprints of a man leaving by the window after he killed himself."

"That," said Bencolin grimly, "was what he forgot. He thought, with the window open, it would seem that Fellowes had left that way, and that the snow would take away footprints. But it stopped snowing before the suicide."

"Why, we must have seen that he couldn't get out that way!"

"*You* didn't, Bishop Wolfe," said the Frenchman, looking at him with steadiness. "Oh, my friend, isn't it so obvious? Isn't it so ridiculously plain a plot? All the mummery, when Darworth could easily have saved himself from Fellowes if he thought the latter meant to kill him? Planting an audience who were not allowed to see him? A murderer handcuffing Darworth without the latter's making a sound, when there were men within twenty yards. How could Fellowes have done it? Why would Fellowes have invented a story so impossible as to be absurd, unless it were true? Darworth was resolved that if he was to die anyway, Fellowes should never live to enjoy the money that was coming to him. He could hardly enjoy the money, Bishop Wolfe, if he was hanging at a rope's end. God! It's so cheap and stagy. . . ."

"But how did you know about his being a handcuff king?" persisted Wolfe.

Bencolin smiled faintly, and said with drowsiness:

"I'm a policeman, monsieur. My business is handcuffs. And I have seen Darworth give one of his séances. . . ."

The sun was coming up, over the blank rows of houses, filling the areaways. A milk wagon clattered past. One sleepy housemaid threw up a window with a bang. And the warm light had something in it that held the heart, as though all the world had stopped its breathing. . . . McShane rattled his glass and mumbled a few words. Then Sir John Landervorne appeared in the doorway. His face was perfectly blank.

"We're too late," he said. "He was hanged ten minutes ago. They haven't cut him down yet."

"I don't see that I'm to blame!" returned Bishop Wolfe nervously. "I merely did my duty to justice in trying to run down—"

"Shut up!" Sir John ordered in a toneless voice. He went aimlessly over to the table and began picking at the scattered toys, and tried to balance a wooden lion on a toy chair. Suddenly he drew a long breath, adding: "Well, he's dead."

A drowsy, deadening hush of summer, ruffled by light winds, was on the street and in the room. Bencolin took off the coat.

"I'm sorry I could not have got here sooner," he observed.

Then Sir John began speaking in jerky bursts:

"They said he—he died very well. He was not crying when he left Miss Melford. He walked out to the scaffold without—you know—stumbling or fainting. They had his coffin there. He smoked a cigarette on the platform and Miss Melford was crying, but she was waving to him. He smiled. . . ."

"Where the hell is the rest of that brandy?" mumbled Dr. McShane, thrashing around him.

"Apparently the phone call that sent him to her house that night came from Darworth," went on Sir John, "and his mimickry! The conversation you overheard, Bishop, was about Darworth's health. . . . Miss Melford will be around here soon. They've told her. We . . . shall have to face that girl, Bishop."

The bishop raised his earnest eyes, one arm up as though he were in the pulpit, the other hand on the lapel of his black coat.

"It is God's will," he said piously. "The ways of the Lord are dark, and His servants can only follow humbly. This thing, which seems so tragic, is but another manifestation of divine intervention for good. We must pray for Fellowes' soul."

Bencolin did not laugh. He did not feel like laughing. But he made a sound that was something like passionate fury, and his hand dropped from the window, and he turned.

"Oh, Bishop," he said, "when will you learn? When will you learn?"

The Haverfordian, May 1927

The Murder in Number Four
Further Adventures of Bencolin and Sir John Landervorne

DURING the night run between Dieppe and Paris, on a haunted train called the Blue Arrow, there was murder done. Six passengers in the first-class carriage saw the ghost; one other passenger and the train guard failed to see it, which was why they decided the thing was a ghost. And the dead man lay between the seats of an empty compartment, his head propped up against the opposite door and his face shining goggle-eyed in the dull blue light. He had been strangled.

This Blue Arrow has an evil name. At twelve o'clock the channel boat leaves New Haven. With good weather, it arrives at Dieppe about 3 A.M. On a wintry night of sleet and dull-foamed waves it is the atmosphere for ghosts. The great echoing customs shed, hollow with steam and the bumping of trunks, the bleary lamps, the bedraggled passengers filing silently up the gangplank, set an imagination running to things weird. Sickness, loss of sleep, the bobbing eerie boat floundering in against the pier, had made a wan crew of these eight people on the night of December 18th. Thus, after a six-hour crossing on which the vessel several times lost the Dieppe light and staggered helpless in the gale, they boarded the Blue Arrow for Paris.

Superstitious porters have many tales about this train. Its engine is misshapen, and sometimes there rides in the cab a blind driver named Death. Along the moonlit waste people have been ground under the wheels, with no sound save a faint cry and a hiss of blood on the firebox. On this run, too, there was once a fearful wreck; they say that on some nights, when you pass the place, you can see the dead men peering over the edge of the embankment, with their smashed foreheads, and lanterns hanging from their teeth.

The testimony of eight witnesses was to be had about the tragedy, on this night of December 18th when the murder was committed. Nobody had particularly noticed the victim; he traveled alone, and in the boat he had sat in a corner of the lounge with his hat pulled over his eyes, speaking to none of them. Sir John Landervorne, on his way to Paris to see his old friend M. Henri Bencolin, had asked this mysterious person what time the Blue Arrow arrived there, but he received only a shrug. Mr. Septimus Depping, another Englishman, had asked him for a match; the stranger merely muttered, *"Je ne parle pas anglais."* Miss Brunhilde Mertz, militant feminist, clubwoman and tourist from the United States of America, had tried to engage him in conversation about the inestimable advantages of prohibition (as she did with everybody), and had been highly incensed when he merely turned his back.

On the Blue Arrow, he went into a compartment by himself and pulled the door closed. He had not changed the blue night lamps; those who passed in the corridor could see his back as he sat staring out of the window. The guard had got his ticket from his skinny outthrust hand while his back was turned. Even during the examination of passports before they boarded the train, although Miss Brunhilde Mertz had earnestly tried to look over his shoulder, nothing was seen. Then there was a dispute in the customs shed, because Miss Mertz shrilly refused to open her trunk ("Do you think I'm going to let that nosy man look at my underwear?"), until, after she had shrieked "No key! No key!" in ever increasing volume, with the idea that the louder she yelled in English the more easily would she be understood, the weary inspector merely sighed and passed her. Under cover of this disturbance, the dark man disappeared into the train.

Now here occurs a random bit of information of which nobody made much. Two of the passengers professed to behold something. These two were M. Canard, one of the most fiery of the French journalists, and his companion, Mademoiselle Lulu, who played a harp. They said that by one pale light on the edge of the pier, they had seen a man standing motionless at the line of the smoky whitish water. He had not been on the boat. He merely stood there, his cloak blown around him, leaning on a cane, and one of his hands clasped over the cane held a cigarette. The next moment he vanished, almost as though he had jumped into the water.

In the train, the midmost compartment was occupied by the man who was to die. That was number four. In number one were M. Canard and Mademoiselle Lulu. In number two, Mr. Septimus Depping and Miss Brunhilde Mertz. Number three was vacant. In number five, Sir John Landervorne. In number six, Villeford, the proprietor of a café in Montmartre of not too good reputation. In number seven, Mr. Charles Woodcock, a traveling salesman from America. Number eight was vacant.

A drowsy hush settled on the train when it started, a drugged chill of spirits and bodies, for the heating system would not work. The blue night lamps flickered a little in the drafty corridor. At one end of this corridor, by the door, stood Sir John Landervorne, tall and gray, leaning against the railing and smoking. The train swayed ever so little in a creaking rush: that was the only noise. At the other end of the corridor, from the second of the two doors opening from the car on that side, appeared the train guard.

Somebody screamed. It was Mademoiselle Lulu. She had had an altercation with M. Canard, and in tearful dignity she had swept out of compartment number one and planted herself in the vacant one, number three. Her cry was dreary and chilling in that cold place, as though produced by nightmare; for she had seen a face pressed against the glass of the door giving on the corridor, a bearded face which looked as though it had its nose chopped off. It disappeared in an instant; she put her head against the cushions in terror.

Someone else gave an exclamation. When everyone came tumbling into the corridor, it developed that the face had looked in at every compartment, as the testimony of witnesses showed later. *Yet neither Sir John Landervorne, who had been standing at one end of the corridor, nor the train guard, who stood at the other, had seen anybody there, though, at the moment Mademoiselle Lulu cried out, they were looking at each other from opposite ends of the car.*

Then Miss Brunhilde Mertz, while they all stood out there shivering, happened to glance into compartment number four. They saw the dark man stretched out between the seats, and he did not move. Then, while they looked at each other with that sinking panic of horror piled on horror, Sir John tried to open the door. It had been bolted on the inside.

Saulomon, the train guard, pulled the emergency cord. With the train stopped on a dismal waste five miles from Dieppe, they investigated. They went round to the other side of the train; it had no door there, but three windows set level together. One of these windows was down halfway, but secured there by its snap; it would go no further. The others were up and locked.

When the corridor door had been pried open, the occupant of compartment four was found with face discolored by strangulation, eyes blood-filled and staring out, the bruises of thick hands on his throat. He was dead.

Now, this man had been seen entering the train, he had been seen sitting at the window, and Saulomon had collected his ticket some ten minutes before. The door was not bolted then. But the door was bolted now, and no murderer could have gone through that door. Nor could a murderer have come through the window. One of the windows was down some inches, but no human being could have squeezed through that space, even if anyone could have reached the window—for it was twelve feet from the ground, and the idea of a murderer clinging to the side of a train was impossible. The other windows were locked.

Two days later, the Parisian police discovered the murdered man's identity. He was traveling under a forged passport as a lawyer from Marseilles; his real name was Mercier, and he was probably the deftest diamond smuggler in Europe.

II

There was a conference of puzzled people in the office of M. Villon, he of the great, bald mechanical head and small body, who may be remembered as having worked with M. Henri Bencolin in the LaGarde murder case. He had never forgiven Bencolin for tricking him into smoking the cigarette which held the identity of the woman spy Sylvie St. Marie; but that was all meaningless ancient history now. For M. le Comte de Villon was now promoted to the position of *juge d'instruction,* the most dreaded police official in France, whose cross-examination of suspects is a process which even American third-degree experts are forced to admire. And now Bencolin was away; for some months he had been in the United States on a police mission. Villon was in sole charge of the Blue Arrow mystery; very spiteful in his quiet, ponderous way, with his pinpoint eyes and big flabby hands.

He sat behind his broad desk, blinking slowly. With him were Sir John Landervorne and Saulomon, the train guard, each bright-featured under a reading lamp in the gloom of the great room.

"It is curious," Villon said slowly to Sir John, "that you should be coming to France to see M. Bencolin, monsieur. He has been away some time. Surely you would know of that?"

Sir John was little grayer, a little more irascible; the rust had got into his voice and the rime on his features. He seemed to be made of wire and iron, gaunt in the leather chair, and the sharp cheekbones threw odd shadows up over his eyes.

"See here," he said. "I have had the honor to be associated with the French police many times, my dear sir. I was with Bencolin when he dug the truth out of that Fragneau stabbing in England, and the Darworth business too. I have yet to be a suspect myself. . . . It's rather a shame Bencolin isn't here now. Would you accept him as a character witness?"

Villon muttered, "Bah! Bungler!" under his breath, and shifted, and played with a penholder. But he continued smoothly: "Monsieur, this is not a question of character witnesses. You must realize that both you and M. Saulomon here tell an extraordinary story. You say that you were at opposite ends of this corridor, and that neither of you saw a person there who was plainly seen by six people in the various compartments." He spread out his hands.

Saulomon, who was tall, smooth-shaven and rather threadbare, ill at ease in Villon's ponderous presence, made a protesting gesture.

"M. le Comte," he remarked, "is justified in calling it extraordinary. But it is true. I swear it is true! I do not lie, I. For ten years I have served—"

"Oh, let him talk! It's true enough," Sir John said irritably.

"Nothing? You saw *nothing?* Come now, my friend: The dim

light, the possibility that you might have looked away . . . eh?"

"Nothing! The light was clear enough for me to see this man Saulomon at the other end. I wasn't looking away, because I was waiting for him to get my ticket."

"But if I may ask, what were you doing in the corridor?"

"Great God! Can't a man step out for a cigar if he likes?"

"You could have smoked in your compartment, if I may mention it. *Peste*, but no matter! You could not have mistaken each other, possibly?"

"No, we could not. Both of us are over six feet; I have a beard, but it isn't black, and neither of us went near the compartments at the time this woman screamed. You want a small man with his nose chopped off. But why concentrate here? If *I* may mention it, why not discover how the person who killed this fellow Mercier killed him, anyway? I had only been standing in the corridor five minutes or so. How did the murderer get in and out?"

"He didn't go through a bolted door," said Villon, smiling. "He must, therefore, have come through the window."

"Wriggling a normal body through five or six inches of space while the train was in motion?"

"Well, he might have been a very small man."

"A dwarf, yes. Where does your dwarf come from? And how is he able to strangle a man?"

"Why, from the roof of the carriage, possibly. They do it frequently in the American moving pictures." Villon's face was a strange caricature of an intelligent man being stupid: the dull-smiling lips and suspicious eyes strikingly naïve. For Villon was baffled, and he was maintaining anything he could think of. Sir John could hardly restrain his bubbling anger, but he asked:

"And the motive for this crime? This phenomenal dwarf who slides down from train roofs, strangles a large man, walks through a bolted door without disturbing the bolt, and parades up and down the corridor to show his beard and his chopped-off nose—what's his motive, if any?"

"His motive," answered Villon with sudden ringing clearness, "was robbery. I have examined the customs officer who looked at the man Mercier's passport. Mercier took his credentials out of a large wallet. The officer saw that the wallet was filled with thousand-franc notes. When the body was examined, the wallet was empty."

Villon got up from the desk. His big head seemed to drag down the weight of his body, and he was peering at them shaggily.

"Messieurs, I don't suspect you. Don't be under a misapprehension. I want to find out who knew this Mercier, and therefore I must see everybody. The other passengers are coming here tonight." He touched a bell. "No; be still, please."

Then Villon went over to the window. Lights were strung over the naked city, following the dark curve of the river and the toy bustle on the Pont Alexandre. He shivered. For a while there was silence. Villon's next remark startled them with its dreary frankness.

"I must confess to failure. I do not seem to handle things the way Bencolin did. He saw to everything. But I'm only human; I have too much work! Work, work, nothing else, and I'm only human, yes. . . . I should have caught this man Mercier. I didn't set the nets, and I should have done so. We were on the watch for him. He had diamonds. This will cost me my position, I fear, messieurs. . . .

"*Bien,* you shall know everything," Villon continued, with sudden doleful helplessness. "Mercier had been in America. He had smuggled six uncut diamonds of great value past the English authorities; he arrived at Southampton two weeks ago on the liner *Majestic.* Scotland Yard lost track of him, but we were warned to watch the channel ports. He had a confederate. It is not known where this confederate is now; it is not known whether the confederate is man or woman. We do not even know whether Mercier was carrying the diamonds, or whether he disposed of them in England, but this latter is considered unlikely. They were not on his person when he was killed, nor were they in his hand luggage. And you should know this. The tide of diamond smuggling has turned to Europe now; the United States has become so rigorous that it is impossible for even the cleverest of them—like Mercier—to do it safely. I did not set the nets. It will cost me my position."

Slowly Villon turned round.

"A few things only are to be known as possible clues. The compartment has been tested for fingerprints, both on the glass of doors and windows and on the woodwork near the windows. The only fingerprints are those of Mercier. His luggage, consisting of a small portmanteau, was found rifled and scattered near the station; it had not been carried into the train. Do you make anything of that? Well, I will go on. Sir John, you were the first to examine Mercier after the murder. Did he wear a beard?"

"Why, yes—a brown beard. It was—"

Saulomon abruptly lifted his head.

"But—that is—are you *sure,* monsieur?" he demanded. "I recall distinctly that the man in compartment four had no beard when I took his ticket."

"Exactly!" Villon cried. "And he had no beard when he was before the passport examiner; the passport picture shows a clean-shaven face. But when he was taken to the morgue after the murder, he was bearded. The attendant doctor discovered that the beard was false. It had been hurriedly put on with spirit gum between the time he left the passport examiner and the time he entered the train. *Why?"*

After a lengthy silence Sir John observed, "He might have been intending to meet somebody in Paris. . . ." Then he stopped, and began drumming on the chair arms.

Villon went to the desk and leafed through some papers.

"Here are our reports. We had six people on that train, aside from yourselves. Four of them we may eliminate as having no probable connection with this affair. They are useful only as corroborating the evidence. With M. Canard I am personally acquainted; in fact, I may say that I am one of his closest friends. He had never before set eyes on this man Mercier, nor had his *petite amie,* Mademoiselle Lulu. M. Villefranche and Mr. Woodcock, the American salesman, you yourself have eliminated, M. Landervorne. As you will see by the records, they occupied compartments where they were under your eye the whole journey until the time of the murder—and we shall be forced to accept you as a reputable witness. Besides, thorough inquiry nets no possible connection between either of them and Mercier, or our agents would have discovered it. *But,* by a curious coincidence, both Mr. Septimus Depping, the Englishman, and Miss Brunhilde Mertz, the American lady, had seen Mercier before; they must have seen him. All three of them traveled to England on the *Majestic* two weeks before." He picked up two type-written sheets. "Here are their records. With your permission, I will read:

"Depping, Septimus. R., Loughborough Road, Brixton, London. Business: jeweler, Bond Street, London. Age, fifty years, appears in comfortable circumstances. Recently returned from the United States. In Paris now on business for firm of Depping & Davis. Occupied compartment number two with Miss Mertz. Testimony: 'I was asleep most of the time, when I could, because the woman kept talking a lot of damned drivel about women's rights, and poked me in the ribs with an umbrella when I dozed off. Once I went out to see whether I could get a drink; that was shortly after the train started, and about ten minutes before we saw the man look in the window. I couldn't get the drink. Yes, I saw the man look in the window, but not very well; I was sleepy. I don't remember the time. All I remember was that that asinine woman talked loud enough to wake the dead, and complained about everything, and said the American trains were comfortable and much faster than anything she's seen over here. Address in Paris: Hotel Albert 1er, rue Lafayette.

"Mertz, Brunhilde Nation. R., Jinksburg, Missouri, U.S.A. Author of 'Woman, the Dominant Sex,' 'What Europe Owes to Uncle Sam.' Age stated as none of our business. Touring the Continent for the purpose of lecturing about it in America. Testimony: 'It's a pity you can't ride on a train in this abominable country without getting murdered! And such service! Did you ever hear of the checking system for baggage?' Examining magistrate: 'Madame will pardon me if I ask her to confine herself to the essential facts?' Witness: 'Well, if that isn't essential, I'd like to know what is—such cheek! I want you to know I'm an American citizen, and you can't bully me, young man, or our ambassador will—' Examining magistrate: 'Madame, I beg of you—' 'Well, what do you want to know? *I* didn't kill the man; I sat right in my compartment the whole time. Certainly I saw the measly, stupid little rat's face that looked in. . . .' "

"And so on," said Villon, putting down the paper. "Miss Mertz was a somewhat difficult witness, as you will perceive. That is all."

He sat down. In the stillness his chair creaked. Taxis hooted along the quai below. Leaning forward, Villon rested his head on his clasped hands.

"It would almost make one think wild things," Saulomon said in a low voice. "If you were aboard the Blue Arrow night after night, you would feel it. Thieves, murderers, ghouls ride it, streams of them, and we don't know them; we hardly see them, in the mist. But their evil remains, like a draft out of a cellar." He looked up suddenly. The sharp features, the long, powerful hands, the eyes of a mystic, made him incongruous in his role. But in the next instant stolidity closed over him, and he stared down at the floor.

It was as though the imagination of all three, focused on a weird train and a strangler's hands, brought a little of the blue mystery of it into that room. A sense of remoteness added to their feeling of nearness to a dead man in a false beard—which somehow made it all the more horrible. A sudden noise would have startled them. They were looking at murder, through the distorted magnifying glass of an eyewitness.

III

It was some moments later that Miss Brunhilde Mertz arrived, escorted by Mr. Septimus Depping. They sat in chairs so that a semicircle was formed round Villon's desk. Miss Mertz leaned forward, a heavy stuffed woman, staring down over the icy bulges of her figure through glasses which made her eyes terrifying in size; she carried her gray hair like a war banner, and spoke with the baffled ferocity of a saint who knows he is right but can convince nobody. A hat resembling a duck under full sail rode aggressively over one eye. Mr. Depping, on the other hand, was uncomfortable; he fidgeted, polished his monocle, stroked his ruddy face, smoothed at the creases of the immaculate trousers on fat legs.

"Er . . . well?" said Mr. Depping.

". . . and furthermore," said Miss Mertz, "if you think you can bullyrag me, I want to tell you you've got another think coming!" She shook her finger, and the duck wagged ominously. "The very idea of this outrage, *the very idea!* Now, none of your parleyvooing on me, sir; you speak English. Everybody ought to speak English over here; the idea of this foolish talk, widdgy-widdgy, and waving your hands, like a lot of crazy people! It isn't natural, *I* say! And—"

"Madame," said Villon, rather awed; he stumbled, and added deftly: "Mademoiselle, of course! I do not wish to offend you. We are merely trying to get at the truth of this matter, you see. Just a few questions."

"Questions! Bah! If you were half a police force, you would have solved this thing long ago. The idea!"

"Perhaps mademoiselle has some ideas?" Villon asked politely.

"I have found the murderer," said Miss Mertz.

There was such an abrupt and appalled silence that Miss Mertz enjoyed the full savor of it before she went on. Then she became theatrical. Flustered, pompous, with glasses and hat coming askew at the same moment, she got up.

"Let a real intelligent person show you how to act, you slow-pokes!" she cried. "I want to tell you, if you had more people from the good old U.S.A. around, you'd soon know how to handle these things—wouldn't they, Depping?"

"Er . . . of course," said Mr. Depping.

"Now I'll tell you how I did it. I was coming down the elevator in the lobby at the Ambassador tonight and right over by the door that runs into a little alcove, I saw a man sitting, and I knew who it was. It was the same one who looked in the compartment at us on the train; I'd swear to it on a stack of Bibles. Well, *I* knew what to do, and I didn't waste any time. I got my porter, and he got a policeman. The porter speaks English, and I told 'em what to do. You never can tell what they'll do against Americans in these foreign cities; if we jumped on the man, he might start a rumpus, and maybe we'd get a knife in us, the way they do in these foreign cities. So I just had the porter call him in the corridor that runs out to the street right by the hotel. They jumped on him, and stuffed a handkerchief in his mouth so he couldn't yell for his friends and maybe get me killed; and I told the policeman I'd be responsible—to bring him right around here with us, and I'd present you with the murderer." Triumphant and breathless, she pointed toward the door. "They've got him right out there now, and your flunkies all round here are trying to keep him quiet."

Villon rose heavily, as though lifted by a sort of slow explosion. His mouth was partly open, and he merely stared. Depping was fumbling to adjust his monocle.

"Bring him in!" shrilled Miss Mertz.

Everybody in the room scrambled up, turning a hodgepodge of astonished faces. An apologetic *agent de police* escorted through the door a very quiet little figure, who was spitting out a handkerchief with gurgles of disgust.

Villon bawled, "Lights! Turn them on over by the door!" When the lights came on, Villon's mouth opened still further. The prisoner gently disengaged his arms from the grasp of the policemen. He stood looking over the group slowly and sardonically—a small man, whose lips were pursed mockingly under his pointed black beard, eyebrows raised in quiet amusement. His careful evening dress was slightly rumpled under the long cape, and he held a silk hat under his arm.

"Oh, my God," Villon said slowly and tonelessly.

"Mademoiselle," explained the stranger, "is not oversupplied with brains."

"Brains? *Brains?*" cried Miss Mertz, glaring around her at the group. "What do you mean, brains? Do you know who I am?"

"Why, naturally," the stranger replied, smiling. "If I may be so bold as to say so, you are the meddling shrew who has nearly ruined a somewhat important piece of work, and I, mademoiselle, am Bencolin, the prefect of police of Paris."

IV

Bencolin went over to the desk. He put down his hat, removed his opera cloak, and put that beside it; then he pulled off his white gloves—quietly, in perfect stillness. Villon had not moved.

The prefect of police faced them, his fingertips spread out on the desk. Under the light of the hanging lamp his head was sharply outlined, with the glossy black hair graying at the temples and parted in the middle; the pouches under the quizzical black eyes, and the wrinkles around them; high hooked nose; curling mustache and short pointed beard—with Bencolin, the caricaturists had always a chance for Mephistopheles.

"I am sorry that I have had to resort to this deception," he said. You noticed not a little of the aristocrat in the back-thrown head, the slow, graceful speech, the faint and dominant contempt with which he faced Miss Mertz. "I have been in France for several days, but few people knew it. I was not prepared to have my presence smashed in on you in such an abrupt fashion, but I had no choice." He smiled suddenly, and exhibited the gag he still held. "Chiefly, my apologies go to M. Villon. But since I am here, I must make my arrest before I should have chosen to do so."

Mr. Depping had the monocle in his eye, and was frankly staring. Sir John's face wore a curious smile. Saulomon was casually searching after cigarettes. Miss Mertz still had her arm extended in the dramatic gesture; she had not straightened the hat over her eye.

"Bencolin," cried Villon, "you were the man in the corridor, then?"

"Yes. That is why I owe you so many apologies. Won't you sit down, Miss Mertz? I have much to explain.

"When I arranged this elaborate bit of deception," he went on, "I did not know that I should have to cope with murder. My intent was to trap the accomplice of the man Mercier. We of the police cannot be content with knowing the identity of our guilty men. Unlike the detectives in fiction, we must have proof. My friends, two months ago I went to America to assist in running down a league of smugglers—that story does not belong here. Four of them are now in the hands of the New York police. The fifth, Mercier, escaped us, and came to England. The sixth and last is here, in this room.

"Please do not interrupt. I knew who he was, I knew that Mercier would meet him, and Mercier walked into my trap. For Mercier sold in England the diamonds he had brought with him from the States. I know to whom he sold them, and I knew that when Mercier came to France and divided his gains with his last confederate, we should be able to arrest that confederate. For Mercier carried marked money.

"There was a trustworthy man in whom I confided, privately; he watched Mercier in London, and followed him on the channel boat, which I met at Dieppe. Of course, Sir John Landervorne's connections with Scotland Yard ceased long ago, but he remains no less valuable for that. I met the boat at Dieppe. *I must not be seen;* if I were seen, it was necessary that my presence be denied. I had confided in Sir John. I also confided in M. Saulomon, the train guard, because I recognized his intelligence, and also because it was such an ironical joke that I should confide thus in the man who murdered Mercier. . . . M. Saulomon," he said quietly, "you are caught. I trust that you will make no resistance."

It would have relieved the tension had anybody exclaimed, or moved, or cried out. Instead, there was such a deadly matter-of-fact calmness in the room that the whole proceeding seemed unreal. Saulomon was lighting a cigarette; his big hands did not tremble, his face was wooden, but under the harsh light the veins were throbbing in his head.

"Proof, monsieur?" he asked.

Abruptly the thought shot through Sir John's mind: "God, something's going to happen!"—the stiffness of Bencolin's pose, the tensity like the sound of drums slowly rising.

"Your strongbox at the Credit Lyonnais," answered Bencolin, "contains the marked money you stole from Mercier's wallet when you killed him. You said that you took Mercier's ticket; you did not, because you never went into the compartment. I found it on him when the body was examined at the morgue. They found none of your fingerprints at the scene of the crime; nevertheless, they were found on the metal clasps of Mercier's rifled portmanteau."

It was rather like handling a bomb. By his shiftings in the chair, the struggle that reddened and pulled his face, they thought for a moment that Saulomon would act. Then, soothingly, the struggle ceased. Saulomon inclined his head.

"I did it, monsieur," he said.

"Let us reconstruct, then. You knew Mercier was coming over, but you did not know on what day to expect him. At Scotland Yard we did not arrest him; we deliberately forced him over on that boat, letting him think he was distancing us, because we wished to use him as stalking horse for you. Mercier and you had been working cleverly. Consider! A train guard, who there in that dimly lighted place could pass for a porter, could take a man's luggage and abstract smuggled stones from them before the luggage went to the customs. A clever plot. But this time Mercier did not play the game. He wanted to get away from you with the money he had gained in England. The false beard? Exactly! He put it on after he had left the passport inspector; he did not turn on the full lights in the compartment, hoping thus to deceive you and slip past. Well, you could play such a game yourself, eh?

"Now! Mercier is already in the train, and you know who this bearded gentleman is. He has bolted his door so that those who got into the train would not enter and see there a man wearing a beard —he did not wear a beard on the boat. You could not enter by the door. But *outside:* the train is waiting there by its platform, and as usual, it is a high platform above the tracks, so that one passing by the train finds the train windows on a level with his breast. Inside one compartment, near the window, which is halfway down, sits Mercier, opening the wallet which contains his winnings. You see him. You are a tall man—your hands through the open window in an instant, there in the darkness of the platform. Mercier sees only two hands, which flash in at his throat. He is still gripping the wallet when the life has gone out of him. Had it fallen on the floor, you would have been baffled, for you knew the money was not in the portmanteau, which you had already rifled. Look! His knees are drawn up in a death agony which is grotesquely like that of a sitting man. Here is an alibi. Mercier propped against the window, sitting there as though he were peering out, with his back to the door—you saw the possibility. Nobody could see that he was dead. He would tumble down, of course, after the train started and the movement dislodged him, but if it could be proved that he was alive when the train started, your alibi could be strengthened all along—it was almost perfect. Your error lay in saying that you had taken his ticket, for you wished to keep him alive as long as possible, and you did not want to discover the body—there might be embarrassing questions."

Bencolin sat down on the edge of the desk and pulled up his trouser leg. He regarded Saulomon thoughtfully.

"I also made a mistake, M. Saulomon. I should not have gone into the train at all. But looking through the window outside and seeing Mercier on the floor, I was not unnaturally startled; I came in to see what had happened, and found the door bolted. Then I began to realize what had happened. I wanted to see who was on the train, and when I foolishly exhibited myself at the corridor window, I had to get Sir John and M. Saulomon to swear that they had seen nobody. Why? Well, was it not good tactics? If I revealed myself to the murderer as the prefect of police, got him in the league with me, and threw myself on his mercy for silence, was it not rather good evidence to him that I suspected nothing? Otherwise he would hardly have been so secure in his position, and he would not have deposited in a bank that marked money which will send him to the guillotine."

Saulomon stood up. His eyes were brilliant, he smoothed at his pale hair, and suddenly he laughed.

"It was admirable, M. le prefect. Well!" He glanced towards the policeman in the doorway.

"I could kill you, Bencolin," said Villon venomously. "If for nothing else, I could kill you for that absurd masquerading as a ghost. Why? Why must you look in and scare everybody to death?"

"That statement," said Bencolin, "is not flattering. Besides, I did not have my nose chopped off; I merely pressed it against the glass." He contemplated the speechless Miss Mertz, raised his eyebrows and chuckled faintly. "Give me pardon for a little curiosity, my friend. I wanted to see whether Miss Brunhilde Mertz had succeeded in getting through the French customs the one of Mercier's diamonds which she had bought from Mr. Depping in London."

V

Bencolin and Sir John Landervorne left Villon's office in the Quai d'Orsay. There had been a somewhat hectic scene, in which Miss Mertz was remembered to have struck somebody with an umbrella. In the midst of it Sir John remembered most distinctly Saulomon's tall, pale figure standing unmoved among the shadows, on his face a dim smile of wonderment and pity.

Muffled in their greatcoats, Bencolin and Sir John crossed over and stood by the embankment at the river. A faint snow hovered in the air, like a reflection of the weird pale carpet of light which flickered on the dark water, and, beyond, on the dull shine of the Place de la Concorde. A necklace of lamps on a soft bosom which shivered with the cold; windy spaces and low gray buildings, twinkling, muttering; the lighted arch of the bridges; farther on, the closed bookstalls where the river curved away. To Bencolin, every house held a quiet mysterious beauty, every street stone was a shining miracle. He leaned on the balustrade and sniffed the sharp wind.

"A pretty enough chessboard, isn't it?" he remarked after a while. "A chess game can be a terrible and enthralling thing, when you play it backwards and blindfolded. Your adversary starts out with his king in check, and tries to move his pieces back to where they were at first; that's why you can't apply rules or mathematical laws to crime. The great chess player is the one who can visualize the board as it will be after his move. The great detective is the one who can visualize the board as it *has been* when he finds the pieces jumbled. He must have the imagination to see the opportunities that the criminal saw, and act as the criminal would act. It's a great, ugly, terrific play of opposite imaginations. Nobody is more apt than a detective to say a lot of windy, fancy things about reasoning, and deduction, and logic. He too frequently says 'reason' when he means 'imagination.' I object to having a cheap, strait-laced pedantry like reason confused with a far greater thing."

"But look here," said Sir John, "suppose you take this business tonight. You gave a reconstruction of that crime, all right, and perhaps that was imagination. But you didn't tell us how you knew that was the way it happened. Reason told you that. Didn't it? How did you get on to the murder, anyhow?"

"It's an example of what I was trying to say. There is so much elaborate hocus-pocus around the whole matter of criminal detection that it makes a detective wonder why people think he acts that way. The fiction writers want to call it a science, and attach blood pressure instruments to people's arms, and give them Freud tests— they forget that your innocent man is always nervous, and acts more like a guilty one than the criminal himself, even his insides. They forget that these machines are operated by the most cantankerous one of all, the human machine. And your psychological detective wants to pick out the *kind* of man who committed a crime; after which he hunts around till he finds one and says, 'Behold the murderer,' whether the evidence supports him or not. I hope you'll permit me to say damned nonsense. There is no man who is incapable of a crime under any circumstances; to say that a daring crime was necessarily committed by a daring person is to argue that a drunken author can write on the subject of nothing but liquor, or that an atheistical artist could not paint the Crucifixion. It is frequently the tippler who writes the best temperance eassay, and the atheist who finds the most convincing arguments for religion.

"And your so-called 'reason,' in an intricate crime, convinces you of exactly what is untrue. It reduces the thing to the silly restricted rules of mathematics. In this Mercier murder, for example, reason said to me Mercier was alive when the train started, because he was seen sitting by the window, and the guard took his ticket; also, somebody must have been in the compartment with him, since no man could have strangled him from outside while the train was in motion. This was perfectly elementary logic, and quite false. Imagination asked me these questions: Why did not Mercier make an outcry when somebody attacked him? Why did he not struggle; does a person sit quiet and unmoving when he is assailed? Why no resistance, then? *Because Mercier did not see the murderer,* a thing impossible if anybody were in the compartment. What does it suggest? Hands through the window, obviously; confirmed by the fact that though Mercier's wallet was robbed, his pockets were not rifled— the murderer's arms would not be long enough to do this through the window. Discount the testimony for an instant, says imagination, and see whether this would have been possible at any time. Yes, before the train started. Did anybody speak with Mercier after this time, or see him move? Nobody except the train guard. Yet this sole witness first says that the man's back was turned when he took his ticket; later he announces that Mercier was wearing no beard. How did he see that, if the man's back were turned and the lights were so dim that you who examined the body face to face could hardly distinguish the features? Then see whether the guard did take the ticket. If not, he lied, and the evidence of the only person who spoke to Mercier after the train started is discounted. I found the ticket.

"Well, then. Who fits all our specifications for the guilty man? We know him to be a confederate of Mercier; it seems likely that he is also the murderer. Who else? Two others on the train had been associated with Mercier. On the boat from New York he had made arrangements with Mr. Depping to sell Depping his diamonds. (I also was on that liner, and it was I who threatened Depping with the law if he did not pay Mercier in marked money.) Moreover, Miss Mertz had bought one of the diamonds. Both these people were on the train. Neither had reason to kill Mercier, so far as I knew, and it was physically impossible for either to have killed him. Depping was too small to have reached that window; Miss Mertz had not the strength."

Bencolin paused, and smiled. *"Voilà!* I'm getting as verbose as a detective in fiction," he said. "I dragged you over here to Paris, and I don't mean to talk shop all the time. Suppose we go somewhere and have a drink. *Taxi!"*

IN THESE early stories Carr already demonstrates a magician's ability to misdirect his audience. For instance, in "The Fourth Suspect" he mentions the mask, but we miss its true significance because he directs our attention to the unimportant similarity between the eyeholes and the bullet hole. "The Ends of Justice" provides a good example of Carr's fair yet misleading use of clues; we should have known the meaning of Darworth's conversation with McShane, but it takes Bencolin to interpret it correctly. (In Carr's novels the misinterpreted conversation becomes a favorite plot device.) Even in the opening statement of a case Carr legitimately directs us away from the key point; reread, for example, the first few pages of "The Murder in Number Four" to see how Carr leads us to conclude that the murder was committed inside the train.

As you read the remainder of the stories and plays in this book, watch for clues and beware of misdirection. But I doubt that anyone will be wary enough to notice when Carr, like a prestidigitator, palms the ace.

RADIO
PLAYS

JOHN DICKSON CARR was unequaled in creating an eerie atmosphere by careful choice of emotive words, and many passages of his novels and short stories are especially effective when read aloud. This ability transferred easily into the preparation of radio dramas. Beginning in 1939, Carr wrote mystery plays and wartime propaganda for the British Broadcasting Corporation. After the United States entered the war, Carr returned to America to sign up for military service, and while waiting for orders from the government, he agreed to prepare radio plays for the Columbia Broadcasting System series *Suspense*. Carr's first episode was broadcast for half an hour on Tuesday, October 27, 1942, and during the next eight months Carr wrote twenty-two original scripts. By that time the government had decided where to assign Carr; he later recalled that the authorities "turned me round and sent me back to London as a staff member of the BBC." In addition to writing and narrating BBC propaganda broadcasts, Carr created a mystery program called *Appointment with Fear*, for which he wrote a new series of plays.

Carr's *Suspense* and *Appointment with Fear* programs are the finest products of the golden age of radio mysteries—an era that also produced such notable series as *The Adventures of Ellery Queen, Sherlock Holmes* and *I Love a Mystery.* More than any other radio dramatist, Carr knew how to create tension merely with sound. "Cabin B-13," the first of the scripts presented in this book, was one of the most popular plays broadcast on the radio. CBS and BBC repeated it several times; it was adapted as a television drama; and in 1953 the script became the basis of a feature-length movie, *Dangerous Crossing,* starring Michael Rennie and Jeanne Crain. The other plays include brilliantly crafted miracle problems, an almost unknown adventure of Carr's great detective Dr. Gideon Fell, and more plot twists than seem possible in a thirty-minute broadcast.

Radio plays induced the listener through dialogue and sound effects to "see" the events. So imagine yourself before a radio; you turn on the set, and with a background of organ chords, *Suspense*'s narrator, "The Man in Black," introduces another weekly episode—a tale, he intones, "compounded of mystery and suspicion and dangerous adventure . . . calculated to stir your nerves."

A Note About "The Phantom Archer"

In the July 1988 issue of *CADS*, the British magazine devoted to crime and detective stories, Andrew Mayot and Mike Brinck pointed out that the radio drama "The Phantom Archer," as printed in the first edition of *The Door to Doom*, contains an error or at least a misstatement that is so serious that Carr's candidate for murderer could not have been guilty. (I can't tell you what this mistake was without revealing the solution.) The error appeared in the *Ellery Queen's Mystery Magazine* publication of the script, but it may not have originated with Carr; the script of the play preserved in the British Broadcasting Corporation's Play Library does not have the error. We have corrected the text on the following pages.

Cabin B-13

NARRATOR: Come, now—in happier, peacetime days—to a great ocean liner on the night of her departure for Europe. There she is at the West Twenty-second Street pier: the twenty-five-thousand-ton *Maurevania,* of the White Planet Line. Smoke from her three funnels coils up lazily in mild October air. You can see the decks, white and shiny like shoe boxes; and the string of lights along them; and the band standing by on A deck to "play her out." You can hear the murmur of an excited crowd and the rattle of steam winches as cargo is lowered into the hold. You can see the bustle of activity, and the second officer standing at the head of the gangplank, as two rather late passengers hurry through the customs shed towards that gangplank, and . . .

(RICHARD BREWSTER *is thirty-five, with a pleasant, assured, but rather worried manner. His wife,* ANNE BREWSTER, *is in her late twenties, and clearly under some emotional strain.*)

ANNE *(breathlessly):* It's all right, Ricky! We're *not* too late!

RICHARD: No, Anne. I thought we'd be in time.

ANNE *(dreaming):* A honeymoon in Europe! Three whole months with nothing to worry about!

RICHARD *(gently):* That's right, dear. And you've been my wife for —let's see—practically five hours now.

ANNE: We did decide to get married rather quickly, didn't we?

RICHARD: So quickly, Anne, that we have to travel on our own passports instead of a husband-and-wife one. *(Amused)* I hope they don't think you're not an honest woman.

ANNE *(with a flash of gaiety):* I'm going to act like a complete wanton, just to devil you! What about our tickets? Do we give them to that officer standing at the top of the gangplank?

RICHARD: No. Keep your ticket. The cabin steward will come around and collect it after we're under way.

ANNE: And . . . the money, Ricky?

RICHARD *(worried):* It's a lot of money, Anne. Twenty thousand dollars in cash. Maybe I'd better turn it in at the purser's office for safekeeping.

ANNE: Yes. Maybe you had. I . . . *(Groping)* Do you mind if we stand here for a second, before we go up the gangplank?

RICHARD *(quickly, concerned):* What's the matter? You're not ill, are you?

ANNE: No. But . . . getting over brain fever isn't any joke.

RICHARD: I know, dear.

ANNE: You see, I ought to be eager and excited. Like all those people up there. But I get fancies. Queer, sick fancies. All I can think of is the night, and the wind, and all the black water in the dark.

RICHARD *(sharply):* That's exactly the kind of morbid fancy I'm trying to cure you of!

ANNE: I know, Ricky. I—I'll be good. Which way do we go?

RICHARD: Up the gangplank, through that door there, then down in the elevator to B deck. And no more horrors, do you understand? *(Music up)*

RICHARD: Here we are, Anne. B deck, and cabin number . . . Good Lord! B-13!

ANNE: B-13!

RICHARD *(uneasily)*: You're not superstitious, are you?

ANNE: No, dear. Not about things like that. Open the door.

RICHARD: Here we are. *(Door opens)* Lights on, and . . .

ANNE *(delighted)*: Ricky! It's a *beautiful* cabin!

RICHARD: Best I could get, dear. They've got our luggage in, anyway. *(Mock solemnity)* And over there, madam, you'll find a basket of fruit and some books from your obedient servant.

ANNE: You *are* nice to me, Ricky! *(Bursting out)* And I'm such a *miserable* little devil!

RICHARD *(gently)*: You're nothing of the kind, darling. But you'll not find any detective novels among those books. Detective stories may be all right for Presidents and college professors; but they're straight poison to *you*.

ANNE: I keep thinking and *thinking* about one.

RICHARD: Now, Anne . . .

ANNE: It's an old one. You probably know it. But it was new to me. A woman and her daughter arrive in Paris and go to a hotel—

RICHARD: You mean the old Paris Exposition story?

ANNE: That's it! The daughter goes out. When she returns, her mother has disappeared and even the hotel room isn't the same. The proprietor of the hotel swears the girl came there alone, and that there never *was* any mother. The girl goes to the police, and *they* won't believe her. Of course, it turns out that the mother has caught bubonic plague and died, and they're hushing it up so that visitors won't keep away from the city. But—

RICHARD: You've got to stop this kind of talk, Anne!

ANNE: I know. But imagine being in a position like that! With all those queer eyes staring at you! Wondering if you'd lost your reason! Wondering if your brain had cracked, and the whole world might dissolve, and . . . Listen! *(The noise of a hollow, brassy gong)*

VOICE: All ashore that's going ashore! All ashore that's going ashore!

RICHARD: That's the last call, Anne. We'll be under way any minute.

ANNE: You know, Ricky, I *would* like to see the skyline go past. And the Statue of Liberty, and the rest of it.

RICHARD: Then why not go up and see it? I've got to deposit this money in the purser's office on C deck.

ANNE: I—I don't like to leave you!

RICHARD: Now look here, my dear. You don't think *I'm* going to disappear, do you?

ANNE: I suppose I don't, really. When I get these ideas—and I can't help it, Ricky!—I wish you'd kick me!

RICHARD: I'm not going to kick you, Anne; but we've got to find *some* way out of this! *You* certainly won't disappear, in a crowded ship with any number of people around you. As for me, I'd defy Houdini himself to make *me* vanish. . . .

ANNE: Don't *talk* like that!

RICHARD: . . . and I hereby challenge any attendant magician to do it. Run along, dear. I'll join you on deck as soon as I can.

ANNE: All right, Ricky. I'll be good. (*Music up. It fades to the murmur of an excited crowd, as though lining the rail of a ship.*)

MAN'S VOICE: In with your gangplank! In with your gangplank!

SECOND VOICE: Gangplank in, sir!

MAN'S VOICE: Close the rails! Stand by!

ANNE (*muttering*): Eager people! Excited people! Happy people! Crowding up to the rail to wave good-bye! Nothing to worry about! Nothing on their minds except—

(DR. PAUL HARDWICK *speaks. He might be any age between thirty and forty; he has the gentle manner of the philosopher rather than the man of action.*)

HARDWICK: Except seasickness, madam?

ANNE: Oh!

HARDWICK: I *beg* your pardon! I hadn't meant to startle you, believe me!

ANNE: Please don't mention it. It was my own fault. I—I haven't been very well.

HARDWICK (*gravely*): I noticed it, madam, if you'll forgive me. That was why I spoke to you. As you see by my uniform, I am the ship's doctor—Dr. Paul Hardwick, at your service.

ANNE: I'm Mrs. Brewster, doctor. Anne Brewster. When does the ship go?

HARDWICK: In a few seconds, Mrs. Brewster, you'll hear the whistle. Then the band will strike up "Auld Lang Syne." (*Two blasts on a loud ship's whistle.*)

ANNE: We're moving, aren't we?

HARDWICK: Yes. This isn't your first crossing, Mrs. Brewster?

ANNE: I'm afraid it is, Dr. Hardwick. My husband's crossed many times, he tells me. But not in this ship.

HARDWICK: Then I hope you're a good sailor.

ANNE: Why, Dr. Hardwick?

HARDWICK: Because we'll run into some very dirty weather, once we're out at sea. October is a bad month for traveling.

ANNE: If I do get seasick, doctor, I'll rush straight to you. And I'll expect to be cured.

HARDWICK: I'll do my best, Mrs. Brewster. How do you like the *Maurevania?*

ANNE: It's a magnificent ship, from what I've seen of it. And they've given us a very nice cabin down on B deck. B-13. *(Pause, then sharply)* What's the matter? Why are you looking at me like that?

HARDWICK: I beg your pardon. Did you say . . . B-13?

ANNE: Yes, of course! Why not!

HARDWICK: You're quite sure of that, Mrs. Brewster?

ANNE: Yes, of course I'm sure of it! I saw the number on the door. Why not?

HARDWICK *(slowly)*: Because . . .

ANNE: Go on, Dr. Hardwick!

HARDWICK: Because there's no such cabin aboard this ship! *(Pause)* I'm not joking, Mrs. Brewster. Some people are superstitious. Many ships, like this one, omit number thirteen on each deck. You *must* have been mistaken!

ANNE *(fiercely)*: What are you trying to tell me? Do you think I saw something that wasn't there?

HARDWICK: Not at all. I only—

ANNE: Then come along with me, and I'll show you! I'll *prove* to you there's a number thirteen! *Will* you come along?

HARDWICK *(slowly)*: Yes, Mrs. Brewster. I think perhaps . . . I had better *escort* you.

(Music up)

ANNE *(calling)*: Stewardess! Stewardess!

STEWARDESS: Yes, miss! Yes, ma'am! Coming straightaway!

ANNE *(desperately)*: Tell me, stewardess. This *is* B deck, isn't it?

STEWARDESS *(puzzled)*: B deck, ma'am? Yes, ma'am. No doubt about *that.*

ANNE: Dr. Hardwick and I have been all over this part of the ship, looking for cabin number 13. But . . .

HARDWICK: Will you please tell this lady, stewardess, that there's no cabin number 13 on this ship?

STEWARDESS (*earnestly*): There sure to 'eaven isn't, ma'am! And never 'as been. I've served aboard the *Maurevania* a matter of eight years, and I ought to know.

ANNE: But I tell you, I saw it! I was in there! A big cabin, with a private bathroom attached. The walls were paneled in light oak; the furniture was rosewood and yellow satin; and the portholes were like real windows!

STEWARDESS (*dubiously*): That's not much good, ma'am.

HARDWICK: No, I'm afraid not. Most of the cabins look like that. What name was the cabin booked in?

ANNE: Brewster, naturally! Mr. and Mrs. Richard E. Brewster.

STEWARDESS: There's no Brewster on my list, ma'am.

ANNE: I tell you, I was *in* there! They'd even delivered the luggage! I saw it!

STEWARDESS (*still more bewildered*): Excuse me, ma'am. But I had a look-see in all the cabins I'm in charge of, just to see if the passengers wanted anything. And *I* don't remember any luggage with a "Brewster" label on it!

ANNE (*sharply*): Wait a minute! There may be a simple explanation of this!

HARDWICK: That's better, Mrs. Brewster. I was hoping you might find one.

ANNE: Ricky—that's my husband—Ricky and I have only been married a very short time. When my maid printed the baggage labels, she may have made them out in my maiden name. I never noticed at the time.

STEWARDESS: Oh? And what name might *that* be, ma'am?

ANNE: Thornton, Anne Thornton.

STEWARDESS (*heartily, relieved*): Lord, miss, why couldn't you 'a' said that before! I remember it well! Two suitcases and a little trunk! They're in B-16.

ANNE: And where's B-16?

STEWARDESS: Right behind you, miss. You're standing in front of the door.

ANNE: But what about my husband's luggage?

STEWARDESS: There's no gentleman's luggage in that cabin, miss.

ANNE *(crying out):* Where's Ricky? What have you done with Ricky?

HARDWICK: Please, Mrs. Brewster! Be quiet! There's one easy way to settle this.

ANNE: Settle it? How?

HARDWICK: Look down the corridor. You notice the man coming towards us—the man with the two gold stripes round the sleeve?

ANNE: Well?

HARDWICK: That's Mr. Marshall, our second officer. Did you ever see him before?

ANNE *(excitedly):* Yes, of course I have! He was standing at the top of the gangplank when Ricky and I got aboard!

HARDWICK: Then he may be able to tell us something. *(Calling)* Mr. Marshall! Mr. Marshall!

MARSHALL: Yes, doctor? What's up?

HARDWICK: Take a good look at this young lady. Have you seen her before?

MARSHALL: Seen her before? As a bloke once said to me at a pub in New York, I should hope to kiss a pig I have! Any passenger as pretty as she is gets special attention from the old Marshall eye.

HARDWICK: You saw her come aboard tonight?

MARSHALL: Yes! Certainly!

HARDWICK *(casually):* And of course, you saw the gentleman who was with her?

MARSHALL *(puzzled):* The . . . gentleman who was with her?

ANNE *(wildly):* Yes! Yes!

MARSHALL: But there was nobody with her. *(Pause)*

HARDWICK: You're quite certain of that, Mr. Marshall?

MARSHALL: My dear doctor, she was the last of 'em to come aboard. And I'll take my Bible oath there was no other passenger with her. Or ahead of her or behind her, if it comes to that!

ANNE: *Why are you lying to me? All of you?*

HARDWICK: Please, Mrs. Brewster! Lower your voice!

ANNE: I know what this is. It's the old Paris trick. But you won't get away with it, do you hear? I'll go to the purser. I'll go to the captain. I'll . . . *(Breaking off, almost in tears)* Dear Father in Heaven, won't anybody believe me?

(Music up)

NARRATOR: Later that night the S.S. *Maurevania* is battling a head-wind twenty miles off Ambrose Light. You can feel the long balloon surge of the deck underneath; then the crest of the wave; then the sudden downward plunge, with a queasiness rising in your stomach, and the crash and hiss of water across fo'c's'le head and forward hatches. In the captain's room, just abaft the bridge, there is a conference of ship's officers. Outside, stung by spray, clinging to the bulkhead rail in the dark, a frightened girl waits until the door to the captain's room opens and . . . *(Door opens.)*

ANNE: Dr. Hardwick!

HARDWICK: You can come in now, Mrs. Brewster. The captain will see you.

ANNE: Does *he* believe me?

HARDWICK: Better hold tight to that bulkhead rail, Mrs. Brewster. We're pitching rather badly. Easy!

ANNE: I'm all right, doctor. Which one is the captain?

HARDWICK: That stout, red-faced man sitting behind the desk.

ANNE: What's his name?

HARDWICK: Captain Wainwright. Just tell your story straightforwardly and don't excite yourself.

(CAPTAIN WAINWRIGHT *is elderly, with a deep, gruff, slow speaking voice. He is not unkindly, but just now he is harassed almost beyond endurance.)*

WAINRIGHT: Will you bring the young lady in, Dr. Hardwick, and close the door?

HARDWICK: Yes, sir. Here we are. *(Door closes.)*

WAINWRIGHT: Then maybe we can get to some decision in this matter. Will you sit down beside my desk, Miss Thornton?

ANNE: My name is Brewster, Captain—Mrs. Anne Brewster.

WAINWRIGHT *(resigned):* Whatever you say, Mrs. Brewster! Now, I might tell you, ma'am, that I've got a lot on my mind already. The first officer comes aboard with an attack of flu; I'm facing an equinoctial gale short-handed; and now *this* has to happen!

ANNE: I can't help that, Captain. I want to know what they've done with Ricky!

WAINWRIGHT: Just one moment, please, while I get this straight. By this time, I understand, you yourself have personally interviewed every single passenger aboard this ship. Is that true?

ANNE: Yes, it's true.

WAINWRIGHT: But your alleged husband is not here. Is *that* true?

ANNE *(desperately):* Yes! That's true! But . . .

WAINWRIGHT: In the meantime the purser has sent a squad of men to search this ship. They've searched every inch of it—you can take my word for that. And there's nobody hidden. Your husband's not here. According to Mr. Marshall, who's standing over there . . .

ANNE *(grimly):* I see him.

WAINWRIGHT: According to Mr. Marshall, he never was here!

MARSHALL *(uneasily):* Hang it all, Miss Thornton, you needn't glare at me like that! I couldn't see the chap if he wasn't there, could I?

WAINWRIGHT: Be quiet, Mr. Marshall!

MARSHALL: Yes, sir. Sorry, sir.

WAINWRIGHT *(remonstrating):* I'm not unreasonable, Mrs. Brewster. I think you'll admit that. But what can I do? What can I say? Can you offer any proof that this "husband" ever existed?

ANNE: Yes, of course I can! I . . . I . . .

HARDWICK: Excuse me for interrupting, but would you mind, Captain, if *I* asked a question or two?

WAINWRIGHT: No, doctor. Go ahead. I tell you, I'm going batty myself!

HARDWICK: If you were married, Mrs. Brewster, you must be carrying a joint husband-and-wife passport. Where is it?

ANNE: There wasn't *time* to get one! We each carried our own passport!

HARDWICK: I see. Still, there must be someone back in America who can confirm what you say, if we got in touch by radiotelephone? Your parents, for instance?

ANNE: I haven't any parents. They're dead.

HARDWICK: What about relatives, then? Or a guardian?

ANNE: My "guardian" is a trust company. The administrators don't know I'm married.

HARDWICK: But somebody must have performed the marriage ceremony! A parson? A justice of the peace?

ANNE: Yes, of course. But . . . I don't remember the name of the town.

WAINWRIGHT *(staggered):* You don't remember the name of the town?

HARDWICK *(quickly):* Hold tight to your chair, Mrs. Brewster! This ship's going to pitch again!

WAINWRIGHT *(sharply):* How's the glass looking, Mr. Marshall?

MARSHALL: Barometer's rising, sir. This weather won't hold long. But we shall be into fog before morning.

WAINWRIGHT: We're in a fog now, if you ask *me*. This lady says . . .

ANNE: It was a little town in upstate New York, where they can marry you at a moment's notice. Ricky kept the certificate. I—I was confused. I haven't been well. Ricky had been away, and he came back, and I was in love with him, and he sort of swept me off my feet, and . . . *(despairingly)* Oh, what's the use?

WAINWRIGHT *(soothingly):* If you'll take my advice, ma'am, you'll go below to your cabin and get some sleep. The doctor can mix you a sedative, and . . .

ANNE *(fiercely):* You think I'm crazy, don't you?

WAINWRIGHT: I think you're a little overwrought, ma'am.

ANNE *(groping):* What I can't understand is *why* you should play such a filthy trick! It can't be the bubonic plague *this* time!

WAINWRIGHT *(startled):* Bubonic plague, ma'am? Who said anything about the bubonic plague?

ANNE: Never mind. You're all against me—except maybe the doctor. But I'll show you! I'll prove it to you! I *am* going downstairs, and I don't want anybody to follow me. Good night, all of you! *(Door opens and closes.)*

MARSHALL *(with relief):* Wow! I'm glad *that's* over!

WAINWRIGHT *(worried):* Look here, Mr. Marshall. Do you think it's quite safe to trust her out there alone?

MARSHALL: I dunno, sir. She's as mad as a hatter, if you ask *me*.

WAINWRIGHT: You think she might . . . do something foolish?

MARSHALL: I think she might chuck herself overboard, if we're not very careful.

WAINWRIGHT: What's your opinion, doctor?

HARDWICK: I can give you my opinion, gentlemen, in a very few words. *(Calmly)* That girl is as sane as you are.

(WAINWRIGHT *and* MARSHALL *exclaim in protest.*)

HARDWICK: Wait! Hear what I have to say! I shared your own belief, at first. But I've been talking to her all evening. I've heard the whole story. And there's not a psychopathic trait in her nature. She firmly believes in this husband.

MARSHALL: Yes, doctor; and a lot of people firmly believe they're Napoleon. But they get stuck in loony bins just the same.

HARDWICK: This matter is not precisely a joke, Mr. Marshall. I tell you this man exists—or did exist.

WAINWRIGHT: What do you mean, doctor, *did* exist?

HARDWICK: Suppose he's been murdered and thrown overboard?

WAINWRIGHT: Murdered and thrown overboard? Why?

HARDWICK: If you remember, Richard Brewster was carrying a very large sum of money in cash: his wife's wedding gift and practically all her inheritance. He meant to go to the purser's office. But perhaps he never got there. That money might have been a great temptation to . . .

WAINWRIGHT (*sharply*): To whom?

HARDWICK: To a stewardess . . . or even (*thoughtfully*) to a ship's officer.

WAINWRIGHT: Exactly what are you getting at?

HARDWICK: Numbers on doors can be changed easily enough. Just print a small card and put it in the metal slot on the door.

WAINWRIGHT: I still want to know what . . .

HARDWICK: If you use your intelligence, gentlemen, I think you can figure out how a man can be made to vanish into thin air—and why Mr. Marshall saw no other passenger!

(*Music up*)

NARRATOR: Four o'clock in the morning—the hour of suicides and bad dreams. The gale has subsided; the sea is calm. But the S.S. *Maurevania* creeps blindly at barely eight knots, through a thick and strangling fog. The whole ship is dark, and sealed up in sleep. There is no sound in all that mournful dimness, except . . . (*Two hoarse blasts on foghorn*) except when the foghorn cries out a warning overhead. Even cabin B-16 is dark. Anne Brewster, still fully dressed, lies in an uneasy doze across one of the berths, her head almost touching the intercabin telephone, when . . . (*Phone rings.*)

ANNE (*starting*): What was . . . ? I thought I heard . . . ? (*Phone rings again.*)

ANNE (*shivering*): The telephone! Yes? Hello?

(RICHARD's *voice speaks.*)

RICHARD: It's me, Anne. *(Warningly)* Take it easy, now!

ANNE *(crying out):* Ricky! Where are you?

RICHARD: Shh! Keep your voice down!

ANNE: What happened to you, Ricky? Are you hurt?

RICHARD: No, I'm not hurt. But . . . he nearly got me.

ANNE: *Who* nearly got you?

RICHARD: Listen, dear. I can't explain over the phone, and I don't dare come down to you. Can you meet me up on deck?

ANNE: Yes, of course! Where?

RICHARD: Do you know the boat deck?

ANNE: Which one is that?

RICHARD: The top deck, where all the lifeboats are slung.

ANNE: Yes! I know it.

RICHARD: Go to the starboard side—that's the right-hand side facing forward—and find the fourth lifeboat from the aft companionway. There's a thick fog and nobody will see us.

ANNE: I'll be right there!

(Music up)

ANNE *(whispering):* This is the boat deck, unless I've completely lost my bearings. You can just barely see the shapes of the lifeboats. One . . . two . . . three . . .

RICHARD: Anne! Is that you?

ANNE: Yes, Ricky! Where are you?

RICHARD: Here! Duck your head under the lifeboat and take my hand!

ANNE: But isn't it horribly dangerous out there on the edge? With no railing along the ship's side?

RICHARD: Don't worry, Anne. I won't let you fall.

ANNE *(bursting out):* Ricky, put your arms around me! I've been so frightened and miserable I almost did throw myself over the side.

RICHARD: Look out!

ANNE *(gasping):* You—you caught me just in time, Ricky.

RICHARD: I'll say I did! What did you trip over?

ANNE: There's a big piece of iron grating with a rope through it, lying on the deck. In this fog . . .

RICHARD: It would be fatal if either of us fell overboard now. We're well aft, near the propellers. The suction would carry us into the propeller blades, and . . . Listen!

ANNE: I can't hear anything except the foghorn.

RICHARD: But *I* can. There's someone walking along the deck. And I can see a flashlight moving in the fog.

HARDWICK: You're quite right, my friend. You *can* see a flashlight.

ANNE: Dr. Hardwick! What are *you* doing here?

HARDWICK: At the moment I am covering both of you with a revolver. Please don't move.

ANNE: So you *were* in the conspiracy, Dr. Hardwick!

HARDWICK: What conspiracy?

ANNE: The whole ship's conspiracy to say Richard Brewster didn't exist!

HARDWICK: My dear young lady, you can set your mind at rest. There never was any ship's conspiracy against you. The people you spoke to were *perfectly honest.*

ANNE *(sarcastic):* Including Mr. Marshall, I suppose?

HARDWICK: Yes. Including Marshall.

ANNE: He was telling the truth when he said nobody came up the gangplank with me—or before or after me?

HARDWICK: That was not what Marshall said. He said no *passenger* came up the gangplank then.

ANNE *(bewildered):* What's the difference?

HARDWICK: A great crime has been arranged for tonight, young lady. Not less than the crime of murder.

ANNE: Murder? Who's going to be murdered?

HARDWICK: You.

ANNE: *What?*

HARDWICK: That, I repeat, is what has been arranged. But there is no conspiracy. There is only one criminal.

ANNE: And who is the criminal?

HARDWICK: The criminal is that man standing beside you. Your so-called husband.

(Pause)

ANNE: Dr. Hardwick! Do you know what you're saying?

HARDWICK: Yes. Marshall, of course, did see *someone* walk up the gangplank—loitering behind you. But he never dreamed of associating that person in any way with *you.* The person Marshall saw was . . . Well? Have you guessed it?

ANNE: No.

HARDWICK: He saw a ship's officer, returning from shore leave in civilian clothes.

ANNE: A ship's officer?

HARDWICK: Yes. That man's name isn't Richard Brewster. His real name is Blaney, and he's the first officer of the *Maurevania*.

ANNE: Are you trying to tell me . . . ?

HARDWICK: The captain can identify him. He's actually British, though he can fake an American accent very well. He's already got a wife in England, and he's planning to join her with the twenty thousand dollars he got from *you*.

ANNE: I don't believe this! *(Desperately)* Ricky! Why don't you say something?

HARDWICK: He planned it very cleverly, I admit. He never let you know he was a ship's officer. He'd been away for some time—naturally! He persuaded you to marry him in a hurry—naturally!

ANNE: Ricky, is this true?

HARDWICK: He had the money, you see. All he did was hang a dummy number on the cabin door, remove it later, put on his uniform, and walk away with his own luggage.

ANNE: Wait! I remember! Captain Wainwright told us the first officer came aboard tonight . . .

HARDWICK: With a bad attack of flu. Yes. Our friend couldn't be seen in public until after he'd disposed of *you*. The best thing was to convince everybody you were insane—as he nearly did. Then, when you went overboard tonight . . .

ANNE: They would all believe it was suicide?

HARDWICK: Exactly. But I suspected this "Brewster" from the beginning because he told such an obvious lie. You quoted him as saying he had never traveled on the *Maurevania*. Yet he could direct you all over the ship, and even knew where the purser's office was.

ANNE *(screaming):* Look out, Dr. Hardwick!

HARDWICK: What's wrong?

ANNE: He's got a piece of iron grating that must weigh fifty pounds. He's lifting it to throw. . . .

HARDWICK: Put it down, you fool! Put it . . . *(A cry and a heavy splash)*

ANNE: He jumped overboard!

HARDWICK: That was the weight he was going to use in sinking *your* body.

ANNE: But they'll pick him up, won't they? They'll stop the ship, and . . .

(Screams, loud and frantic, then choked away as though bubbling under water)

HARDWICK: What's that?

ANNE *(realizing):* The propellers! The ship's propellers!

HARDWICK: They have sharp blades, Miss Thornton.

ANNE: I can't stand this!

HARDWICK: It won't be easy, I know. But that cold-blooded swine planned a crime in the fourth dimension which for you would have been death in the fourth dimension. Believe me, my dear, it is better this way. . . .

(Music up)

Suspense (CBS), March 16, 1943
Ellery Queen's Mystery Magazine, May 1944

The Hangman Won't Wait

The Characters

Dr. Gideon Fell	the detective
Helen Barton	the accused
Colonel Andrews	governor of Maidhurst Prison
Herbert Gale	brother of the victim

Harris, the warder; women prisoners, etc.

NARRATOR: He comes striding towards us now, beaming like Old King Cole. You can probably hear him chuckle. If he wheezes a little, that's due to his weighing more than three hundred pounds. (DR. FELL *is faintly but sternly heard in the background. He has a powerful voice; its uproaring mannerisms suggest a combination of Dr. Johnson and G. K. Chesterton.*)

DR. FELL: Slander, sir. Gross slander.

NARRATOR: You notice the three chins, and the bandit's mustache, and the eyeglasses on the black ribbon. He removes his hat with old-school courtesy. Don't try to bow, doctor! He is Gideon Fell, doctor of philosophy and expert in crime. If he tells us something about the Barton case . . .

DR. FELL *(majestically):* Sir, I have only one remark to make about the Barton case. Everybody was wrong.

NARRATOR: I don't quite follow that.

DR. FELL: The judge was wrong. The jury were wrong. The prosecution was wrong. The defense was wrong.

NARRATOR: But, Dr. Fell, you can't have a murder case in which everybody is wrong!

DR. FELL *(proudly)*: In *my* cases, sir, you can have practically anything.

NARRATOR: Yes. That's true. But . . .

DR. FELL: I want you to imagine yourself in the position of that girl, Helen Barton.

NARRATOR: Well?

DR. FELL: Imagine yourself waking up suddenly, in the middle of the night. You're terrified, but you don't know why. The room is cold and nearly dark. All of a sudden you realize it's a room you've never seen before. There's a queer smell, like old stone and disinfectant. And there's no sound except . . .

(As the voice fades, we hear the notes of a heavy bell—suggesting a clock in a tower—strike four.)

(HELEN BARTON speaks. She is about twenty-five; she has a pleasant voice.)

HELEN *(dazedly)*: I . . . I . . . *(With a start)* What is it? What was that? *(The first woman who speaks gives the impression of being elderly, stout and motherly: subdued but cheerful. The second woman is more thin and acid. They are Londoners, not quite cockney.)*

FIRST WOMAN *(soothingly)*: Now lean back in your bed, dearie. It's all right!

SECOND WOMAN: Yes, take it easy, miss.

HELEN *(still dazedly)*: I . . . I was dreaming.

FIRST WOMAN: You were having a nightmare, dearie. But it's all right now. Nothing's going to hurt you.

SECOND WOMAN: Not yet.

FIRST WOMAN *(fiercely)*: Be quiet, Hannah!

SECOND WOMAN *(sulkily relenting)*: All right, all right! Would you like us to turn on all the lights, miss?

HELEN: Please—would you do that? You see, I don't understand this! Where am I? And how did I get here? And who are *you?*

SECOND WOMAN *(wearily)*: Now don't start that all over again, please!

HELEN *(crying out):* Start *what* all over again?

SECOND WOMAN: Saying you've lost your memory, and don't even know what your name is.

HELEN: Are you insane? Of course I know what my name is! I'm Helen Barton.

SECOND WOMAN: Ah!

HELEN: But it's all I do know. Where am I? And why on earth is it so cold?

SECOND WOMAN: Well! That's not unusual, you know, for England in the middle of December.

HELEN *(slowly):* Did you say . . . December?

FIRST WOMAN *(falsely cheery):* That's right, dearie. Eighteenth of December.

HELEN: You're fooling me. You're playing a trick on me. *(With growing wildness)* My head feels queer, and I want to start crying, but I won't. It's not December! It's the end of August. I was going up to see Philip. That's it! I was going up to see Philip!

FIRST WOMAN: Philip?

HELEN: Philip Gale. The man I'm going to marry.

SECOND WOMAN *(awed):* 'Struth!

FIRST WOMAN: Be quiet, Hannah! And don't turn on these lights yet!

SECOND WOMAN *(alarmed):* She's having us on! She . . .

FIRST WOMAN: Hannah, this child's shaking all over; and so help me, she *don't* know where she is! *(Cajolingly)* Listen, dearie. I'm going to sit down on the bed beside you. *(A creak)* Now take my hands. Hold 'em. Tight!

HELEN: What's wrong? Why are you looking at me like that?

SECOND WOMAN: This is Maidhurst Prison, miss.

FIRST WOMAN: Steady, dearie!

HELEN: I'm still dreaming! I must be! You can't mean *I'm* in prison?

FIRST WOMAN: Now look, dearie. I'm afraid it's worse than that.

HELEN: Worse than that?

FIRST WOMAN: Look over there. You see where there's a little bit of fire in the grate?

HELEN: Well?

FIRST WOMAN: And paper on the wall, and pictures? And a carpet on the floor . . .

SECOND WOMAN *(fiercely):* Why can't you come out straight and tell her? *(Flatly)* They're going to hang you in the morning, miss. This is the condemned cell.

(Strong, harsh music up. As this fades, we hear the voice of DR. FELL*)*

DR. FELL: "With sudden shock the prison clock
           Smote on the shivering air . . ."

(Five slow notes of a heavy bell)

DR. FELL: But I won't quote that any further. I have too vivid a memory of sitting up that night with Colonel Andrews, the governor of the prison. Over here you'd call him the warden. It was in a little office, with the lampshade tilted so that I could see his face. And he said . . .

*(*COLONEL ANDREWS' *voice suggests a thinnish middle-aged man with a military curtness but a fussy and worried manner.)*

ANDREWS: I hate executions. Loathe 'em! Can't even sleep the night before. If you hadn't offered to come here and save my life . . .

DR. FELL: This is a strange place, sir, to talk of saving lives.

ANDREWS: It's no good being sentimental about the thing. That's the law. *I* didn't make it.

DR. FELL: But I gather you're not exactly happy about this case?

ANDREWS *(abruptly):* I'm not, and that's a fact. Mind you, there's no doubt whatever about the girl's guilt!

DR. FELL: I am gratified to hear it.

ANDREWS *(querulously):* But if only she'd confess! Most of 'em do, you know.

DR. FELL: They confess to you?

ANDREWS: To me or to the hangman. Not often to the chaplain, because they think he'll threaten 'em with the hereafter. But when Kirkwood goes in with the strap to bind their arms, he says to 'em, "I don't like to think I'm doing something that would be on my conscience. So if you'd care to tell me . . ."

DR. FELL: Quite a sensitive fellow, your hangman.

ANDREWS: Look here, I'm serious!

DR. FELL: So am I.

ANDREWS: Sometimes I wish I had any job in the world but mine. If only the girl would confess! If she'd just stop this nonsense about "not remembering."

DR. FELL: Not remembering what?

ANDREWS: Not remembering how she shot Philip Gale! Not remembering anything, even her own name! Total amnesia.

DR. FELL *(gravely):* Sir, you frighten me. Do you mean to say that a woman suffering from loss of memory can be tried and sentenced to death?

ANDREWS: No! Not if she really *has* lost her memory.

DR. FELL: Well, then?

ANDREWS: But this defense was a fake.

DR. FELL: You're quite sure of that?

ANDREWS: Naturally! The judge would never have allowed it to come to trial if he hadn't been convinced she was shamming. Even then, she might have got off with a life sentence or even with manslaughter if it hadn't been for the nature of the crime.

DR. FELL: She didn't cut anybody up, I hope?

ANDREWS: No; but it was almost as bad. She shot a man who had raised his hands and begged for mercy. That completely damned her in the eyes of the jury.

DR. FELL: And yet you have doubts.

ANDREWS *(angrily):* I tell you, I *haven't* any doubts! And in any case, it's none of my business.

DR. FELL: How has she acted since she's been here?

ANDREWS: Oh, a model prisoner. But I wish she'd stop this business of seeming to be in a daze. It's getting on my nerves.

DR. FELL: I rather think the prison itself would get on *my* nerves. I looked into your execution shed once, and I didn't want to look again.

ANDREWS: You get used to it, after a while.

DR. FELL: Helen Barton won't. Tell me about her.

ANDREWS *(brooding):* Nice girl, too. I knew her grandfather.

DR. FELL: She lived near here?

ANDREWS: Yes! Born and bred in Maidhurst. She got mixed up with a thoroughgoing swine named Philip Gale. Crazy about him. Wouldn't hear a word against him. Then he threw her over for a woman with money.

DR. FELL: I see.

ANDREWS: He had a bungalow on Whiterose Hill. She went up there one Sunday afternoon.

DR. FELL: Alone?

ANDREWS: Yes. Herbert Gale, Philip's brother, heard them screaming at each other. He ran in to see what was wrong. Philip was
trying to chase the girl out. She grabbed a .32 revolver out of a table
drawer, and told Philip to put up his hands. That scared him, and
he did put up his hands. Then she shot him dead.

DR. FELL: And afterwards?

ANDREWS: Afterwards she "couldn't remember."

DR. FELL: Couldn't remember anything?

ANDREWS: Pretended she didn't even recognize her own family. She
said, "Who is Philip Gale?"

DR. FELL (reflectively): And you hang her tomorrow morning.

ANDREWS: Yes.

DR. FELL: Without ever hearing her side of the case.

ANDREWS: Confound it, man, there's no doubt about the evidence!

DR. FELL: Are you sure?

ANDREWS: She killed Philip Gale. Gale's brother Herbert saw her do
it. This hypocrisy about "not remembering" . . .

DR. FELL: Emotional shock could do just that, you know.

ANDREWS: She wasn't so emotionally shocked that it disturbed her
aim. She drilled him clean through the heart at fifteen feet. The
bullet entered in a dead straight line through coat, waistcoat, shirt
and heart. You could have run a pencil through the holes. (Angrily)
Now don't sit there puffing out your cheeks and waving a cigar at
me! I'm only . . .

DR. FELL (quietly): Tell me, Colonel Andrews. Aren't you talking to
convince yourself?

ANDREWS: No!

DR. FELL: I was thinking of that girl. Suppose she is telling the
truth. Suppose she has lost her memory. (ANDREWS protests.) All
right! You don't believe that. But suppose it! And then suppose, in
some black hour just before the hangman comes, that her memory
returns.

ANDREWS: Don't talk rubbish!

DR. FELL: Sir, I have lived long enough to know that mental suffering is the cruelest form of suffering on this earth. Imagine yourself in that position. You come out of a daze, into what you
thought was a safe and pleasant world. You don't know where you
are. You don't know what's happened. You only know that when

the clock strikes eight they are going to take you out and—
(A scream, very high and shrill, heard at a distance. Short pause.)
ANDREWS *(clearing his throat):* Did you hear that?
DR. FELL: Yes.
ANDREWS: Are you thinking what I'm thinking?
DR. FELL: Yes.
ANDREWS *(shakily):* It isn't possible . . . ?
DR. FELL: I very much fear it is.
ANDREWS *(blankly):* Sometimes, you know, we have to use drugs.
DR. FELL: Drugs?
ANDREW: Yes. When we take them to the execution shed. It's only a short distance, and we try to get it over in a matter of seconds. But sometimes they can't walk.
(Sharp rapping on a door.)
ANDREWS: Yes? What is it?
(The door opens. A WARDER, *middle-aged and rather hoarse, speaks.)*
WARDER: Beg pardon, sir. But I thought I'd better get you. Or the doctor. Or the chaplain. Or both.
ANDREWS: What's the matter with you, man? You're as white as a ghost!
WARDER: Can't 'elp that, sir. I've been a warder at this place for a matter of fifteen years; but I never knew anything like *this.*
ANDREWS *(noncommittally):* It's the . . . upstairs room, I suppose? Miss Barton?
WARDER: Yessir.
ANDREWS: Hysterical?
WARDER: Yessir. She says . . . well, she *(significantly) says* she remembers now.
ANDREWS *(still noncommittal):* I see.
WARDER: She's carrying on something awful, sir. But that ain't all. She claims she never done it.
DR. FELL *(sharply):* What's that?
WARDER: She claims she never killed Mr. Gale at all.
DR. FELL *(explosively):* Never killed . . . ?
ANDREWS: Any other disturbances in the building?
WARDER: Well, sir, they're a bit restless in A wing.
ANDREWS: That's usual.

WARDER: Yessir. And there's a bloke—outside the prison, I mean— who keeps hanging about in front of the main gate. You can see him by the street lamp. First he'll take a few little quick steps back and forth. Then he'll run and stick his face against the bars of the gate. Then he'll go back to pacing again. Fair gave me the creeps, even before this other thing.

DR. FELL: You don't happen to know who he is?

WARDER: It's the other Mr. Gale, sir. Herbert Gale. I hadn't the heart to chase him away.

ANDREWS: All right, Harris. Go ahead. I'll be along in a minute.

WARDER: Yessir.

(The door closes.)

DR. FELL: So the girl claims to be innocent! You heard that, eh?

ANDREWS: Yes. I heard it.

DR. FELL: What do you mean to do?

ANDREWS: I'll see the girl, of course. But it won't affect the issue.

DR. FELL: Not even if she does happen to be innocent?

ANDREWS *(breaking out):* Fell, in the name of heaven try to under- stand my position!

DR. FELL: Believe me, I do understand it. A jury convicted this girl of murder. Her appeal was dismissed. The Home Secretary has refused to intervene on behalf of the King. You couldn't do any- thing, even if you wanted to. You couldn't even appeal to the Home Secretary without new evidence. . . .

ANDREWS: Exactly!

DR. FELL: And it's too late for new evidence, because you can't just accept the word of Helen Barton.

ANDREWS: All the same, I'm dreading this interview, It's against regulations, but I wish you'd come along with me.

DR. FELL *(roaring):* If there were only *something . . .*

ANDREWS *(querulously):* There isn't. Where's that whiskey? I think a little stimulant . . .

DR. FELL: *She* will need the stimulant.

ANDREWS: It's a cold night.

DR. FELL: It will be colder yet, where *she's* going.

(Strong, harsh music up. This fades into the heavy notes of the prison clock, striking six.)

HELEN *(moaning):* But I didn't do it! I tell you, I didn't do it!

SECOND WOMAN: Steady, miss.

FIRST WOMAN: It's all right, dearie. The governor and the big stout gentleman believe you didn't do it.

HELEN: Oh, no they don't! You needn't try to fool me! Look at them over there in the corner, whispering!

ANDREWS *(under his breath):* Fell, she's lying.

HELEN: I heard that! You said, "Fell, she's lying." But I'm not lying! I'm not!

SECOND WOMAN: Miss, you've got to pull yourself together.

FIRST WOMAN *(heartily):* And have a nice breakfast. What would you like for breakfast?

HELEN *(bewildered):* Breakfast?

FIRST WOMAN: You can have anything you want for breakfast this morning. Anything at all!

HELEN: Please listen to me! When I first woke up, I didn't even remember Philip was dead. I thought I was still . . . going to marry him. Then it came back to me.

ANDREWS: Yes?

HELEN: I remember standing outside Philip's bungalow, on a hot day with the sun in my eyes. I heard a shot inside the bungalow. I ran into the living room, and found Philip lying on the floor by the couch, with his mouth open and blood on his chest. But that's all I do remember. Something hit me.

ANDREWS: Something *hit* you?

HELEN: On the head. Or that's what it seemed like. Please!

ANDREWS: The doctors found no injury to your head, you know.

HELEN *(desperately):* I tell you . . .

DR. FELL: One moment!

(Dead silence. We hear slow, heavy, lumbering footsteps crossing the floor, and the bump of a cane. DR. FELL clears his throat.)

DR. FELL: Miss Barton, can you forgive the intrusion of an old duffer who sincerely wants to help you?

HELEN *(controlling herself):* I'm s-sorry, Dr. Fell. I'll try to be sensible.

DR. FELL *(surprised):* You know who I am?

HELEN: Everybody knows those eyeglasses and that mustache. But I thought you were always laughing. *(Bitterly)* If you can find anything to laugh at in *this* situation . . .

DR. FELL: Believe me, Miss Barton, I am not laughing. Now tell me. When you arrived at the bungalow, Philip Gale was already dead?

HELEN *(fiercely):* Yes!

DR. FELL: You didn't go up there to quarrel with him?

HELEN: No! And why should I have killed him, anyway? I only went to tell him I was through. Finished! Fed up with him! I . . . Oh, what's the use?

DR. FELL: They haven't told you, then, that there's a witness who claims to have seen you shoot Gale?

HELEN *(astounded):* A witness? Who?

DR. FELL: Herbert Gale.

HELEN *(not even angry, merely wondering):* But that's a lie!

DR. FELL: You didn't take a .32 revolver out of the table drawer?

HELEN: This is the first time I've even *heard* of any revolver! Please believe that!

DR. FELL: You didn't order Philip to put up his hands? And then, when he did put up his hands . . .

ANDREWS *(interjecting):* . . . high above his head . . .

DR. FELL: . . . you didn't shoot him from a distance of about fifteen feet?

HELEN: No! No! No!

ANDREWS: Your fingerprints were on the revolver. You were still holding it in your hand when Herbert brought a policeman.

DR. FELL *(thoughtfully):* Just who is this brother, this Herbert Gale?

HELEN *(starting to laugh):* He's the good member of the family.

FIRST WOMAN *(urgently):* Now steady, dearie!

HELEN: I c-can't help it! Herbert is the good boy, where Philip was the bad one. Younger than Philip. Terribly respectable; pillar of the church; never smokes or drinks. Has to work hard, because Philip inherited what money they had. Oh, let me laugh! It's too funny!

ANDREWS *(guardedly):* Herbert's word certainly carries weight.

HELEN: It's carried weight against me, hasn't it? Why should he want to get me hanged? Why should he tell such a complete pack of lies?

DR. FELL: Yes. I wonder why.

HELEN: Every second I imagine I'm going to wake up and find myself back in that living room again. Looking at Philip's body! Just standing and staring at it, and feeling sick! And—of all things to think of at a time like that!—wondering why he was wearing a waistcoat on such a hot day. . . .

(Slight pause)

ANDREWS *(sharply):* What's the matter with you, Fell?

FIRST WOMAN *(under her breath):* Why is that stout gentlemen rolling his eyes like that?

SECOND WOMAN: Off his rocker, if you ask me.

DR. FELL *(explosively):* Archons of Athens! What an idiot I've been! What a turnip! What a dunce!

ANDREWS *(scandalized):* Lower your voice!

DR. FELL: The murdered man was wearing a waistcoat! You told me so yourself.

ANDREWS: Well? What if I did?

DR. FELL *(as though awed):* The murdered man was wearing a waistcoat on a hot day! Grasp that beautiful fact! Keep it in splendor before you! Three hours of sheer nightmare, and all because I never thought of the waistcoat?

FIRST WOMAN *(under her breath):* Lummy, Hannah, he really *is* off his chump!

DR. FELL *(eagerly):* Let me ask you just one thing. What happened to the court exhibits in the Gale case?

ANDREWS: As a matter of fact, we've still got 'em. The case was tried at the Maidhurst sessions house, you know.

DR. FELL *(pouncing):* You've still got 'em?

ANDREWS: Certainly, but . . .

DR. FELL: Sir, let me shake your hand. Let me slap you on the back. Let me, if necessary, set you on my shoulder and carry you out of here in triumph. Let me . . .

ANDREWS *(definite cold water):* Just a minute, my friend. Stop a bit!

DR. FELL *(suddenly deflated):* I . . . I beg your pardon.

ANDREWS: Have you forgotten where you are?

DR. FELL: No.

ANDREWS: Let's face facts. The prisoner has been told that there's . . . well, no hope.

HELEN *(crying out):* Please!

ANDREWS: I'm sorry, but there it is! The cruelest thing you could do now would be to raise hopes that I can't fulfill. Do you understand that?

DR. FELL: I understand it only too well.

ANDREWS (*fidgeting*): This can't be pleasant for any of us. There's nothing in the evidence that justifies any change of plan. . . .

DR. FELL: Except, of course, that the girl isn't guilty.

ANDREWS: Can you prove that?

DR. FELL: To my own satisfaction, yes.

ANDREWS: That's not good enough.

DR. FELL: Very well, suppose I proved it to you—conclusively, mind! —out of evidence you gave me yourself. What would you do?

ANDREWS: Are you bluffing?

DR. FELL: No. Speak up, man! What would you do?

ANDREWS: That's easy. Phone the Home Secretary and ask for a stay of execution.

DR. FELL: Could you get in touch with him at this hour of the morning?

ANDREWS: Easily. There's a private line from my office to his country house. But I warn you . . .

HELEN: Dr. Fell, is there any hope for me? Is there *any* hope for me?

ANDREWS: I warn you. They won't accept fancy theories. They'll only accept facts.

DR. FELL: I shall be happy, sir, to cram the facts down their throats. One final point, Miss Barton. How tall is the estimable Mr. Herbert Gale?

HELEN (*blankly*): How tall?

DR. FELL: Yes! Is he anything like the same height as his brother Philip?

HELEN: They're about the same height. Five feet ten. But I don't see . . .

DR. FELL: If I remember correctly, one of the warders told us that Herbert Gale has been hanging about the front gate all night. I should very much like to speak with him. Colonel Andrews, will you send someone out and ask him to come into your office?

ANDREWS: I can't do that!

DR. FELL: Why not?

ANDREWS: It's against regulations. He'd have to get a special pass.

DR. FELL: Then write him one. Curse it all, can't you get it through your correct military head that an innocent person is going to swing in less than two hours?

HELEN: Dr. Fell, I don't know what you're trying to do. But *can* you do it?

DR. FELL: My dear, I can't tell.

HELEN: But you *are* going to try?

DR. FELL: I am going downstairs now. Maybe, in a very short time, a certain gentleman will be entering this institution without any need of a pass. But don't hope for anything. Don't hope for anything! *(Strong, harsh music up. The prison clock strikes seven.)*

DR. FELL *(muttering):* Seven o'clock. Seven o'clock. Less than an hour to go. *(His voice rises.)* Why doesn't that warder come and bring the exhibit I want? What's delaying him?

ANDREWS: Probably he can't find the stuff.

DR. FELL: But you said you had it here!

ANDREWS: Things like that are apt to get mislaid. It's been a month since the trial. *Must* you have these exhibits?

DR. FELL: In order to prove it to you fully, yes. But if he doesn't come in two seconds more . . .

ANDREWS: I can't stay here much longer myself. The chaplain is with her now, but I'll have to take over before the end.

(Sharp rapping at the door.)

ANDREWS: Yes? Come in! *(Door opens.)*

WARDER *(breathlessly):* Sorry to 'a' been so long, sir. I could 'a' sworn it was in one place; and, lo and behold, it turned up somewheres else.

DR. FELL: Never mind that. Did you get the exhibits?

WARDER: It's all 'ere, sir, in this suit box. Where shall I put it?

DR. FELL: Put it on Colonel Andrews' desk. Now let's see. Move the lamp over here, will you?

WARDER: And about Mr. Herbert Gale, sir . . .

ANDREWS: Where is he?

WARDER: Out in the 'all, sir. Do you want to see him now?

DR. FELL: Yes, my lad. Very much so. Ask him to come in!

WARDER *(calling):* You can come in, sir. This way.

(HERBERT GALE is about twenty-eight. He has a light voice, giving the impression of earnestness and sincerity. He is rather nervous.)

HERBERT: Thank you. *(Door closes.)*

ANDREWS *(uncomfortably):* Morning, Herbert. Glad to see you. Sit down.

HERBERT: Thank you, Colonel Andrews.

ANDREWS: Let me have your hat and coat. This is Dr. Gideon Fell. *(Both men murmur.)*

HERBERT: The warder said you wanted to see me. I came, of course. But . . . do you think it was quite the right thing to do?

ANDREWS: Why not?

HERBERT: Well! People might think I was holding a grudge against Helen. Because of Phil, you know.

DR. FELL: And you don't hold any grudge?

HERBERT *(earnestly):* Good lord, no! I really don't! I pity that poor girl from the bottom of my heart! I only wish I hadn't had to testify against her. But what else could I do?

DR. FELL: You mean you'd like to help her? Even now?

HERBERT: Of course! If there were anything I could do to—to soothe her last moments on earth . . .

DR. FELL: There *is* something you can do, Mr. Gale.

HERBERT: Well?

DR. FELL: You can come with us to the condemned cell.

HERBERT: Are you joking?

DR. FELL: No.

HERBERT: But wouldn't it be pretty horrible for Helen?

DR. FELL: Yes. Probably. But as you point out, she has only a very short time to live.

HERBERT *(sharply):* Excuse me. What have you got in that suit box?

DR. FELL: In *this* suit box, Mr. Gale? A flattened bullet—the bullet that killed your brother. A .32 revolver. A tweed coat, bloodstained. A tweed waistcoat, also bloodstained.

ANDREWS: Look here, Fell! What do you expect to *prove* with that stuff?

DR. FELL: One moment. *Will* Mr. Herbert Gale go with us to the condemned cell?

HERBERT: Yes! If you think I can do any good there.

DR. FELL: Then, with your permission, I propose to prove that a straight line is the shortest distance between two points. Will you walk into my parlor?

(Music, out of it the single note of the prison clock.)

FIRST WOMAN *(under her breath):* Seven-thirty! Half an hour to go! *(Aloud)* Easy, dearie! Easy!

(A heavy door is unbarred, opens, and closes again.)

HELEN *(terrified):* They're not coming already to . . . Herbert Gale!

HERBERT: I'm very sorry for you, Helen. Please believe that.

HELEN: *Th-thank you!*

HERBERT: I shouldn't have intruded at this painful time, believe me. But Dr. Fell and the colonel here made me come to see you.

HELEN *(eagerly):* You mean . . . you've come to confess?

HERBERT *(sharply):* Confess? What should I confess?

HELEN *(fiercely):* You didn't see me shoot Phil. You *know* you didn't!

HERBERT: I'm sorry, Helen. I pity you, and I bear no malice. But you *did* shoot poor old Phil, after you'd asked him to put up his hands. . . .

DR. FELL *(quietly):* How high did he put up his hands?

HERBERT *(startled):* I beg your pardon?

ANDREWS: Dr. Fell said: How high did he put up his hands?

HERBERT: Really! *(Wearily)* Is there any purpose in going over all this in the last few minutes before the hangman—

HELEN: *Please!*

DR. FELL: We can demonstrate still further with a little experiment. I have here a bloodstained tweed coat and a bloodstained waistcoat. You see them, Mr. Gale?

HERBERT: I see them, yes.

DR. FELL: Take off your own coat and waistcoat. Put on *this* coat, and *this* waistcoat.

HERBERT: I'll do no such thing!

DR. FELL *(quickly):* Why not?

HERBERT: Colonel Andrews, I appeal to you!

ANDREWS: Where's the harm in it?

HELEN: Unless he *has* got something to hide!

HERBERT: I've got nothing to hide! Give me the things! I'll put them on!

DR. FELL: Thank you.

HELEN: I don't know why you're doing this. It's the nightmare again. But if something isn't proved very soon . . . *(Quickly)* What time is it?

FIRST WOMAN: Twenty minutes to eight, miss. Easy, now!

HERBERT: There! Does *that* satisfy you, Dr. Fell? Philip's coat and waistcoat fit me very well.

DR. FELL: So I was told. Would you care to tell us, now, why you killed your brother? *(Pause)* It was the money you inherited, I suppose. When Helen Barton walked into the middle of your crime, you knocked her out with a weapon that left no bruise, and put the revolver in her hand. Then you discovered, as a gift from heaven, that she really had lost her memory. Mr. Herbert Gale could tell any lying story he liked.

HERBERT: Be careful! You can't prove that!

DR. FELL: Would you like to make a small bet I can't prove it?

HERBERT: Yes!

DR. FELL: Very well. . . . I am threatening you with a gun, Mr. Gale. *Hold up your hands!*

HERBERT: No! Oh . . .

HELEN: You'd better do it, Herbert! You'd better do it!

DR. FELL: Hold up your hands! That's it! But higher! Higher! Now look at his coat, everybody! Look at his coat!

HELEN *(dazedly):* The coat is . . . it's rising!

DR. FELL: Of course it is. The bullet hole in the coat—you notice?—rises with it. But the waistcoat doesn't move.

ANDREWS *(explosively):* I think I begin to see . . . !

DR. FELL: The bullet hole in the coat has risen at least four inches above the corresponding hole in the waistcoat. Yet the bullet, you told me, penetrated in a dead straight line. Therefore Philip Gale could not possibly have had his hands raised when he was shot.

(Rapping on heavy door, which opens.)

WARDER: Colonel Andrews, sir!

ANDREWS: Yes, Harris?

WARDER: I thought I'd better tell you, sir, that the hangman's here.

DR. FELL: Herbert Gale told you he saw Miss Barton shoot a man whose hands were raised high in the air. It prevented any possible plea of manslaughter. It condemned that girl to death. Destroy that single lie, and you destroy the whole case.

HELEN: Is it true, Colonel Andrews? *Is* it true?

WARDER: I tell you, sir, the hangman's here!

ANDREWS: Harris, do you know the private telephone line in my office?

WARDER: Yes, sir?

ANDREWS: Get me the Home Secretary.

DR. FELL: Fine. And—ah—oh, warder . . .

WARDER: Yes, Dr. Fell?

DR. FELL: Tell the hangman he'll have to wait. This young lady has most inconsiderately been proved innocent. *(Cheerfully)* But his services will be required just the same. It will be a little later . . . and with a new client.

(Music up to curtain.)

Suspense (CBS), February 9, 1943
Ellery Queen's Mystery Magazine, September 1944

The Phantom Archer

The Characters

Lady Drew	owner of St. Ives Castle
Christopher Drew	her nephew
Charles Norman	her solicitor
Professor Ballard	caretaker of St. Ives Castle
Sally Ballard	his daughter
Caesar	his parrot

NARRATOR: Such a mysterious, unusual crime. Such an extraordinary way to commit a murder. In London homes everywhere, people were reading about it in the newspapers. . . .

WOMAN'S VOICE: St. Ives, Cornwall. July 15, 1938.

MAN'S VOICE: Harriet, Lady Drew—elderly widow of the late Sir George Drew—was mysteriously slain tonight at St. Ives Castle, on an island off the Cornish coast.

SECOND MAN'S VOICE: The means of death is said to have been an arrow.

WOMAN'S VOICE: An *arrow!*

SECOND MAN'S VOICE: An arrow fired from the end of the portrait gallery, and in the presence of two witnesses.

MAN'S VOICE: Historic St. Ives Castle, though still the property of the Drew family, is no longer lived in. It has been converted into a public museum . . .

WOMAN'S VOICE: And is in charge of two caretakers, who were witnesses to the killing. But both witnesses swear . . . *(Hesitates.)*

MAN'S VOICE: Well? What's next?

WOMAN'S VOICE *(slowly):* Both witnesses swear that the arrow was fired by no human hand.

NARRATOR: In the red sunset of one evening a week later, the Cornish coast looms dim and forbidding as two men walk out on the little pier that juts into the steel-dark sea. A motorboat is waiting there. One of the men is young and puzzled. The other is stout and elderly, and carries a briefcase. And as they meet suddenly at the end of the pier . . .

CHRIS: Excuse me, sir. Are you going to St. Ives Castle too?

NORMAN: I am, young man.

CHRIS: May I ask . . . if you're related to the family?

NORMAN *(amused):* Not exactly. But let me see if I can't make a guess as to who *you* are.

CHRIS: Well, sir?

NORMAN: You're Christopher Drew, Lady Drew's nephew. She sent you packing off to America fifteen-odd years ago.

CHRIS: That's right. But *you* . . . ?

NORMAN: Take a good look, and see if you don't remember.

CHRIS *(surprised):* Good lord!

NORMAN: Got it in one. I'm "Old Charley" Norman, the family solicitor. A little stouter, a little grayer, but the same person you used to devil years ago.

CHRIS *(worried):* Look, Mr. Norman. I took the first ship from New York, as soon as I got your cable. But what I want to know is—

BOATMAN *(calling):* The boat's ready, gen'l'men, if you are. The boat's *ready!*

NORMAN: The boatman seems to be getting impatient, Chris. You'd better jump in.

CHRIS: Right. Can *you* manage?

NORMAN: I'm not quite as unwieldy as that, thanks. *(They both get in the boat.)*

CHRIS: We're in, old man. Let her rip. *(Boat starts.)*

NORMAN: You know, Chris, you *were* a young limb of Satan in those days.

CHRIS: I liked *doing* things!

NORMAN: Don't we all?

CHRIS: I mean, I liked tinkering with things—bells and locks and toy planes and all that. I'm an aircraft designer now. But would that suit Aunt Harriet? Oh, no! I had to be a lawyer.... I *beg* your pardon, Mr. Norman!

NORMAN: That's all right, Chris. A lawyer is always the first to be sworn at and the last to be paid. So you and Lady Drew parted company?

CHRIS: When I was barely more than a kid. Yes.

NORMAN: And I gather you're not exactly ... glad to be back?

CHRIS: Would *you* be? Look out there!

NORMAN: I see it.

CHRIS: Same old desolate, rocky island, with the surf boiling over it ...

NORMAN: As a matter of fact, there's a bad surf boiling now. I hope we can make the landing stage.

CHRIS: Same old shell of a castle, towers and battlements and slimy walls, up against an ugly red sky. It was bad enough when we lived there, before the place was turned into a museum. But now ...! Tell me, Mr. Norman, is Professor Ballard still the caretaker?

NORMAN: Yes. The professor is still there.

CHRIS: Why a cultured old guy like that should want to bury himself just to take care of the so-called Drew treasures ...!

NORMAN: You remember Professor Ballard?

CHRIS: Very well. He used to own a parrot named Caesar.

NORMAN: Yes. Caesar's still alive.

CHRIS: I used to throw water over that parrot to make it swear. *(Reflecting)* Oh, yes! Professor Ballard had a daughter.

NORMAN: You mean Sally?

CHRIS: That's it! Sally! Scrawny, long-legged kid. I used to pity her, she was so ugly. ...

NORMAN: "She was so ugly," you say. Yes.

CHRIS: I pitied her for having to live in a place where you always imagined something was following you along the halls, and might tap you on the shoulder one night when you went upstairs.

NORMAN: You were rather a nervous kid, weren't you?

CHRIS: I don't know. But I didn't like it. Even now, when we come near the place, I have a feeling I might be getting into a ghost story.

NORMAN *(quietly)*: As a matter of fact, Chris, you already have.

CHRIS *(sharply)*: Have what?

NORMAN: Got into a ghost story.

CHRIS: Now look, Mr. Norman—

NORMAN: Haven't you seen the London newspapers?

CHRIS: No, I've just come straight from Southampton.

NORMAN: Then you don't know how your aunt died?

CHRIS: That's what I've been trying to ask *you!*

NORMAN: Just a minute, Chris. Boatman, do you think we can get through to the landing stage?

BOATMAN: Easy, sir. We'll be through the jetty and into calm water in half a tick. Hold tight!

NORMAN *(with relief)*: There! That's better!

CHRIS: Just one other thing, Mr. Norman. I don't have to *stay* at the castle, do I?

NORMAN: It would certainly be advisable, Chris, until the estate's wound up. You're the heir.

CHRIS: But I don't want the old shrew's money! Or those "art treasures," either!

NORMAN: All the same, Professor Ballard and I have to make an accounting to you.

CHRIS: Hang it, I don't doubt your honesty!

NORMAN: That's not the point, Chris.

CHRIS: And as for staying at the castle, I'll stay there one night out of . . . well, call it respect. But not an hour longer! I tell you, sir, I wouldn't stay another night at this place if . . . Hullo!

NORMAN: Anything wrong?

CHRIS: Who's that? Standing on the stone pier, with a lantern in her hand? Just about the prettiest girl I ever saw!

NORMAN *(dryly)*: That, Chris, is the "scrawny, long-legged kid."

CHRIS: Not Sally Ballard?

NORMAN: The very same.

CHRIS: She looks scared half to death.

NORMAN: She *is* scared half to death.

NORMAN *(reassuringly)*: Now, take it easy, Sally! It's all right!

SALLY: Mr. Norman, I'm so glad you're here, I could break down and cry. M-maybe I will.

NORMAN: There's nothing to be afraid of now. Sally, this is—

SALLY: I can guess—you're Christopher Drew, aren't you? I'd have known you anywhere.

NORMAN: That's more than Chris himself could have said.

CHRIS: Never mind that. Give me the lantern, Sally. Your hand's shaking.

SALLY: Is it? I . . . suppose it is.

NORMAN: Yes. And what are you doing out in this wind without a hat or coat?

SALLY: I'm afraid to stay in the castle. I'm afraid I might hear it again.

CHRIS: Hear what?

SALLY: I wish I could describe the sound to you. It's a sound like . . . *(Pause)* The bowstring twangs, and the arrow sticks in the door. And then the parrot screams. But when you go to look, *nobody's there!*

CHRIS: Wait a minute! What *is* all this?

NORMAN: The phantom archer.

CHRIS: Phantom archer?

NORMAN: That's the newspaper's sobriquet. But, Sally, what about the police? Aren't they here to see that nothing else happens?

SALLY: The police have gone.

NORMAN: Gone?

SALLY: Yes. There's nobody here but my father and old Maggie, who does the cooking and cleaning.

CHRIS: How *is* your father, Sally?

SALLY: He's well enough, for a man over seventy, except that his eyesight's going. And . . . he broods. Over all this, Mr. Drew!

CHRIS: Chris is the name, Sally. It always used to be.

SALLY: All right, Chris. It *is* nice to see you again.

NORMAN: That's better!

SALLY: You may not know it, Chris, but your aunt was thinking of selling the castle to a millionaire named Mr. Singleton, who wanted to tear it down and put up a summer residence on the island. *(Intensely)* I don't think my father could have stood that! This castle is his whole life.

NORMAN: That's true, Chris.

SALLY: Now that you're the owner . . . are *you* planning on selling it off?

CHRIS: My dear Sally! You can keep the place, or tear it down, or do anything you like with it! But . . .

SALLY: Yes, Chris?

CHRIS: I shouldn't think *you'd* like to live here.

SALLY: *Like* to live here? With death striking out of the dark before you can move a finger?

CHRIS: Striking out of the dark . . . from where?

SALLY: People can go mad when they're alone. They don't go mad when they have friends with them. I can face it now. Come along. I'll show you.

NARRATOR: Take care how you walk, now. Walls and towers and battlements whipped by the east wind. Twisting staircases, that once echoed to the clank of armor, and a hundred lightless rooms. True, the castle is supplied with electricity from its own power plant, but only a few of the rooms—the showplaces—have even that life which is the life of death. In the core of all this damp stone is the sitting room of PROFESSOR BALLARD and his daughter. A pleasant room, furnished in almost modern style, despite its stone floor. First of all, as we approach, you might notice the ancient parrot, its cage swung from the ceiling, and . . .

SALLY: This is our sitting room, Chris. Mr. Norman knows it well. *(The parrot lets out a horrible shriek of laughter.)*

CHRIS: Good lord! What's that?

SALLY: Be quiet, Caesar!

CAESAR: Die and rot! Die and rot! Die and rot! *(CAESAR screeches again.)*

CHRIS: Same old parrot, I notice.

SALLY: Do you remember how you used to throw water over him, Chris? And imitate him?

NORMAN: He's got a wicked-looking eye, that parrot.

CAESAR: Stow your gab! Blast your eyes! Die and rot! *(Laughs again.)*

CHRIS: Doesn't Caesar get on your nerves, Sally?

SALLY: He never used to. He does now. That's what I was going to tell you. You see that big door over there?

CHRIS: Well?

SALLY: Do you remember what that door leads to?

CHRIS: Let me get my bearings for a second. . . . Yes! That door leads into the portrait gallery.

SALLY: Yes. And do you remember what the portrait gallery looks like?

CHRIS: Well . . .

SALLY *(insistently):* Do you?

CHRIS: It used to be a long, narrow room without any windows and only this one door. Pictures hung up on each side.

NORMAN: Including a Rubens, a Rembrandt and a Van Dyck.

SALLY: Please, Mr. Norman!

NORMAN: I'm sorry, my dear.

SALLY: Finally, do you remember what used to stand at the other end of the narrow gallery, facing this door?

CHRIS: Now wait a minute! That's going too far!

NORMAN: What is?

CHRIS: Mr. Norman, she's talking about a wooden figure—a dummy! It was dressed up as a medieval archer. It used to stand at the other end of the gallery. It held a bent bow with an arrow on the string. You're not going to tell me that blasted dummy started firing arrows?

CAESAR: Caesar eats flesh! Caesar eats flesh! Caesar eats flesh! *(Laughs again.)*

NORMAN: Throw the cloth over his cage, Sally. That ought to quiet him down.

CAESAR: You're a thief! You're a thief! You're a— *(Squawks.)*

SALLY: There, Caesar! Now you be quiet!

CHRIS: But what I want to know is . . .

SALLY: One night about two weeks ago, I was sitting in here alone. Father had gone to bed. I . . .

CHRIS: Go on!

SALLY: The door to the portrait gallery, of course, was locked. It's got a rather elaborate lock, because the paintings are so valuable, and Father has the only key.

CHRIS: Well?

SALLY: That was when I heard the sound. If I could describe it to you, it would be a sound like . . . a twang. And Caesar screamed. And I—I don't know why—I was so terrified I couldn't move. I knew there couldn't be anybody *in* the portrait gallery. But I didn't dare open the door to see.

CHRIS: What did you do?

SALLY: Nothing. I didn't say anything about it. But the next morning, when we opened the door . . .

NORMAN: The next morning, Chris, there was no arrow on the bowstring of the wooden dummy. The arrow was buried in the door forty feet away.

CHRIS: Now look! That is impossible!

SALLY *(quietly):* It's true, though.

NORMAN: And it happened on *three successive* nights.

SALLY: Some local paper got hold of the story. Finally, my father telegraphed to Lady Drew. And on the night of the murder . . . *(Pause)* Just a moment, please!

CHRIS: Anything wrong?

SALLY: No. But I think I hear my father coming. *(Door opens and closes.)* Hello, Father.

*(*PROFESSOR BALLARD'S *voice, though thin and elderly—in sharp contrast to* NORMAN'S—*is by no means weak or senile. It has strength, and more than a little dignity.)*

BALLARD: Hello, my dear. I—I heard voices, but I wasn't aware we had visitors. Who are these gentlemen?

NORMAN: You surely know *me,* Professor Ballard!

SALLY: And this is Chris Drew, father. The new owner!

BALLARD: Indeed.

SALLY: And he's *not* going to sell the castle to Mr. Singleton after all! Let me help you across to that chair.

BALLARD: Thank you, Sally, but I am not quite as blind as all that. Christopher Drew, eh?

CHRIS: That's right, sir.

BALLARD: I was afraid it might be our friends the police back again. It is one thing to have a suspicious mind, and quite another thing to be paid to have one. Still, I suppose they must do their duty. *Fiat justitia, ruat coelum!* I think I *will* have that chair.

SALLY: Here you are, Father. I was just telling them about how you telegraphed to Lady Drew, and how she came down here . . .

BALLARD: Oh, the night of the murder. Yes.

SALLY: I can tell you everything that happened that night. Father and I were in this room when Lady Drew came storming in here. You remember what a strong-minded person she was, Chris. No nerves or nonsense about *her!* In she came, with her umbrella and that funny hat of hers. . . .

(Music bridge to flashback)

BALLARD: If you would allow me to explain, Lady Drew . . .

LADY DREW: I don't want explanations, Professor Ballard! I want an end to this tommyrot! *(*CAESAR *screeches.)* Hasn't somebody strangled that parrot yet?

CAESAR: Ugly old mug! Ugly old mug! Ugly old mug!

DREW: I'll take this umbrella to you, you beastly little—

SALLY: Please, Lady Drew. Caesar doesn't mean any harm!

DREW *(grimly):* Neither do I, my girl. But I very often do harm.

BALLARD: I can easily believe your ladyship.

DREW: Ghosts in the portrait gallery! Wooden dummies firing arrows! Never heard such stuff-and-nonsense in all my born days! *(As she speaks, she keeps pounding on the stone floor with her umbrella.)*

BALLARD: It is not really necessary, Lady Drew, to keep hammering the ferrule of that umbrella on the floor.

DREW: It is necessary, Professor Ballard, if I *think* it's necessary! And it's easy enough to see what's happened here. Somebody's playing a trick on you.

BALLARD *(wearily):* Yes. I'd already thought of that.

DREW *(surprised):* You had?

SALLY: Father prides himself on his detective wits, Lady Drew. You have to have that quality, you know, to be a decent research historian. But a trick . . . how?

DREW: Oh, some contraption rigged up to fire an arrow when nobody's there.

SALLY: Father thought of that too. Only . . . it won't work. *(*CAESAR *laughs.)* Be quiet, Caesar!

BALLARD: My daughter is quite right, Lady Drew. The wooden figure *is* a wooden figure, without any mechanism inside or outside. The rest of the gallery is as bare as your hand. But what makes you so certain this is a trick?

DREW: Because there's somebody hiding in this castle!

SALLY: *What!*

DREW: Don't argue with me! I *know!* *(Hammers with umbrella.)* I *saw* him dodge round the corner of the stairs just outside the armor hall, and a nasty ugly look he had too!

BALLARD: You must be mistaken, Lady Drew. There's nobody here except myself and my daughter and old Maggie, who does the cooking and cleaning.

DREW: I know what I know, Professor Ballard. Have you the key to that portrait gallery?

BALLARD: Of course.

DREW: Give it to me, please.

SALLY: Don't go in there, Lady Drew! Don't do it!

DREW: And why not?

SALLY: Because . . . (*A small clock begins to strike nine.*)

DREW: Well, my girl? Why not?

SALLY: Because this is the time the arrow is usually fired. And when you open that door, you'll be facing the archer forty feet away.

DREW (*snorting*): You mean *I* might get an arrow through *my* neck?

SALLY: Yes. You might.

CAESAR: Die and rot! Die and rot! Die and rot!

DREW: I've had just about enough of this! Professor Ballard!

BALLARD: Yes, Lady Drew?

DREW: *You* don't believe in this tommyrot, surely?

BALLARD: I have no belief in the supernatural, if that's what you mean. At the same time . . .

DREW: *Will* you give me that key?

BALLARD: If you insist.

DREW: Then hand it over.

BALLARD: One question, please, before I do. Are you still determined to sell this castle to Mr. Singleton?

DREW (*surprised*): Yes. Naturally. I told you so.

BALLARD: Then here is your key.

DREW (*changing mood*): No you don't! You're coming with me, both of you! You take that key, Professor Ballard, and you open the door for me!

BALLARD: Just as you like.

DREW: It isn't enough—oh, no!—to have my life half worried out with rates and taxes that would ruin Croesus! *This* has to happen on top of it, and maybe spoil a good sale! *Will* you open that door so I can go in?

BALLARD: Certainly.

CAESAR: Die and rot! Die and rot! Die and rot!

(Ballard puts key into lock.)

SALLY: Stand to one side, Father! *Please* stand to one side!

BALLARD: Will you go first, Lady Drew?

DREW: Yes, I will! And don't think I won't!

BALLARD: As you know, this part of the castle dates back to the twelfth century. *(He turns key and opens the door, then stands aside.)*

SALLY: Father!

BALLARD: What's wrong?

SALLY: All the lights have gone out!

(The parrot shrieks on a long, sustained note. Then a choking noise, and a heavy thud.)

BALLARD: Lady Drew! *Lady Drew!*

SALLY: We were all so shocked we couldn't move, Chris.

CHRIS: But . . . well, what happened then?

SALLY: Twenty seconds later the lights went on again.

CHRIS: Well?

SALLY: Lady Drew had been shot through the chest with an arrow. She was lying across the threshold, already speechless and dying. But there was nobody in the portrait gallery!

NORMAN: Excuse me, Sally. But . . .

SALLY: Yes, Mr. Norman?

NORMAN: I've been over the evidence many times, of course. All the same, are you *sure* there was nobody in the gallery?

SALLY: Absolutely sure.

CHRIS: Why, Sally?

SALLY: As soon as Lady Drew was hit, Father moved over and stood in front of the door. Nobody came out. And the lights went on twenty seconds later. Isn't that true, Father?

BALLARD *(blankly):* Eh?

CHRIS *(whispering):* Sally, what's wrong with your father? He's sitting at that table with his hand shading his eyes, as though he were a million miles away.

SALLY: He *is* a million miles away . . . in his own thoughts. Father!

BALLARD: Yes, my dear?

SALLY: Isn't it true that there was nobody in the portrait gallery after Lady Drew was shot?

BALLARD: Oh, yes, Sally. That's true enough.

CHRIS: Then how in all blue blazes was Aunt Harriet killed?

NORMAN: That, Chris, is what the police want to know. Speaking as a mere lawyer, I'm a little out of my depth. If Professor Ballard has any ideas . . .

BALLARD: I beg your pardon for my discourtesy, gentlemen. I was merely sitting here thinking about the nature of evidence, and the curious ways in which the human mind can be misled.

SALLY: Misled, father?

BALLARD: Into error. And into great crime.

SALLY: Yes, but . . .

BALLARD: I was also wondering, if you will forgive me, whether this young man is really Christopher Drew.

SALLY: Father!

CHRIS: Great Scott, sir, you don't think I'm an impostor? Your own daughter can identify me! So can Mr. Norman!

BALLARD: At the same time, I move in a world of visual shadows. And I have a great trust to hand over before I . . . speak.

SALLY: Before you *speak?*

BALLARD: I should prefer some more formal identification of Mr. Drew. A passport, for instance?

CHRIS: I have a passport.

BALLARD: May I see it, please? . . . Thank you.

NORMAN: This isn't necessary, is it? Even I . . .

BALLARD *(sighing):* No. It is all correct. Photograph, fingerprint, height, age, weight. Landed Southampton July first; immigration stamp. You are Christopher Drew. I have here the keys to all the inhabited parts of the castle. I take great pleasure in turning them over to you.

CHRIS: Tell me, sir. Is the key to the portrait gallery among them?

BALLARD: It is.

CHRIS: Which key is it, Professor Ballard?

SALLY: Chris: What are you going to do? *(The clock begins to strike nine.)*

NORMAN: I think *I* can guess. But are you sure it's wise?

CHRIS: You can't tell me arrows can be fired out of empty air! Either

Aunt Harriet was killed by some mechanical contrivance rigged up in there . . .

BALLARD: On my solemn word of honor. Mr. Drew, there was nothing of the kind.

CHRIS: . . . or else she was killed by a ghost. And I'm going to find out which. Mr. Norman?

NORMAN: Yes, Chris?

CHRIS: We might have the conditions as they were before. Would you mind taking the cover off the parrot's cage?

NORMAN: I'm a sensible man. I'm a practical man. But I still don't like this! If . . .

CHRIS: Would you mind, Mr. Norman?

NORMAN: If you insist. But . . .

CAESAR: You're a thief! You're a thief! You're a thief!

SALLY: Why do you jump back, Mr. Norman? You're *not* a thief, are you?

NORMAN: No, of course not. But this infernal bird gets on my nerves even more than it must get on yours. It's got the eye of a rattlesnake and the face of a mummified pharaoh.

SALLY: Maybe Caesar knows the truth.

CHRIS: Maybe he does. But we won't count on it. Which is the key to the portrait gallery, Professor Ballard?

SALLY: Don't do it, Chris! Don't *do* it!

BALLARD: This is the key, Mr. Drew.

CHRIS: Then stand back, everybody, and let's have a look at the ogre's den. If any wooden dummy starts shooting arrows at me, you can call the wagon for the loony bin. *(He starts unlocking the door.)*

SALLY: Chris! Please! Don't do it!

CAESAR: Die and rot! Die and rot! Die and rot!

(Chris turns the knob.)

BALLARD: Just one moment, please!

CHRIS: Yes, Professor Ballard?

BALLARD: It will not be necessary to expose yourself to any danger.

CHRIS: No? Why not?

BALLARD: Because I should prefer to tell you who killed Lady Drew, and how it was done.

NORMAN: You *know?*

BALLARD: My dear Mr. Norman, there is one obvious question for the research student—or detective, if you prefer—to ask himself in this matter. That question is why the lights went out before Lady Drew was killed, and on again twenty seconds later.

NORMAN: Well? Why did they?

BALLARD: They were extinguished because someone pulled out the switch of the fuse box, which is just outside the door of this room. They went on again because someone threw back the switch twenty seconds later.

NORMAN: Someone?

BALLARD: Yes, someone.

SALLY: That's all very well, Father, but it doesn't tell us anything!

BALLARD: You think not, my dear?

SALLY: It certainly doesn't tell us, for instance, who fired an arrow from the portrait gallery.

BALLARD: There never was any arrow fired from the portrait gallery.

CHRIS: *What?*

BALLARD: On what grounds, Sally, do you assume that there was? Did you hear any sound of the bowstring?

SALLY *(bewildered)*: No, I—I didn't.

BALLARD: Why not?

SALLY: Because just at that moment, just as Lady Drew was going in, Caesar—*(The parrot screams.)* Like that!

NORMAN *(shakily)*: Very convenient for the murderer, wasn't it?

BALLARD: Not convenient. Arranged.

CHRIS: Go on, Professor Ballard!

BALLARD: Let me repeat. Why did you assume an arrow was fired from the gallery? Simply because, on three successive nights, an arrow *had been* fired in there by someone who detached the bow from the dummy figure and aimed at a locked door.

SALLY: But somebody had to get into the gallery to do that.

BALLARD: Of course. With a key, for instance, like mine.

SALLY: Father!

CHRIS: Look here, sir, do you know what you're saying?

BALLARD: I am saying that our minds were prepared for it. We expected it. When Lady Drew was struck down by an arrow in the dark, we assumed that the arrow had been fired from the gallery. Of course, the arrow was never fired at all.

NORMAN: Never . . . fired . . . at all?

BALLARD: Does it surprise you, Mr. Norman?

NORMAN: Very much.

BALLARD: That arrow, you see, was in the *hands* of the murderer—it was used *like a dagger.* When those lights were out, the murderer simply caught Lady Drew from behind and drove the arrow into her chest.

CAESAR: Die and rot! Die and rot! Die and rot!

BALLARD: It was all over in less than twenty seconds. Much less.

NORMAN: See here, Professor Ballard. Are you confessing to this murder?

BALLARD: *I?* Confessing to the murder? *(Chuckles.)* Sir, you amuse me.

SALLY: But you must be accusing somebody!

BALLARD: Does Mr. Norman forget so easily as that?

NORMAN: Forget what?

BALLARD: Does he forget, for instance, the man who was hiding here in the castle? The man seen by Lady Drew herself?

CAESAR: You're a thief! You're a thief! You're a thief!

NORMAN: Are you accusing *me?*

BALLARD: Sally, my dear! I have trained you well. Can't you use your reason even yet?

SALLY: But I don't see . . .

BALLARD: I am accusing the man who liked to tinker with locks and could have made a key like mine. I am accusing the man who could and did imitate Caesar, to cover any absent noise of a bowstring.

SALLY: You mean . . . ?

BALLARD: I am accusing the man who claims to have arrived in England only today, though his passport stamp—look at it!—bears the date of July first, two weeks before the murder. I am accusing . . .

SALLY: *Chris Drew! You wanted the money! You killed that old woman yourself!*

(CAESAR *screams.*)

Suspense (CBS), March 9, 1943
Ellery Queen's Mystery Magazine, June 1948

The Bride Vanishes

The Characters

Tom Courtney	a newlywed
Lucy Courtney	his wife
Harry Granger	a retired oilman
Countess Luchesi	a devotee of excitement
Dr. Rutherford Davis	a specialist in brain diseases

A boatman, a dog named Tiberius, etc.

NARRATOR: Italy, in the springtime; Italy, as we used to know it before the jackal struck. And the island of Capri, twenty miles out across the Bay of Naples . . . Blue water adazzle under the sun. Behind you the bone-white beaches, and Vesuvius dull purple in a heat haze. Ahead, as the little steamer from Naples chugs out across the bay, rises Capri. . . . Olive trees and white roads and vineyards above the cliffs. Could young Americans find a better place to spend their honeymoon? While the guitars sing, and the warm winds blow, and the little steamer carries them?

(TOM COURTNEY *is about twenty-eight;* LUCY, *his wife, is four years younger. Both are trying to be very casual.*)

TOM: Well, Mrs. Courtney?

LUCY: Well, Mr. Courtney?

TOM: I can't keep it up, Lucy. I'm going to break down and ask if you're happy.

LUCY: I'll break down too. I want to walk up to everybody I meet and say "Whee!" Just like that.

TOM: What *I* want to do is turn somersaults, myself.

LUCY: I want to say, "I've been married to Tom Courtney for practically two weeks. And now we're going to have a villa at Capri for a month." Oh, Tom, I ought to be the happiest woman in the world, only . . .

TOM *(sharply):* You shivered! What's wrong?

LUCY: Ever since we got aboard this ship, people have been staring at me.

TOM: I can't blame 'em for *that.*

LUCY: No! I mean . . . in a funny way! And muttering! Even your American friend—what's his name?

TOM: Granger?

LUCY: Mr. Granger. When you introduced him to me at Naples, I thought his eyes were going to pop out.

TOM: Be careful, dear! He's standing over by the rail now. He lives at Capri.

LUCY *(giggling):* I'd like to see him wearing that white ten-gallon hat in Italy.

TOM: Before Granger made money in oil wells, he was a real old-fashioned cowpuncher. And he's proud of it. Good fellow too.

LUCY: He's too polite to say anything, but he keeps looking around at me, just the same as the rest of them do, Tom.

TOM: Well?

LUCY: They look *scared.*

TOM *(worried):* You know, Lucy, this isn't the time to start imagining things.

LUCY: I know. Maybe I'm just so happy I'm afraid it can't last.

TOM: Don't *say* that!

LUCY: But wouldn't it be awful if something did happen? And we weren't together any longer?

TOM: Wait a minute. Hasn't this ship stopped?

LUCY: Yes. That *is* Capri up ahead of us, isn't it?

TOM: It can't be anything else. But it seems a funny place to stop.

No sign of a harbor—only rocks and little gray cliffs. *(Calling)* Mr. Granger! Mr. Granger!

(GRANGER is about sixty; he is a robust, genial, good-natured man with a natural courtesy of manner; just now he is very worried.)

GRANGER: Yes, young fellow?

TOM: Do you happen to know why we're stopping here?

GRANGER: That's an easy one, son. We're stopping so that you and your good lady—and anybody else who's curious—can get a look at the Blue Grotto.

LUCY: The Blue Grotto! Of course!

GRANGER: Shade your eyes with your hand, ma'am. You see that tiny little arch under the cliff?

LUCY: Yes?

GRANGER: And all the little white rowboats coming out towards us?

LUCY: Yes!

GRANGER: When the first boat comes alongside, climb down that iron ladder and get in. The boatman'll row you out and through the arch into the grotto. It's a big dark cavern. The water in there looks as though it's lit up underneath with blue fire.

TOM: Like to go out and see it, Lucy?

LUCY: I'd love to!

GRANGER: Let me give you a little tip, though. The current's pretty fast out there. You'll go shooting under that arch like sixty.

LUCY: Are we likely to upset?

GRANGER: No. But the arch isn't as high as your head. When you see it coming, lie back flat in the boat. That is, unless you want your block knocked off.

TOM: Thanks, Mr. Granger. We'll remember.

TOM: Easy on the ladder, Lucy. Don't look round yet!

LUCY: I'm all right, darling, and just as good a swimmer as you are.

TOM: I'm in the boat now. Take one more step . . . steady . . . now turn around, facing the boatman, and sit down here beside—

BOATMAN *(terrified)*: *Corpo di Bacco!*

LUCY: What's the matter with the boatman?

TOM: Easy, man! Do you want to upset us? Sit down!

BOATMAN: *Si, signor. (To LUCY)* You . . . come . . . back. Yes?

LUCY: Come back? I've never been here before in my life!

TOM: Push off, man! Start rowing! The other boats are piling up behind you!

BOATMAN: You . . . come . . . back.

TOM: Start rowing, can't you? *Andare subito! Basta! (The boat starts moving.)*

LUCY *(whispering):* Tom, he can't take his eyes off me!

TOM: I wish he'd watch where he's rowing!

BOATMAN: You come to live at the Villa Borghese, yes?

LUCY: Tom, how does he know that?

BOATMAN: Theesa lady . . . she eesa not dead?

TOM: Dead? Of course she's not dead! What are you talking about?

BOATMAN: She never come to Capri before?

TOM: Never!

BOATMAN: Then I tella you. She will disappear, justa like de other one.

LUCY: Disappear?

BOATMAN: I rest on my oars, and I tella you.

LUCY: Tom, aren't we moving rather fast?

TOM: Yes. That's the entrance to the grotto ahead.

BOATMAN: I tella you. There was a lady. So mucha like you it—*corpo di Bacco!*—It scare me.

TOM: Look, old man. I don't want to teach you your business, but you've got your back to that grotto!

BOATMAN: Take theesa lady back where she came from! Don't take her to the Villa Borghese!

TOM: Down, Lucy! Flat on your back! Down!

(A loud rushing of water, then the noise of water fades)

BOATMAN *(contritely):* Signora! Signora! I am sorry! I almost make you get hurt!

TOM: Do you know you nearly got your own head knocked off?

BOATMAN: Scusa me, no! I am used to it! Now I weel row you round the Blue Grott'. *(The boat starts again.)*

LUCY: I don't think I like the grotto much, Tom.

TOM: Neither do I.

LUCY: Dark—except for that blue light under the water. It's transparent. You can see the fish swimming.

TOM: Just a minute, boatman! This lady who disappeared from the Villa Borghese . . .

BOATMAN: Two, three year ago she disappear.

TOM: You say she looked exactly like my wife?

BOATMAN: *Sì, signor!* She wasa going to be married. She was trying on what you calla her wedding dress. Her mother anda sisters, they were in da room with her. She walk out on a balcony over da sea. You know what I mean by a balcony over da sea? And nobody has ever heard of her again.

LUCY: You mean . . . she jumped over into the sea?

BOATMAN: A young girla going to be married? Keel herself? No, no, no!

TOM: Then what did happen?

BOATMAN: *Corpo di Bacco,* I don't know! But somatimes, they say, you can meet her ghost. Ina here. She float just under the water, where you can see her. And turn over and over. And the wedding veil is still round her face.

LUCY: Tom—let's get out of here!

BOATMAN: You want to go? *Yes?*

TOM: Lucy, if this fellow is stringing us along—

LUCY: He's not—I'm sure of it!

TOM: Then somebody ought to know what this means. If we've inherited a haunted balcony, where people disappear like soap bubbles, I say it's too much! Let's get back to our ship and talk to Granger! Yes, boatman, take us back. . . .

LUCY: Mr. Granger! Mr. Granger!

GRANGER: Climb aboard, ma'am. And you too, young fellow. This ship's starting in half a second.

LUCY: Didn't anybody else go to the Blue Grotto?

GRANGER *(embarrassed):* Well, ma'am . . . no. *(Hesitates.)* Not after they saw *you* go.

TOM: It's all right. We've just heard the story, Mr. Granger.

GRANGER: I ought to have told you about it myself! All the way out here I've been cussing myself, and thinking what an ornery old badger I am, for not telling you when I first met you in Naples!

TOM: The girl *did* vanish, then?

GRANGER: By a miracle, yes. In broad daylight, and within twenty feet of her mother and sisters.

TOM: You don't look like a man who believes in miracles, Mr. Granger.

GRANGER: I'm not, son. I'm just telling you what happened.

TOM: But why is everybody so excited? Somebody must have thrown her off the balcony.

GRANGER: Josephine Adams was all alone on a balcony forty feet up a cliff smooth as glass. She didn't fall, and she wasn't thrown, because there was no sound of a splash. She didn't come back from the balcony, because her mother and sisters were in front of the only door. Yet within fifteen seconds—*fifteen seconds,* mind you—she vanished!

TOM *(incredulously):* You believe that?

GRANGER: Sure I believe it, son. It's a fact.

LUCY: Did you know the girl's family?

GRANGER: Very well. We've got a real English-speaking colony here. In about half a minute now, I'm going to show you your new home.

LUCY: Can we see it from the ship?

GRANGER: You sure can, ma'am. It's on the edge of the cliff. Dr. Davis's house is on one side of it, and my shack's on the other. *(Hesitates.)* That's why I want to ask you a question.

LUCY: Of course. Ask anything you like.

GRANGER: I'm an old stager, ma'am, and not exactly up to the high-toned society around here. But . . . do you trust me?

LUCY: Yes, I think so.

GRANGER: Then promise me something. Unless you're with somebody you trust, *keep away from that balcony.*

TOM: Do you honestly think there's danger of . . . ?

GRANGER: I don't know, son! If I did know, I wouldn't have to talk this way!

(Barking of a dog)

LUCY: That sounds like a dog barking! I thought I heard it before.

TOM: It is—a big police dog. And led by a very handsome woman, if you ask me.

GRANGER: Oh, Lord! Here she is again!

TOM: Who?

GRANGER: The countess. She's one of our colony.

LUCY: She looks like an American. *(Whispering)* You take your eyes off her, Tom Courtney!

GRANGER: She *is* an American. Married a Count Parcheesi, or something like that. Just call her Nellie.

(NELLIE *is in her late thirties; she has the breezy, drawling, offhand voice of someone eagerly interested in everything.*)

NELLIE: My dear Mr. Granger!

GRANGER: Hello, Nellie.

NELLIE: It's true! Everybody told me so, but I couldn't believe it until I saw her! She *does* look exactly like poor Josephine Adams. Just as small, just as dainty, and just as pretty. . . .

LUCY: Please! Is *everybody* trying to give me the jitters?

GRANGER: Nellie, I want you to meet some friends of mine.

NELLIE: You don't need to introduce me! I know who they are! You're the nice young couple who've taken that villa. I'm Nellie Luchesi. . . . (*The dog barks.*) And this is my dog, Tiberius. Named after the wicked Roman emperor, you know, who used to live at Capri. I must confess I'm terribly fascinated by wicked things. Aren't you, Mr. Courtney?

TOM (*muttering*): Lucy, stop digging me in the ribs! I haven't done anything!

LUCY: No, and you're not going to.

NELLIE: Tiberius seems to have taken quite a fancy to you, Mrs. Courtney. I've never known him to go up to a stranger before.

LUCY: I only wish I could borrow him. He might be a charm against . . . oh, I don't know!

NELLIE: We'll be at the harbor in a few minutes. Then you must let me drive you up to the villa. You won't be able to get any servants, I'm afraid, because they won't stay there. But you can camp out. . . . Look! There's the villa! We're passing it now.

LUCY: Where?

NELLIE: On the cliff! Where I'm pointing.

TOM (*sharply*): Wait a minute. There must be some mistake. That's not the Villa Borghese . . . ?

GRANGER: It sure is, son.

TOM: But that's a palace! Like all the other houses there. And I rented it, furnished, for about twenty-five dollars a month!

GRANGER: Can't you guess why you got it so cheap, son? If you take my advice, you'll turn around and go back to Naples by the next steamer!

NELLIE: Harry Granger, don't be an idiot! Let's have some excitement! *(Through her teeth)* Let's have some *excitement!*

LUCY: Tom, it *is* beautiful!

TOM: Too infernally beautiful, if you ask me.

NELLIE: There's the balcony!

GRANGER: It's all right by daylight, son—marble and tapestries and whatnot. But at night, when you've got to put out the lights, and you start thinking what happened there, what *might* happen . . .

NARRATOR: The moon, over Capri, makes a deathly light. You could see clearly enough to read on that balcony—if anyone went out there. Frosted-glass doors open out on it from a big room on the ground floor, where two determinedly calm persons—and a dog—sit looking at each other. It is that evening. . . .

TOM: Lucy, stop it!

LUCY: Stop what?

TOM: Stop looking over at that balcony!

LUCY: I'm sorry, darling.

TOM: Why are we sitting here, anyway? There's an outer room that's much more comfortable.

LUCY: It's like having a toothache. A very *little* toothache.

TOM: I may be dense, angel, but I don't follow you.

LUCY: You put your tongue against the tooth, to see if it'll hurt. You know it will hurt. But you go on doing it just the same. That's us.

TOM: Maybe you're right.

LUCY: Tom, did you ever think we'd live in a lovely house like this?

TOM: The house is all right. But they have to go and spoil everything—our honeymoon—with this blasted tommyrot about—

LUCY: Tom, you're as jittery now as I was this afternoon! Even Tiberius is jittery.

TOM: Yes, I guess I am. . . . Easy, boy! Easy!

LUCY: There's whiskey on the table. They call it veeky here. Mix yourself a drink.

TOM: In a minute. Not just now . . . Lucy, there's nothing wrong with that balcony. Suppose you walked out there this minute . . .

LUCY: I've had a horrible longing to try it, just because I know I shouldn't.

TOM: Nothing could attack you. All you'd have to do would be yell. That would bring Mr. Granger out on his balcony like a shot. And the neighbor on the other side of us. Who is on the other side, by the way?

LUCY: A loony-doctor.

TOM: A *what?*

LUCY: A specialist in brain diseases. Dr. Davis. He's English. *(Pauses.)* Listen!

(The dog begins to bark furiously. This is followed by a scratching sound from outside.)

TOM: It's somebody in the outer room. Easy, Tiberius, easy!

LUCY: Tom, I'm afraid!

TOM: It's all right. You hold Tiberius's collar while I open the door. We don't want him to fly at anybody. We're going into the other room and stay there. Ready?

LUCY: Yes. *(Door opens. DR. DAVIS enters. His voice suggests a thin, middle-aged man with a dry, precise manner.)*

DAVIS: Good evening, Mrs. Courtney. Good evening, Mr. Courtney. I am no ghost, believe me. I am merely your neighbor, Dr. Rutherford Davis.

LUCY: Oh! Yes, of course. Mr. Granger mentioned you.

DAVIS: I trust you will pardon this intrusion? No one answered my knock, so I ventured to come in.

TOM: It's no intrusion, Dr. Davis. We're . . . a little disorganized here, that's all.

DAVID: Naturally. Mr. Courtney, I wish I could say, "Welcome to Capri." But I have a very different message.

TOM: Yes?

DAVIS *(with great intensity):* If you value Mrs. Courtney's life, sir, go back to Naples immediately.

TOM: Not you too!

DAVIS: I do not say that as a ghost-hunter, sir. I say it as a medical man. May I sit down?

LUCY: Of course! Please do!

DAVIS: Thank you.

TOM: We seem to be forgetting our manners, Dr. Davis. Will you . . . have a drink?

DAVIS: Thank you. Perhaps a small whiskey?

LUCY: *I'll* get it, darling. You sit down and talk to Dr. Davis.

TOM: You're not going back into that room alone?

LUCY: I'm only going to get the drinks, Tom! I promise to be good. And Tiberius can come with me. Won't you, Tiberius?

DAVIS: You've borrowed Tiberius from the Countess Luchesi, I see.

LUCY: Yes. She was kind enough to offer him. Excuse me. I'll be back in a minute. Come on, Tiberius!

(Dog barks. Door opens and closes.)

TOM: I hope this is all right!

DAVIS: No, sir, it is *not* all right. Your wife is in very great danger.

TOM: But why? Because of that balcony?

DAVIS: No. Because she looks exactly like the late Josephine Adams.

TOM: I don't get it.

DAVIS: Mr. Courtney, did you ever hear of paranoia?

TOM: It's some kind of mental disease, isn't it?

DAVIS: The paranoiac begins by imagining that he—or she—is being persecuted by someone. First he hears things. A voice in his brain whispers, "You'll be killed, you'll be killed, you'll be killed." He hears it in the tick of a clock, in the rattle of a train, in the footsteps on a street. There are holes in the walls through which his enemy is always watching. Invisible speaking tubes bring him messages. There are pains in his joints, and nightmares of attempts to poison. His brain bursts, and he kills—kills—kills. Excuse me for speaking so . . . strongly.

TOM: But how does this affect us?

DAVIS: Mr. Courtney, will you examine this sheet of paper?

TOM: What is it?

DAVIS: The fragment of a typewritten diary. I found it on the cliffs months ago. Don't ask me who wrote it! But I know there's a criminal lunatic on this island. He imagined that poor, inoffensive Josephine Adams was his enemy. So he killed her.

TOM: Killed her? *How?*

DAVIS: I don't know.

TOM: And what happened to the girl's body?

DAVIS: I'm not a detective, sir. The body was carried out to sea, perhaps. Or washed along the cliffs and into the Blue Grotto to be lost. But don't you understand the danger to your wife?

TOM: You're not suggesting . . . ?

DAVIS: To somebody's cracked brain, your wife is Josephine Adams all over again.

TOM: Kill Lucy? It couldn't be done!

DAVIS: It *was* done, my friend— Listen!

TOM: That sounded . . . like a dog howling.

DAVIS: Mrs. Courtney is rather a long time in getting that whiskey.

TOM: She wouldn't go near the balcony! She promised not to go out on the balcony!

DAVIS: People sometimes do perverse things, my friend.

TOM: Lucy! *Lucy!*

DAVIS: That seems to be Tiberius, out on the balcony. I can't see anything else from here.

TOM: She's gone. She's gone. She's . . . *gone!*

NARRATOR: An empty balcony. A howling dog. And a sea turned clear silver under the moon. Then, after the tumult and the shouting, there are other pictures. Do you hear the noise of that motor-launch, with a half-demented young man at the wheel? Three other familiar figures are gathered round it. Don't you recognize the brunette prettiness of Nellie Luchesi? And the white ten-gallon hat of Harry Granger? And the neat pointed beard of Dr. Davis?

NELLIE: But what on earth is he going to *do* out here in this motor-boat?

GRANGER: I'd like to know too.

TOM: Listen! Please! All of you!

GRANGER: Take it easy, son.

TOM: What time is it?

GRANGER: Time?

TOM: Yes! What time is it?

NELLIE: It's half-past two in the morning.

TOM: Then the tide ought to be just where it was this afternoon.

GRANGER: What's the tide got to do with it?

TOM: A whole lot. Somebody set a trap and made Lucy fall off that balcony. I know it.

NELLIE: That's absurd!

TOM: If Lucy's been carried out to sea, there's nothing we can do about it. But if she's been carried along with the current, and into the Blue Grotto . . .

NELLIE: The Blue Grotto?

DAVIS: One moment, sir. You are not proposing to run this big launch under that arch after dark?

TOM: Yes, doctor. That's just exactly what I do propose.

NELLIE: Go on! Do it! I'll back you up! Let's have some excitement!

DAVIS: It will be exciting enough, I assure you. Mr. Courtney, have you some wild hope of recovering your wife's body?

TOM: I've even got a wild hope she may be alive. Lucy's a very strong swimmer.

GRANGER: You're acting like a nut, son!

TOM: Get set, everybody. I'm going to swing around.

NELLIE: We're in the current now. Better hold tight.

TOM: I've got to duck my own head when we go through. Everybody else—flop down!

DAVIS: I still protest! Don't you understand, Mr. Courtney, that—

TOM: Get ready. Here we go!

(Long pause)

NELLIE: What on earth is wrong? There's no Blue Grotto. It's as black as pitch in here!

DAVIS: My dear Nellie, I kept trying to tell all of you. The "blue grotto" effect is caused by the sun's rays. There never is a "blue grotto" except when the sun is out. Just how does our friend expect to find anything in this pitch-black darkness?

TOM: *Listen! (Sound of splashings)*

NELLIE: Something's got hold of the side of the boat! I felt it move!

DAVIS: Not the dead girl, I trust?

TOM: There's a hand here . . . a wet hand. . . . *Lucy!*

NELLIE: She's not . . . *alive?*

TOM: Mr. Granger, help me lift her up over the side. Easy! Don't tip the boat! Lucy! Are you all right?

LUCY: To-om! To-om! *(Coughs.)*

TOM: Are you all right, Lucy? Can you hear me?

LUCY *(panting):* All ri'. Jus' exhausted. Got in here . . . couldn't . . . swim out . . . 'gainst current.

TOM: Don't try to talk. . . .

LUCY *(desperately):* Got to talk. Going to faint. Tom! Who's with you?

TOM: Only our friends.

LUCY: Who's with you? Is . . . the murderer with you?

DAVIS: I was just wondering the same thing. To be shut up in the dark, at nearly three o'clock in the morning, with a criminal lunatic . . .

LUCY (*terrified*): Who spoke then?

TOM: Lucy, don't hold me so tight! Let go! I'll get the boat started and have you out of here in a second!

LUCY: Who spoke then?

TOM: Only Dr. Davis.

LUCY: Tom . . . got to tell you. . . . Know how that girl, Josephine Adams . . . died. . . . Almost killed . . . *me.*

TOM: Has anybody here got some brandy? Or a flashlight?

DAVIS: I have a flashlight. Will you allow me, as a medical man, to examine Mrs. Courtney?

TOM: She's hysterical, doctor. Try to calm her down. Here, give me the flashlight.

LUCY: I walked into . . . other room. Nobody with me. All alone. Except Tiberius.

DAVIS: Yes, Mrs. Courtney?

LUCY: Somebody . . . called my name. From the balcony, I thought. Very soft. "Mrs. Courtney!" it said. "Mrs. Court-ney!"

TOM: Did you recognize the voice?

LUCY: Yes. That's why I went.

NELLIE: Hadn't you better start up this boat and get out of here?

LUCY (*terrified*): Who spoke *then?*

TOM: Don't pay any attention, Lucy. Nobody can hurt you now.

LUCY: I went out on the balcony. Bright moonlight—bright as day. But there was . . . nobody there.

TOM: Nobody on the balcony?

LUCY: No. I looked out over the sea. And something came at me. Something flew out of the air and came at me!

DAVIS: Just one moment, before Mrs. Courtney goes on. Is anybody in this boat carrying a revolver?

TOM: Not that I know of.

DAVIS: Excuse my mentioning it, but I felt something like that—metal, and in the shape of a revolver—brush past my hand.

NELLIE: It was only the flashlight, probably.

DAVIS: Excuse me, it was *not* a flashlight. Mr. Courtney's got the flashlight.

TOM: Will you please let Lucy go on and finish? Lucy, you were on the balcony, and something came at you—

LUCY: Yes! Like a snake! Sideways. Out of the air. It went over my head and fastened round my neck. It was a rope. . . .

TOM: A rope?

LUCY: That's it! A rope. It was thrown . . . from another balcony. I'm small and light. Like Josephine Adams. It pulled me sideways, and over the rail. I fell.

TOM: I think I begin to understand.

LUCY: They couldn't see what happened to Josephine Adams. Frosted-glass doors to balcony. So they couldn't see.

TOM: Take it easy now—you're perfectly safe, Lucy.

DAVIS: *Is* she perfectly safe?

LUCY: The murderer . . . let her fall. But the rope was jerked tight long before she struck the water. That broke her neck! Then the murderer lowered her, softly.

TOM: So there wasn't any splash! And the current took her away, rope and all.

LUCY: That's it! It would have happened to me, only . . . the rope must have slipped through the murderer's fingers.

TOM: Through *whose* fingers?

(A pistol shot)

DAVIS: What did I tell you? Somebody in this boat *has* got a revolver!

(A heavy splash)

TOM: Who went overboard?

DAVIS: Switch on that light and shine it on the water!

TOM: All right, doctor. There's your light. *(Pause)* Look at it! Turning over and over! The water in the Blue Grotto is red now.

LUCY: Tom! Stay close to me!

TOM: It's all right, Lucy. I swear you're safe now.

LUCY: Did he . . . shoot himself?

TOM: Yes.

NELLIE: Did *who* shoot himself?

TOM: Who had a balcony exactly like ours, on the house next door? Who began life as a cowpuncher, and would have known how to use a lasso?

DAVIS: Who knew Josephine Adams well, and got it into his maniac head that Mrs. Courtney was Josephine Adams all over again?

Том: Harry Granger! Look! There's his ten-gallon hat floating away!

(Music up)

Suspense (CBS), December 1, 1942
Ellery Queen's Mystery Magazine, September 1950

Will You Make
a Bet with Death?

The Characters

Betty Andrews	who visits the Haunted Mill
Robert Penderel	who meets her there
John Destry	Penderel's stepfather
A barker, an inspector, a sergeant, etc.	

NARRATOR: Coney Island on a summer day . . . There's the beach, bright-colored with bathing suits. There's the boardwalk, all straw hats and summer dresses. There's the Ferris wheel and the roller coasters and the merry-go-round. There's all humanity eating hot dogs and having a good time. And over there, beyond that souvenir shop, is the Haunted Mill. You get into a little boat that holds only two. You float through a narrow tunnel into the dark, while witches scream. But that doesn't fool anybody, does it? There couldn't be any real terror—could there?—while the bands are playing, and the crowd goes by, and we hear . . .

BARKER: I'm telling you, ladies and gentlemen! A *u*-nique attraction! It hurts me, I say it hurts me, to see you stand there and miss this! Only ten cents, one dime, the miserable tenth part of a dollar, to go through the old Haunted Mill and get the thrill of your lives!

BETTY: An overstatement, if you ask me. One ticket, please.

BARKER *(startled):* Did you say one ticket, lady?

BETTY: That's right. One ticket. What's the thrill?

BARKER: I beg pardon, lady?

BETTY: I said, what's the thrill?

BARKER: Lady, the gals who come here with their boyfriends don't have to ask that. Ten cents, please. This way, and mind the gate. *(Louder)* Step right up, ladies and gentlemen! Get your tickets for the old Haunted Mill, where ghosts walk and corpses—

PENDEREL: Give me some tickets. Hurry!

BARKER: Now just a minute, young fellow! I know you want to get into the old Haunted Mill, but there's plenty of time! How many tickets?

PENDEREL: *I* don't know. Better give me ten.

BARKER: Ten tickets? *(Louder)* You hear that, ladies and gentlemen? Here's a young fellow who likes the old Haunted Mill so much he buys *ten* tickets!

PENDEREL *(under his breath):* Don't call everybody's attention to me! Listen: I've got a better idea. Whatever boat comes *after* mine . . .

BARKER: Yeah?

PENDEREL: I'll give you an extra dollar to send that boat through empty.

BARKER: What's the matter, son? *(Under his breath)* The cops ain't after you, are they?

PENDEREL: No, no, it's nothing like that! Will you do it?

BARKER: Money talks, young fellow. O.K. Go ahead . . .

PENDEREL: Isn't there an empty boat here?

BETTY: Well, really! If you've got such a great objection to riding in the same boat with me . . .

PENDEREL: I—I'm sorry! I didn't mean that at all.

BETTY: Then you'd better get in, if you want to go at all. This boat's starting to move.

(Faint splashing and slapping of water, as in a narrow tunnel)

PENDEREL: Look here, I want to apologize!

BETTY: That's quite unnecessary. This place is rather childish, isn't it?

PENDEREL: Yes. Isn't it?

BETTY: But I've seen everything else, so I may as well see this. Here we go, into the dark.

(They hear a loud burst of machinelike, brassy laughter.)

PENDEREL: What was that?

BETTY: One of the ghosts, I imagine. From a machine.

PENDEREL: It sounded like *him* laughing. There isn't anybody in the boat behind us, is there?

BETTY: I can't see. It's pitch dark.

PENDEREL: Listen, Miss . . . Miss . . .

BETTY: My name is Andrews, Betty Andrews—if it's customary to exchange names in a place like this.

PENDEREL: Mine is Penderel, Bob Penderel.

BETTY: Did you say Penderel?

PENDEREL: Yes. Do you know it?

BETTY: Not—not exactly. It's an unusual name, that's all.

PENDEREL: I don't want you to think I'm out of my mind, though I very nearly am. But I've got five hours to go. Just five hours! At the end of that time, either I'll have won twenty-five thousand dollars, or else . . .

BETTY: Or else?

PENDEREL: Or else I'll be dead.

(Another burst of brassy laughter)

BETTY *(frightened):* You know, I wish I had kept you away from this boat!

PENDEREL: There's nothing to get alarmed about. For *you.* I had to tell somebody or I'd have started yelling. There's just one other thing.

BETTY: Yes?

PENDEREL: In these places they've usually got little dim-lighted rooms along the way. Exhibits.

BETTY: Yes. Ghosts and things.

PENDEREL: When we come to one, I'm going to get out of this boat and hide there. Don't be afraid—and don't tell anybody when you go out.

BETTY: But why should you *do* that?

PENDEREL *(absent-mindedly):* I think I see a light ahead.

BETTY: It *is* a light. But . . .

PENDEREL: Dim too. That's all to the good. It's . . . yes, we're coming round the corner. It's the old mill loft, with a wax dead man on a pile of straw. Goodbye, Betty Andrews. I wish we'd met at a different time.

BETTY: Watch out! *(Splashings)*

PENDEREL: Here! What are *you* doing?

BETTY: Getting out too.

PENDEREL: Don't be an idiot! What's the idea?

BFTTY: You need looking after, Mr. Bob Penderel. If we must hide, I suppose this is as good a place as any.

PENDEREL: I won't have it!

BETTY: Quick! There'll be more boats along any moment! Over behind the dead man on the straw. Hurry! *(Footsteps)* Now, Mr. Bob Penderel, what is this all about?

PENDEREL: I can't tell you!

BETTY: You said yourself that if you don't tell somebody, you'll go crazy!

PENDEREL *(with a deep breath):* Maybe you're right. It's against the strict terms of the bet, but this is the last day and I tell you I can't hold out much longer!

BETTY: Lower your voice—there's a boat coming.

PENDEREL: I wonder if you've ever heard of my stepfather, John Destry?

BETTY: Yes.

PENDEREL: I imagine everybody has. He's a millionaire and . . . I'm not. I'm a chemist, an analytical chemist. Not very successful. If I'd had time, if I'd had money, I might have worked out a process that would have . . . Well, anyway, Destry's a big, white-haired, fine-looking man. You'd think butter wouldn't melt in his mouth. He's got an apartment in the East Sixties, and a secretary—I never met her—valet, cook, that kind of thing. He used to invite me there, but I wouldn't go. Then he got hold of a book I had to have—a German work on chemicals. So I went. After dinner, in that study of his, over the brandy . . .

(Flashback)

DESTRY: My dear Robert, you're quite welcome to the book! Don't mention it! What do you think of this brandy, by the way?

PENDEREL: It's excellent, thanks.

DESTRY: Yes. Yes. I thought you'd like it. And now that we're all relaxed and comfortable after dinner, tell me something.

PENDEREL: Yes, Mr. Destry?

DESTRY *(changing his tone):* You hate my guts, don't you? *(Laughs.)*

PENDEREL: Frankly, I do. And always have.

DESTRY: Good. Then you'll be relieved to hear I've always felt the same about you. But tell me something else. Did you ever know me to break my word?

PENDEREL: No, I never did. I'll give you that.

DESTRY: I asked you that, Robert, because I want to make a little bet with you. That is, if you have the nerve. Which I doubt.

PENDEREL: I'm afraid I can't afford to make bets.

DESTRY: You always were careless with money, Robert, where I've been thrifty. I saw that while your mother was still alive. But you can afford to make this bet. Look here! In my desk.

PENDEREL: Well?

DESTRY: Twenty-five thousand dollars, Robert. Twenty-five thousand dollars, in five-hundred-dollar bills.

PENDEREL *(bitterly):* And what would I have to bet against that?

DESTRY: Your life.

PENDEREL: My *life?*

DESTRY: There's the money on the table. Look at it. What wouldn't you give for that money? What wouldn't you give to have it for this precious work of yours that you're so fond of? And that you've failed in.

PENDEREL: So far I've failed! Yes!

DESTRY: Robert, I've had a fairly good life, as lives go. My heart isn't as good as it might be, but the doctors say I'll last a long time yet. And before I go there's one pleasure, one little exquisite thrill, I would like to experience. I want to commit a murder.

PENDEREL: *Murder!*

DESTRY: Yes, I said murder! I'll bet you that I can kill you within six months, that you can't stop me, and that I'll never be punished for it. What do you say? Yes or no?

PENDEREL: I believe you mean that!

DESTRY: Of course I mean it.

PENDEREL: And just how would you propose to . . . kill me?

DESTRY: Ah! That would be telling.

PENDEREL: You know, if I had time to think this thing over . . .

DESTRY: There's no need to think it over. Now! Yes or no?

PENDEREL *(after a pause):* Yes.

DESTRY *(chuckles):* You must need the money badly, Robert.

PENDEREL: I do. But oddly enough, Mr. Destry, that isn't why I'm doing this.

DESTRY: No?

PENDEREL: No. I want to show you you can't play the Lord Almighty and get away with it.

DESTRY: Are you challenging me?

PENDEREL: Yes!

DESTRY: You don't think I can do it?

PENDEREL: I know you can't.

DESTRY: You understand, of course, that there will be conditions to the bet.

PENDEREL: What conditions?

DESTRY: First of all, you will never mention this matter to anyone.

PENDEREL: All right. That seems fair enough.

DESTRY: You will remain within the city limits of New York for six months. You will spend at least one hour of every day walking the open streets—alone.

PENDEREL: Agreed.

DESTRY: You will spend at least one hour every evening in your own room—alone. I may come to see you, or I may not—as I please.

PENDEREL: Trying to scare me already?

DESTRY: Finally, you will write out a little note, and give it to me. There's pen and paper on the desk in front of you. Write it now.

PENDEREL: First let me hear what I have to write.

DESTRY: You will write: "I am a failure—"

PENDEREL: You can't stop harping on that, can you?

DESTRY: "I am a failure, and this was the only way out. I wouldn't have done it otherwise."

PENDEREL: A suicide note?

DESTRY: Yes. I intend to use it when I . . . operate.

PENDEREL: And if I won't write it?

DESTRY: Then there's no bet.

PENDEREL: All right, I'll do it.

DESTRY: It is now—let's see—nine o'clock on the night of January tenth. If you are alive, and not in a madhouse . . .

PENDEREL: Is that part of the bargain too?

DESTRY: Yes. At nine o'clock on the night of June tenth, given those conditions, you will receive twenty-five thousand dollars. Can't you hear the dice rattle, Robert? You're playing with death now.

PENDEREL: I know it.

DESTRY: Er . . . aren't you going to finish your brandy?

PENDEREL: No, thank you.

DESTRY: Then pour it back into the decanter. . . . You heard me. Pour it back into the decanter. If you were as careful as I am, you wouldn't be where you are now. *(Sound of liquid poured into glass)* That's right. Always be thrifty. I can promise you, by the way, that you'll be perfectly safe as long as you're in this apartment. But that's the only concession I make. I notice your hands are steady, at the moment. I wonder what they'll be like a month from now. . . .

(Back to the Haunted Mill)

BETTY: So you were fool enough to make a bet like that with John Destry?

PENDEREL: Let me tell you what else happened that night. I left his place carrying that book he'd got for me. Remember?

BETTY: I remember.

PENDEREL: It was a damp, foggy night, and I was cold even under my overcoat. I got into a Fifth Avenue bus. I climbed to the top and sat down. . . .

(Flashback)

CONDUCTOR: Hey! Young fellow! You!

PENDEREL: Yes?

CONDUCTOR: Your fare, please. Put a dime in the slot. Say, what's the matter with you?

PENDEREL: That . . . *book* . . .

CONDUCTOR: Here, wait a minute! You've got blood all over your thumb!

PENDEREL: It's a book on . . . poisons.

CONDUCTOR: You'd better wrap a handkerchief around that thumb of yours.

PENDEREL: There are safety-razor blades sewed in a line down the inside edge of the cover. When you open the book . . . Listen, conductor! Listen!

CONDUCTOR: I'm listening.

PENDEREL: A little white card, with something written on it, fell out of the book. Do you see it?

CONDUCTOR: Yeah, I see it.

PENDEREL: Will you pick it up and read it for me?

CONDUCTOR: What's the matter? Can't you read yourself?

PENDEREL: Please pick it up and read it. Will you?

CONDUCTOR: All right; keep your shirt on! It says . . .

PENDEREL: Yes?

CONDUCTOR: It says, "See how easy it is to take you off guard?"

PENDEREL: Anything . . . else?

CONDUCTOR: Yes. It says, "Those razor blades aren't poisoned. But they might have been. Take warning." Say, what is this? A joke?

PENDEREL: Yes, it's a joke.

CONDUCTOR: Some people got a queer idea of what's funny, haven't they? And I still want that fare, mister. . . .

(Back to the Haunted Mill)

PENDEREL: Betty, that was six months ago. Six months less five hours of careful, refined torture. And now I've got only five hours to go.

BETTY: What has he done in the meantime?

PENDEREL: Nothing.

BETTY: I don't understand.

PENDEREL: Nothing at all! That's the cleverness of it. He's left me waiting, waiting, waiting. . . .

BETTY: Expecting something?

PENDEREL: Expecting it every hour of the day or night. Once, at the laboratory where I work, I opened a box that I thought came from a chemical supply house. And a Mexican tarantula, one of those furry spiders about as big as your fist—

BETTY: No!

PENDEREL: —ran out across my hand. *(Pause)* It was a toy tarantula. He enclosed a card asking if I admired it.

BETTY: Bob, this can't go on!

PENDEREL: I used to think I didn't have a nerve in my body. I could hold a test tube at arm's length, absolutely steady, for minutes at a time. Now look at me.

BETTY: Don't, please.

PENDEREL: But the waiting's almost over now. Walking the streets, wondering who is behind you . . . sitting alone at night, listening for every step on the stair. He's got very little time left now, and he's got to *do* something. The question is—what's he going to do?

BETTY: Maybe he didn't mean it. Maybe he only meant to scare you.

PENDEREL: And lose all that money? You don't know my stepfather.

BETTY: Listen!

PENDEREL: I—I don't hear anything.

BETTY: That's just it. There's no sound of running water. The boats have stopped.

PENDEREL: Then we're all alone in here. Or with him.

BETTY: Yes.

PENDEREL: Lord, how I wish I hadn't made that silly bet! You know, I thought I saw him in the crowd outside. But I wasn't sure. I see him everywhere.

BETTY: Bob, tell me something. Did you ever see Mr. Destry—I mean, face to face—after that first night?

PENDEREL: Many times.

BETTY: He came to see you?

PENDEREL: He came to my laboratory once, yes. But mostly, I went to see him. And why? Because it was the only place in the world I could feel really safe.

BETTY: He promised nothing would happen to you while you were in his apartment?

PENDEREL: Don't you see it was part of the torture? Night after night he'd invite me—and I'd go to visit him. As a matter of fact, I saw him only last night. We were in that study of his, with the devil masks on the walls. And he was sitting behind the big ma-hogany desk. . . .

(Flashback)

DESTRY: My dear Robert! I'm pleased and even touched to have you here on the last night before you . . . before you . . .

PENDEREL: Why don't you say "die" and get it over with?

DESTRY: Well! Let's not say die.

PENDEREL: No?

DESTRY: The clergy contend that we never die; we only change. Let that be a consolation to you. And must you be going so early?

PENDEREL: There's that "one hour at home," you remember.

DESTRY: I remember. You're keeping to the rules?

PENDEREL *(fiercely):* Keeping to the rules? I mean to beat you at this if it's the last thing I ever do!

DESTRY *(reflectively):* "The last thing I ever do." That's an unfortunate choice of phrase, Robert. My boy, you haven't a chance. Something is going to happen to you within the next twenty-four hours, when you least expect it.

PENDEREL: Will you answer one question?

DESTRY: If I choose.

PENDEREL: Have you decided *how* you mean to kill me?

DESTRY: I decided that six months ago.

PENDEREL: And you still think you can get away with it?

DESTRY: It's a method which has never been known to fail. I give you my word of honor on that.

PENDEREL: Is it . . . sudden?

DESTRY *(thoughtfully):* Yes . . . and no.

PENDEREL: Good night, Mr. Destry. I think I'd better be leaving.

DESTRY: No, my dear boy! No! You mustn't go yet. Sit down and pour yourself a glass of brandy.

PENDEREL: No, thanks.

DESTRY: Then perhaps you wouldn't mind pouring a glass for *me? (Rattle of glass against glass)* I notice your hands are shaking. They didn't six months ago, did they? No. You were full of confidence then. And it grieves me to see you waste tobacco by lighting a cigarette and then putting it out immediately.

PENDEREL: It's no use lying to you. But I'm going to beat you just the same.

DESTRY: You wouldn't like to back out now?

PENDEREL: After what I've been through?

DESTRY: You'd still have your life.

PENDEREL: I'll keep it, thanks.

DESTRY: That's very unwise of you, Robert. Still, it is you who must decide. I was expecting my secretary a little later, to dictate some letters. But now I think I'll leave her a message that I've gone to bed. Tomorrow is likely to prove an interesting day for both of us. Here's your hat . . . your briefcase . . . and let me wish you a fond, peaceful and happy night. . . .

(Back to the Haunted Mill)

PENDEREL: That was last night, Betty, and only five hours to go. . . .

BETTY: Less than five hours now.

PENDEREL: If I can keep away from the old devil until nine o'clock . . .

BETTY: I wish those boats would start running again!

PENDEREL: Why?

BETTY: Because it's almost as spooky in here as in a real mill. And even that wax dummy on the straw . . . At any minute now . . .

PENDEREL: You're expecting to see it move? So am I.

BETTY: Don't stand up!

PENDEREL: It doesn't matter. If the boats aren't running, we can hear anybody who comes along.

BETTY: I hope so.

PENDEREL: Do you think Destry got in?

BETTY: Bob, he couldn't have!

PENDEREL: Why not?

BETTY: Because today Mr. Destry intended to— *(Stops dead.)*

PENDEREL: Go on, Betty, go on. How do *you* know what Mr. Destry intended to do?

BETTY: Because I'm his secretary. I was going to tell you. *(Pause)*

PENDEREL: You know, Betty, I'm sorry it was you who did this.

BETTY: Did what?

PENDEREL: You can't guess?

BETTY *(crying out):* I didn't come here to trap you or spy on you, if that's what you're thinking. I swear I didn't!

PENDEREL: No. You only got me to tell you all and lose my bet.

BETTY: I haven't heard a single word you've said, Bob Penderel. Please believe that!

PENDEREL: He didn't send you here?

BETTY: No! No!

PENDEREL: And you didn't see me at his apartment last night?

BETTY: No, I swear I didn't! I got there late. He'd gone to bed. I didn't even take off my hat or gloves before I left again. Don't you understand, Bob? I hate him, and . . . I rather like *you.* I want to see you beat him! You've got to beat him!

PENDEREL: You mean that?

BETTY: Look at me and see if I mean it!

PENDEREL: Betty, I almost believe you.

(Slapping and splashing of water)

BETTY: We'd better hide—the boats have started up again. Come on
—hurry!

(A man's voice shouts from a little distance.)

VOICE: Wait a minute, you two! Stay where you are!

PENDEREL: Where's that voice coming from?

BETTY: From back in the tunnel, I think.

PENDEREL: But it's not Destry's voice.

BETTY: No, it's a man standing up in a boat. He's coming around the
bend. I can see him now.

(Splashings and the bump of a boat)

STRANGER: The Old Haunted Mill, eh? By golly, if *this* ain't some
place to make a pinch, *I* never heard of one!

PENDEREL: What do you mean—make a pinch?

STRANGER: Just what I said. Your name Robert Penderel?

PENDEREL: Yes. Who are you, and what do you want?

STRANGER: I'm from police headquarters. You're to come along with
me. They want to see you over in New York.

BETTY: About . . . what?

STRANGER: I wouldn't know, lady. But it *might* be about the murder
of John Destry. *(Brassy laughter)* Sweet howling catfish, what was
that?

PENDEREL: Did you say the *murder* of John Destry?

STRANGER: That's right. Somebody poisoned him last night with
mercury cyanide. I wouldn't have got on your trail at all, if the
barker outside hadn't thought the cops was after you to start
with.

PENDEREL: Betty.

BETTY: Yes, Bob?

PENDEREL: He's beaten me. I know now the weapon Destry planned
to use in killing me.

BETTY: What weapon?

PENDEREL: The electric chair. It never fails.

BETTY: You mustn't *talk* like that!

PENDEREL: Don't you see? He never once intended to kill me in the
way I thought.

STRANGER: Are you comin' quietly, Mr. Penderel?

PENDEREL: He poisoned himself. But he left evidence to show *I* did
it. He's killed me just as effectively as if he'd used a gun. The money

doesn't matter now. If I'm in the death house for murder, what use would I have for all the money in the world?

(INSPECTOR MULLAN *is fiftyish; he has a gruff voice, patient and almost friendly.*)

MULLEN: Mr. Penderel, let me introduce myself. My name's Mullan. Inspector Mullan.

PENDEREL (*sardonically*): It's a pleasure to meet you, Inspector. It's a pleasure to be . . . safe again.

MULLAN: I've had you brought to my office for a quiet little talk. You're in a jam, son, and I want you to realize how bad it is.

PENDEREL: You think I don't realize it?

MULLAN: John Destry was poisoned with mercury cyanide administered in a glass of brandy. . . .

PENDEREL: And only my fingerprints were on the glass besides his own.

MULLAN: Mr. Destry's body was found this morning, lying behind the desk in the study. There was an empty glass, with traces of brandy and cyanide. We haven't had the full autopsy report, but the smell of that stuff is pretty distinctive. They tell me you're a chemist, Mr. Penderel.

PENDEREL: That's right.

MULLAN: The boys find that eight grains of mercury cyanide are missing from your laboratory.

PENDEREL: Where he visited me a month ago.

MULLAN: And in your briefcase, which you took away from his apartment last night—

PENDEREL: He handed it to me.

MULLAN:—we found over a thousand dollars in cash. Now take a look at this note. Ever see it before?

PENDEREL: Yes. I wrote it.

MULLAN: It says: "I am a failure, and this was the only way out. I wouldn't have done it otherwise."

PENDEREL: Where did you find it?

MULLAN: Torn up in little bits. You started to write a confession, then couldn't face the consequences. But you shouldn't have left the pieces. You're in for it, my lad. Too bad you had to go and kill him, son. Didn't you know he had an aneurysm—a fatal heart disease?

PENDEREL: He said he had heart trouble. But . . .

MULLAN: Heart trouble! His doctor says he couldn't have lived more than eight or ten months. And you might have got something in the will.

PENDEREL: So *that's* why he did it!

MULLAN: Did what?

PENDEREL: Killed himself.

MULLAN: You still stick to that crazy story you told the boys?

PENDEREL: He's *going* to kill me, isn't he? With three thousand volts of electricity?

(Sharp rapping on the door, which opens)

MULLAN *(angrily):* What are you doing, sergeant? Didn't I say I wasn't to be disturbed?

SERGEANT: All the same, Inspector, I thought I'd better do it. There's a young lady here—a Miss Betty Andrews. I think you'd better see her. We've just heard from Mr. Destry's lawyer.

MULLAN: Well?

SERGEANT: He says that young fellow there, Mr. Penderel, inherits twenty-five thousand bucks in Mr. Destry's new will.

MULLAN: Do you hear that, son? Do you see what you'd have got, if you hadn't gone and killed him?

PENDEREL: He was "keeping his promise," that's all. And a fine lot of good it'll do me now!

SERGEANT: But look, Inspector. I've just talked to the medical examiner. And he says there's no poison in Mr. Destry's body. *(Pause)*

MULLAN: Somebody's kidding you! An empty glass with the smell of mercury cyanide, and a dead man with a congested face behind the desk . . . What *did* kill him?

SERGEANT: If you'd like to talk to Miss Andrews, Inspector, she's right here.

BETTY: I think you'd better, Inspector. I've been trying to tell you all afternoon.

MULLAN: Come in, Miss Andrews.

BETTY: I've been over and over it! But until they got the medical report, nobody would listen.

MULLAN: Can you tell us what killed John Destry?

BETTY: Yes. Poison.

MULLAN: But the sergeant just said there was no poison in the body!

BETTY: Inspector, *will* you listen? I was at Mr. Destry's apartment late last night. The servants said he'd gone to bed. I looked into the study, to see if there were any instructions.

PENDEREL: You didn't see . . . ?

BETTY: I couldn't see his body, because it was hidden behind the desk. I didn't even know he was dead until late this afternoon! But I did see a full glass of brandy.

MULLAN: A *full* glass, did you say?

BETTY: Yes! So I picked up the glass and poured the brandy back into the decanter. That's what he always did himself. And I didn't leave any fingerprints because I was still wearing my gloves. And that was the same glass you later found empty.

MULLAN: But you're still not telling us! *What was the poison that killed John Destry?*

BETTY: The poison of his own character. Don't you see? He worked out this plot to frame Bob Penderel. Only, just as he stretched out his hand to drink the cyanide . . .

PENDEREL: Inspector, I think I see it! It was his last great moment— he sat there gloating—

BETTY: That's it! His bad heart couldn't stand it, and he fell dead behind the desk. And from the expression on his face now . . .

MULLAN: Yes?

BETTY: I think he died laughing.

(Music up)

Suspense (CBS), November 10, 1942
Ellery Queen's Mystery Magazine, April 1954

The Devil in the Summerhouse

The Characters

Joseph Parker	the family lawyer
Captain Burke	of the New York homicide bureau
Jerry Kenyon	who died nearly thirty years ago
Isabel Kenyon	his wife
Paul	her brother
Angela Fiske	the other woman
Kitty	the maid

NARRATOR: Somewhere along the Hudson, perhaps not far from Tarrytown, there is a modest house in its own grounds. Behind it, in a spacious garden, stands a summerhouse of evil memory. More than twenty-five years ago, a man shot himself, or, at least, died in that summerhouse. They found Major Kenyon with a scorched bullet hole in his head, and the weapon beside him. But we are in the present now. The latticed summerhouse has grown heavy with vines. And only the other evening, two men came into that garden at twilight, over the shaggy grass, as a storm was brewing along the Hudson. . . .

PARKER (*elderly, very much the conservative family lawyer*): Who's there?

BURKE (*worried*): Easy, my friend! Easy! I was just going to ask you the same thing.

PARKER: My name is Parker. I'm an attorney. That's not . . . *(as though peering)* that's not Captain Burke?

BURKE: The very same and no other, I thought I recognized you, Mr. Parker.

PARKER: And what is a captain of the homicide bureau doing so far from New York?

BURKE: We're only at Tarrytown, you know. I've just come from . . . *(hesitates)* up the river a ways. They told me there'd be a housekeeper her, but I don't see any lights.

PARKER: You've got business here?

BURKE: In a way. Have you?

PARKER *(blankly):* I don't know.

BURKE: You don't *know?*

PARKER: Tell me, Captain, did you ever get an anonymous letter from a dead man? *(A long roll of thunder)*

PARKER *(insistently):* Did you?

BURKE: No, I can't say I did. If the letter's anonymous, how do you know the man's dead?

PARKER: Because they're all dead. Every last one of them. Dead and under the ground, where they can't be hurt any longer. Look! There's the summerhouse where Jerry Kenyon used to work. There are the windows of the library and the dining room, looking towards it. Confound this lightning!

BURKE *(matter-of-factly):* Makes the windows blaze, don't it?

PARKER: Jerry Kenyon hadn't a care in the world. And yet he shot himself. I'll show you the letter.

BURKE: I can't read anything in this light. But if we can get inside the house . . . ?

PARKER: Of course we can get into the house. I've got the keys. But *why* should a dead person send me a letter?

(Music up)

PARKER: This is the library, you see.

BURKE: I notice they've left the lights working.

PARKER: Yes. Same old heavy furniture. Same old thick carpet. Same old globe map.

BURKE: But this letter you were talking about . . . ?

PARKER: It's in my briefcase. Here. Read it.

BURKE: Wait a minute! This thing is dated . . . November 2, 1918!

PARKER: That's right. But it was mailed *yesterday!*

BURKE: From where?

PARKER: I don't remember. I didn't keep the envelope. Read it!

BURKE: "Dear Joe"—

PARKER: In case you didn't know it, "Joe" is your obedient servant.

BURKE: You look more like J. Witherspoon Parker than Joe Parker. "Dear Joe. If you want to know how Major Kenyon really died . . .

PARKER: But we know how he died!

BURKE: "If you want to know how Major Kenyon really died, look in the third drawer of the desk in the library. Press hard at the back of the drawer. Yours very truly—" And then nothing. No signature. Written in block capitals.

PARKER: Look! There's the chair where Isabel sat on the afternoon it happened. Isabel was Jerry Kenyon's wife. Beautiful woman even though past forty. There's the door that the maid let me in by. *(Vacantly)* You know, Captain, it seems to me they're all here tonight.

BURKE: Who?

PARKER: "We stand 'neath the sounding rafter,
    And the walls around us are bare;
  As they echo our peals of laughter
    It seems that the dead are there."

BURKE: "Yet we stand to our glasses steady—"

PARKER: You know it too?

BURKE: It was in my school reader. How does the rest of it go?
    "Yet we stand to our glasses steady,
      And drink to our comrades' eyes;
    Here's a glass to the dead already—
      Hurrah for the next that dies!"

(A heavy crash of thunder)

PARKER *(ashamedly):* I don't know what's come over me, talking that way. But I was very fond of those people.

BURKE: Are you going to look in the desk drawer?

PARKER: This is all a lot of nonsense!

BURKE: Then why are you here, Mr. Parker?

PARKER: Jerry Kenyon was always a happy man. At least, that's what I thought. Big, boisterous fellow—

BURKE: Yes?

PARKER: He had a good position with Vitatone. You know, the phonograph company. But he'd just been made a major in the Army. Nineteen seventeen—there was a war on then, if you remember.

BURKE: I remember. To make the world safe for democracy.

PARKER: Old days. Old heartaches. Old memories. I remember a blazing hot day in August when all the windows were up. I remember this room. And Isabel—that was Jerry's wife—sitting in that chair, knitting. I remember ... *(As his voice fades, there is a knock at the door, which opens. KITTY, the maid, is young and has a faintly insolent manner. ISABEL KENYON is in her forties; she has a very pleasant voice.)*

ISABEL: Yes, Kitty? What is it?

KITTY: There's a man to see you, Mrs. Kenyon. He says his name's Parker.

ISABEL: Mr. Parker's an old friend of ours. Show him in, please.

KITTY: All right, ma'am. Shall I take your knitting and your knitting bag?

ISABEL *(astonished):* Why on earth should you take my knitting?

KITTY: I dunno, Mrs. Kenyon. I just wondered. *(Over her shoulder)* You can come in now.

PARKER: Thank you. *(Door closes.)*

ISABEL: Hello, Joe.

PARKER: Hello, Isabel.

ISABEL: Joe, I must apologize for Kitty. Servants are getting to be a problem nowadays.

PARKER: *She* looks pretty enough to get along.

ISABEL: Oh, Kitty's got large ideas. She wants to go on the stage, if you please, and do imitations. Like Miss Draper. *(Tensely)* If she knew how hard it was, *acting* all your life ...

PARKER: Isabel. You've been crying.

ISABEL: I have *not!* At least ...

PARKER: Is it about Jerry?

ISABEL: Isn't it always about Jerry?

PARKER: Where is he? I want to see him before I go.

ISABEL: He's probably out in the summerhouse. He's got a lot of work to catch up with. He's—he's going overseas before long.

PARKER: Yes. I know.

ISABEL: If you look out of the window, you can see the door of the summerhouse. *(Pettishly)* Go and get Jerry. Go on, get him! Everybody who comes to this house comes to see Jerry. Nobody comes to see *me*.

PARKER: That's not true, Isabel, and you know it.

ISABEL *(checking herself)*: I'm sorry. I didn't mean it. It's this heat, or . . . other things. But sometimes I'd like to put a gun to my head, and—

(A sharp pistol shot)

PARKER: That sounded like a shot!

ISABEL: It *was* a shot, Joe, dear.

PARKER: In the house? It doesn't seem to worry you.

ISABEL: It's only Paul. My brother Paul. I'm not sure if you've met him.

PARKER: I don't think so.

ISABEL: He's staying with us. Jerry's fixed him up a pistol-shooting range in the cellar. Poor Paul's a terribly bad shot. Not like the rest of us. I doubt whether he could hit anything unless he actually got dead on the target and—

(Four shots, spaced in twos)

ISABEL: You don't seem to like it, Joe. Shall I have Kitty go down and tell him to stop?

PARKER: No, no. I suppose young America ought to learn how to use a gun.

ISABEL: Of course.

PARKER: But about Jerry . . .

ISABEL: *Must* we talk about Jerry?

PARKER: You'll feel better. Who is it this time?

ISABEL: Jerry's been home on leave for five days. But he's spent four of those five evenings with *(spacing the words)* that Fiske woman.

PARKER: Angela Fiske? The redhead with all the money?

ISABEL: Has she got money? She must have *some* attraction. Please understand me, Joe. It's not that I'm particularly jealous.

PARKER: No, of course not.

ISABEL: Jerry and I understand each other. He goes his way and I go mine. I may not be without admirers myself, if it comes to that.

PARKER *(quietly)*: You've got no idea how true that is, Isabel.

ISABEL: Haven't I, Joe? Haven't I?

PARKER (*confused*): I mean—

ISABEL: No; I was thinking about poor Jerry. He may not always be lucky. He may meet some little girl who's not as broad-minded as I am. And then, when he gives her the go-by—

(*Six shots, rapidly fired*)

ISABEL: Paul must be getting really furious, down in that cellar. Not hitting anything.

PARKER: He's using a lot of ammunition.

ISABEL: Now, your trouble, Joe, is that you're too much of a gentleman. . . . (*Suddenly changing her tone*) And if you *really* want to see Jerry, there he is now.

PARKER: Where?

ISABEL: Just going down the path to the summerhouse. Look out the window.

PARKER: It's infernally bright out there.

ISABEL: Doesn't he look noble in his new uniform? Sam Browne belt and revolver and everything. Look how he turns round and waves his cap at us like a real soldier!

PARKER: Real soldiers don't exactly wave their caps, do they?

ISABEL: *He* does. (*Calling*) Jerry! *Jer*-ry!

(JERRY KENYON *calls back from a distance.*)

JERRY: Hello, there!

ISABEL (*calling*): Jerry, Joe Parker's here!

JERRY: (*As though unable to hear*) Who?

ISABEL: Joe Parker! He wants to see you.

JERRY: Well, give him a drink or something. I'll be up in a minute.

ISABEL (*tensely*): Into the summerhouse again. Not a care in the world, has he?

PARKER: Now listen, Isabel: you've got to slow down. You'll be crying again in a minute.

ISABEL: The—the light hurts my eyes.

PARRKER: Then we'll pull down these linen window blinds. We'll still be able to see. . . . There! How's that?

ISABEL: Better.

PARKER: Can I get you anything?

ISABEL: Oh, no. You heard the Great White Chief's orders. I'm to get *you* something. What will you have? Highball?

(*Two shots, spaced*)

PARKER: Don't bother about a drink.

ISABEL: It's no bother. The stuff's out in the dining room here.

(Three shots)

ISABEL *(from the adjoining room):* The iceman didn't deliver today, of all days, and I'm afraid I can't give you any. I read in the paper yesterday that we're likely to have automatic iceboxes any day: you know, things that freeze ice by electricity or something. Do you believe that?

PARKER: I doubt it. But listen, Isabel . . .

ISABEL *(returning to the library):* Here you are. Not very cold, but the best I could do.

PARKER: Thanks. What I wanted to say was: couldn't you get that brother of yours to give up practicing now? Hasn't he done his good deed for the day?

(A single shot)

ISABEL: I'll ring for Kitty.

(Sharp knock on door, which opens)

KITTY: You don't have to call me, Mrs. Kenyon. I'm here.

ISABEL: Yes, Kitty? What is it?

KITTY: It's only to tell you there's another visitor. This time it's a woman.

ISABEL: *Lady,* Kitty! Call her a *lady,* please!

KITTY: Well, ma'am, I wonder if you'll think so. She says her name's Fiske. Angela Fiske.

ISABEL *(startled):* Angela Fiske! Tell her I'm not in.

KITTY: It's too late, Mrs. Kenyon. She's comin' down the hall now.

ANGELA *(deferentially):* My *dear* Mrs. Kenyon!

ISABEL: How do you do, Angela? This is a friend of ours. Miss Fiske, Mr. Parker.

ANGELA: I don't want to intrude, really I don't! I wouldn't have intruded for worlds, especially on a day like this—isn't it awful?—but your husband simply insisted. My dear Mrs. Kenyon, he simply wouldn't take no for an answer.

ISABEL: I'm sure he wouldn't.

ANGELA: Do you know what he's brought from his office, as a surprise?

ISABEL: No.

ANGELA: A phonograph recording machine! And he's going to let us use it!

ISABEL: So that we can all hear ourselves talk twice? How nice. *(Four shots)*

ISABEL: In heaven's name, can't somebody stop that firing?

PARKER *(fiercely, under his breath)*: Don't fly off the handle! Take it easy, now!

ISABEL: Kitty!

KITTY: Yes, ma'am?

ISABEL: Please go down in the cellar and tell my brother he's driving us all crazy. Tell him to stop!

KITTY: Yes, ma'am. *(She leaves.)*

ANGELA: My dear Mrs. Kenyon, I do hope I haven't offended you in any way! I know I'm a silly little chatterbox. They say people who have red hair often are, and of course, at your age, you must find the heat very trying.

PARKER: Don't you think we'd all better sit down? *(Heartily)* I was very much interested in what Miss . . . Fiske said about a phonograph recording machine. Mrs. Kenyon . . . er . . . was just talking about a machine to make ice.

ANGELA: Isn't science wonderful? But I *do* think it was mean of Major Kenyon to invite me out here and then fall asleep in the summerhouse.

(Two shots)

ISABEL *(slowly)*: Did you say . . . *fall asleep?*

ANGELA: Yes! Of course!

PARKER: But how do you know?

ANGELA *(surprised)*: I came up the back way. I saw him in the summerhouse, with his head forward on the table.

PARKER: That's queer.

ANGELA: Of course, I couldn't see much, except in the bright light at the door. But I *think* I saw him there.

ISABEL: I think I'd better go and look. *(She leaves.)*

ANGELA: Oh, dear! Somehow I always manage to offend people, being so dependent and everything. Except men, of course. I couldn't offend *you,* Mr. Parker, could I?

PARKER: Madam, I'm not sure.

ANGELA: Of course, the person I really came to see was Paul. Mrs. Kenyon's brother. He's a little young, of course. But he's joining up next month—I think we should all do our bit, don't you?—and he has such a pleasant personality. I think he likes me. If he walked in at that door this minute—

(Door flung violently open. Paul is a tall, gawky young man of twenty.)

PAUL *(in a rush):* Now look here, sis. I think it was a low-down trick to interrupt a fellow's revolver practice just when I'd got to the point where . . . Hullo!

ANGELA: Paul!

PAUL: Oh, lord! Are *you* here again?

PARKER *(placatingly):* Did you have a good day's shooting?

PAUL *(through his teeth):* Swell. One of the best.

PARKER: Hit the target?

PAUL: On the only shot that mattered, I hit the target dead center.

(Distantly, a shrill scream, then another)

PAUL: That sounded like my sister!

PARKER: I think it *was* your sister.

(He runs to window, raises blind, looks out.)

PAUL: *What is it? What's wrong with you, over at that window?*

(Music up)

PARKER *(reflectively):* That was more than twenty-five years ago, Captain Burke.

BURKE: Yes. It's a long time.

PARKER: We found Jerry Kenyon lying across the table in the summerhouse. He'd shot himself through the head with his own revolver. It was lying on the floor beside him.

BURKE: Shot himself. I see.

PARKER: When Isabel found him, he'd been dead about half an hour.

BURKE: The doctors proved that?

PARKER: Yes. That shot had been fired against his head. The front of his uniform cap was powder-burned where the bullet entered.

BURKE: There's no doubt about that?

PARKER: None at all. We never noticed the real shot because—

BURKE: Because that young lad was shooting like a maniac in the cellar.

PARKER: That's right. And now they're all dead. By accident, or ill-

ness, they're all gone. Isabel Kenyon died less than a year afterwards. I think she died just because she was so fond of Jerry.
Er . . . I suppose you've guessed *my* little secret?

BURKE: I think I can read between the lines. You were in love with
Isabel Kenyon, weren't you?

PARKER: Yes.

BURKE: Well, these things happen.

PARKER: I never let her see it, you understand!

BURKE: Women *know.*

PARKER: They're all gone—all but me. And I'm left alone with old
tunes, and old ghosts, wondering *why* the fellow ever killed himself. *(Fiercely)* Why? Why? *Why?*

BURKE: Uh huh.

PARKER: And this morning, out of a clear sky, I get this letter.

BURKE: "If you want to know how Major Kenyon really died, look in
the third drawer of the desk in the library. Press hard at the back
of the drawer." Are you going to do it?

PARKER: Naturally! I've got a key here somewhere that fits the
drawer.

BURKE: Listen, Mr. Parker. In my father's country, in Ireland,
they've got a saying that when a man's going to commit suicide, the
devil comes in, and takes him by the hand, and talks to him. They
say you can see the devil as plain as I see you . . . just before you pull
the trigger.

PARKER: The devil must have been in the summerhouse *that* afternoon, then.

BURKE: Oh, no, he wasn't.

PARKER: What do you mean?

BURKE: Major Kenyon didn't kill himself. He was murdered.

(PARKER begins to laugh.)

BURKE: What's so funny?

PARKER: Because the police covered all that at the time. And everybody had an alibi.

BURKE: They did, did they?

PARKER: Well, think of what I've told you! Isabel and I were together
all the time. Paul, her brother, was shooting constantly in the cellar.
Angela Fiske—

BURKE: What about *her?*

PARKER: She had a chauffeur who drove her here, and he swore he saw her from the moment she left the car until she entered this house.

BURKE: So.

PARKER: Even Kitty the maid could prove she'd never stirred out of the house, until just a minute or so before Isabel went herself—

BURKE: Oh? And why did the maid have to leave the house at all?

PARKER: She was taking Jerry the black coffee he drank every afternoon. But remember, he'd already been dead half an hour then. And that disposes of everybody.

BURKE: Listen, Mr. Parker, I say Major Kenyon was murdered because I *know* he was murdered.

PARKER: By an outsider, of course.

BURKE: No. By one of the people in that house.

PARKER: That's impossible!

BURKE: Is it? Why don't you open that desk drawer and see?

(A clock strikes the three-quarter hour.)

BURKE: What's that?

PARKER: Only the clock. It's been kept running. Let's see—a quarter to eight.

BURKE: A quarter to eight? Then I haven't got much time!

PARKER: For what?

BURKE: Holy St. Patrick, *will* you open that drawer?

PARKER: If it's waited more than twenty-five years, my friend, it can wait another minute. I've got the key somewhere in this bunch. *(He goes on muttering to himself as he finds the key.)* Everything the same. Paul didn't change after he inherited. Same old desk. Same old phonograph. Same old . . . I think this is the key. Yes! It opens. It's a deep drawer, Captain, but there's nothing in it!

BURKE: The letter says to press hard at the back. Have you tried that?

PARKER: It doesn't seem to . . . *(Excitedly)* Yes, by George, it does work!

BURKE: Well?

PARKER: There seems to be a movable back on a hinge.

BURKE: What's inside?

PARKER: Some sort of flat brown-paper parcel sealed with wax . . .

BURKE: Open it, man! Open it!

PARKER: It's a phonograph record! *(Pause)* There's a plain white label and something written on it in pencil. But I don't see too well nowadays without my glasses.

BURKE: Give it to me. I'll read it to you. "A Record of How I Killed Jerry Kenyon." *(Another pause)* Don't you get it, Mr. Parker? This is the real goods! The murderer's going to tell us his own story more than twenty-five years after the fact!

PARKER: Be careful! Whatever you do, don't drop it!

BURKE: You seem to be interested enough *now*.

PARKER: I don't say I'm not interested. I say I can't believe it!

BURKE: There's the phonograph. Put on that record and let's hear what the ghost says.

PARKER: Any of them could have made the record. The apparatus was all here.

BURKE: Won't the phonograph work?

PARKER: Oh, yes, it works.

BURKE: Is it wound up?

PARKER: Yes. It's wound up. *(With a deep breath)* Here goes.

BURKE *(suddenly apprehensive):* But look, Mr. Parker. Whose voice do you think it's going to be?

PARKER: I don't know.

BURKE *(urgently):* I ought to warn you. The voice you're going to hear is . . .

PARKER: Please be quiet and listen! I've started it!

(A measured scratching, as of a needle on an imperfect surface)

PARKER *(speaking to the phonograph):* Well? Speak up! Who killed Jerry Kenyon?

(A woman's voice, clearly heard despite the scratching, seems to reply.)

VOICE: *I* killed him, Joe, dear.

PARKER: Isabel!

BURKE: Mr. Parker, for the love of the saints, listen to me!

PARKER: Shh!

VOICE: I'm sorry about it, Joe. But I had to have you for an alibi. And you were so terribly easy to fool.

BURKE: It's only a phonograph record, man! Don't look at it as if it were alive!

VOICE: You said you and I were always together, Joe. But that wasn't quite true. I left you to go into the dining room and mix a highball. Remember?

PARKER (*hoarsely*): Yes . . . yes . . .

VOICE: And I was carrying my big knitting bag. Remember? But there was something else in it besides knitting. I'm an awfully good revolver shot, Joe. I told you we were all good, except Paul. And the back windows of the dining room face the same way as the back windows of the library.

PARKER (*bitterly*): Thank you, Isabel. Thank you very much.

VOICE: Jerry was in the summerhouse. I made a sign to him from the window, and he came to the door there. In bright sunlight, fifty feet away.

PARKER: So that was how you—

VOICE: Joe, don't you know what August heat is in a wooden summerhouse? Didn't you—didn't anybody—see that no man would be wearing a cap *inside—on a day like that?* Jerry had taken his cap off before he went into the summerhouse. We saw him do it. He was bareheaded when he came to the door. So I lifted the revolver and shot him through the head. Then I dropped the gun back in my knitting bag, and went back to the library with your drink.

BURKE (*hoarsely*): I'm going to turn the thing off!

PARKER: Stay where you are!

BURKE: But it's not—

PARKER: I have a right to hear it.

BURKE: Then don't talk back to the thing, man, or you'll drive me crazy!

VOICE: There was something else in my knitting bag, too. I had to use it. It was a duplicate of Jerry's army cap, with a powder-burned hole already fired through it in exactly the place I wanted.

PARKER: Very clever of you, Isabel.

VOICE: I waited for some time, and then slipped out to "find" the body. I fitted the new cap over Jerry's head in the place where it ought to go. I put the old cap in my knitting bag. I took his real revolver out of the holster and kept it. The gun that I'd used I dropped on the floor beside him. So I proved it was "suicide," you see.

PARKER: You proved it to *me.*

VOICE: Joe, listen. I'm very sick. They tell me I'm going to die.

PARKER: You *are* dead.

VOICE: Joe, I'm afraid. I'm going out in the dark, and I don't know what's there.

PARKER: Don't go away, Isabel! Come back! Just for a minute!

BURKE: I've had about enough of this.

VOICE: I want you to tell everybody about it, Joe. I want you to tell them how a jealous woman couldn't stand it any longer, and— *(Voice and scratching stop abruptly.)*

BURKE: There! It's cut off, and it's going to stay off.

PARKER: I've heard enough, anyway. But you can't arrest her now, my friend. You can't arrest her now.

BURKE: I don't want to arrest anybody!

PARKER: Captain Burke, did you know what was on the record?

BURKE: Yes.

PARKER: And was that your idea of a joke?

BURKE: No, so help me! I may have been trying to have a little bit of fun with you at first . . .

PARKER: Ah!

BURKE: But I never guessed how you'd take it. Then, when I did try to tell you, you wouldn't listen. Man, don't you get it even yet?

PARKER: Yes, I get it.

BURKE: Oh, no, you don't. You don't see anything. That was how the fake "suicide" was managed, yes. That's just *how* it was all done, bar one or two little things. Only . . .

PARKER: Only what?

BURKE: Only it wasn't Isabel Kenyon who committed the murder.

PARKER: What! Did I hear you correctly?

BURKE: You did.

PARKER: This is another of your little jokes, I suppose. Can't you let me alone?

BURKE: Hold it! You're going to hear the real truth now, if I have to hold you down in that chair. I know Mrs. Kenyon didn't kill her husband because I've just come from talking to the real murderer . . . up the river.

PARKER: But they're all dead!

BURKE: Oh, no, they're not. And I haven't got much time, either. That clock's just going to strike eight.

PARKER: What's the time got to do with it?

BURKE: A good deal, if you'll follow me. Mrs. Kenyon died less than a year after her husband, didn't she?

PARKER: Yes.

BURKE: But it wasn't Mrs. Kenyon's voice you just heard on that record.

PARKER: *What?*

BURKE: I'm telling you! The real murderer hated her. Hated her like poison. And wanted her blamed for the crime. When Mrs. Kenyon died, the real murderer wrote a letter to you . . .

PARKER: The letter I received today?

BURKE: Yes. But the murderer never dared to mail the letter. She made a lying "record" of Isabel Kenyon's voice as evidence. Now figure it out for yourself. Who *was* pretty enough to take Major Kenyon's eye, and strike back like fury when she got thrown over? Who wanted to go on the stage and "do impersonations"?

PARKER: *Kitty, the maid.*

BURKE: Now you understand!

PARKER: *She* shot Jerry from the dining room window. . . .

BURKE: Yes, it was Kitty who shot Mr. Kenyon from the dining room window, a half hour before Mrs. Kenyon ran out to the summer house. But a minute or two before Mrs. Kenyon ran out, Kitty took the black coffee out to the summerhouse, as she was accustomed to every afternoon. She carried the duplicate gun and the prepared cap wrapped in a napkin on the coffee tray—remember, she hadn't been able to get hold of Mrs. Kenyon's knitting bag.

PARKER: She *did* go out just before Isabel—I remember!

BURKE: When Mrs. Kenyon entered the summerhouse, Kitty was still there, but it was dark inside and Mrs. Kenyon never noticed her. . . . Kitty kept the letter until the day before yesterday. Then one of the boys at Sing Sing—

PARKER: Wait a minute!

BURKE: One of the boys at Sing Sing, thinking he was doing a kind deed, put a stamp on it and mailed it.

PARKER: Did you say Sing Sing?

BURKE: Yes. They're electrocuting her tonight for the murder of a lover down at Collyer's Hook. But she made me promise to get that lying record and *destroy it* before they turn on the juice at eight o'clock. And here it goes—forever.

(Crash of record breaking. The clock slowly strikes eight.)

(Music up)

Suspense (CBS), November 3, 1942
Ellery Queen's Mystery Magazine, September 1946

"OLD DEVOTEES of blood and thunder" (to adopt words that John Dickson Carr used to describe himself) realize that each of Carr's radio plays has enough sheer inventiveness to form the basis of a full-length detective novel. In fact, at least four of Carr's later novels are elaborations of plot elements which he first used in his *Suspense* and *Appointment with Fear* scripts. Only one of these plays is included in this book; the central idea of "Will You Make a Bet with Death?" was recycled as *The 9 Wrong Answers* (1952), but the setting and the denouement are quite different. Although "Cabin B-13" did not become the basis of a short story or a novel, CBS in 1948 broadcast about twenty Carr plays under the series title *Cabin B-13.* In each of the episodes the ship's doctor tells of bizarre crimes, often in exotic settings, with such titles as "The Street of the Seven Daggers" and "The Island of Coffins." *The Encyclopedia of Mystery and Detection* describes *Cabin B-13* as "among radio's very best mystery series."

STORIES
OF THE
SUPERNATURAL

THROUGHOUT his life, John Dickson Carr was fascinated by tales of witchcraft, demonism and ghosts. "Crime and the occult," remarks a character in one of his novels; "these are the only hobbies for a man of taste." Thus when Carr submitted stories to the pulp magazines, he emphasized the supernatural. The pulps were all-fiction magazines with garish covers and sensational contents which flourished in America between the two world wars. They published a wide variety of stories, from science fiction to westerns, from weird fantasy to war stories, from tales of superheroes to adventures of hard-boiled private eyes; in short, as Carr put it, the pulps featured "any kind of lurid excitement."

The three heavily atmospheric tales that follow take place in locations which Carr knew well. "Terror's Dark Tower" occurs at Exmoor, fairly near Bristol, where the Carrs lived during the 1930s. Sometimes during these years, Carr worked out the plots of his stories while wandering over the moors. The setting of "The Door to Doom" is derived from Carr's experiences in France about 1928. "The Man Who Was Dead" begins in the comfortable quarters of an English club, the Naughts-

and-Crosses. In several of his stories, Carr, who was himself a member of the Savage and Garrick clubs in London, contrasted the traditional solidity of English club life with the terror of violent and perhaps supernatural crime. Long-time readers of Carr novels will recognize the Naughts-and-Crosses Club as the setting for the opening scene of *The Plague Court Murders* (1934). "The Man Who Was Dead" is interesting in another way to students of Carr's writings: The situation which confronts the protagonist must have fascinated Carr, for he wrote several tales using the same motif. The earliest version of the story appeared in *The Haverfordian,* March 1927, under the title "The Legend of the Cane in the Dark," and for the Christmas 1939 issue of *The Illustrated London News,* Carr used some of the same plot elements for a short story, "New Murders for Old." The version he wrote in 1935 for a pulp magazine seems to me the most effective, and that text has been chosen for this book.

Each of Carr's pulp stories is based on the relation between the supernatural and our everyday world. From their compelling opening lines, the stories build suspense as Carr, like a literary necromancer, conjures nameless horrors before dispelling them. . . .

Or are quite all the horrors dispelled?

The Man Who Was Dead

IT WAS NOT until the boat train came in at Waterloo station (said the man in the smoke room at the Naughts-and-Crosses Club) that I read in the newspaper about my own death. Then, if I had not been compelled to go home by Underground . . .

Night and rain and weariness helped the illusion. You see, I was returning to England from South Africa after three weeks on the water. The ship was late in docking at Southampton; there had been delay and irritability at the customs house. So it was nearly midnight before a slow train, ill lit and overcrowded, started for London. I contrived to get a newspaper, although I could not get a sandwich. We passengers were unutterably tired of each other after the voyage. We growled, retired behind our papers, and the train clanked on through rainy blackness.

I did not read for a time, because I tried to brighten the outlook by thinking what a lucky dog I was. Of course, there had always been at the back of my mind the hope that Judith *might* be waiting for me at the dock. She hadn't been there, but what could you expect with these late landings?

Ever since the boat had left Durban, I had been picturing her there, waving to me frantically from the crowd as the liner drew in, her head thrown back, her blue eyes shining as of old. That picture created a sort of ache as I saw it again in the blurred window of the compartment. It drained the joy out of seeing England after four months' absence.

Also, to tell the truth, I was worried. Judith had always been an indifferent letter writer—she usually put it off until the last minute, and even then sent a telegram instead. But she might have written at least one note in four months. She had been affectionate enough that night when she saw me off at the boat, for a voyage which I would have refused to take had it not been for the doctor's orders. I was sound enough now, anyhow. No more of the lung complaint that was a relic of gas during the war, no more struggle and worry over halfpennies! I had Judith, I had money to burn from the dead uncle I had never seen, and no liabilities but the vast, heavy, ugly house in Chelsea that had been my uncle's.

And then I saw it—that headline. NICHOLAS LESSING DEAD was the way they worded it—and it gave me a jump which blurred the type before my eyes. Almost at once I thought: some poor devil with the same name as my own, of course; nevertheless I still felt some peculiar, cold shock of fear. Then I found myself staring at the incredible words underneath.

> London, March 15th. Mr. Nicholas Lessing, the surprise heir to the Douglas Lessing fortune, who figured so prominently in the news a year ago, died last evening at his home in Cheyne Walk, Chelsea. His illness was of brief duration, and was made fatal by chronic weakness of the lungs. The most tragic feature of the affair, his physicians state, was that this weakness could have been cured if he had followed their advice and consented to take a long sea voyage. At the last moment he refused to do this, and was stricken with pneumonia only a week ago. . . .

Reading, I felt very calm, although I could feel my heart pound. It did not even occur to me that this might be a monstrous hoax. My only sensation was one of complete unreality—that the words were unreal, and the jolting train, the dull lights, the somnolent passengers—all were unreal.

> With him to the end were his fiancée, Miss Judith Rogers; his younger brother, Mr. Stephen Lessing; and his aunt, Mrs. Ann Henderson.
>
> He was heir to the greater part of the fortune left by Mr. Douglas

Lessing, whose estate of £800,000 was derived from land development and the financing of the Metropolitan Underground Railway. Mr. Douglas Lessing will be remembered as one of Britain's most eccentric and secluded capitalists. Few people ever saw him. He twice refused a peerage, and his famous remark about the Underground being "halfway to hell" caused controversy some years ago. His freak will left the bulk of his property to the eldest of any surviving children left by a brother whom he had not seen since his youth.

The romantic feature of Mr. Nicholas Lessing's inheritance lay in that fact that, until found by his uncle's solicitors while teaching at a school in the west of England, he did not even know of the relationship. Mr. Nicholas Lessing was thirty-two years old. He was a graduate of Winchester. . . .

My funeral, said the closing words of the article, would take place tomorrow.

Staring at the insane gabble, I had a wild impulse to thump the back of the man beside me and say, "Look here, you know me! I'm Nick Lessing. I'm not lying dead in London; I played deck tennis with you on the ship only yesterday." It was that look of *unreality* about them which stopped me—that, and the sudden hot fear that somebody else would see the item. The fear was so strong that I got up and went out into the corridor to be alone.

We were nearing Waterloo. Through a mist of steam and rain, I could see lamps reflected in the black river. A blast of the whistle was torn behind in the clackety-roar of the train; yet, coming home at last, I suddenly felt I was traveling on a train full of ghosts. That was rather a horrible thought. But, fortunately, rage began to supersede panic.

"With him to the end were . . ." Why, Judith, and fussy Aunt Ann, and my stolid younger brother Stephen all knew where I was. They had all been down to see me off when I sailed, as well as half a dozen friends and the doctor who had attended me in my "last illness." The whole thing couldn't be a fantastic plot of some sort! But the alternative was madness. To fight down that grisly suggestion, I carefully went over every event of the past months. I remembered the lazy days of the voyage out, the blaze of tropic waters, the pokergames, the sneak thief who was caught rifling cabins and came close to shooting me before they cornered him. I remembered every hot day on the veldt, the mild hunting expedition into the Rhodesian game preserves, the jaguar I got with a lucky long shot. . . . Damnation! This was real, and the other was foolery. As soon as we were in, I would jump into a cab without even bothering about my luggage. I would pelt for Chelsea to find out what the foolery meant.

That is exactly what I didn't do. I was in nearly the last compartment of the last carriage. Down swooped the crush when we rolled into the station; I fought and I offered wild tips to porters, but every taxi of the few thereabouts at that time of night was already snapped up. I found myself standing outside in the gusty darkness, with a pavementful of luggage at my feet—and London looked unreal. Yes, I was shivering. Ahead were the blue lights of the Underground. I gave some directions to the porter, and hurried down unencumbered.

There were echoes in the white-tiled tunnel, a distant stir and rumble of trains, and a breeze of stale, warm air. But no other traveler except myself. The uncanny quietness of the place struck me before I understood why, because I had never yet felt *alone* in the Underground. There were the gaudy posters on the walls, my own footsteps echoing, but no life except the ticket seller in his booth under the green-shaded lamp.

"Sloane Square?" repeated the man. I thought he looked curiously over my shoulder and ahead of me, but he was brisk. The ticket machine clanked, and coins rattled back at me. "Sloane Square? Right. That's sixpe—"

"Sixpence?" I said, and stared. "What the devil's the matter with you? You've given me two tickets."

"Well, dontcher want two tickets?" he demanded, and stared down himself. He looked beyond me again. It may have been the effect of the green light, but I thought he changed color. "Sorry, sir. My mistake. One ticket."

Distantly, a train rumbled. I walked off quickly enough; but I thought I saw him looking out of his cubbyhole after me with his face the same color. He called out, "Change at Charing Cross!"—to make me look around, I think. But that was the first time I felt the terror, for I had a sensation that I was being followed.

Although I could identify no footsteps, I was certain of it. I went down the slope of the white tunnel, down endless steps. But I was the only passenger I could see. You seem to be shut and hemmed in, and I thought they must turn off many of the lights after midnight. Heralded by a sharper wind, a train roared in just as I reached the platform. I was running now—I admit it—with a feeling that I had distanced somebody. The train stopped with a kind of sigh; the doors rattled open; silence. Looking for company, I hurried along past the line of cars. Only one was occupied, by a faded woman with a flower basket and a young man in evening clothes; she was motionless, he was asleep, and they both looked dead under the harsh lights.

I bolted inside, shaken with relief because I had distanced pursuit. It was confoundedly quiet, and I prayed for the train to start. Sitting down near the doors, I lit a cigarette and waited for the starting whir to tremble through the car. It hummed at last; the doors began to close; I was free.

Then the doors, within an inch of being shut, stopped. Something began to scratch and tap at the glass. It tapped invitingly, that thing.

Now, it is all very well to talk about your heart "rising in your throat." But mine seemed to do so in a really literal sense. Beyond the glass there was nothing to be seen except the dim platform; yet something was clawing at those doors, trying to wrench them open. Something tapped, first weakly and then with growing anger, as though thin knuckles were knocking.

The wavering doors closed with a snap, and the train rolled out. It had not got in—yet. I felt fury in the air.

Next stop, Charing Cross. After changing trains, I should surely be among crowds on the westbound line. Whatever it was, it was behind me now. All the way, though, I could hear those fingers tapping on the glass just over my head.

There were crowds, although they seemed very quiet under the murky glow. I jostled through the maze to the upper level, and leaped on a train just as it was pulling out. Through the forward windows I could see comfortable, upholstered cars well filled; windows gleaming with friendly welcome in the red sides. Conquering panic, I let my breath slow down as the doors closed. Then I saw that —in this car, at least—I was alone.

Easy enough. I could go through the door to the next car, which, I saw through the glass, was crowded with placid people reading newspapers. But I could not do that, I found. The door was either locked or stuck fast, and I was cut off. It seemed very cold in here. As the train swayed on through its tunnel, I turned back to the bright empty car. . . .

Somewhere, there was a rush of air and a thump, as though a door had opened and closed again. Also, there was a strange smell in the air now.

Sitting down, or huddling down, I waited. Silence but for the creak and roar, while station after station fled past. I sat up quickly when that (locked?) door opened, and somebody stumbled through. It was only the train guard, but he was white in the face. He stared round the car, looked at me, then walked to the end and closed again. Also, there was somebody under the seats. He was a very tall man, whose face must ordinarily have been tipsy reddish. He halted.

"God," said the guard, and wiped the back of his hand across his forehead. "I must have had the horrors. But I'll swear I saw it."

"Saw what?" I shouted back.

He looked at me. " 'Ere! Don't you go and say anything. *I* don't know how he got in. He was big, much bigger than me," said the guard. "And I think he was *blind.* Don't you stay 'ere alone, sir. You come along o' me." Then, with a start of disgust, he reached down and brushed off his sleeve a small, yellowish-black spider.

When I first heard the tapping of the cane, and knew that it was gaining on me, I am not sure. I think it was when I was past Chelsea Bridge on the walk home, almost in sight of my own house. For a time after leaving the tube, I had a feeling of being free from pursuit. I walked along the Embankment, where the sky was strangely light and the wet pavements glimmered. But despite intense loneliness, I felt safer. Some distance behind me, I could discern a tall policeman. In a city that is bulwarked by those guards, we feel that even horror cannot gain.

You have heard of people who repeat prayers or hold up a crucifix. When I believed, now, that the powers of hell were real, what I held up before me was Judith's face, because she could not think I was dead. A few minutes more, and I should see her. She was at my house, as my aunt's companion. That was my prayer and my crucifix: Judith's smile, and Judith's tremulous lips, and Judith's soft blue eyes. She was ahead. Behind me walked the symbol of British law, the policeman with his slow footfalls.

I walked on more slowly. The footsteps were gaining, although they seemed to halt and stumble. Only when I heard the tapping of the cane did I look over my shoulder.

It was not a policeman who was following me.

My latch key was in my hand when I ran up the steps to the big, somber, dark house. In darkness I dodged inside and slammed the door, but I heard it fumbling in its blind, endless patience to come up the steps after me. Home!—to what a home! There was the same dank smell of heavy curtains and muffling carpets; of furniture polish on the massive old wood; but now I could scent a thick odor of flowers. The air was sickly with them. Trying to blunder towards the stairs, I lost my way. I stumbled and nearly fell over baskets, banks of flowers, as though I were to be stifled in them. My hand shook so that I could hardly strike a match. The thin flame showed that I was in the drawing room, but I was not alone.

I had stumbled against what I thought was a table, and was looking down at the other occupant of the room. He lay against shiny white satin, in a long, massive box with a forest of pale flowers built up behind him. He was myself—scrubbed and neat in evening clothes, his cheeks rather sunken and his bloodless hands molded in his lap. The match went out. My hand brushed his face, my face, in the dark; and then I bolted.

I must get to Judith. I felt physically sick, with a hammer beating in my head, yet I must get to Judith because she would know. She was sanctuary, she was security, and against that love all the powers of hell could not prevail. Unless the whole thing was a horrible illusion, who lay in that coffin? I tried to think it might possibly be somebody else. I remembered one poor gassed devil I had known during the war, who looked exactly like me and who had often cadged a few shillings on the strength of it. I remembered another member of the Naughts-and-Crosses Club who was sometimes mistaken for me. But this was different. Besides, what of the thing that was following me?

Suppose, then, that the purpose of the follower was not malevolent? Suppose the follower was merely one of the undead, like my-self, and was friendly because we walked the same lonely heath? Yet there was horror and evil in that follower, I knew—for some-body.

I heard it tapping at the outer door now, and I ran for the stairs.

Somebody upstairs had heard me. A dim lamp shone out in the upper hall as I reached the top. The door to my aunt's bedroom was open; and there stood Aunt Ann, a wrapper drawn about her scrawny body, her hair in curl papers, her face ugly with terror. For a moment we looked at each other across the dim-lit hall, yet from her posture I knew I was cut off from humankind.

"Don't you know me?" I said, and felt a sting behind my eyes. "Don't you know me? For God's sake have pity and say you do!"

She opened her mouth as though to scream, but no sound came. She dodged inside and slammed her door. What, then, would my stolid, black-haired, blue-chinned brother Stephen say? I did not care. I stumbled towards Judith's room, fumbled at the knob, and with a kind of sob fell inside.

The bedside light was on. Judith sat up in bed with her hand still on the chain of the lamp. I saw her under the massive canopy, her heavy yellow hair down on her shoulders, her heavy-lidded blue eyes wide; pale, and the mouth trembling, but with such a blaze of joy in her face that the sickness left me.

"*You* know me," I said. "Don't be afraid of me, Judith. Please don't be afraid of me!"

She conquered her faintness. "I loved you all your life," she said in a low voice, and her eyes brimmed over. "Do you think I am afraid of you now?"

I started towards her, and then drew back; but she held out her hands. When I had grasped them, I knew that she and I were both flesh and blood; that I was not mad or a ghost; and suddenly I think she knew so too, for I had to support her. But that joy was worth all the terrors.

"Alive," I said. "I'm alive, Judith! My hand—my coat—feel! I can't believe it myself. But it's true."

"Hold me," she said in a rapid voice. "Hold me, and don't speak. I don't want to faint. . . ."

Then we heard the thing coming up the stairs outside. Its cane knocked against the banisters as it mounted. I had never seen it in the light, I had seen only the huge, grinning, evil bulk of the blind thing behind me, yet it had to be faced now.

"That's dead," I said wildly, and pointed to the door. "That's the thing that's dead. And it's got to be sent back ... where it came from. Quiet!"

When I looked out into the dusky hall, the staircase was empty. The door to my brother Stephen's room stood a little ajar. Stephen stood flat back against it, his arms outspread like a figure on a cross. He wore striped pajamas, which showed off his paunch. He tried to speak, but he could only jerk his head. His blue-chinned face had gone sickly and his mouth was pulled square like a Greek mask. His stare was fixed on the shadows behind me.

I turned round, and saw it almost at my elbow. The damned thing towered over me so far that its shoulders were stooped, although I am not small like Stephen. It had on a long, blackish coat and a shapeless hat. Against the shadows I could see nothing of its face—except that it was grinning with horrible pleasantry, and wore great black spectacles. Turning its head a little, it seemed to listen between Stephen and me, moving its cane like a feeler.

My brother's scream became a croak.

"Who are you?" And: "What do you want?"

It stiffened. Then I knew it was Stephen's voice it listened for; the grin grew wider, although you could see no teeth. It lifted one hand and removed the black spectacles. Then we could see the cobwebs in the eye sockets.

"You," it said, and leaped.

Whether the sweep of its coat knocked over the lamp, I am not sure. But I felt the brush of the coat, and a strand of cobweb across my face, as it went after Stephen. I saw it at the door, which Stephen was trying to slam against it, a moment before the lamp went out.

Long afterwards, I still heard Stephen screaming beyond in the dark, while I pounded at the door. Always before me there swam that face, a broad face with cobwebs in its black eye sockets, and a small yellow-black spider clambering down from one eye across the cheek. . . .

Then I heard a shot fired, and the screaming stopped.

When I smashed the lock of the door with a heavy chair, and put on the electric light inside, it was all over. Stephen had put his own service revolver to his chest and pulled the trigger. He was still conscious, although he died before morning. Lying across the rumpled bed, with a handkerchief to his mouth, he told the story to Judith and me while Aunt Ann was downstairs rousing the servants and telephoning for a doctor. There was nobody in Stephen's room —nothing, that is, except a biggish spider, which I crushed with my foot.

Stephen, of course (I suppose you might call it his confession, even though not the doctor or the coroner or any outsider has ever yet been told the truth), Stephen had put up the game on me. Under the law of primogeniture, he had inherited not a penny of our uncle's fortune. But he was my brother, and would inherit it if I died.

I think it was one of the most ingenious murder plots ever contrived. He knew the man of whom I have spoken, the one who bore so exact a resemblance to me and whose lungs had been shattered by gas during the war. He knew that this man was dying—that he could live, at most, only a few months more. Suppose, then, this man could be substituted for me, and die a natural death in my place? If Stephen were to kill me at home, in however clever a way, suspicion would be roused and he would probably hang.

But suppose, on the other hand, I were to go to South Africa for my health. The boat would sail at night. On that ship Stephen had planted a hired murderer. (You recall my mentioning the thief and almost-killer we caught rifling our cabins aboard?) My loving brother and all the relatives should be down to see me off. They should be shepherded away a few minutes before the ship sailed. That same night—before I had time to make myself known on the boat as being on it after its sailing—the thug would batter in my head and send me overboard.

In the meantime, Stephen would have my double, fully coached and in my clothes, at the dock. Just as the family party left the dock after thinking they had seen me off, up would come running my double. "I've changed my mind," says he. "I couldn't go after all. I got off at the last minute, and I'm going back home with you." And when I, the real Nicholas Lessing, turned up as missing aboard the boat, the ship's officers would have a radiogram from Stephen saying that I had changed my mind about sailing after all. When a bogus Nicholas Lessing died a perfectly natural death in his own house, a death that no police could ever question, who could accuse his stricken brother of murder?

"But you're not dead," said Stephen, coughing, with his hands against the bandages on his chest. He lolled back on the bed, still coughing. "You did me down after all, didn't you? You turned my own damned games on me, didn't you? Speak up!"

"Your own games?"

I looked at Judith, who was trying to quiet him, but he fought her off.

"Don't you try to scare me!" he cried, but his face was an ugly color all the same. "Why am I here with a bullet in *my lung?* Because I lost my nerve. Because you got a dummy of an actor to dress himself up like—"

"Listen!" said Judith.

The cane was tapping again. We heard it above Stephen's wheezing breaths, rattling against the banisters out in the hall. Stephen seized my arm and tried to hide behind me.

"It's going downstairs," he said. "You did do that, didn't you? You hired somebody to do that? It's real, it was real, wasn't it? I'm dying, Nick. I couldn't stand the thought of having to meet him *again.*"

"Yes, it was a hoax," I lied.

"And he's gone now?"

"Yes, he's gone."

I walked to the door and peered out. Hall and stairway were deserted. A light shone from downstairs, where Aunt Ann screeched among a terrified group of servants. Also, the front door was open. But he had not gone. He did not go until just before daylight, when Stephen died. A policeman on that beat (they say) saw a very tall man hurrying towards the station of the Underground Railway. This man was trundling along something in a striped costume, like a bag with its top crushed under his arm, and he was tapping ahead of him with a cane. The policeman—who had known the neighborhood for a long time—said that this big man wore something that looked horribly like old Mr. Douglas Lessing's coat and hat.

Dime Mystery, May 1935

The Door to Doom

"IF MONSIEUR takes the shortcut through the wood," said the taller of the two peasants, "he will arrive at his destination before sundown."

"And at his last destination," said the shorter one, "before moonrise."

Peter Maynard turned around quickly. His French was not good enough to make him certain that he had understood the idiom of the thick-wooded province of Orléans. And anyway, the words were of no importance. But it was the tone he did not like, with its dry chuckle and smacking of lips.

The two peasants were on the overhanging bank beneath which the road twisted—the taller leaning against the brown earth of the slope; the shorter silhouetted against a murky sky at the top. He stood amid blowing grass, with the wind fluttering his clothes like the trees behind him. And he chuckled those words as though into the neck of his blouse.

Maynard hesitated. Shifting the knapsack on his back, he took a step forward down the road that led to the wood; stopped, turned, and stared up at the peasant.

"You said?" he asked sharply.

It was as though the other had been caught off balance. The taller man, who was reflectively running dirt through his brown fingers, came to his aid. His wheezy rumble followed a shrug.

"Monsieur heard, then. Louis-Cyr will have his joke. Monsieur is an American, is he not? Yes. Then he would not understand. That is the way to the town of Chartres—there." He pointed at the wood.

"But I only meant," croaked his companion, smiling, "a very little joke! Blood of the world, I am not without courtesy! Monsieur will see, *voyez,* that a storm is coming. Wherever he is going, he can assuredly reach there before the moon rises on a night like this. *Ohé!*"

This was true enough. Maynard, who was tired and hungry and strangely cold, heard the hiss of wind rise in the trees and saw a flicker of lightning in the tumbled sky. It was growing so dark that he could barely see the shorter man grinning at him. Still, there was nothing for it but to push on to Chartres; nine kilometers by the highroad, but only four, according to these men, if he took the shortcut. He paused again.

"There is, perhaps, an inn along this way?"

"Ah! The best in France, monsieur! . . . Thanks, monsieur!"

The coin Maynard tossed was caught, and he trudged on. But he could still feel the short man grinning behind him. It affected him unpleasantly; the more so as the whole sky went white with lightning. The wood affected him unpleasantly too, where the soggy grass-patched path bred gnats under the shadow of soggy maple trees. It grew darker as he plodded on, stamping ahead of him with his ash stick. There was an unclean smell about the place, and more of a rustling than should come from silver birches. Once he could have sworn that something was following his passage from tree to tree, keeping out of sight. But he had little time to observe. The wood glared with lightning; thunder rattled and split down the sky; and, with a sudden rush growing to a roar, the storm tore down.

There was little protection from the trees. They seemed all trunk and no leaves. When they did not let the blast drench him, they found crevices in his clothes for the rain to soak in rivulets. His shirt was black with water in two minutes, but he splashed steadily on, cursing this walking trip and the uproar of the rain. A walking trip through France, eh? Jim Hanwick had suggested it, had he? The drowsy countryside, eh? He was to meet Jim Hanwick that night at the Hotel du Grand Monaque in Chartres. He was to walk on through the rain, was he, while Jim came down comfortably from Paris on a train? Now, if he could only find that inn . . .

He blundered into a tree trunk, and stopped.

"Hell," said Maynard aloud, and very distinctly. "I can't stand this."

Then the lightning flared again, and he saw that there was somebody standing almost at his elbow.

For a second it brought the heart into his throat. Then he saw a woman's face, and dark eyes, and rain-wet lips drawn back from her teeth in terror. He saw this small face against a shapeless cloak with a hood, motionless in the flooded path, before it went dark. She cried out something, and he heard a splashing of footsteps.

"*Madame!*" he shouted. "*Mademoiselle! Restez tranquille, je vous en prie!* Wait, I beg of you. I'm hunting for the inn. Could you direct me to it?"

The footsteps stopped. He felt someone staring through the darkness. Then, to his astonishment, a low voice spoke in excellent English.

"What is it you wish?"

"Mademoiselle," said Maynard, and in that wild moment he remembered solemnly lifting his sodden hat in the dark, "this is much better. I am soaked to the skin, as I imagine you must be, and I am looking for the inn. Where is the inn?"

The rain lashed steadily through a brief pause. Then: "Inn? What inn? There is no inn."

"But they told me—"

"They would tell you anything!" the voice called. "There is no inn, I tell you! Go back the way you came; go to Chartres by the highroad. Go!"

Maynard replaced his hat. "Mademoiselle," he said politely, "I have been in this infernal wood over half an hour, and I must be more than halfway through it. I do not intend to go back now, inn or no inn. Besides, if you don't mind me saying so, where do *you* go?"

He felt her close to him. She spoke low and fiercely. "Please don't be a fool. Do you want it to catch you and crush you to death?"

Then she had vanished—and he wondered if he had suddenly

gone mad. He called to her, and was answered only by the roar of the rain. He cursed her, yet she did not appear. Finally he resumed his march; angry, puzzled and uneasy.

He had walked only a hundred yards more when he saw lights. It was the inn, no doubt. He could see nothing except yellow light shining through chinks in the shutters, on stone that might once have been whitewashed, and a banging sign above the door. Ducking up against the entry, he found a heavy iron knocker and hammered it sharply. There was no answer. Yet he had a strange feeling that the moment before there had been movement inside; that this was suddenly hushed and tense, waiting. He knocked again, and one of the shutters opened a crack.

"Who is there?" a man's voice asked, gruff but suddenly whining, filled with a kind of surly terror.

"A traveler. I am looking for shelter. . . ."

"Hah," said the voice, with a little grunt like relief. "One is sorry, monsieur, but the inn is full. You must go away."

As the shutter began to close, Maynard's wrath boiled. "My friend," he yelled, "an innkeeper must at least give a hot drink and provide a fire. That is the law. Will you let me in, or shall I mention you to the police?"

Behind the shutter he thought he heard voices murmuring: queer, ugly, glutinous voices. Then he heard a brief smack of laughter, abruptly strangled. The shutter closed. The door opened. . . .

When he dodged inside, he took a moment to shake himself and brush the water out of his eyes before he looked around.

He was in a low passage with a stone floor, smelling none too well, and lit only by the oil lamp in his host's hand. His host was a squat, powerful man with a blue-chinned jaw and a moist reddish face. The little black eyes looked unwinkingly at Maynard as he held the lamp high. He wore a dirty white apron which covered most of his clothes, and Maynard saw that its grime was spotted with brownish stains, and that his hairy arms were bare to the elbows.

"Bear witness, then," he said abruptly, "that you have been let in." He followed Maynard's look towards his apron. "Ah! Monsieur must excuse me. I have been butchering."

He turned back to the door with great urbanity and slowly shot the bolts. "It is safely locked now. This way, if you please."

He led Maynard, who had an impulse to look over his shoulder, into a long, low room with greasy walls and a sawdust-sprinkled floor. Maynard saw a bar counter with a few bottles stacked behind, and a board of hooks on which hung one solitary key. Though he had a feeling that there had been several people here, the room was now deserted except for a woman sitting before a fire in the big stone chimneypiece. She was fat to shapelessness, and wore a shawl over her head. He could see only a faint blackish mustache on her upper lip, and a grin. The rain drove and rustled against the house.

"Monsieur is welcome," continued the innkeeper—his nervousness had come back—"to the Inn of the Beautiful Prospect. There is the fire. Make way for the gentleman, madame my wife. Monsieur would like some rum, perhaps, with hot water?"

Maynard unslung his knapsack. He was shivering.

"Yes. And a room where I can change my clothes . . ."

The innkeeper turned. "I have told you that it is impossible. Impossible, do you hear! We have no rooms. We are full."

By this time more curious than insistent, Maynard pointed to the one key on the rack. The innkeeper stared at him a moment, then glanced behind; when he turned back again, his face was white.

"God of mercy," he said very softly, and jabbed his hand across his eyes. "It is there again, yes." He turned to the woman. "Do *you* do this to torment me? Do you wish to drive me mad? It was not there a moment ago, that key. Did you put it back?"

"No," said the woman. She did not turn, but Maynard saw the whites of her eyes flash. She giggled. "Not I, my heart's desire. The one who put it there is crushed and mangled, *voyez*, long ago. He cannot be far behind you now."

For the first time, real terror came to Maynard, and he felt a jerk of shivering that was not cold. A voice in his brain said: You've been a fool. Don't be a fool any longer. Get out of this house. Hurry! Get—

But he could not prevent himself from saying: "I don't think I understand. Why can't I have that room?"

The innkeeper walked behind the bar counter. From a stone bottle he filled two glasses with rum, and drank one greedily. Then he put his hands flat on the counter.

"Listen, monsieur. We give nobody that room; we do not dare. There is—how shall I put it?—a horror there. For myself, I would not sleep there for a thousand francs. Nowadays, we call our place the Inn of the Beautiful Prospect. It used to be . . ."

The fat woman said some words to herself, which sounded to Maynard like "The Inn with the Twisted Doors," but he was not sure. Her husband interposed with repressed fury.

"Be quiet, fool. I do not mean *that.*" He swallowed. "Listen, monsieur. Myself, I am not a scholar like my niece Elise, and I do not know the rights of it. Many years ago—they say it was the time when the people of France made revolution against their king—this wood was a park. It belonged to a fine nobleman, whose chateau was here. This man was"—he made a slight gesture—*"bad.* He practiced the black arts, and they say he knew the devil. But I know he brought people here, and killed them."

"Here?"

"Our little inn, monsieur, stands on a part of the foundations of that place. It stands on what was left when they burnt it. They did burn it, the people. They caught this man, and what they did to him I am not sure—"

"Thou liest, my heart's desire," said the woman. "But it must have been a pretty sight. Everywhere there were bits of bone sticking up through the blood and silk and ruffles."

Maynard saw sweat on the innkeeper's forehead, and his fixed, unblinking eyes. Again Maynard heard the voice whispering: Get out of here! These people are mad! Get out of here. Hurry!

He felt his heart knocking, and he had risen with the ash stick gripped tightly, when a door opened across the room and a girl came in. She was holding another lamp, so that he saw her face clearly. He saw pink lips and dark eyes: he saw a face of such startling beauty, against the chipped oak door, that he stared. It was not a peasant beauty. There was a quality of repose about her, as though she were always ready to smile; a force and delicacy, a poise even in the lift of her shoulder or the way she held the smoking lamp. She was coarsely dressed, in a heavy skirt and blouse open at the neck, or he might not have believed his eyes. But he knew two things: first, that she was the girl he had met on the road in the rain; and second, that he must stay here to see her.

He was about to blurt out some remark about the road, when her eyes warned him. He caught himself in time, and said to the land-lord: "I will pay you as much as you like. But I mean to have that room."

The other hesitated, breathing deeply. He pointed his finger.

"Soit-il!" he said with abrupt decision. "As you like! To have someone here in the house . . . Well! Remember, you asked. And there is one thing you must promise. . . ." He turned, saw the girl, and his face changed. "Elise! Great name of the devil, what do you do here?"

She did not look at Maynard.

"I cannot stay in my room, Uncle, and I will not," she answered. "You said you would have the roof repaired, but you did not. I will bring my books here."

The innkeeper made another decision. And he seemed very anx-ious to keep this girl in the background. He growled something over his shoulder, took the lamp from her with a sharp gesture, and faced Maynard.

"Let monsieur follow me. Madame will prepare an omelet while monsieur is changing his clothes."

Maynard had an impulse to back out of this, but he was commit-ted now. And his uneasiness increased as he followed the other upstairs. The inn was larger than he would have suspected: a hive of low passages, thick walls and crooked-paned windows with the green damp crusted under their sills. The woodwork, he saw, was alive with black beetles, which rustled and scurried as the lamp-light moved. As they mounted three staircases, he noted with aston-ishment the fine carving of the balustrades. He mentioned this to the innkeeper; and either the sound of his voice or a sudden spatter of rain on the windows made the man jump.

"Ah!" he said, looking over his shoulder. "We are now, you under-stand, in the only part left standing of the old chateau. If monsieur will look closely, he will still see the scars of fire. The old Comte de Villefleur walked up these stairs every night, in his wig and bed-gown. It was down these stairs that the mob dragged him, headfirst, before they burnt the place. He could not walk, because most of his bones were already smashed—"

"Look out!" Maynard suddenly cried, leaping forward to seize at the lamp.

His host had missed a step and nearly pitched head foremost over the balustrade. Maynard went hot with fear, and felt his arm shaking when he steadied the man's shoulder. He heard the breath go out of the landlord's lungs like a man hit in the stomach. Slowly his host turned around with a pale wavering grin.

"I thank you, monsieur. And now listen to what I tell you. I, Paul Maillot, swear to it. There is something on this staircase now. It is crawling. I felt it pluck me by the back of the coat. Can I not prevail upon monsieur to return—"

"Lead on, damn you," said Maynard through his teeth. *"I didn't see anything."*

"But this you must promise," insisted the other. "My place is full of guests. If at any time you hear or see anything you should not, you must hurry out and call to us, eh? You promise that?"

"Steady with that lamp," Maynard said sharply. "You'll have the place afire again. Yes, I promise. Another staircase?"

They must have come to the top floor, for the noise of the storm flapped loudest now. At the end of a long corridor lined with doors, they came to an oak door with a white porcelain knob, beside a projecting stone buttress. Then Maynard remembered that his guide had neglected to bring the key—but the door was open. The lamp burned as though in a gulf when they went into a high room paneled to the ceiling in oak, so that even the door and the fireplace were a part of the paneling. Maillot lit a couple of grimy candles, which he stuck in their own grease to the marble top of a rather fine boule table with blackened gilt carving. They gave a little light; the forms of gilt furniture swam big and indistinct, and the bed curtains wavered in shadow. Yet, to Maynard's surprise, the place was quite clean. He looked at the windows, which were shuttered; he looked at the rotted flooring, which seemed to have been scrubbed in uneven patches. And slowly a heavy, sickly odor in the room, which might have been a disinfectant, gagged in his throat.

"Never mind a fire," said Maynard, although he was cold to the heart. "But I shall want hot water and towels. Then I will go down to dinner. Wait!" His voice went high as the innkeeper made for the door. "A question or two, my friend. Was this the room where *he* lived?"

"So they say, monsieur. At least, it was where he . . . disposed of his victims."

"How?"

"Nobody has ever known. Of course, he was mad."

"One more question," Maynard said. "Is it also a part of the same superstition, or is there some real thing in these woods that catches people and smashes them to death?"

Maillot cried, "Who told monsieur that?"

"A man on the road," the other lied. "Well?"

"Ah, that! What do these imbeciles know of real fears, I ask you?" He spoke contemptuously, swabbing a hand across his forehead. "One spoke there of the gully, the ravine, half a kilometer from here. Sometimes people stray off the road on dark nights, and—" He gestured. His voice rose. "Excuse me! I will go and get monsieur's hot water."

When he was alone, Maynard stared around. He flung back the red brocade curtains of the bed—suddenly, as though to surprise an intruder. Yet he saw nothing. Stripping off his wet clothes in a hurry, he took a clean blanket from the bed and wrapped himself up. He wanted to keep close to the candle flames. What had Maillot said? "A horror there." Power of suggestion! Yet why must he keep constantly whirling and looking over his shoulder?

When he rummaged through his knapsack after soap, he felt some consolation in finding his flashlight. He darted a beam round. Why was the damned place so *quiet?* If all these rooms were occupied, they must be occupied by dead men. The ugly thought grew and flowered. Above all, if they never used this room, why was it kept swept and polished in its decayed finery, as though to receive the eighteenth-century nobleman whose devil house had been cleansed by fire?

He saw the candle flames reflected in the dark mirror over a bureau, and walked over to stare at his own face. . . .

The next moment he felt his stomach turn to water, and his legs began shaking so much that he had to sit down. He shut his eyes, opened them, and peered again. It was gone. It had been no phantom; it had been suggestion. But—for just one second—he thought that he had seen another face reflected in that dark mirror as well as his own. This imaginary face had been flabby and pinkish in color. The white eyeballs were upturned, the mouth hung open, and a thin trickle of blood ran down from one corner of the mouth.

To banish these hobgoblins, he got up stiffly and paced around. Where the devil was Maillot! A sort of fury rose in him at Maillot's slowness. Maynard glanced over at the white porcelain knob of the door. He strode over, threw it open, and flashed his light up and down the corridor.

One or two of the doors in this corridor were open. His suspicions became almost certainties, but he had to know. Drawing the blanket close, he tiptoed down, pushed one door open, and flashed his light inside. It was a bedroom, empty and unused. He looked at the next—and the next. . . .

All were empty.

And faintly now, from downstairs, he heard a murmur that rose in a thin gust of laughter. . . .

A hand was put on his shoulder from behind.

"Monsieur's hot water and towels," said the voice of the innkeeper, blandly. "Let me conduct monsieur back to his room."

And his fingers closed firmly round Maynard's arm.

When he got down to dinner a little while later, Maynard hoped he had himself under control. To Maillot he pretended that he had noticed nothing, and hoped that he had been believed. The consciousness of danger—and not danger from ghosts—was clear-cut now.

A silence fell on the smoky kitchen at his entrance. The fat hag still rocked before the fire. Maillot, drinking heavily out of the stone jug, leaned his elbows on the bar counter and grinned. At one side of the fireplace sat the two peasants who earlier in the evening had directed Maynard here. The shorter one, squatted with his legs under him, was whittling a stick; his clasp knife glittered by the red firelight, and he also grinned. The taller one, still impassive, got up and went over to bolt the door into the outer passage. Everybody laughed.

"Your comrade is nervous, Louis-Cyr," said Maillot jocosely. "He

fears burglars, eh? . . . There is your dinner, monsieur. Good appe-
tite!"

The squeal of mirth that went up seemed to distort their faces;
Maynard saw eyes everywhere, and flourishing hands. But he steadied himself. Over in the corner he saw now the girl who had made
him resolve to stay. She was regarding him calmly, over a book
opened on the table, but he thought her mouth trembled. Something
inside him cried wildly: Good God, *she* can't be a part of this! And
all the while he was moving across casually, to a table on which
they had set out a smoking omelet, a long loaf of bread and a liter
of wine. The ring of eyes grew larger.

"I have met these gentlemen before," Maynard heard himself
saying. "They directed me here. It was a long, long four kilometers,
my friend."

Maillot, who had been sucking at the stone jug, set it down with
a thump. He pointed abruptly, and blinked reddish eyes. "So, so! It
was you, then, who were indiscreet, Louis-Cyr? You mentioned
something which catches and crushes—"

"Ssst!" said the taller peasant.

"No, my faith, I did not!" declared Louis-Cyr. He stared, brushing
his knife across his cheek like a razor. "I had my joke, you understand. *Ohé!* I appeal to Gerrold here! I directed monsieur to the best
inn in France, and he gave me a two-franc piece . . ."

"Ah, bah! Yes, you would accept tips," grunted Maillot, and mim-
icked the mincing air of a servant girl. He drank again. His fury
grew. "So you did not speak of it? Then who did, I ask you? It is plain
. . . *Where are you going, Elise?*"

The girl had risen. The ring of eyes moved towards her, and
Maynard felt a stab of fear.

"You asked me to get some eggs," she answered, raising her eyebrows as though in surprise. She was not flustered. "Madame used
the last in making the omelet."

"Sit down," said the innkeeper. "You, Louis-Cyr, you and your
damned tips! Why, look there! Look at Elise. This is the first time she
has set eyes on you and your kind since she was a child. Haven't I
kept her at the best schools in Paris itself; hasn't Papa Maillot made
her a scholar—yes, faith, and a great lady? *Enfin,* won't she have a
tidy bit when I am dead? Come here, Elise! Come here and show

yourself." He turned eagerly. "There is monsieur our guest, Elise. Speak English to him!"

"Take care, I say," growled the man called Gerrold.

Elise obeyed. She was composed and smiling; she looked significantly at all of them, winked at Louis-Cyr—who guffawed—and squeezed Maillot's arm. Her eyelids drooped in what to Maynard's fuddled wits was a horrible coquettishness as she sidled up to him. Then she spoke in English.

"Laugh," she said. "Laugh, and pretend to pay me compliments. Otherwise we are both done for. They mean to kill you. Why were you such a fool?"

He kept his head, made believe he was flirting back. "Right. What's the game? That ghost story of your uncle's . . ."

She looked arch. "There is no ghost, or any story of one. My uncle was pretending; he thinks he is an actor, and he likes to pretend. He does it as bait for Americans and English, with money, who come alone. You are a mad people. They tell you that a room is haunted, and you will insist on sleeping there. Eh, monsieur?"

"*Vraiment, mademoiselle.* That is true—but why that room? Why all the fancy business? Can't they get me anywhere?"

She winked at the others behind her, and he took her hand. "They will not touch you, unless you try to escape. They never touch anybody. There is some mechanism in that room which—"

"Catch and crush?"

"Yes. Of itself. It caught a man last night, and I saw the body afterwards. It is the first I had heard of it. I was trying to run away tonight when I met you. I don't know what to warn you of, because I don't know what the mechanism is or how it works. It breaks—"

"Steady!"

"What does he say?" demanded Louis-Cyr eagerly.

Suddenly he saw that she was trembling beyond control, that her lips moved and jerked without sound. He saw her wavering, her glazed eyes squeezing shut.

"What does he say?" Gerrold repeated, very softly. In the midst of an abrupt silence, he yanked the poker out of the fire and stood up.

"I say," cried Maynard in French, "that mademoiselle is the most beautiful, the most—" He lunged out, grinning foolishly, and made a clumsy play of seizing her in his arms. The rest of his sentence was lost in the roar of laughter that exploded from all of them.

"Oh, that!" said Gerrold, and flung down the poker.

The wing of terror brushed and passed. Flushed, she drew away from him with an air of chiding delicacy.

"Come, monsieur! Truly, that is too much!" She changed quickly into English. *"Don't let them suspect you know. Go to the room tonight, but don't touch anything or go near anything."* Then in French she said: "I am sure, Uncle Paul, you will excuse me now of my duties." She gave him a brilliant smile, and paused at the door. "A very good night, monsieur; sleep well. *You must try to hang on until I return. I am going for the police."*

She was halfway to the door when the immense woman by the fire stirred. She peered around under her grimy shawl. Getting up with a heavy wheeze, she waddled towards Elise.

"Ah, now, there, my dearest!" she urged. "That is very well, but first you must take off poor old Tante Marie's shoes, eh? I am tired, Paul. Good night."

And as she grinned and thumped past Maillot, she spoke in such a low voice that ordinarily Maynard would never have heard her: "You are stupid, my heart's desire. I know no English, but the word 'police' is like ours. . . . Come along, dearest Elise! Come along! Be sure that your old Tante Marie will attend to you."

She towered over Elise, clucking, and Maynard saw the brownish stains on her own apron. The door closed after them.

He could do nothing, Maynard realized—that was the baffling and maddening thing. The trap had caught the girl as well. If he provoked open war now, he could not help her and it might mean certain death for both of them. A fool's face was the only chance— a fool's face and an outwitting.

He stood gripping the edge of the table, smiling fatuously. Didn't they suspect he knew? It was an even chance—and if so, why didn't the pack close in and tear his throat out? Why bother with their crushing mechanism, whatever it was? Unless they enjoyed the view of the fool in the mousetrap, pattering round until it snapped his neck; or unless—

The ugly answer came to him as he saw them laughing and wagging their heads before the fire. Maillot had mentioned a gully or ravine near here, over which lost travelers had gone to death on rocks. They were not lost travelers; Maynard knew now what had happened to them. Kill a man with knife, gun or poison, and you have the police at your heels. But smash him in some clever snare, place his body at the foot of a ravine on a rainy night, and you have nothing but the accidental death of a careless (probably drunken) tourist.

Through a mist he heard the innkeeper speaking. "Come, monsieur must drink some wine!" he urged. "And eat before the food grows cold, eh? There is good cognac to follow. As for you others—"

"Cognac and a hand at cards," crowed Louis-Cyr, jingling his pocket. "There is plenty here; plenty. You play, monsieur?"

Maynard ate a mouthful, although it choked him. "Not tonight, unfortunately. You see, my friend is carrying all my money. But then, I expect him here tonight, so M. Maillot need not worry about his bill."

He felt the silence after this double-barreled bluff. Then he saw Maillot smirking. Maillot was amiably drunk now.

"Eh, but monsieur is cautious about play! When he offered me any amount to sleep in my haunted room, he displayed a well-filled wallet."

"If I offer—" said Maynard, and stopped. He could offer nothing. Doing so would not help a determined, rebellious girl, nor would it help him; it would only show that he knew too much. He shut his teeth hard.

"And this friend of yours?" Louis-Cyr suggested silkily.

"Go to hell," said Maynard, with calm suddenness. He drained a glass of wine and sat back amid an explosion of laughter.

"I begin to think, really, that our guest does not trust us," said Maillot, shuffling a pack of cards. "Yet he shall go up to his room when he likes, and lock himself in. That is fair, eh?"

The minutes dragged, and the storm did not decrease. Fair! With every tick of the clock, the time came nearer when he must go upstairs to face that unknown trap that caught and crushed. Where was it? What was it? The room had seemed harmless enough. It must be something that worked by itself, like a live thing. Somehow, he had to outwit it and find a way to Elise. For of one thing he was now sure: it was not merely for a franc or two that these men played murder in good earnest. They were out here where the ghosts and hobgoblins had crept into their own brains; they liked to spring their trap, and their most unholy mirth was derived from it.

Maynard thought he couldn't stand it any longer. He sprang up.

"I will go to my room, if you don't mind," he said, "and see whether the Comte de Villefleur will pay me a visit tonight."

Maillot sprang up. "I will accompany monsieur. Come along, Gerrold, and carry the lamp."

"And if the Comte de Villefleur really is here . . ."

"Our ghost? *Hé, hé,* yes," chuckled Maillot. But he looked a little pale nevertheless. What, thought Maynard, was the good of acting now?

There was no chance for a blow or an escape. They were on either side of him, and just behind, and he saw that Gerrold had a knife. Yet when they went up those windy staircases, amid the rattle of windows, once the innkeeper clutched at Maynard's coat. Even Gerrold didn't look so stolid when they came into the room.

Nothing—nothing yet. Gerrold relit the candles, while Maynard stared round and Maillot stood with his back to the door. Now Maynard did not want to be alone. The shadows swayed with monstrous concealments, the red curtains seemed to grow larger; and, without warning, Maillot screamed.

"It looked out from the bed curtains," he said, and pointed. "I saw it just then."

Maynard's rage flared uppermost. He flung the man back against the wall and pinned him by the throat. He spoke in English, heavily, because all French had fled his wits. Then he heard himself yelling.

"Now, then, we'll stop this filthy pretending if I have to strangle you here and now. Let's have it out, shall we? If—"

He stopped. He held one of Maillot's limp wrists against the wall; and there was barely a pulse beating. He saw a bitten tongue and staring eyes. The man was not pretending.

"Shall I . . . ?" breathed Gerrold. Maynard heard the click of a clasp knife. The innkeeper's eyes came into focus. He was wheezing.

"No, my child. No. We will leave him to the Comte de Villefleur."

He wrenched himself free, grinning out of a mottled face. Inserting the key in an almost invisible keyhole, he locked the door.

"We, monsieur," he explained shakily, "we will get out by another door—behind that hanging over there. I have no desire to go down those front stairs again. But monsieur need not worry about our exit. He can lock *that* door too."

Raising a tapestry in the far wall, he disclosed a door with heavy bolts. He and Gerrold were out of it before Maynard could speak; Maynard fell against it, shot the bolts behind them, and stood for a second motionless, with his head down.

Steady! Pull yourself together! The thing that catches and crushes will be here now, if it is anywhere. They were right in one thing: this door was solid, as he proved by examining it and testing the bolts. He went to the other door, which was also locked and solid. Nobody could get in, then. Whatever it was must be here in the room with him.

With his back to the wall, he studied the place, until he remembered that he must touch nothing. There was a leprous look about it, as though fungus would come off in his fingers. If he could find out where Elise was . . .

Then he suddenly thought of the windows. He laid hold of the shutters, and with a savage wrench opened the bar that held them. Outside was dusty glass; and beyond it iron bars. But he had been warned not to touch anything! Again he remembered it, backing away.

Then one of the candles on the table went out.

He had forgotten that. They were both stumps, carefully given him, and both almost burned to flat masses of grease. The other would not last much longer. He had his flashlight; but there was a horror in the thought of pressing darkness. If he could—

Steady! He felt that he must be losing his wits. Were they so confident that their mechanism would get him that they had not locked the doors on the outside? If they had not, and he could get out into the house unobserved, it was his best chance. The second and last of the candles went out in a puff. Darkness was like strangling water here; the thought of what Maillot might have seen looking out from the bed curtains nearly brought on panic. But he groped over quickly to his knapsack and took out the flashlight. One brief flash showed him the porcelain knob. He twisted the key, and, with a kind of profane prayer, pulled. The door was not locked on the outside.

He stepped out into the corridor, and nearly smashed head foremost to his death. Maynard heard himself screaming. . . .

There was no corridor there at all, and no floor. He stepped forward into nothing with his hand still on the knob of the door, and that saved him from falling immediately. He felt himself reeling when nothing met his foot; he swayed on a hair tread, sick at the stomach, and slid down on one knee while he still gripped the knob. He thought, now, that he could not get back. Still overbalanced, if the strength went out of that hand he would go down. He cried his profane prayer aloud; swayed again, and with slow wrenches forced himself to tumble down inside the room.

After an interval he shakily got out his flashlight. The sickness and dizziness had passed, but he could not believe what he saw. The corridor had vanished—and in its place was only a stone-walled room perhaps ten feet square, and without a floor. He turned the light downward. It did not go to the depths, sixty feet or more, but he thought he could discern rocks in the steamy mist at the foot, and a pulpy mass spread-eagled there. He smelled something too.

Now, this was madness, unless . . .

Wait a bit! Just outside this room, he remembered, there had been an immense stone projection beside the door. Well? And the door was set so closely into the oak panels that you could see where it was only by the *white* knob. His brain bursting, he moved the beam of light along the wall.

Yes. Just beside this door he had opened on the pit, there was another keyhole and another spindle for a knob. There were two doors, set side by side: one to the corridor and one to the pit beside it. To set your trap, you had only to shift the knob from one spindle to the other, a few inches, as Maillot had done while his confederate had been lighting the candles. Then they started (say) a fire scare, and let your victim kill himself. But in his case, they had only to wait; for they knew that he was frightened and would try to escape.

The Inn with the Twisted Door . . .

"Thing that catches—" Maynard said aloud, and froze. He could hear a movement out in the real corridor, and stealthy footfalls. It came back to him with a shock of realization that he had cried out when he lost his balance. They had heard him. They were coming to see the result.

There was only one way out now! It might work. He'd get behind the real door when they came in; then slip out into the corridor when they went to look for a crushed pulp at the bottom; and he'd try to find Elise. . . .

A lock clicked, and the real door began to open almost in his face. Still sitting on the floor, Maynard twisted frantically to one side, gasped, and rolled behind as the door brushed within an inch of his fingers. The glow of a lamp showed in the aperture. He heard voices muttering, a smack of laughter that he identified as Tante Marie's. But he did not dare look.

"He is down, my heart's desire?" asked Tante Marie.

"He is down," said Maillot, shakily. "Ah, God, that *swine!* We can rejoice. You, Louis-Cyr! You, Gerrold! Go down into the cellars and see what he has in his pockets."

Tante Marie said: "Let us look. It will be pretty, but it is good also. The little Elise liked him. She would betray us for him. She wept, until I smashed in her mouth and beat her to submission. Thou art sure he is finished, my husband?"

"Nothing ever comes up out of that pit," said Maillot. He repeated, "Nothing ever—" and stopped.

There was such a dead silence that Maynard could hear them breathing. Then a wild, long, queer, whimpering noise, like the cry of a beaten dog, began to bubble through Maillot's lips. It rose. "No!" cried Tante Marie. "No, no, no. Not me too. Not me. Go back. Go back. . . ."

"Mercy," said Maillot. "Mercy on me, in His name. Oh, in His name—"

The lamplight jumped and vanished, and Maynard heard a muffled crash. Above it he heard Louis-Cyr and Gerrold crying something. He heard the thud of their feet as they ran down the corridor in a black terror that made them wail louder than the two by the pit. A scuffling, sobbing noise beat in the darkness, as though fighting people were being dragged somewhere. . . .

Maynard risked a flash of his light. He saw two figures, Maillot and Tante Marie, on the edge of the pit. Before them was a third figure, which he could not see distinctly; but it was crumpled like a laundry bag, and had bits of bone sticking through ruffles and silk of an ancient bedgown, and a once white wig that was blood-matted. He saw, also, a pinkish flabby face whose eyes were now wide open in a stare of the dead, and the thing had its broken arms around them. . . .

There was a moment's scuffle and screaming. Then the mouth of the pit was empty. He heard the thud from the rocks below.

The police *commissaire,* in dull light that struggled through broken shutters at dawn, stood with his notebook at attention.

"Deceased," he repeated formally, "Paul Descartes Maillot, 55, and Marie Agnes Maillot, 52. Injuries . . . hm." He cleared his throat, and looked at Elise, who sat very pale in the kitchen, a handkerchief over her bruised mouth and Maynard's arm round her shoulder. "Of course, you understand, mademoiselle," he continued with a trace of awkwardness, "it is better so. It would have been necessary to . . . well, we have caught the men Louis-Cyr Fley and Gerrold Cocteau, and you may safely wager that their heads will go into the guillotine basket."

"How can I have sympathy?" she asked quietly. "I never knew . . . them. He used my mother's money, and boasted of educating me. He . . ."

"Ah, *ça!*" muttered the *commissaire,* as the girl's eyes brimmed over. He shifted uncomfortably. "Doubtless M. Maynard will . . . But back to our sheep! There is just one thing, you see, which will not quite square with our police records, or our common sense. . . ."

"Yes?" said Maynard.

"Not that I would doubt your word, you perceive! But when the two bodies were picked up, a third figure was found . . . a figure that looked very much like the old Comte de Villefleur, who was killed there a century and a half ago. . . ."

"I see!"

"No, no, M. Maynard misunderstands. I said 'figure.' For we all know the dead stay dead." He spread out his hands. "Mme. Maillot, when she came upstairs, was carrying with her . . . a scarecrow, very . . . shapeless in its old garments, and doubtless she wished to take

M. Maynard's garments for it." The *commissaire* cleared his throat, smiled faintly. "When the two miscreants missed a step and fell to accidental death, it was doubtless this scarecrow which constituted the third figure that M. Maynard saw. We agree it was a scarecrow?"

"Doubtless," said Maynard firmly, though he had been there and seen and knew that he could never believe.

They all looked at each other. Elise shrank inside Maynard's arm. The police *commissaire* bowed very low.

"That is wise, my friend. We are sensible, in France," he said.

Horror Stories, June 1935

Terror's Dark Tower

LOUISE turned her lovely face so that her dark, troubled eyes looked directly into my own.

"Could you believe," she said, "that though a woman locked and barred herself into a room beyond any possible attack, nevertheless something came from the air and tore out her eyes?"

They were wild words to have been said at that time and place—and yet they were spoken so quietly!

We sat in a rustic summerhouse down the slope of the hill. The oak trees had gone dull scarlet with October, but the leaves underfoot were yellow, and a wet wind stirred them. On an autumn afternoon there is no place in England more mournful than this brown fold of the hills where Somerset becomes Devon, and northward the waters of Bristol Channel make a chilly gleam. My arm was around Louise, and I felt her shiver. She got up suddenly. She went to the door, and stood staring at the brown road that wound up the hill to Moat Hall.

"I don't know whether I believe it," she went on quietly. "But if you marry me, you marry a family curse. And I do know that I'm horribly afraid."

She had never spoken like this before. The words were all the more startling because they had come in the midst of a happiness such as I had never known before, when Louise's eyes and Louise's cheek were close against my shoulder. I had ridden over that afternoon, singing aloud in the joyous air, from Sir James Fenwick's place on Exmoor. Singing—because Louise would meet me when I tethered my horse by the little spring they called Goblin Water.

Her dark hair would be blown back like the gray scarf around her neck, her hazel eyes shining, and her lips parted in that half smile which had completely upset my universe when I first met her a month ago. Then we would walk up the brown hill to our summerhouse. Well, I had asked my question, and had been answered. So the whole dark afternoon had turned to gold—until now. For here was Louise staring at me with a white, serious face.

"Do you mean what you're saying?" I asked. "Afraid? What have you to be afraid of?"

"I'm afraid for my sister Anne. You met her, remember? Yes, and I'm afraid for myself too. Afraid that something will come and tear out our eyes. No, no, please don't think I've gone mad!" Her face became whiter yet as I got up and took her hands. "You see, it isn't merely a thing like a curse. But Anne is to be married next week. She's marrying a very decent chap, one of the Gordons of Hope Grange. My Uncle Harry is furious—I shouldn't mind that, if he didn't keep on smiling. He says nothing, and makes no objection. He simply smiles."

"Object? Why should he object?"

She did not answer. I looked at the dull-red brick house on the hill, with its latticed windows winking in the afternoon light, and its broad moat where the swans floated. A crooked tower rose from it like a deformity. Louise Mortlake was no product of that gloom. But there had been Mortlakes at Moat Hall since the reign of Queen Elizabeth. The line had decayed; they had closed themselves in behind shutters; the clean winds that blew across the moors did not touch them. With my friend Sir James Fenwick, I had dined there one night—it was the night I first met Louise.

We dined in shabby pomp, under the oak paneling and candles. Besides Louise, there were four in the family. There was her quiet sister Anne. There was a high-nosed Aunt Kate, with a dark face like an old painting. There was an eighteen-year-old cousin Richard. But most of all I remembered Henry Mortlake, fat and sweating and soft-voiced, smiling as he cracked walnuts with a big fist.

"Anne is to be married a week from today," Louise went on blankly, without answering my question. "If the thing should creep up and catch her this evening, as Uncle Harry says it might—"

"You've got to stop this!" I said, and gripped her shoulders hard, for she was trembling on the edge of hysterical tears. "The place has poisoned you. Shall I tell you what we'll do? I'll swing you up on that horse and we'll ride over and put you in the charge of Lady Fenwick. They have such things as special licenses in England, haven't they? Tomorrow Sir James and I will see about getting one. Then I will come back and undertake the pleasant task of telling Uncle Harry exactly where he can jump in the moat."

She smiled, shakily. "All right; I'll be good. But I want you to listen to something. I want you to listen as carefully as though you were reading evidence in a court case. For it *is* evidence. This isn't the legend and the curse. It's something that happened less than fifty years ago, and there are people alive who can swear to it."

"Yes?"

"You see that tower?" She pointed. "At the top of that tower there is one room. It is a bare brick room, with no furniture except a table and a chair. There is one door, and one window. The window faces this way; it is heavily barred, and below there is a smooth face of brick sixty feet down. You can see that from here.

"In June 1886, one evening just a week before her wedding day, my grandfather's sister Ellen went into that room alone. The door isn't of the ordinary sort; since that room occupies the whole top of the tower, it's a trap door in the ceiling of the room below. You understand, don't you? Like going up into a loft. You must use a ladder for it.

"Well, Ellen Mortlake climbed up there. She shut and bolted the trap door on the inside. Just below her, watching the trap door all the time, were four people whose truthfulness is beyond question. She had been there only ten minutes when they heard her scream, horribly, and the table overturn. When they got a ladder and smashed in the bolted trap, they found her lying in the middle of the room with both eyes jaggedly torn out. She died of shock, without speaking, only a few minutes later."

Louise was speaking very quietly, her lips barely moving in the gloom of the summerhouse, and the hazel eyes never left my face.

She went on: "Oh, do you think they didn't try to make it a police case? They did. But what could they find out? ... There was nobody in that room except poor Ellen. Nobody! Not even a place to hide, and they searched immediately. There was nothing in the room that could have given her such wounds. Nobody left the room while they were searching. There was no such foolish thing as a secret entrance or panel; they examined every inch of the room. They even took the table and chair apart, looking for a possible weapon. Nothing! Yet the door was bolted and watched by four people. The window was solidly barred, and sixty feet up a wall that a fly couldn't have climbed. Tom, no human murderer could have done it. But it was done."

Now the wind rose in a great gust through tattered oaks, and the yellow evening light struck full across on the tower up the hill. I felt that from happiness I had slipped into a nightmare. For Louise believed this. The thing had to be gripped and faced.

"And you really believe," I said, trying to keep my voice steady, "that a curse did that? What was the woman doing in that room?"

"She didn't believe in the legend. She was trying to show it was all nonsense."

"What is the legend?"

Louise turned away to look at the road. "I—I can't tell you all of it now. But this much you ought to know, Tom. A horrible thing was done three hundred years ago, by a woman who wanted her own way. Her name was Vivian Mortlake; she was a shrew and a beauty. Because she hated a man whom her family wanted her to marry, she had him killed in such a way that the crows of the field tore out his eyes while he was still alive."

"Go on," I said "Give me your hand. At least it will do you good to talk."

"Before he died, he said that if she ever married, he would pay her a visit a week before the wedding. She watched for him from that tower window. A week before her wedding, the crows came to her —" Louise drew a deep breath. "You see, it was said she saw him coming back from his grave, groping his way up this road in the twilight, with the blood soaking out of his empty eye sockets, and the great crows clustered on him like pets. Anyway, Vivian Mortlake went mad with blindness and pain."

She swung round to face me.

"And this is the tale, Tom: that if any Mortlake girl marries against the will of her family, as Vivian did, those blind things shall fly from the air and stab out her eyes. . . . Don't laugh. Whatever you do, in God's name don't laugh! I don't know anything, except that it *has happened.* My sister, you see, will be marrying against the family's will."

I had no inclination to laugh. I wanted only to curse "Uncle Henry" Mortlake's smug and unctuous ghost stories, his poisoning of two girls in a lonely house as surely as though he had done it with cyanide.

"And he doesn't want you to marry, either?" I asked.

"No. You see—both Anne and I have a little money held in trust for us till we marry. As it is, the money supports all of us. . . ."

"Held in trust by him?"

"Yes."

"Damn his soul," I said. "He can have all the money he wants, crammed down his throat. But there are other things to settle with him."

"There are," spoke up a great voice in the road behind us, "if it's not too late to do any good."

It was the familiar, quiet, curt voice of Sir James Fenwick. Neither of us had heard him ride up, though Queen of Clubs was blown as though from a long gallop. He sat motionless on the great horse, outlined against the yellow sunset, but his voice shook like the hand on his bridle rein. He wore his old tweed cap and coat; in his big lined face the eyeglass was stuck in his left eye, and the corners of his mouth were turned down. He took one look at us.

"So," he said. "She's told you about the bogey, eh? Then you're just in time to hear the latest development." He stabbed his finger towards the house. "Louise, did they tell you that Henry M. has persuaded—or goaded—Anne to try her luck in the tower room? No, by God, they wouldn't! Well, he has. She's there now. Your cousin Dick just telephoned me on the quiet to come and do something about it. He's too afraid of Henry to put in a word. He tried to get in touch with Anne's fiancé, but young Gordon's in London and I was the only one left."

"You mean . . ." said Louise. "No! *No!*"

"I mean some deviltry. Come on! I'm off to see if I can—"

The great horse reared, monstrous in the twilight, but not from his urging. It was sixty yards up the hill to Moat Hall, yet we heard the screams plainly. A woman in the tower room was screaming in such hideous pain or terror that it dislodged wheeling birds in a fluttering cloud from the eaves. The screams abruptly stopped. Fenwick cursed only once. His horse pawed the air, came down with a strike of sparks from the flints, and was off like thunder up the road.

II
THE BIRDS OF HELL

Louise and I ran hard. When we reached Moat Hall, the startled swans were still flapping the water in the moat. Fenwick was already across the stone causeway; he was standing at the big door furiously banging its knocker. Nobody answered. But it was unlocked, and Louise led us inside. In the dark oak hallway there was —I don't know how to describe it—a kind of ringing stillness, as of evil sinking back after it strikes. A dim figure almost walked into us, and my heart rose in my throat.

Then the figure began to laugh hysterically. It was the eighteen-year-old cousin, Richard. His callow, sensitive face, with the shrunken good looks of the Mortlakes, rocked back and forth in the gloom.

"You're too late," he said. "The crows dug through into the brain. She's dead."

I thought Louise was going to faint. She turned round and put her head against my shoulder. It was Fenwick's strong presence that kept us sane; he had Richard by the collar, choking off his laughter.

"Pull yourself together," he said harshly. "Quiet, do you hear? Now tell me: Why was she fool enough to let Henry persuade her to . . . go in there?"

Richard looked at Louise. "She did it for *you*," he answered. "She said you had found somebody you had fallen in love with. She said that she wouldn't have you terrified, and she was going to break the curse forever. You see, there's trust and honor—even among the Mortlakes."

"Henry is up there now, is he?" asked Fenwick, after a silence. "And your Aunt Kate too?"

"Yes. If they were the only ones!" said the other bitterly. "But they're not. There's Mr. Walters, and Dr. Porter, and Squire Brixley; the vicar, the doctor, and the chief magistrate of the county. All men whose word is above reproach. They were summoned to see it. They can swear—we'll all have to swear—they saw an impossible thing done. Anne went up the ladder, she bolted the trap; we never took our eyes off it. All those men can testify. . . ."

"His witnesses," Fenwick groaned. "And yet nobody tried to stop it?"

Richard stopped, as though he had said too much. His head was shaking with a terrible motion like a paralytic's.

"The vicar tried to. But Anne insisted. Also, Dr. Porter said it was a lot of damned nonsense, and Squire Brixley was half drunk and didn't care a hoot either way. So she went in. I—I can't stand this. You see, she trusted me. You'd better go upstairs."

Two minutes more, and we were climbing the stone staircase that curved up into the tower. We emerged into the room where the watchers had waited, the one just below the room of the curse. A ladder ran up to a trap in the ceiling; the trap door was splintered through where they had smashed it in. From the room above we could hear footsteps moving about, and the mutter of voices.

This lower room was square, with diamond-paned windows through which the sunset light had turned reddish. The furniture was black Jacobean oak, and the silver candlesticks caught a glitter. Beside the table sat Kate Mortlake, Henry's wife, with her high-bridged nose and darkish face. Her hands were folded quietly, as though the matter did not concern her.

"Good evening," said Henry Mortlake's smooth voice from the western window. "Ah, but isn't it sad—sad! Louise, my dear, I am sorry to tell you that your poor sister is . . . gone. I warned her, but she was foolish and headstrong. I ask you to remember that she did this of her own free will."

He was standing by the open window, big and shapeless, with the reddish light shining on his face, and he was smiling. On his face there was a thin oil of sweat. He was eating walnuts; I saw his black fingernails as he broke a walnut in one hand, and delicately shook out the kernel. His little eye gleamed like a crumb of glass. Although he tried to be impassive, he could not keep the loose mouth from broadening into a grin.

"Gone," echoed Aunt Kate, without inflection.

"Mortlake," said Sir James Fenwick calmly, "I think you know what I believe. It's not necessary to go into that now. . . ."

"Yes, yes! By all means tell me what you believe," said the other, with agreeable surprise. "Please tell me. Then I can institute a suit for slander, and the court will award me several thousand pounds. Eh, Kate? My niece Anne chose to disobey my orders about marriage. So she suffered—but not through me. No human intelligence can explain how she was struck down in an empty, sealed room. Three unprejudiced men will swear that the room was both empty and sealed. They will tell you that all the while I stood before their eyes, and did not move from here. Eh?" He smiled again, and spoke very softly as he thrust out his head. "So? You are James Fenwick, late of India, and retired chief of the Indian secret police? Then see if you can explain the magic of the supernatural. . . . You poor bloody fool, if you so much as dare mention what you may be thinking, I'll go to court and have the very shirt off your back."

He chuckled. Fenwick's face was gray, and he was gripping his riding crop hard. Mortlake's indifferent eye turned round towards me.

"And now I hear," he added pleasantly, "that there is talk of more marriages against my express wish. An American visitor comes and makes love to our little Louise. Can I humbly ask you to take a warning? Louise has pretty eyes too—"

There was a riding crop slung by a loop round my own wrist. I gripped the butt and took a step forward, but Fenwick seized my arm.

"Don't do it!" he snapped. His voice broke the mist of wrath that had taken all of us. "Don't you see you'd be doing exactly what he wants you to?"

"There is talk of a marriage," I said, releasing the crop. "Have you any objections?"

"I? *I?* Of course not. You do not understand, I fear. But then you Americans, who have not even any grandparents you can identify, would not understand such things, would you? There is a blight on that girl. It is a part of her; it is in her blood, and her destiny, and the sticks and stones of this house. If she will not obey our wishes, then *it* will—"

"I don't think it'll have the chance."

"Well, I'm going up there now, in any case," said Louise, and her eyes brimmed over. "She did that for me."

She was climbing the ladder before anybody could stop her. But we did not realize the worst of the business until we stood in the bare black room above. The evening light was almost gone. A wet wind blew through the bars of the one small window, and made a vast seething in the trees below. It was not merely what we saw there. . . .

Dr. Porter was bending over the body on the floor, and at first we did not see the ruined face. At one side stood the lean old vicar, Walters, in his clerical black; at the other side was the stout Major Brixley, in dark riding clothes, and now quite sober. They looked themselves like three birds of prey.

Dr. Porter held up his hand. "Don't look, Louise," he cried, but he was too late.

Anne Mortlake had been a small, fragile girl, dressed in gray silk. I need not describe her injuries, except to say they were such that Louise could not remain very long, and Major Brixley had to take her downstairs. After Anne had been attacked, she had evidently run and stumbled wildly round the room in her blindness—there were stains on the wall in several places—before she fell. Her dress was stained, and ripped down from the shoulder as though she had torn loose from something. But this was not the terror which made our skins crawl. It was the realization that this attack must have been conjured up by powers from hell, because it could not have been done by man.

It was Dr. Porter, with his black pointed beard and his Ascot tie, who spoke first.

"I don't believe it!" he said wildly, and stared round. "I see it, and yet I don't believe it. Look round you. Blank walls—not even a place for a rat to hide. No furniture—not even the chair and table they talked about. There was nobody here before she came up—we saw that. There was nobody here when we smashed that trap door after she screamed. And we never took our eyes off that trap door, either.

As for the window, look at it! Bars too close for a midget to get through, set solid in stone, and sixty feet up a wall smooth as glass. Well?"

"You've tested the walls?" asked Fenwick sharply.

"Been over every inch of 'em," nodded the doctor, and Walters agreed. "The ceiling too. There's no secret entrance, and no hocus-pocus mechanical device to attack her, if that's what you're thinking."

The old clergyman rubbed blurred eyes.

"This is my fault," he said with an unsteady look round. "I protested, but I should have *done* something . . . something . . . You see, I was a boy when Ellen Mortlake died here nearly fifty years ago. I remember it well. It was exactly like this."

"So I've heard. That," said Fenwick, "is what makes me wonder. But suppose we get things straight, gentlemen, before we have to send for the police. I suppose you're all provided with . . . alibis?"

"Eh? Alibis?" said Porter, startled. "Good God, yes! That is, I suppose so. We were all together down there. None of us came up with her."

"You were all down there, including Mr. Henry Mortlake?"

"Yes, certainly."

"Thank you," said a smooth, fat voice from the trap door. "Thanks very much." Mortlake's head appeared in the opening. "It will set the good Sir James's doubts at rest. Would you like to telephone the police now?"

And he laughed in our faces.

III
A CHALLENGE TO DEATH

"Have you gone mad?" cried Walters. "Do you realize, or don't you, that your niece is . . .?"

Mortlake became contrite, with a sudden change like fear. "Excuse me, gentlemen. Of course I am sorry. But you d-don't understand. She paid a penalty, that is all."

"You honestly believe that?" snapped the doctor.

"Can you prove anything different? Prove it, I said?" the other asked composedly. "I advise you to be careful."

"We'll try," said Fenwick grimly. He paused as the thin, drawn face of Richard Mortlake appeared in the trap. "To get this in order, doctor: when did Anne come up to this room?"

Porter looked at his watch. "About half an hour ago. Say six o'clock or thereabouts."

"Did anybody come up here with her?"

"No. Not up here. Except that . . ."

"Yes?"

"Well," grunted the doctor uncomfortably, "as she was climbing up the ladder, Dick Mortlake here climbed up a few rungs and whispered something to her."

The young man, who was climbing over the edge of the trap, stumbled. His face went white with the implications of this.

"*I* didn't have anything to do with it!" he cried. "Don't look at me like that! I—I was trying to help her. All I said was not to worry, and that I had telephoned Sir James to come up as soon as he could—"

"So," interrupted Henry, and showed his teeth, "you are the reason why our estimable neighbor pays us this visit, eh? I shall remember that."

Fenwick kept his eyes on Porter. "But he didn't actually come up into this room with her?"

"Oh, no."

"Was anything else said to her before she went up?"

Porter hesitated. "Henry here said, 'If you see Rupert and his pets coming up the road, my dear . . .' "

"What did he mean by that?"

"You had better let *me* explain that," nodded Henry, and giggled.

He moved over softly against the gray light from the window. The wall was very thick, so that the window sloped outward, and the bars—set three inches apart—were fixed immovably in stone. Nevertheless Henry made a great show of shaking them and winking at us.

"It is a pretty story, gentlemen," he went on. "Some of you may have heard it. It does not concern the modern crow, but the carrion crows of 1621, which were used to gorging themselves on battlefields. In 1621 Rupert Henley was the suitor of Vivian Mortlake, the red-haired devil, and he was the man her family—her wise family, gentlemen—ordered her to marry. She hated him. She even hated him for his devotion. It is evil blood, I tell you, in the women of our race!"

He pointed at us. His face was like pale butter in the gloom.

"She would scream at him, 'Will you never tire of following me wherever I go?' And he would answer, 'Madam, love has four faces, like a compass; and I am the needle to be drawn wherever you are. You will never be rid of me.'

"Do you know what she had done to him? He was waylaid one night when he rode home past the great acres of cornfields that used to lie at the bottom of this hill. He was stripped of his clothes, and bound round in surgical bandages and splints so that he could not even move his body. He was a living mummy. Even his head was bound in splints, with only the eyes and nose showing. Then they dressed him in the rags and straw and hood of a scarecrow, and propped him up on sticks high in the field. All the world could pass by and see him, yet no one would know the scarecrow was a living man. The exposed part of his face was slashed so that the blood should be there to attract the carrion crows. . . .

"The next day she could sit in this tower room and look out to where the scarecrow hung in the blaze of sun. She sang at her needlework, and jabbed her needle as the cloud of crows came down there. It is said he endured two days of it, while nobody ever knew. They did notice, however, that the crows swarmed in such fashion that the head of the scarecrow seemed to be covered in moving black fur. And thus it was discovered. When two farm hands came to beat them away, they discovered . . .

"Still he was not quite dead. He never betrayed her, and nobody at the time knew she had been responsible. He only said to tell Milady Mortlake that if she ever married, he would visit her a week before the wedding. 'And she will find,' he said, 'that death has four faces too.' "

Henry drew a deep breath. Then his voice rose almost to a scream.

"Can anybody deny the truth of that? You blind fools, don't you know that the Devil is as real in this world as the beef you eat at dinner or the lamp that lights your room? The Devil *is* real. I have seen him lurk behind the hedges. Can you deny that he sent a dead Rupert Henley riding up that road on a dead horse, with his blind eye sockets fixed on this tower; and that the cloud of crows left his

head to fly up here through this window and covered Vivian Mortlake's face as though with moving black fur?

"And if you do not believe that," he said, very softly now, "remember what happened tonight. You all heard it. We were down there
listening. And just as Anne screamed, can you in your sober senses
deny that we all heard a *great beating of wings?*"

We had all drawn back. The man was cool and smiling now,
mopping at the oil of sweat on his face, but his smirk looked more
fanatical than any rage. Dr. Porter looked hard at him.

"I'm not sure," said the doctor, "whether it ought to be Walters or
myself who prescribes for you. I don't know whether you need a
doctor or a clergyman. . . . Beating of wings! Yes, we heard it. But
I know what it was. It was the swans down below, that got a scare
when she screamed; I heard them splashing as well, and I can
swear to that. *You* ought to know. You were standing by the window
down there."

"So," said Fenwick, in such a queer voice that we all whirled
round. "He was standing by the window, was he?"

Fenwick's big face was impassive, but he stared straight at the
trap door in the floor near Mortlake.

"He was," said Porter. "But what of it?"

"Mr. Walters," Fenwick went on, and turned to the vicar without
raising his voice, "you said that you were a young man when Ellen
Mortlake died in this room in 1886, and that you remember the
case? Good. Who objected to Ellen Mortlake's marriage? Her father?"

"Her . . . ?" The vicar seemed sunk in apathy, and he raised his
white head vacantly. "Her father? No. He was dead. The one who
objected was her brother Henry. Come to think of it, he was the
father of Mr. Henry Mortlake here."

"And what," asked Fenwick in a curious tone, "was his profession?"

"I believe he was a jeweler."

Fenwick slashed his riding crop across his knee. "It tells us nothing! Damnation, he could not have been a jeweler! I tell you he
couldn't—" He broke off as Mortlake's assured, contemptuous grin
defied him to do anything whatever. But I noticed that Fenwick had
caught my eye as though asking me to agree with anything he said.

He went on: "Now shall I tell you something, Mortlake? The curse is broken. Your poor little bogey is smashed to blazes, and we can laugh at it. Do you know why? Louise came into this room a while ago, and was unharmed. . . ."

"Naturally," said Mortlake. "We must patiently wait—and I hope she enjoys the prospect—until a week before her wedding."

"It is just a week before her wedding," said Fenwick politely. "Didn't you know that she and my friend Tom Brocklin had arranged this afternoon to be married on the same day as Anne and her fiancé?"

At this thumping lie, Mortlake's loose mouth fell open a little.

"It's against all decency," Fenwick's cold voice went on, "with Anne dead, but you might be interested to hear that they are going through with it. Why? To save Louise's reason. To show that this tuppenny curse can be smashed for the turnip ghost it is. Better violate a few conventions rather than have Louise in a madhouse. . . . But you didn't know that, did you? And your ghosts didn't know it, either. This is the last night Louise will spend under your roof. Good afternoon, gentlemen."

He strode across and began to descend the ladder. I followed him. We were in the room below before Mortlake stuck his head down the trap.

"A last word, my friend," he said silkily, and pointed with the stained point of the walnut pick. "Put a guard of police round me, if you like. Let every move I make be watched. Put her into a room with all the doors and windows bolted, and a guard around her. *They* will come after her just the same. As for you, dear Mr. Brocklin—"

"Don't answer him," snapped Fenwick, and dragged me away from that reddish face peering down, while Mortlake went on smiling. Fenwick and I were going down in the gloom of the tower stairs before my friend spoke.

"God help us, Tom. I mean that in a literal sense. I'm afraid he will keep his word."

"You mean Louise . . . ?"

"Yes."

"But the man's not supernatural!" I cried. "He can't command black magic and turn loose a cloud of devils. Or can he? He can't commit murder in a locked and sealed room while he's still standing before the eyes of all those witnesses! Unless, of course, the witnesses were lying."

"The witnesses were not lying," said Fenwick quietly. "But if it's any consolation to you, I think I can tell you there's nothing supernatural about it. It's only a very brilliant and very horrible trick. But he may work it again."

"You mean a device hidden in that room?"

"No, Tom. The room is as harmless as—as a nursery; there's nothing there. But don't be confident when you learn it's not supernatural. There are worse things. I think that Mortlake already had a crack in his brain, for the dark world to press through. It split wide when I challenged him; he'll go to any lengths now, and it's our only chance to catch him. Don't argue! We must find Louise."

We found her in the dusky lower hall.

"I'm sorry I was weak," she said, and took my hand like a child. "It was . . . everything at once. I am strong now."

"That," said Fenwick quietly, "that is good news. Because, Louise, I am going to ask you to be stronger still. Tonight, after the police have gone, I am going to ask you to go up into the tower room . . . alone."

IV
RENDEZVOUS IN THE TOWER

Even as he said it, I realized that the whispering old house was not so quiet as we had thought. Somewhere, on the stairs or in one of the tapestry-hung rooms, there was the sound of a footfall: a creaking as someone stalked us. It was as though the whole house were listening.

But I heard for only an instant—and then forgot, for Fenwick's words were too startling to allow anything else to remain in my mind.

"Go up into that room alone tonight?" I said. "Look here, have you gone crazy too? If she ever goes up into that room alone, there's just one precaution we'll take first: we'll strangle Uncle Henry."

Fenwick turned round. I saw the gleam of his eyeglass, but his lips did not move against tightened jaws when we heard the whisper: *"Agree with anything I say, you fool."* He turned back to Louise, and spoke in an audible mutter.

"Now listen carefully, and whatever you do, don't fail me in any particular if you value your life or your reason. Got it? Got that? I don't want you to go up there to break the curse. I want you to go because it's the highest point in this house, and the only place from which you can see across the moor to Fenwick House—"

"Your own place?"

"My own place. At eleven o'clock I want you to go up to the tower room. The police will have gone by then; and until then you'll be safe. You will take no light, understand? But you will be armed. Go up there and watch for my signal. At eleven I'll put a lamp in the highest window of the east wing of my house. If you see one light, that means that no matter what happens, you are to remain absolutely still in that room until ... something happens. But if you see two lights, that will mean my plan has miscarried. In that case you are to get out of the house instantly, and shoot without question anyone who tries to stop you."

He paused, staring straight at her.

"I know it's a lot to ask, Louise. I know it would break the nerve of anybody with less at stake than you have. Believe me, I should not ask you to trust me blindly—"

"Blindly," said Louise in a low voice.

"That," said Fenwick, and made a fierce gesture, "was the wrong word. I should not ask you to trust me if I did not know—*know*, do you hear?—that it's the only way to bring you out of the shadow and into clean air. . . . Well?"

"She did it for me," Louise answered, after a pause, and nodded. "It's the least I can do for her. Of course I will. I—I— What now?"

"Outside," he muttered. "Both of you. Quickly!"

We hurried out on the causeway in the thickening dusk. Fenwick made certain the big door was shut, and then peered up and down the moat.

"We were overheard," I said. "You knew that?"

"Of course. I intended that we should be."

"Then the plans are changed?" Louise asked quickly.

"Not at all. Do just as I told you, with one addition. You are to conceal Tom somewhere in the house. Can you do that? Good! Tom, you know the way up to the tower room. You are to get up there, secretly, at least fifteen minutes before she does. Show no light, and watch. If everything goes well ... Ah! Found it! Look there, both of you!"

Abruptly he pointed up the shadowy stretch of the moat, now gray and ruffled in its fringe of reeds. He indicated a point at a great distance away from the big tower, and I could see only a white blur on the water. We followed him round to look at it from the bank. It floated shapeless and dead: a swan whose long neck was outstretched snakily, and whose head was severed in a red pulp that still stained the water. Nothing brought out the intrinsic horror breathing from this house more than that sodden white mass floating in the dusk.

"Someone's chopped off—" muttered Louise, and stopped. "Uncle Harry is very fond of the swans. He has names for all of them."

"It's the last link," said Fenwick, closing his fist. "The last piece of evidence we need. First, the direction of the sun this afternoon. Second, the fact that his father was a jeweler. Third, that dead swan. Does he have names for all of them? By God, he ought to call that one Justice. It is going to hang him."

That laugh went echoing and twisting in my mind through all the long hours between then and eleven o'clock. As each clock tick drew us nearer the time for Louise's vigil, my own fear grew to more grotesque shapes.

Worst of all, I could not see Louise during those hours. She had hidden me in a little back library, where neither of the two old servants ever came. She went about her tasks with a white face but a steady smile. Hidden away in her bureau upstairs, she said, she had a Browning .22 for pot shots at rabbits. Meanwhile the police had been summoned from Porlock, the nearest town.

So I waited in the dark, not daring to smoke and hardly daring to move, while the phantoms gathered. When a clock out in the hall chimed ten-thirty, I almost jumped out of a crawling skin.

I allowed five minutes more, and then crept out. I groped my way upstairs, keeping to the wall and testing every tread. The closer I crept to the tower door, the more hot grew my fear of discovery.

Nearly there! Watch out for chairs. Ten feet more, and bear to the right—

I climbed the tower stairs, slipped into the lower tower room, and groped for the ladder. Two seconds more, and I was in the loft, where the rain blew through open bars. No gleam yet showed across the moor in the direction of Fenwick House. This rain, I realized, would play the devil about seeing that signal. I crouched back against one wall away from the trap, and waited.

The direction of the sun, a jeweler, and a dead swan . . . These strangely unrelated things hammered over and over in my brain, but they conjured up a thousand incredible shapes in the dark for the Death with Four Faces. . . .

Somebody was coming up the ladder. I heard it above the splashing of the rain, a mere rustle of sound. A shadow moved on lighter blackness; the shattered trap door creaked slightly.

"Tom . . ." whispered Louise's voice, and something wrenched in my throat.

"Take it easy," I whispered. Those threads of sound moved and crossed.

Only blackness showed at the window. If Fenwick failed us now . . .

"I asked," she whispered, "because, Tom, there was somebody following me up the tower stairs."

The roar of the rain grew, but it did not quite blot out the noise of someone crossing the floor of the room below. Whoever it was, I was a little surprised to find that he was not trying to walk softly. The ladder shook, just as Louise seized my arm and seemed gesturing towards the window. Far down the hill and out across the moorland, there was a blurry gleam.

Someone was climbing the ladder. I motioned Louise to the far side of the room, and crouched ready behind the trap. A head came through. The beam of a flashlight struck across the room on Louise's face.

"It's all right!" came an agonized whisper. "Louise! Are you there? It's all right! I know about it! Sir James told me. It's Dick."

"What do you want?" she whispered. "Don't you know you'll break up—"

"I had to help you! Don't you know you'll never see that light in this rain, unless . . ." He held out his hand, and there was a dark gleam. "I've brought you a pair of binoculars—night glasses. You'll be able to pick it up now."

"Thanks, Dick. Give them here, quick! It's past elev—"

She screamed.

Out of the dark a few feet to my right sprang the straight white glare of a bull's-eye lantern. It fastened on young Mortlake's fallen jaw as he whirled round with the small binoculars in his hands.

"Don't touch those glasses," said the voice of Sir James Fenwick. *"That's what killed Anne. Grab him, Tom, and don't let him yell for help. Steady, now."*

V
DEATH'S BINOCULARS

Richard Mortlake showed no fight. He backed against one wall, pushing his hands out feebly before him, like a child under hypnosis. Fenwick kept the light steadily in his eyes, propping the man's own flashlight on the floor.

"Oh, no," said Fenwick, who himself was breathing heavily, "he's not the king devil, though he may hang for all of that. You see, he was too afraid of Henry to refuse. But our young friend was used because Anne trusted him. He planted the glasses. Like to see how the damnable trick was worked? . . . Give me those glasses!"

Richard Mortlake handed them over. His thin chest heaved, and his tongue seemed too big for his mouth, so that he could not speak.

"Somebody gives you a pair of binoculars, or you find them on a window ledge," Fenwick went on, very quietly. "You put them to your eyes, and you can see only a blur. What do you immediately do? While you keep on looking, you put your hand up and start to turn the focus wheel in the middle, to put the glasses into focus. Only, in this case . . .

"There's a good reason why you see a blur. It's worked on the principle of a compressed-air gun, and only a touch of the focus wheel is necessary, like a trigger. When you turn it, two jagged steel points about an inch and a half long strike out from the lenses and drive through your eyes. There's your bogey and your curse, Louise, and that's *all* there is to it."

Louise could not speak, but her breath came in a shuddering gasp.

"And yet," Fenwick went on evenly, "no glasses were found in this room afterwards. That's the brilliant part of the whole scheme. Without it, there would have been no curse and no mystery when Henry Mortlake's father took advantage of an old curse and devised these glasses to kill his sister fifty years ago. And since a jeweler is usually also an optician . . .

"Think how it was done! A woman is told to watch a road for a phantom rider coming up a road towards evening, and she finds a pair of binoculars conveniently left there. . . . You see, what young Dick really whispered to Anne—when she was going up the ladder —was that he had left a pair of glasses up there for her. And she trusted him. . . . Well, what happens? Strong evening light is beating straight through that window into her eyes. She can't see very well. But suddenly she notices, far down the evening road, a horseman. She sees—"

"She sees *you*," Louise interrupted, and in the shock of realization our eyes turned—I don't know why—to a slobbering Richard Mortlake.

Fenwick passed a hand over his eyes. His voice was heavy and bitter.

"She sees me—for I have been summoned, just at the right time, by a telephone call. The recollection of that, the knowledge that *I* was responsible for that girl's death . . . ! But to explain. Let's suppose you saw, dimly against the sun, just that. You want a good look. But though you can get a shaded look with those binoculars, *the bars are in your way* and impede the glasses. What do you do?"

I felt a little sick. By turning those glasses sideways, they could be passed out through the bars.

"In that case," I said, "you'd pass those glasses *out* through the three-inch space between the bars. You'd hold the middle part of the nose against one bar, with the eyepieces outside the bar on either side, and look through. But when you turned the wheel—"

"We needn't dwell on it," said Fenwick savagely. "I only dwell on it now to show Louise what thin tissue paper all the terrors were built of. Oh, evil enough! But not supernatural. The steel points go through. In that sudden blast of agony, the victim releases the glasses. They go down, sixty feet, and sink to the bottom of the moat. Any splash they may make—which is carefully listened for by

Henry Mortlake, standing by an open window to make sure his plan has succeeded—any splash is explained by the beating of the swans. As it happened, those glasses smashed off the head of a swan when they fell. It was simple enough; all clues led straight to the moat. But we had to get a confession. We had to find somebody tonight fishing up those glasses from the moat. And last of all we had to catch somebody, before witnesses, handing those glasses to Louise. Hence my scheme to misdirect attention to the lights at my house.

"As for you," he snapped, and walked slowly towards Dick, "I rather thought your excellent master and devil's advocate would be too canny to do the work himself. So we can't implicate him, eh? Well, *you're* going to implicate him now, unless you want to swing for murder."

Dick was wiping a hand aimlessly across his mouth, his eyes roving. But when he heard this he burst out. It was to Louise he spoke.

"You—you don't understand," he said, in a shaky voice that was like a child's puzzled hesitation. "I—yes, I admit I did that. I couldn't help myself. He's mad. He'd have sneaked in, if I refused; he'd have sneaked in, while I was sleeping, and put those glasses over my eyes. I was going to kill myself, anyway, after what I did to Anne. But you don't understand, Louise. I was going to save your life. I tried to save your life. Honestly and truly, Louise, I was going to—"

"You're going to talk," said Fenwick. "Speak up! Do you admit, before witnesses, what I've just been saying?"

"Yes!"

"Then we'll round it out. Why was Henry standing by the window all the time? Wasn't it because he wanted to see the glasses fall? And if by any chance his scheme didn't work, and the glasses fell inside the room, he had a duplicate harmless pair in his pocket? He was going to be the first to rush up that ladder, and substitute the harmless ones for the others? Is that right?"

"Yes!"

"And if I write all this down, here and now, you'll sign it?"

"Yes!"

A soft, heavy voice spoke behind us.

"That, of course, is open to debate," it said. "No, I wouldn't move, if I were you."

We had not even heard him come up the ladder, or seen his light. He was squatting beside the trap, smirking and wagging his head over a lantern before him. It outlined every bloated feature of the moist face; it made monstrous the flabby bald head, and threw a slow-wagging distortion of shadow on the wall behind. I got Louise behind me. But we looked into his eyes, and we saw death.

"I have here," he said, opening his eyes wide, "an air pistol. I think it is more powerful than the German type you remember from the war, although it is much older. My father made it, as he made that air-gun mechanism in those glasses. It is almost noiseless. It also fires an expanding bullet, and I shall be able to blow your guts wide open if any of you so much as moves a finger. Is that clear?" He put his tongue in his cheek and smiled thoughtfully. He was in no hurry. "I have said," he went on, "that this is a more powerful air pistol than the German. Let's test it, shall we?"

I don't know what happened, except that I saw the thing come round in a half circle. I cannot remember any sound at all, although there must have been one. The lantern light spun sideways and seemed to pitch forward. The full weight of my shoulder had come down on the floor, and I was looking at that broad reddish face from underneath. They say there is no pain, which is a lie. It went over my brain in a sick heat like sunstroke.

"Don't try to get up," said Mortlake. "Your right leg is smashed just below the knee. But you will be feeling a trifle dizzy now. . . . I am not going to hurt any of you, with bullets. You will simply be put out of commission, until I can make you . . . look at the stars through my telescope. Eh? Eh? You know, I rather fancy myself as a humorist. Eh?"

"No, you won't hang," Fenwick observed. "Unfortunately, I think you'll only go to Broadmoor. In case you don't know it, that's where they put the criminally insane."

"I shouldn't talk like that, if I were you," said Mortlake coolly, and pulled the trigger again.

I heard a scraping noise on the wall, as though Fenwick were trying to hold himself up. He said nothing, but I heard the little tinkle as his eyeglass broke on the floor.

"That was a worse one," Mortlake said, "but still not serious. You'd better let go that wall, my poor bloody friend, the head of the secret police, or I shall have to give you another." A snarl suddenly came up behind his grin. "You're all going to look through my telescope, you know. As for you, Louise, don't try to use that little toy pistol. I unloaded it early this evening."

His voice rose querulously.

"Do you think I didn't know what you were planning? I prepared for it. Something had to be done. I could see the great Sir J. had spotted my little optical device. We might as well have a banquet, eh? And if you had every policeman in the West Country surrounding the place at this moment, I fail to see how it could help you— do you?"

I was thinking that if I could get any leverage for my body in my wobbling arms, I might pitch forward into him and carry him through the trap door. Unfortunately, he saw the intention just as I jumped. Something else went into my arms. He lowered the air gun and got to his feet.

"It's all right, Dick," he said to that stricken young man, who was praying now. "Take it easy, and you may not be hurt—yet. Don't be a fool like this one. Will you obey me now?"

"Yes!" The boy meant it; we all knew that.

"There is just one thing I should like to know. *You!*" He screeched the word at Fenwick, and I thought he was going to fire again. "What did you mean by that little trick and fancy with those lights at your place? What *do* you mean by it? Eh?"

"Suppose," Fenwick's voice said coolly, "you try to find out."

"I will. *These* glasses," said Mortlake, tapping the case at his side, "are harmless. "We'll have a look. We—" He screamed.

I could not see him where he was, but something grimy yellow spilled across my line of sight just as there was a metallic crash on the floor. The yellow blur became distorted, seemed to strike the floor and roll from side to side before it lay breathing but unconscious. Over that room where the terrors had lately choked and blasted, there was now only the cool rush of the rain. Two people spoke.

Fenwick said: "Pick up that gun of his, Louise. Take it easy, now. He'll give very little trouble."

And, rising to the breaking point, Dick Mortlake's voice went on in its puzzled babble: "I told you I tried to save your life. Honestly,

I tried to save your life. You see, Louise, I wasn't lying. Tonight, before I came up here, and when he didn't know it, *I switched the two pairs of glasses.*"

I remember grinning at Louise, who was running towards me. Then it is possible that the whole nightmare ended in a bad faint.

Detective Tales, October 1935

I SUGGESTED in the introduction to this book that the effect of Carr's stories is to confirm the orderliness, rationality and fundamental justice of the universe by presenting logical and human explanations of all the apparent impossibilities. The conclusion to "Terror's Dark Tower" agrees with that generalization, but "The Door to Doom" and "The Man Who Was Dead" depend on the reality of the supernatural. It seems to me, however, that even Carr's ghosts support order; by punishing the criminals in singularly appropriate ways, they are much more efficient than human law in restoring justice. But the ideas of a creative author cannot be easily pigeonholed, and evidence for a different interpretation of Carr's use of the supernatural can be found in one of his greatest novels, *The Burning Court.*

SHERLOCKIAN PARODIES

AT THE END of the Second World War, a Labour government was elected in Britain, and John Dickson Carr believed that traditional England would be destroyed by
socialism. "I could take war," Carr remarked; "I can't
stand the bloody Socialists." He remained in England a
few more years to complete his definitive biography of
Sir Arthur Conan Doyle, before moving to Mamaroneck,
New York, in 1948. He became active in the Mystery
Writers of America, and in 1949 he was elected president
of that organization.

At its annual meeting held each April, the Mystery
Writers of America presented a humorous playlet under
the general title "The March of Crime." The authors of
the plays included such important writers as Clayton
Rawson, Harold Q. Masur and Kelley Roos. Carr had
recently completed his biography of Doyle when he
wrote his contributions, and naturally his plays were
Sherlockian. Carr disliked the idolatry with which some
Baker Street Irregulars approached "the sacred writings," and on several occasions he criticized the attitude
that Holmes and Watson were real people and Doyle only
their agent. "Let's not, even in jest," he said, "make the

flesh-and-blood of Sherlock Holmes and John H. Watson an obsession very near religious mania." Carr found nothing sacrosanct in Holmes's adventures, and the two plays exhibit what Robert E. Briney calls Carr's "irreverent and rowdy sense of humor." Holmesian experts will immediately recognize several sly and not-so-sly references to the canon.

"The Adventure of the Conk-Singleton Papers" was performed in April 1948, and "The Adventure of the Paradol Chamber" a year later. In both plays, Clayton Rawson portrayed Holmes, Lawrence G. Blochman played Watson, and Carr assigned himself the role of the visitor. Audrey Roos was Lady Imogene Ferrers in "The Paradol Chamber."

The Adventure of the Conk-Singleton Papers

NARRATOR: Crime marches on! ... A long, thin silhouette emerges against the gaslight. Here is an unpublished record: "In turning over my notes of some twenty years I cannot find any startling event on New Year's Eve except that which is forever associated with the Conk-Singleton Papers. On New Year's Eve of 1887, it is perhaps unnecessary to state, Mr. Sherlock Holmes did not wear a paper hat and blow squeakers at the Hotel Metropole. Far into the night, while the wind howled round our sitting room in 221B Baker Street, Holmes sat bending over a microscope. ..."

(SHERLOCK HOLMES *at microscope,* WATSON *immersed in a copy of H. Rider Haggard's* King Solomon's Mines)

HOLMES *(after a moment looks up and stares glassily out at audience):* It is spinach, Watson. Unquestionably, it is spinach!

WATSON: Holmes, you amaze me! What new wizardry is this?

HOLMES *(rising):* It means a man's life, Watson. The gardener was lying when he said he found Riccoletti's body in the gooseberry bushes. *(He rubs his hands.)* I think, perhaps, a note to our friend Lestrade ...

WATSON *(jumps up):* Holmes! Merciful Heaven. I had forgotten!

HOLMES: Forgotten what?

WATSON: A note for you was delivered by hand this morning. You must forgive me. I was attending the funeral of my last patient.

HOLMES *(impatiently):* The letter, Watson! The letter! *(*WATSON *takes note from his pocket, hands it to* HOLMES, *who examines postmark, holds letter up to light, then opens with care and reads.)* "There will call upon you tonight, at three o'clock in the morning precisely, a gentleman who desires to consult you about a matter of the deepest moment. Be in your chamber at that hour, and do not take it amiss if the visitor wears a mask."

WATSON: This is indeed a mystery. What can it mean?

HOLMES: These are deep waters, Watson. If Porlock had not warned me about the Scarborough emeralds . . . *(Thoughtfully)* Three o'clock . . .

(Clock strikes three. Bong! Bong! Bong! Immediately followed by three loud raps on door in same tempo)

WATSON: And that, if I mistake not, is our client now.

(Enter visitor dressed in evening clothes but covered with medals —decorations, stars, ribbons, etc.)

VISITOR: Mr. Sherlock Holmes?

HOLMES: I am Mr. Sherlock Holmes. This is my friend and colleague, Dr. Watson.

VISITOR: You will forgive me, Mr. Holmes, if I do not reveal my identity. I also wear plain evening dress so as not to be conspicuous.

HOLMES *(coldly):* You would be better served, My Lord, if Your Lordship removed the mask.

VISITOR *(staggering back):* You know me, then?

HOLMES: Who could fail to know Lord Cosmo Conk-Singleton, third son of the Duke of Folkstone and private secretary to the Prime Minister?

WATSON: You mean . . . Mr. Gladstone!

VISITOR *(finger at side of nose):* Sssh!

HOLMES *(same):* Ssssh!

WATSON *(same to audience):* Sssssh!

VISITOR: The matter upon which I have come to consult you, Mr. Holmes, is no ordinary one.

HOLMES: It seldom is. Pray be seated.

VISITOR *(sits):* It will be not unknown to you, Mr. Holmes, that for some time there has been—shall we say—disagreement between Mr. Gladstone and Her Gracious Majesty, Queen Victoria. I have here a diplomatic communication in Her Majesty's own hand, sent to Mr. Gladstone on December 15, 1886. You are empowered to read it. *(Hands important-looking document to* HOLMES.*)*

WATSON: These are deep waters, Holmes.

HOLMES: Her Majesty, I perceive, was not amused.

VISITOR: She was indeed *(hesitates)* somewhat vexed. *(Then suddenly amazed)* But how could *you* possibly know—

HOLMES: Her Majesty has twice underlined the word "bastard." And she has placed three exclamation points following her instructions as to what Mr. Gladstone should do with the naval treaty involving a certain foreign power. Surely our inference is obvious.

WATSON: Excellent!

HOLMES: But very superficial. *(Reading again)* "Even that German sausage, my late husband, could have done better." Hmm! Yes! But how do these diplomatic matters concern me?

VISITOR: Mr. Holmes, the Prime Minister has been poisoned!

WATSON: What?

VISITOR: On December 24th Mr. Gladstone received—apparently as a Christmas present from Queen Victoria—a case of Scotch whisky.

HOLMES: I see. And did the case indeed contain whisky?

VISITOR: Whisky, yes. But each bottle was most unhappily charged with two ounces of prussic acid!

WATSON: Merciful heaven! The man is dead!

VISITOR: No, Dr. Watson, no! *Dei gratia,* he still lives! The strength of the whisky neutralized the poison.

HOLMES *(blandly):* Come, come, this is most disappoi—most interesting. Have you any proof, My Lord, that the Prime Minister drank this particular whisky?

VISITOR *(producing document):* Here is a letter of thanks, in Mr. Gladstone's own hand, written on Christmas Eve. Pray read it aloud.

HOLMES: Will you oblige, Watson?

WATSON *(very dignified, clears throat gravely, and reads):* December 24th, 1886. Illustrious Madam: How extremely kind of you to send me this case of whisky for Christmas! I have never tasted such superb whisky in my life. The whisky you have sent me for Christmas is superb. I keep tasting it and how kind of you to sen me thish wondrous whichkey which I keep tasting for Xmas. It really is mosh kind of you to keep sending me this whisky in cases which I kep tashing for whichmas. Hic! Dock, dickory dock, and kissmus.

VISITOR: Can there be any doubt, Mr. Holmes?

HOLMES: None whatever. Then it is your belief, My Lord, that Queen Victoria herself is the poisoner?

VISITOR: No, Mr. Holmes! *(Horrified)* A thousand times, no! But think of the scandal! It bids fair to rend asunder the fabric of the Empire! You must come down to Sussex and investigate. Will you come?

HOLMES: No, My Lord. I will not.

WATSON *(amazed):* Holmes, this is unworthy of you! Why won't you go?

HOLMES: Because this man is not Lord Cosmo Conk-Singleton! *(Sensation.* HOLMES *produces revolver.)* Let me present you, Watson, to none other than Professor Moriarty.

WATSON: Professor Moriarty!

HOLMES: Your double disguise as a younger man, my dear Professor, deceived me for perhaps ten seconds. The note from Mr. Gladstone seems quite genuine. But the letter from Her Majesty is a manifest forgery.

WATSON: Forgery, Holmes?

HOLMES: Her language, Watson! Her language!

WATSON: You mean—

HOLMES: Queen Victoria, Watson, would never have written in so slighting a fashion of her late husband, Prince Albert. They intended the letter to lure me to Sussex while the Scarborough emeralds were stolen from Yorkshire, not knowing *(*HOLMES *produces emeralds from his pocket)* that Lord Scarborough had already given them to me for safekeeping!

VISITOR *(in a grating voice):* One day, Mr. Holmes, you will try my patience too far!

(Curtain)

The Adventure of the Paradol Chamber

NARRATOR *(reading):* "I find recorded in my notebook that it was after dark on a hot evening in August 1887. All day Sherlock Holmes had been moody and distraught. That evening he took up his violin. Leaning back in his armchair, he would close his eyes and scrape carelessly at the fiddle, which was thrown across his knee. Sometimes the chords were sonorous and melancholy. *(In pitch blackness, a few unearthly chords from violin)* Occasionally they were fantastic and cheerful. *(Chords hop.)* I might have rebelled had it not been that he usually terminated them by playing in quick succession a whole series of my favorite airs."

(Violin plays a few bars of Mendelssohn's "Spring Song," then fades. Lights slowly come up. HOLMES *and* WATSON *are sitting on opposite sides of stage, facing audience; table at* HOLMES's *side.* HOLMES *has violin across knee, bow in right hand; lighted pipe in mouth; eyes fixed glassily ahead.* WATSON *wears expression of ecstasy, hand in air as though it has been keeping time to music; copy of* Daily Telegraph *in his lap.)*

WATSON: My dear Holmes, your virtuosity is unrivaled. Pray continue!

HOLMES *(grim; on edge):* I am in no mood for it, Watson. *(He puts down violin and bow on table; gets up.)* My mind is tortured, *obsessed!*

WATSON *(amused):* Surely not—again!—by Professor Moriarty?

HOLMES: He is the Napoleon of crime, Watson! You will find his spider trace, I dare wager, in that very newspaper. What is the first item on which your eye falls?

WATSON *(scanning paper):* By Jove, Holmes, this *is* curious!

HOLMES: Quick, Watson, the item!

WATSON *(reading):* "Lord Matchlock, the Foreign Minister, collapsed in a faint as he was walking up Constitution Hill after leaving Buckingham Palace."

HOLMES: Ah!

WATSON: "We are happy to report, however, that Lord Matchlock's condition is not serious."

HOLMES: I wonder!

WATSON: "Messrs. Lestrade, Gregson and Athelney Jones, all of Scotland Yard, pronounce it a heat stroke. Lord Matchlock, on a hot day, was wearing a heavy frock coat, bombazine waistcoat, wing collar and Ascot tie, long flannel underwear, woolen socks, and Hessian boots. He therefore—"

(Violent reaction from HOLMES: WATSON *starts.)* My dear Holmes! What can be wrong with you?

HOLMES: *There's villainy here!*

WATSON *(taken aback):* You jest, my dear fellow!

HOLMES: He was wearing no trousers, Watson! Lord Matchlock was wearing no trousers!

WATSON *(pause; stunned):* Holmes, this is marvelous!

HOLMES *(waving it away):* Elementary! But not uninstructive. Scotland Yard, of course, observed nothing.

WATSON: But why should Lord Matchlock, the Foreign Minister, have been walking up Constitution Hill without his britches?

HOLMES *(somber):* There lies our problem. If only . . .

(Sharp knocking is heard off.)

WATSON: A client, Holmes!

HOLMES: Perhaps even the answer to our problem. Come in!

(Enter LADY IMOGENE FERRERS, *in a state of restrained terror. She carries a paper parcel. In violent agitation, she looks from* HOLMES *to* WATSON: *finally chooses* HOLMES.)

IMOGENE: *You* are Mr. Sherlock Holmes! Every fiber of my woman's instinct tells me so! *(She rushes to seize* HOLMES *by the shoulders.)* Help me, Mr. Holmes!

HOLMES *(austerely):* Pray compose yourself, madam. I shall do my best. A chair, Watson! *(He leads her to* WATSON's *chair, and goes to his own.)* A cup of hot coffee, too, might be not unwelcome. I perceive that you are shivering.

IMOGENE: Alas, sir, it is not the cold which makes me shiver!

HOLMES: Not the cold? What then?

IMOGENE: It is fear, Mr. Holmes. It is terror! I am Lady Imogene Ferrers. My father is Lord Matchlock, the Foreign Minister.

WATSON *(bursting out):* They have stolen your papa's britches!

IMOGENE: I think you must be wizards, both of you! For I came here, Mr. Holmes, to show you . . . there! *(Rising dramatically, she opens the paper parcel and holds up in majesty a pair of trousers.)*

WATSON *(amazed):* Merciful heaven! Britches!

HOLMES *(exalted):* It is for these dramatic moments that my soul lives! Tell me, Lady Imogene: are they your father's trousers?

IMOGENE: No, Mr. Holmes! No! I had not thought, until this moment, that dear Papa was trouserless.

HOLMES: Ha! Then how came the trousers into your possession?

IMOGENE: This morning, Mr. Holmes, they were thrown from an upper window at Buckingham Palace. I saw them fall.

WATSON: Holmes, some fiend is snatching the britches from half London!

HOLMES: Good, Watson! But not, I think, quite good enough. May I see the evidence? *(She hands over the trousers.* HOLMES *scrutinizes them through a magnifying glass. Then to* LADY IMOGENE*)* Buckingham Palace, I think you said?

IMOGENE: Yes. Mr. Holmes. My father had gone there for a conference with the new French Ambassador, M. de Paradol, and Her Majesty the Queen. *(Faltering)* It—it concerned, I think, a secret treaty between France and Great Britain. Can you picture my dread —nay, my terror!—when I saw the trousers take wing from Her Majesty's window?

HOLMES: These are deep waters, my lady. Were you followed here?

IMOGENE: I hope not, Mr. Holmes! All day I have been riding in four-wheelers! And yet . . . *(Off, heavy and elaborate knocking)*

HOLMES: Quick, Watson! Make haste and hide the evidence! *(*HOLMES *hands the trousers to* WATSON, *who thrusts them inside his frock coat.* WATSON *turns and moves towards door.)*

WATSON: Holmes, this is no ordinary client! This is . . .

HOLMES: Speak out, man!

WATSON *(stepping back to one side like a court chamberlain):* His Excellency the French Ambassador!

(Enter M. DE MARQUIS DE PARADOL: top hat, frock coat, imperial beard. He swoops forward, center, removing hat, and adopts posture of immense dignity.)

PARADOL *(drawn up):* Messieurs! *(To IMOGENE, different tone)* Mademoiselle!

IMOGENE *(crying out):* You have come here, sir, about the hideous enigma at Buckingham Palace?

PARADOL *(fierce dignity):* I 'ave come 'ere, mademoiselle, to get *my pants!*

HOLMES: Are we to understand that Your Excellency's trousers have disappeared too?

PARADOL: No, no, no! Not deesappear. At Buckingham Palace, in de presence of Her Majesty de Queen, I 'ave remove my pants and throw dem out of de window!

WATSON: No!

PARADOL: But yes! All of a sudden I see—in a mirror!—six men in de masks and de false whiskers, which are creeping up on me to attack me. I cry: *Vive la France!* and do my duty. No pants.

IMOGENE: You performed this in the presence of Her Majesty?

PARADOL: I regret! She pushes a great cry and faints—boum!—on a gold sofa. And to you, mademoiselle, I weesh also to apologize.

IMOGENE: You owe me no apology.

PARADOL: I regret! It is I who have pinch the pants of your papa! I conk him on de onion wit a blackjack—*voilà!*—because I must 'ave pants to follow *you.*

WATSON: The diplomatic service is sadly changed. But why should these wretches wish to purloin your britches?

PARADOL: You 'ave 'eard, perhaps, of the Paradol-Matchlock Treaty between England and France?

IMOGENE: The secret treaty! Yes!

HOLMES *(to Paradol):* And the secret treaty, I think, is in Your Excellency's trousers?

PARADOL *(staggered):* Quel homme! Quel homme magnifique!

(As he speaks, HOLMES takes the trousers from under WATSON's coat.)

HOLMES: A secret chamber—two thin plates of copper—hides the secret treaty. May I return these valuables to Your Excellency? *(Bowing)*

PARADOL *(receiving trousers):* Monsieur! In de name of my government, in de name of all France, I . . . *(He breaks off, staring; and begins to examine the trousers feverishly.)*

IMOGENE: You are agitated, M. de Paradol. Is the copper chamber not there?

PARADOL: The copper chamber, yes! But de treaty . . . is gone!

IMOGENE: *Gone!*

WATSON: *Gone!!*

HOLMES: Have no fear, my dear sir. The secret treaty is still in *this* room. It has merely been abstracted by a thief and a traitor!

WATSON: Not Professor Moriarty?

HOLMES: Not Professor Moriarty, no. But his chief lieutenant—and the second most dangerous man in London—stands—here! *(He whips the false mustache off WATSON, who stands snarling.)*

IMOGENE: But that's Dr. Watson!

HOLMES: No, Lady Imogene. The real Watson lies bound and gagged in some den of infamy. May I introduce you to Colonel Sebastian Moran.

WATSON *(shouting):* Curse you, Holmes! May you die of a bullet from my air gun!

PARADOL: But how—why did you suspect de wretch?

HOLMES: A very simply matter, I assure you. When he recognized a *new* French Ambassador, whose appointment has not yet been announced, I knew him for the villain he is. I gave him an opportunity to steal the treaty *(reaches into WATSON's inside pocket and produces impressive-looking document)* and he has done so.

PARADOL *(exultantly):* The Adventure of de Paradol Chamber!

WATSON *(snarling):* No, curse you! The Adventure of the Copper Britches!

The Unicorn Mystery Book Club News, 1949

CARR INTENDED these parodies as no disrespect to the writings of Sir Arthur Conan Doyle or to Watson and Holmes, whom Carr described as "the stout-hearted doctor and the greatest detective of them all." In 1959, in honor of the one hundredth anniversary of Doyle's birth, he edited a collection of Doyle's tales. "Here in these stories," Carr wrote in the introduction, "you will find that sense of wonder that keeps joy and zest alive, and the picturesqueness we have all but lost, and the humanity which (it is to be hoped) we shall never lose." This admiration for Doyle's works was reflected in Carr's adaptation of Holmes stories for BBC radio and in the 1954 book *The Exploits of Sherlock Holmes,* written by Carr and Doyle's son, Adrian Conan Doyle. In this book, which contains the finest serious pastiches of Holmes, the great detective solves cases which Watson alluded to but never recounted in Doyle's original stories. Two of the *Exploits* contain Carr's hallmark, the impossible crime. "The Adventure of the Sealed Room" tells of a locked-room murder, and "The Adventure of the Highgate Miracle" concerns the disappearance of a man almost before the eyes of the onlookers. Holmes is thus confronted with what might be called Carrian crimes.

ESSAYS

"TO WRITE GOOD HISTORY," John Dickson Carr remarked, "is the noblest work of man." Throughout his writing career, Carr was fascinated by the past. He described his first novel-length manuscript, written in Paris about 1928 and later destroyed, as "an historical romance with lots of Gadzookses and swordplay." In his later career he became the master of the period detective novel, but even his early stories, which take place in the present, are dominated by a sense of the past. For example, the crimes in the first Sir Henry Merrivale novel, *The Plague Court Murders* (1934), seem to have been committed by the ghost of a seventeenth-century hangman's assistant, and in other Carr stories modern murders imitate centuries-old crimes.

Carr was entranced by what one of his characters calls "the dusty records of the past where so much sparkle of life is imprisoned." Through his wide reading in the literature of ancient dirty work, Carr in his essay "Stand and Deliver!" was able to release that sparkle of life in a series of colorful vignettes of seventeenth- and eighteenth-century highwaymen. This article, which was Carr's last work except for his book reviews in *Ellery Queen's Mystery Magazine*, was intended as the first installment of a series that was to include (in Carr's words) "discussions of pirates, murderers, housebreakers, roaring girls, and other wearers of the motley." Unfortunately, his increasingly poor health prevented him from completing the series, but what a book that would have made!

As the final John Dickson Carr work in this book, we include "The Grandest Game in the World," which summarizes Carr's attitude toward the craft of detective fiction. He wrote this essay in 1946 as the introduction to what was planned as an ambitious anthology, *The Ten Best Detective Novels.* He chose, as what he preferred to call "ten *of the* best" detective novels, A. Conan Doyle's *The Valley of Fear,* Gaston Leroux's *The Mystery of the Yellow Room,* A. E. W. Mason's *At the Villa Rose,* Agatha Christie's *Death on the Nile,* Ellery Queen's *The Lamp of God,* Anthony Berkeley's *The Poisoned Chocolates Case,* S. S. Van Dine's *The Greene Murder Case,* Philip MacDonald's *Murder Gone Mad,* Rex Stout's *The League of Frightened Men,* and Dorothy L. Sayers's *The Nine Tailors.* All excellent choices, but as Ellery Queen pointed out, there is one notable omission: "Where, oh, where in Mr. Carr's anthology is a writer named John Dickson Carr, or his *alter ego,* Carter Dickson?" Although obviously a Carr story belongs in a collection of the ten greatest detective novels, Carr's anthology would nevertheless have been a notable achievement. But three of the original publishers refused to grant reprint rights, and the book never appeared. In 1963, however, Queen rescued Carr's introductory essay from oblivion, and Carr added a postscript for its publication in *Ellery Queen's Mystery Magazine.*

I envy anyone coming upon Carr's essays for the first time. The reader feels that he is listening to a fine raconteur at an English club (say, the Naughts-and-Crosses) talking about those perpetually fascinating topics, crime and the authors who write about it.

A Note About the Complete "Grandest Game In The World"

In the preface to the 1947 collection, *Dr. Fell, Detective and Other Stories,* Ellery Queen said that Carr's choice for the Sayers novel to appear in *The Ten Best Detective Novels* was *The Nine Tailors.* He repeated that statement when half of "The Grandest Game in the World" appeared in a 1963 issue of *Ellery Queen's Mystery Magazine,* and as indicated in the epilogue ("Second Thoughts—After Seventeen Years"), Carr himself had come to believe that he had chosen *The Nine Tailors.* In fact, however, Carr had discussed a different Sayers novel, *Strong Poison,* in the full "Grandest Game in the World." We have decided to let this contradiction remain.

Stand and Deliver!

THE TITLE PAGE of my own five-volume edition impressively reads: *The Complete Newgate Calendar,* being: *Captain Charles Johnson's* General History of the Lives and Adventures of the Most Famous Highwaymen, Murderers, Street-Robbers, and Account of the Voyages and Plunders of the Most Notorious Pyrates, 1734; *Captain Alexander Smith's* Compleat History of the Lives and Robberies of the Most Notorious Highwaymen, Foot-Pads, Shop-Lifts and Cheats, 1719; The Tyburn Chronicle, 1768; The Malefactor's Register, 1796; *George Borrow's* Celebrated Trials, 1825; The Newgate Calendar, by *Andrew Knapp and William Baldwin,* 1826; *Camden Pelham's* Chronicles of Crime, 1841, etc., collated and edited with some appendices by J. L. Rayner and G. T. Crook (London: privately printed for the Navarre Society Limited, 23 New Oxford Street, W.C. 1, MCMXXVI).

Frequently I dip into it; here is dirty work in plenty. Beginning with Thomas Dun, the probably mythical monster who led a lunatic band of robbers in Bedfordshire during the reign of King Henry the First (1100–1135), this rodeo of villainy comes whooping down the centuries to James Inglett, a venerable "cow-leech" or vet ninety-four years old, who carelessly administered arsenic to a young girl among his patients at the full tide of Victorianism in 1841.

One great charm of the earliest compilers, Captains Smith and

Johnson in the eighteenth century, is their delightful gullibility. They will swallow any tale and relate any anecdote, from the merely far-fetched to the outrageous, provided it makes a good story. So far as entertainment goes, who cares? At the same time, if we are to study these cases as fact, we must apply the test of historical research no less than the test of common sense. There are many classifications: murderers, housebreakers, roaring girls who combined prostitution with thievery. And we can do worse than begin with those polished aristocrats of roguedom, the highwaymen of the seventeenth and eighteenth centuries.

He was one hell of a fellow, this highwayman, idol of small boys and darling of the ladies. They liked to think of him as a gentleman; usually, whatever his background, he affected the airs and dress of one. His brutality they accepted with tolerance; it was a brutal age. Modern verses give us a picture of the highwayman for the delight of romantic people.

> He'd a French cocked hat on his forehead, a bunch of lace at
>   his chin,
> A coat of the claret velvet, and breeches of brown doeskin:
> They fitted with never a wrinkle; his boots were up to the
>   thigh,
> And he rode with a jewelled twinkle,
>   His pistol butts a-twinkle,
> His rapier hilt a-twinkle, under the jewelled sky.

That costume suggests middle eighteenth century, when the huge periwigs of Stuart times had dwindled into more manageable hairpieces under the first two Georges. Though the most fashionable highwayman is unlikely to have worn jeweled sword or pistols, pistols he assuredly did carry: two in saddle holsters, with four to six more stuck through his belt. On the roads and heaths round London, his career was generally a short one. He trusted a friend or a mistress, who betrayed him; he got drunk and betrayed himself; he took on odds too heavy and was brought down after firing his last pistol.

Followed trial, sentence, the few sweet days of lording it among admirers at Newgate Prison. Then, one morning, the great bell boomed at St. Sepulchre's. They put our hero into a cart, the sheriff going before and the javelin men around. Seated on his coffin, with chaplain and hangman in attendance, he was driven the mile and a half along Tyburn Road, now Oxford Street, to three-armed Tyburn gallows. That little procession would halt more than once on the way. Like the gallant in the ballad, who "rode stately to Tyburn to die in his calling,"

> He stopped at the "George" for a bottle of sack,
> And promised to pay for it when he came back.

Easygoing custom allowed him to get royally loaded before Tyburn hove in sight. They saw no harm in this; the parson and the executioner were apt to be drunk too. At Tyburn, if he played the game according to the rules, he made an affecting speech to the spectators, repented in tears, and was jerked into hell before an appreciative crowd.

The first noted highwayman to have his exploits recorded was one Isaac Atkinson, who flourished during the first fifteen years of Charles the First's reign, and had a longer career than most. Son of a well-to-do landowner of Faringdon in Berkshire, young Isaac did little good at Brasenose College, Oxford. There he learned chiefly to "rail at the statutes of the university, lampoon the rulers, wear his clothes after the mode, curse his tutor, and sell his books," before being hauled home by an angry and disappointed father.

At home he did no better. Addicted to "extravagance and lechery," any convenient woman serving his turn, he painted the countryside red until his outraged parent disinherited him and turned him out of doors. Making for London, Isaac soon spent what little money he had. A desperate young man returned forthwith to Berkshire. Arrived back home, he broke into the house one night, robbed his father—who by this time must really have been in a state—of "fifty pounds in silver and one hundred and twenty broad-pieces of gold," left some jeering doggerel in the family Bible, and decamped with the best horse in the stables.

The following Sunday, passing through Uxbridge on his way to London, Isaac went to church in a mood less than reverent. The parson preached from 1 Thess. 2, "For ye know that the day of the

Lord cometh as a thief in the night," a sermon so full of zealous and pious exhortation that, muses the compiler, "any man less hardened in impiety than Atkinson must have gone away deeply affected."

It had indeed affected Isaac. When the service was over, and the clergyman had set off alone across the fields, our hero dogged the parson along the same path and overtook him half a mile from town.

"Stand and deliver!" says Isaac.

"Young sir, what do you mean by this?"

"I mean," replied the prodigal, "to let you know that all thieves do not come in the night. The next time you preach, you may tell the people that the day of the Lord cometh like a thief at noon: which, in my opinion, is a much better simile. At night we are led to expect thieves; but who the devil ever feared being robbed at noonday so near a town?"

Though unconvinced by this interpretation of Scripture, the dominie had no choice. He delivered up a silver watch and one pound eighteen shillings in cash. Forcing him off the path and trussing him securely with strips torn from the clerical gown, Isaac bolted in triumph with the fruits of his first daylight robbery.

Another of his victims is said to have been no less a personage than "that great Gamaliel of the law" William Noye, attorney general to King Charles. Both were on horseback when Isaac accosted him a mile or two outside London.

"Sir," began the highwayman, a flowery sort of fellow, "I have a writ of *Capias ad Computandum* against you, which requires an account of all the money in your pocket."

If you must put the heat on an eminent lawyer, no doubt this is the way to address him. Asked on what authority he served the writ, Isaac produced a brace of pistols.

"These weapons, sir, have as much authority in them as any tipstaff in England. Of this you shall be convinced, if you make any delay."

William Noye is described by his contemporaries *(Dictionary of National Biography,* vol. xiv, p. 699) as a man of humorous mind. Here his nonchalance seems to have been superb. "The Attorney-General had no more to say," our chronicler explains, "but very contentedly gave him a purse well lined, and they parted with mutual compliments."

Whether or not we believe this story, certain it is that Isaac Atkinson became the terror of all lawyers. He rode the circuits like any barrister or solicitor, plundering whom he would. In one eight-month period he is supposed to have held up more than 160 lawyers in the county of Norfolk alone, for an estimated haul of £3000. Finding the gentlemen of the long robe easy game, he would attack three, four, even five of them at once. And always he escaped, until tripped by an encounter from which he could have gained little profit.

The intended victim was an old market woman mounted on a white mare. Cantering magnificently through Turnham Green one wet, muddy afternoon in the summer of 1640, Isaac saw in her hands a purse full of halfpennies. Imagining it contained more than it actually did, he crowded her towards the hedge. With much spirit the old woman flung the purse over the hedge into a field beyond and rode hard for the neighboring town of Brentford to give the alarm.

It would get him nothing to pursue her; Isaac wanted the money. Dismounting, he climbed through the hedge into the field. His horse, having taken a fancy to the market woman's white mare, and as alert for venery as Isaac himself, instantly galloped off in pursuit of the mare. Deprived of his horse, our hero was now in trouble. Rain had made the field a quagmire in which he sank to the calves of his fine jackboots. However he writhed and cursed, he could pull neither his boots from the mire nor his feet from the boots, and he lacked a knife to cut himself free. The scourge of lawyers was stuck like a fly in treacle. At this juncture he heard the view-halloo bellow of ten men racing out from Brentford to take him.

Isaac's temper boiled over. "God damme! Must I lose my liberty to a parcel of clods like these?" With the four pistols in his belt he slaughtered four of those who closed in, badly wounding a fifth with his sword. The other five set on him and pulled him down.

That finished Isaac Atkinson. In prison he tried and failed to kill himself before sentence could be carried out. He was hanged at Tyburn in that same summer of 1640, cursing the chaplain and jeering at authority until the end. Just two years later King

Charles's standard went up at Nottingham, and civil war ripped apart the nation into camps of Roundhead and Cavalier.

During the next two decades—troubled days of war, and of the Commonwealth under Oliver Cromwell after wheeling and dealing Parliament men had cut off the king's head—any tales of highwaymen must be approached with great caution. Most of these swashbucklers were, or professed to be, fire-eating Cavaliers. They loved to rob a canting Puritan, whom they called (often with justice) a canting hypocrite, and to quote Scripture back at him while they robbed. But the chroniclers of their adventures had royalist sympathies too. So numerous are the legends of highly placed Roundhead officials waylaid, mocked and plundered that to accept all such accounts were to show the rest of us as gullible as the chroniclers themselves.

On the other hand, it is quite possible that "Captain" James Hind —no captain, but a butcher's apprentice before he took to the high toby—really did hold up the coach of Colonel Harrison, most fanatical of all the regicides, and of John Bradshaw, presiding judge at the trial of King Charles. He may well have shouted to Bradshaw, as they say he did, "I fear neither you nor any king-killing son of a whore alive. I have now as much power over you as you lately had over the king. Your money or your life!"

Such incidents have been called possible, even probable. James Hind merits special mention; no other mere outlaw was treated with such ferocity by the Roundhead government. Hind had committed several murders. If they had merely wanted him disposed of, this charge (or robbery itself) would have been enough. Instead they went out of their way to be merciless. Convicted of high treason, Hind was hanged, drawn and quartered—the whole filthy sentence—on September 24, 1652.

Exploits still more sensational are credited to Captain Zachary Howard, who really was a captain, and had raised a troop of horse for King Charles. He is also supposed to have fought valiantly in 1651, when the man who afterwards became Charles the Second tried in vain to topple Oliver Cromwell at the battle of Worcester. In the king's cause young Zachary Howard had mortgaged his estate for £20,000. Having lost everything when the Saints triumphed, he swore vengeance against Cromwell and all the tribe.

Zachary Howard is said to have waylaid the Earl of Essex, "Traitor Essex," one of the original Roundhead commanders. Perhaps so. But his escapade against the wife and daughter of "Black Tom" Fairfax, a still more eminent Roundhead general, followed by the robbery and humiliation of great Cromwell himself, forms a tale so tangled and confused that no study can set the record straight. Some truth there may be in all this, but how much?

For the tale tells, James Branch Cabell–wise, that in the summer of 1650 "Black Tom" Fairfax was being feted at Newcastle-on-Tyne by the mayor and aldermen, who presented him with a gift of silver plate. Recently Fairfax had sent his wife and his only daughter south to Faringdon in Berkshire (to Berkshire, so very far from their home, and to Faringdon, birthplace of the late Isaac Atkinson?). Wanting to send the silver service too, he told his newest servant to pack it in a portmanteau, choose a good horse, and carry the gift to his wife.

Redoubtable Zachary Howard, shadowing Fairfax in hope of revenge, heard of this errand at a tavern. He rode after the servant and, pretending to be the most canting of Puritans, struck up an acquaintance with the Roundhead messenger. They journeyed together amicably until they were within a day's ride of Faringdon, at which time Zachary revealed himself and demanded the portmanteau.

The servant, as resolute as Captain Howard himself, wouldn't give in. Both men drew and fired. Since neither seems to have been what today would be described as a Top Gun, they exchanged shots until the servant drilled Zachary's horse and Zachary drilled the servant's head.

On the body of the slain Roundhead, Zachary found a letter from Fairfax to his wife. The contents of this curious document are given in full. Dated at Newcastle on August 12, 1650, it is supposed to have said:

> My dear—Hoping that you and my daughter Elizabeth are in good health, this comes to acquaint you that my presence is so agreeable to the inhabitants of this place, that their mayor and aldermen have presented me with a large quantity of plate, which I have sent to you by my man Thomas, a new servant; whom I would have you treat very kindly, he being recommended to me by several gentlemen as a very

honest, worthy man. The Lord be praised, I am very well, and earnestly long for the happiness of enjoying your company.

Back to bold Zachary Howard! Hiding the portmanteau in a hollow tree, he rode on to Faringdon. Here he presented the letter, introducing himself as Thomas, the new servant, and explained that because of the danger from robbers he had lodged the silver for safekeeping at an inn along the road. Pleased at such sober, prudent behavior, Lady Fairfax ordered him to bed so that he might rest from the fatigue of his journey.

The household at this time, says our chronicler, consisted only of the wife, the daughter, two maids and two menservants. When everybody had turned in for the night, Zachary Howard intimidated the servants at pistol point; he bound and gagged them all. Proceeding to the bedroom of Lady Fairfax and her daughter, he bound and gagged them too. He then raped both ladies, beginning with the daughter, and concluded by rifling the house of "two thousand broad-pieces and some silver." But a reward was posted for his capture, so he fled to Ireland.

Let's test the story a little.

It must be remembered that in 1648 "Black Tom" Fairfax had succeeded to his father's title as third Lord Fairfax. In June of 1650 he gave up his commission in the Commonwealth Army and retired permanently to a country house in Yorkshire. Just possibly the ex-general owned another house in the south, sending his family there for the summer. And the Fairfaxes did have one daughter, though at the time of the alleged rape she would have been only twelve years old. This need not embarrass belief; *Lolita* has prepared us for anything. But the young lady was named Mary, with no Elizabeth in her baptismal register, and presumably papa knew his daughter's name.

In Ireland, we are told, Zachary Howard robbed so many dupes and made his name so notorious that he thought it safer to return. He landed at Highlake and put up at an inn in Chester, where chance gave him the opportunity for his boldest stroke. To that same inn came none other than Oliver Cromwell, old Noll in person, visiting Chester with "a troop of horse."

By other dates of the narrative this must have been in 1652, a year before Cromwell became Lord Protector. Zachary played his usual trick: affecting to be a man of the deepest piety, he gained the dictator's ear and confidence. Late one night, alone with his victim in the latter's room, he walloped Cromwell over the head with a pistol butt and tied *him* up. "In a couple of trunks" Zachary found "about eleven hundred jacobuses," quite some haul. As a last humiliation he emptied on Cromwell the contents of a close stool, the vehicle for indoor sanitation in those days, and escaped with the 1100 jacobuses (or jacobi).

This takes some believing too. The Cromwell it pictures is as unconvincing as the sentimental Cromwell of *Curfew Shall Not Ring Tonight.* Though no domestic ogre, old Noll, in addition to being extremely tough and suspicious, had alert guards in uneasy times. And the jacobus, a gold coin worth from twenty to twenty-four shillings, was minted only in the reign of James the First (1603–1625). Unless Cromwell had been hoarding them, a trait foreign to his character, he is far from likely to have carried such a load in his luggage.

Zachary Howard's career was nearly over—something of a relief, since the record has grown far too scrambled. Our chronicler keeps his hero in Ireland between 1650 and 1652, forgetting that he has already placed Zachary at the battle of Worcester in 1651. Not long after the humiliation of Cromwell, if in truth anything like it ever occurred, the real-life Zachary was unwise enough to challenge half a dozen former Roundhead officers on Blackheath. One he killed, two he wounded in the ensuing fight; the rest haled him before a magistrate, who committed him to Maidstone Jail.

Trial and sentence followed swiftly. He suffered in 1652, the same year as James Hind. Eternal legend, of course, has Cromwell present at the execution. But there was no charge of treason; he would hang, without trimmings, for robbery and murder.

"Good people," Zachary said on the scaffold, "I am truly sorry for the murders I have done. And yet, since they were done only against a crew of cursed Roundhead rogues, I must own I regret them less than I should. God save the king!"

And so they hanged him at Maidstone, when he was only thirty-two.

In May of 1660, King Charles the Second, "the best that ever reigned over us," was restored to the throne of his fathers. Henceforward, for his reign at least, there was a pattern less crude. The highwayman dances to a merrier measure under the Merry Monarch, even when he dances on air. Which leads us inevitably to Claude Duval.

No pop singer of today has made so many feminine hearts flutter as did handsome Claude. Born in France, by trade a footman, he learned much of the English language and still more of polite deportment in the service of British masters in Paris. Not yet twenty, already a skilled performer on the flageolet and on females, he crossed the Channel in the Duke of Richmond's household, but soon broke free for other business.

And he became quite a lad; we can't doubt it. His own little gang of highwaymen elected him their leader. In a proclamation listing the malefactors most wanted by the law, Claude's name, like Abou ben Adam's, led all the rest. For indoor work he was a practiced cardsharp, and his technique with women proved irresistible. "Those eyes of yours, madam, have undone me!" Or, "Oh, that I could by any means in the world recommend myself to your ladyship's notice!" One adventure of his, true or false, has been repeated persistently for three hundred years.

To Claude at the Tangier Tavern came word that a certain wealthy knight and his lady would enter town by way of Hampstead Heath, with a cache of £400 in their coach. Under bright moonlight that night, as the coach jolted across the heath, its occupants saw three or four mounted men, Claude's gang, skulking ahead. The lady in the coach with her husband—or her boyfriend, this part is not clear—immediately took up a flageolet and played a lively air.

Well, anyway, the story says she did. *The Concise Oxford Dictionary* describes the flageolet both as "a small flute blown at the end" and as "a kind of kidney-bean," though we must suppose this lady played the former. Up galloped Claude Duval, resplendent with periwig and feathered hat, himself playing a flageolet in reply.

"Sir," said he to the knight, "your lady plays excellently, and I make no doubt she dances as well. Will you both please to step out of the coach, and let me have the honor of dancing with her on the heath?"

This sounds like Charles Boyer at his best. Down climbed the lady and her escort. Claude, after leading her through one coranto, with great politeness handed the lady back.

"But, sir," pointed out Claude, "you have forgot to pay for the music!"

The poised nobleman, replying that he never forgot such debts, reached under the back seat of the coach; he took out and handed over £100.

"You are liberal, sir," courteously continued Duval, "and shall have no cause to regret it. This hundred so generously given has excused you the other three hundred pounds, which you have with you in the coach at this moment. Keep them safe for your comfort; a good journey, sir, and now good night!"

All right, so they danced in the moonlight; but one question must still provoke curiosity. Who played the flageolet for that impromptu coranto? Was it some member of Claude's gang, another musical virtuoso? Or the accommodating knight who saved three hundred of his four hundred quid? Whoever piped or whoever paid, they could do things handsomely in good King Charles's golden day.

Other episodes show Claude in a light less amiable, as when he stripped the trinkets from a whole coachful of ladies and wouldn't even give back a child's silver sucking bottle. His full story has never been told; it has never been known. The law took him one day when he was drunk, at the Hole-in-the-Wall in Chandos Street. But everybody forgave him when he had been sentenced. His levees at Newgate were great social occasions. So was his execution.

They gave him the business at Tyburn on January 21, 1670. Ladies of quality thronged to the gallows, their eyes blind with tears behind the vizard masks they wore to any dubious spectacle like a hanging or a theatrical performance. Nor did his honors end when his legs ceased to twitch. Borne in a mourning coach to Claude's favorite tavern, his body lay in state in a black-draped room with tapers burning round the bier and black-clad mourners openly weeping. He was buried in Covent Garden Church, itself a social achievement, under a stone with this epitaph:

> Here lies Duval. Reader, if male thou art,
> Look to thy purse; if female, to thy heart.

Much havoc hath he made of both, for all
Men he made stand, and women he made fall.

It would please me to linger on the career of William Cady, a true
hellion who roved, robbed and died in the reign of James the Second. Will Cady, son of an eminent surgeon, earned a B.A. at Trinity
College, Cambridge. Left impoverished by his father's death, he
bought pistols, took to the highway and showed his mettle first
crack out of the box. Riding across Hounslow Heath one summer
afternoon in 1685, he overtook two horsemen with whom he fell into
talk: a gentleman whose name is not given and one Captain Chevalier, a Frenchman with a commission in the First or Grenadier
Guards. Will waited until nobody else was in sight. Without more
ado he shot the civilian dead and whirled on the other with an order
to stand and deliver.

"I am a captain in the Guards," the Frenchman snapped at him.
"Any rogue who wants my money must fight for it."

"If you are a soldier," quoth Will, "you have learned to obey a
command. Hand over!"

Roared Captain Chevalier, "You are an unconscionable son of a
bitch—"

In passing, let's consider that term "son of a bitch." Though today
never heard in Britain and unknown except as an Americanism, it is
in actual fact old English. Characters in the uninhibited novels of
Tobias Smollett (1720–1770) frequently wallop out with it. Sir Walter
Scott records a conversation alleged to have been held between Dr.
Samuel Johnson and Adam Smith, author of *The Wealth of Nations*.
According to this account, Adam Smith told Dr. Johnson that David
Hume, the Scots historian, had died very tranquilly though still
abjuring all religious faith. Whereupon Dr. Johnson called Adam
Smith a liar, and Adam Smith called Dr. Johnson a son of a bitch.
This seems to have been the only meeting or exchange of compli-
ments between the great lexicographer and the great economist.

But we have left Will Cady and Captain Chevalier astride their
horses, glaring at each other on Hounslow Heath.

"You are an unconscionable son of a bitch," roared Captain
Chevalier, not without reason on his side, "to demand money of me,
who never owed you any."

"There's not a man travels the road but owes me money," retorted Will, with less cogent reasoning. "Pay me; pay instantly!"

Captain Chevalier fired from the hip and missed; Will shot the captain's horse. Now less bold, the Frenchman disgorged. Nailing his victim's coattail to a nearby tree (did he carry ironmongery as Claude Duval carried a flute?), Will rode away with a watch, a diamond ring and a purse of twenty-six guineas.

Following a too-daring robbery soon afterwards, it is related that he fled abroad and took refuge at an English seminary in Flanders. Our chronicler, much impressed by Will's Cambridge degree, calls him a scholar and says he was "admitted, upon the superior's examination" into the fraternity of Benedictine Friars, where he remained for two years. We may well believe Will had no liking for poverty or chastity, and schemed only to ease out of the seminary as soon as he could raise the cash for getting back to England. It is in explaining Will's departure that the chronicler seems to skid and land on his ear.

Among the fair penitents who had chosen Will Cady for their confessor, he declares, were two young gentlewomen as handsome as they were rich. (Even if the Benedictines let Will stay there, would they have allowed him to hear confessions?) Anyway, the next time these young ladies visited the seminary, it is related, Will heard their confessions separately; then, bringing them together and covering both with a pistol, he swore they must hear *his* confession.

He was in great need of money, he said. Unless they supplied him at once, or if they made any noise at all, they should have a bullet for their pains. The girls, terrified, between them yielded up a sum in French money equal to more than £40 sterling, as well as two diamond rings. Will had not finished. Putting both victims on the bed, he debauched them both (double rape again, egad!). He tied them neck and heels, gagged them, and made haste out of the seminary before any alarm could be raised.

Will's subsequent career was as brief as it was violent. In background ranging from Durham to his favorite stamping ground of Hounslow Heath, in the few months before they caught and hanged him in 1687, one murderous incident blatters after another. On the robbery of a middle-aged hop merchant and his wife, Mr. and Mrs.

John Sandal, the chronicler dwells with a horrified fascination easy to understand.

Mr. and Mrs. Sandal were riding one horse across Hounslow Heath when Will accosted them and ordered them to alight. He also dismounted. The hop merchant provided a good haul, some £28 pounds, but the wife had only half a crown. And Will lost his temper.

"Is this your way of traveling?" he yelled. "What! Carry but half a crown in your pocket, when you are to meet a gentleman collector on the highway? But I'll be even with you, madam; therefore off with that ring on your finger."

"Oh, sir," pleaded Mrs. Sandal, "I entreat you to spare my wedding ring. I would not lose this for double its value; I have kept and worn it above twenty years."

By this time Will was raging. "You whining bitch! Marriage be damned, and you too. What! Because you are a whore by license, must I be more favorable to you than to another woman? Give me the ring this moment without more cant, or," says he, displaying a knife in his left hand, "I'll cut off your finger with the ring on it, as I have served others of your sex before this."

Mrs. Sandal pulled the ring from her finger; but instead of handing it over, she instantly popped it into her mouth and swallowed it. And Will Cady went completely round the bend. Raving, stamping, he swore he would still send her to the devil without her wedding ring, and forthwith shot her through the head. When she lay dead in the road, with his knife he slit her up from navel to chin, and then cut the ring from her innards. This is rough-and-ready surgery with a vengeance, anticipating Jack the Ripper (1888) by almost exactly two hundred years.

Let me repeat that I would linger on Will Cady. Or on Edward and Joan Bracey, who kept an inn by day and went forth for highway robbery by night. Or on Jocelin Harwood, so tough a cookie that his own associates feared him and gave him up to the law. Or on half a dozen more of their kind, as the 1690s rolled into the new century. But it is time to end this survey. We are carried forward to the year 1739, and to the most famous highwayman in history. I refer, of course, to Dick Turpin.

No other outlaw-hero has become so celebrated for something he didn't do. Ever since Harrison Ainsworth published the immensely popular novel *Rookwood* in 1834, it has become fixed in many minds that Dick Turpin on his mare Black Bess for some reason rode from London to York in one day, and that on reaching York the gallant horse fell dead.

Ainsworth dreamed all this. And yet, though Turpin himself never made the famous ride, it has been maintained that somebody else did: one Samuel Nicks, an earlier outlaw of good King Charles's golden day, who by the king himself was dubbed "Swift" Nicks. The distance from London to York is 188 miles. "Swift" Nicks, it has been claimed, did even better.

At Gad's Hill in Kent, some twenty-odd miles *south* of London, Nicks committed a robbery at four o'clock on a summer morning, when it was light enough for his victim to identify him. An alibi must be established, or he was a gone goose.

Crossing the river to Gravesend, Nicks galloped north at such a pace that he reached York in late afternoon, changed his clothes, and appeared on the bowling green to ask what time it was—a quarter to eight—of no less a dignitary than the Lord Mayor. When eventually he was charged with the holdup at Gad's Hill, the jury acquitted him because they wouldn't believe such a feat of horsemanship could be accomplished.

We needn't believe it either. The only authority is Daniel Defoe, who turned out so much fiction disguised as fact that every tale becomes suspect. And that any man covered such a distance in less than fifteen hours—on one horse, over the appalling roads of the time—must be considered, as Huckleberry Finn considered the *Pilgrim's Progress,* "statements interesting, but steep."

What was the truth about Turpin? *The Newgate Calendar* features him, and there is a full record of his trial. Both accounts appeared nearly one hundred years before Ainsworth's novel credited him with the ride to York.

Our story soars to its climax in the third decade of the bawling, brawling eighteenth century. The king was fat little George the Second, jabbering broken English at St. James's Palace; the prime minister was corrupt Sir Robert Walpole, who pretty well proved his thesis that any man may be bought for a price. Rich people could occupy themselves with such stimulating japes as the Hell-

Fire Club or with such charmers as Elizabeth Chudleigh, afterwards Duchess of Kingston, who appeared "all but naked" at a public ball. Poor people got fuddled on cheap gin—"drunk for a penny; dead drunk for twopence; straw for nothing"—and scratched a living as best they could. To the latter class Dick Turpin belonged.

He was born in 1706. His father, a country innkeeper, apprenticed him to a butcher in Whitechapel. When his apprenticeship was finished, Dick married a girl named Joan Palmer. Already he had been stealing sheep and oxen. Nearly nabbed for this, he borrowed some money from his wife and joined a gang of smugglers in Essex, with a sideline in stealing deer. The venture brought little profit; Dick, as leader of four other hard nails like himself, set up a career of robbery and terror.

In this they were more successful. Choosing a lonely farmhouse at nightfall, they would knock at the door, burst in when it opened, and rip the place to pieces. At their first try Dick sat an old woman on the grate over the fire to make her tell where the family's money had been hidden. But a reward of 100 guineas was offered for the gang's arrest; in 1735, when the others had been hanged or dispersed, Turpin retreated to Cambridgeshire and joined forces with a highwayman called Tom King.

Tom King was the character who figures in all romances as Turpin's "great friend." A silent film of many years ago, in which the cowboy star Tom Mix played Dick Turpin, sent him through hair's-breadth escapades to rescue his friend from prison. Reality was a little different.

The firm of Turpin & King did fairly well on the highway until Dick stole a fine horse from a landowner in Epping Forest and had it sent to his favorite haunt, the Red Lion in Whitechapel. A constable named Bayes traced the horse there. Bayes crossed the stable yard and came face to face with Tom King, a much-wanted man. Turpin, galloping into the yard at that moment, saw the constable closing in on his friend.

"Shoot him, Dick, or by God we're taken!" Turpin fired, missed the constable, and shot his friend through the chest. King died the next day, perhaps letting slip enough to put the bloodhounds on Dick's track. Turpin fled to Yorkshire, which may have inspired Ainsworth in the next century. Under the name John Palmer he combined highway robbery with horse stealing. Arrested for horse stealing, he was tried before Sir William Chapple at York Assizes in March of 1739, and turned off at Eastertide as another moral lesson for that moral age.

Legend dies hard. Round London there are still places associated with the name of Dick Turpin. At York, up to a generation ago at least, they would point out to you the exact spot on which Black Bess fell dead under her master. Most of the highwaymen mentioned here, even the most bloody-minded, have shown some spark of imagination or picturesqueness. Turpin showed none; anyone who called *him* a son of a bitch could have pleaded full justification.

Whether or not we are all lawbreakers at heart, certain it is we cherish them whenever we can. It has been done in America with the Western bad man, even with the gangster; England will always have Dick Turpin and Claude Duval. Sixty years ago there was a toast much given at convivial gatherings. Our band of highwaymen never heard it. Two, perhaps three, of its desiderata they never attained or could have hoped to attain. Yet it seems probable that Isaac Atkinson, Zachary Howard, Claude Duval, William Cady, even Turpin himself, would have raised their glasses right lustily to

> A long life and a merry one,
> A quick death and an easy one,
> A true girl and a pretty one.
> A cold drink—and another one.

Ellery Queen's Mystery Magazine, March, April 1973

The Grandest Game in the World

"Do YOU solemnly swear never to conceal a vital clue from the reader?"

"I do."

That is the first article in the oath taken by members of the Detection Club. The candidate, placing his hand upon Eric the Skull, swears this with fervency. He swears it with stern looks fixed on him. He swears it while Eric's eyes (thanks to John Rhode) glow with red electric lights. He swears it even before he promises to honor the King's English, use legitimate detective methods in his stories, and refrain from pinching his fellow members' plots.

And this rule, the *sine qua non* of the profession, must be emphasized at the beginning to explain my choice of stories in *The Ten Best Detective Novels*.

For the once humble detective novel has come a long way. It has gone up hill, down dale, over the plain and through the sewer. In fifty years it has undergone so many changes, not to say disguises, that sometimes we quite literally don't know what we are talking about. A new novel is praised because it is well written, because the characters are admirably drawn, because it is "tough," because it is experimental in technique, because it is written sideways or upside down: on any grounds, in short, except that it is a good detective story.

If the term means anything at all, it means this:

The detective story is a conflict between criminal and detective in which the criminal, by means of some ingenious device—alibi, novel murder method, or what you like—remains unconvicted or even unsuspected until the detective reveals his identity by means of evidence which has also been conveyed to the reader.

That is the skeleton, the framework, the Christmas tree on which all the ornaments are hung. If the skeleton has been badly strung, or the tree clumsily set on its base, no amount of glittering ornament will save it. It falls over with a flop. Its fall may create a momentary sensation, especially among children; but adults are only depressed when they see the same sort of thing happen in fiction.

The author of the book hasn't bothered. He has decided that good construction is of no consequence, or that nobody cares any way. Far from planning in advance every move, every speech, every detail, he has roared ahead on inspiration and trusted to luck. And his attitude is understandable if he is writing a straight thriller, where rapid-fire action swallows up everything. But it becomes merely bad craftsmanship if he thinks he is writing a detective story.

We might postulate, to begin with, that the detective novel at its best will contain three qualities seldom found in the thriller. It will contain the quality of fair play in presenting the clues. It will contain the quality of sound plot construction. And it will contain the quality of ingenuity.

Ingenuity? Do we start an argument here?

It seems remarkable that this need for ingenuity in the *outstanding* detective novel has been so strangely overlooked. Perhaps the reason is that you cannot turn it into a "must"; you cannot lay it down as a rule of the game. You cannot say to an author, "Look here, sit down and be ingenious." Maybe he can't be. Maybe he doesn't want to be. His interests may lie along other lines, such as the hero slugging the police or (more pleasant to read about) the police slugging the hero.

But though this quality of ingenuity is not necessary to the detective story as such, you will never find the great masterpiece without it. Ingenuity lifts the thing up; it is triumphant; it blazes, like a diabolical lightning flash, from beginning to end.

It is not of intrinsic interest to read that X has been stabbed to death in a hotel room, and that the police—after rewinding the clock, or studying the bloodstains, or any of the stock tricks in vogue since the time of Gaboriau—have proved the guilt of Y the waiter. This is all very well; it may be competent work; it will serve to be read if we have nothing better at hand. But in pitting our wits against the masters of the trade, we require something very different.

We require, for instance, the superb explanation of the clock alibi, in A. E. W. Mason's *The House of the Arrow.* Or the means used to conceal the identity of the criminal, in Agatha Christie's *Murder in Mesopotamia.* Or the reason why the corpse wore its clothes the wrong way round, in Ellery Queen's *The Chinese Orange Mystery.* Or the ironic brilliance of Anthony Berkeley's *Trial and Error,* in which a man who has confessed to the murder tries to prove himself guilty and can't do it.

These writers (with others like them) are the aristocrats of the game, the old serpents, the gambit-devisers and trap-baiters whose strokes of ingenuity make the game worth playing at all.

For what, after all, is the game itself?

It is a hoodwinking contest, a duel between author and reader. "I dare you," says the reader, "to produce a solution which I can't anticipate." "Right!" says the author, chuckling over the consciousness of some new and legitimate dirty trick concealed up his sleeve. And then they are at it—pull-devil, pull-murderer—with the reader alert for every dropped clue, every betraying speech, every contradiction that may mean guilt.

Nothing, in fact, shows more clearly the difference between the expert craftsman and the novice than his manner of presenting this evidence. The novice, even when he is anxious to include a clue, develops a case of acute self-consciousness about it. He feels naked before the reader's eye. He is much too afraid of being caught with the goods. So he hurls the clue into the story and then runs like a maniac, as though he had thrown a bomb.

The result is that the clue, one or two words at most, will flash past and become lost among sixty or seventy thousand other words. This is painfully evident during the detective's summing up in the final chapter.

"The whole question of Dagmar Doubledick's guilt," declares the detective, "turns on the kind of necktie he was wearing when we met him that day at Wemmerly Park. Of course you remember it was a green tie?"

To which the honest reader is compelled to answer: "No, I'm damned if I do!"

And then, if he is conscientious, he will turn back through the book to discover whether Dagmar Doubledick's tie really was green. Perhaps he finds this clue, a violet by a mossy stone, half hidden somewhere in the dusky recesses of Chapter Six; perhaps he misses the page and does not find it at all. In either case he is left with a vague feeling of dissatisfaction: as though he has been, if not swindled, at least outtalked.

Now, it may be argued, and reasonably, that the author here was playing perfectly fair. He was not compelled to repeat it, or even stress it. Thus when the whole solution of Earl Derr Biggers' *Charlie Chan Carries On* is based on the single word "stuffy," or when Carolyn Wells in *The Luminous Face* argues guilt from the thesis that no gentleman would wear a wrist watch with evening clothes, these novels are at least technically within the rules.

But the masterpiece of detection is not constructed from "a" clue, or "a" circumstance, or one single inconsistency of any kind. Such methods, dubious enough in a short story, become grotesque when they are applied to a full-length novel. It is too reminiscent of those minute mysteries, vignettes accompanied by paralytic-looking photographs, with which we are so familiar in magazines.

"You stated, Leonard Andreas," thunders the Inspector, "that you drank a Scotch-and-soda in the bar parlor of The Flaming Bishop at nine o'clock, whereas we know the pub ran out of spirits at half-past eight. It proves, Leonard Andreas, that you committed the murder."

Now, this is a bit rough on poor old Leonard Andreas, because it doesn't prove anything of the kind. It proves only that the witness told a lie, or that the landlord (as usual) was keeping his whisky under the counter for favored customers. We are dealing, here, with murder; and we can hardly let a man's life, even that of a character in fiction, depend on such flimsy evidence.

The fine detective story, be it repeated, does not consist of "a" clue. It is a ladder of clues, a pattern of evidence, joined together with such cunning that even the experienced reader may be deceived: until, in the blaze of the surprise ending, he suddenly sees the whole design.

Your craftsman knows, as Dr. R. Austin Freeman long ago pointed out, that it is not at all necessary to mislead the reader. Merely state your evidence, and the reader will mislead himself. Therefore, the craftsman will do more than mention his clues: he will stress them, dangle them like a watch in front of a baby, and turn them over lovingly in his hands. He will give not only the clue physical, but the clue psychological and the clue atmospheric.

No speech in the book is included just because it sounds mysterious, or because it makes a given character look guilty, or because the author doesn't know what the devil his character does mean and simply throws in the words to fill up space. Not at all. In turning over the pages afterwards, the reader can see for himself—how rare it is!—just what each character was *thinking* at any moment.

And the result?

That is why the story pulses with vitality all the way through, and springs into living vividness at the end. The veil is twitched away; the masks are removed. Human beings walk here, and no sawdust dolls, because the author has described voice inflections, shades of feeling, as well as Inspector Hogarth's discovery of the blunted thumbtack under the sofa. He has not forgotten to study his characters merely because he is writing about them in reverse. That turn of the eyes—of course! That momentary hesitation, when Betty puts her hand on the window ledge as though to steady herself—naturally!

Each small detail glitters now with an effectiveness it should have had, and would have had, if the story had been written straightforwardly. It is in the mood, in the tempo, an arrow whang in the gold. And when, in addition to this, we find ourselves flumdiddled by some master stroke of ingenuity which has turned our suspicions legitimately in the wrong direction, we can only salute the author and close the book with a kind of admiring curse.

There, good friends, *is* a detective story.

But who writes such stories nowadays?

In considering this question, on a terrain where it is to be feared that bricks are apt to fly, we might do worse than examine the wide difference which has developed nowadays between the British and the American type of detective novel.

During the good (or bad) old days twenty-five years ago—let's speak first of the everyday mediocre practitioners rather than the great ones—these novels were of much the same kind. Both sides were content to write the English language, even when they wrote it badly. Both sides made some mumbling acquiescence in the matter of rules, even when they broke rules all over the place.

Their plots, too, were the same. Alter the locale from Long Island to Surrey, substitute "baronet" for "industrial magnate," and the stories were almost interchangeable. This change, in fact, was actually made when the thrillers about Frank L. Packard's Jimmie Dale were published in England, with the redoubtable Jimmie living in Park Lane and battling against an evil, conscienceless gang of robbers called (it is regrettable to state) the Crime Club.

But the pattern of the average detective story ran thus: The victim, on the eve of making a new will, was found murdered in his library. He had been stabbed with an Oriental dagger, customarily used as a paper knife on his desk. The whole room was strewn with cuff links, bus tickets, lace handkerchiefs and cigarette ends, in the fine artistry of a paper chase.

Inspector Brace, summoned hastily to the scene of the crime, found only the beginning of his troubles. The baronet or industrial magnate—in addition to his ne'er-do-well son, his rebellious daughter and his invalid wife—was afflicted with such a household as nobody, even in the days of the servant shortage, would tolerate for five minutes. The butler was a blackmailer, the chauffeur an ex-convict, the housekeeper a religious maniac. If this were not enough, investigation discloses that no less than eight other suspects, at the time of the murder, were skulking in one long procession past the library windows.

"This situation," says Inspector Brace, "is hopeless!"

And it is difficult not to agree with him, since the various cuff links and cigarette ends are proved to have been dropped innocently by one or the other of the suspects, popping at intervals in and out of the windows like Box and Cox. Inspector Brace, desperate, is about to arrest the ne'er-do-well son when the latter's fiancée calls in that gifted gentleman, the private detective Reginald Du Kink.

Then we get real business. It is Du Kink who discovers that the established time of the murder is all wrong, due to an effect of ventriloquism or a phonograph record of a voice, and at a dramatic gathering of suspects he fastens the guilt on the dead man's secretary. The secretary, haggard and foaming, waits only to scream out a confession before he drinks off the contents of a small vial and instantly falls dead.

And that was that.

Now the above, so help me, is not written in ridicule. It is not meant as burlesque. You and I, who have been improving our minds with sensational fiction for so many years, are much too fond of detective stories. We are aware that all the above plot tricks were used long before 1920, have been used since, and are still in use today—often by the very best practitioners in the business.

Seldom are they lumped together in one story, as was formerly the case, nor is the clue so näive as a broken cuff link. And the ghost of Dr. Freud haunts everything today. But the old elements remain. The millionaire's home, the threatened disinheritance, the rebellious family, the enigmatic servant, the multiplicity of suspects, the wrongly accused, the wrong time of death—how many novels can you name in which not one of these elements is to be found?

Why, then, do we protest at the adventures of Inspector Brace and Reginald Du Kink? Why do their frenzied activities hover always on the edge of comedy, not to say broad farce?

We don't find them funny because they are what our age likes to call "period pieces." Far from it. One glance at a list of the detectives who were practicing long before them, a list which includes short stories as well as novels, will convince us of that.

There is nothing in the least funny about the great stories of Sir Arthur Conan Doyle. Nobody smiles today at G. K. Chesterton's Father Brown, though the stumpy little priest first appeared in 1911. The same applies to Inspector Hanaud, whom A. E. W. Mason introduced in *At the Villa Rose* a year earlier; and Dr. Freeman set the experienced John Thorndyke to solve his greatest problem, *The Eye of Osiris,* in the same year. E. C. Bentley, in 1913, was a comparative latecomer with his brilliant tour de force of *Trent's Last Case.* On the other side of the Atlantic, an underrated genius named Jacques Futrelle had created Professor Augustus S. F. X. Van Dusen as early as 1907, whereas Melville Davisson Post was already an old craftsman when he gave us the classic book of short stories about the far-from-comic Uncle Abner in 1918.

And here we begin to see the explanation of why, as early as the 1920s, the intelligent reader was getting fed up with the adventures of Inspector Brace and Reginald Du Kink.

"Oh!" said the reader. "I'm tired of just guessing who the criminal is. Instead of these sleight-of-hand half clues, so that it's never properly explained at the end how the detective knew, let's have some real evidence.

"Furthermore," continued this reader, "it's all very well to have your eight suspects parading in their endless ring-around-the-rosebush outside the library. That's fine. But give some sensible reason why they were there. If you must shower the room with bus tickets, provide a reason for that too. In other words, construct your story. Your present problem is not to explain the villainy of the guilty: it's to explain the stupidity of the innocent.

"Finally, your 'amazing revelation' at the end was so soggy, so lacking in essential cleverness, that I couldn't care less. Haven't you a new idea tucked away somewhere? Can't you wield even a minor thunderbolt? It was far different, believe me, from that joyous shock when Father Brown unmasked the Invisible Man, or Uncle Abner showed the meaning of the Straw Man, or Sherlock Holmes, in an unforgettable moment, swept the disguise from the Man with the Twisted Lip."

Holà! Wow!

Please pardon these exclamations. It is only that I, who write this introduction, feel warm with pleasure merely to recall, and taste in memory, those great moments of fictional crime. Once more, in memory, we see the gaunt figure of Holmes with the bath sponge in his hand, and shock-haired Hugh Boone writhing on the bunk. Or Father Brown, under a lurid sky in the waste of snow, with the giant hall porter between whose very feet runs the straggle of tracks where no man has passed; and out across the snow rings that despairing cry:

"God! The invisible man!"

Such moments, then, aid us in summing up the reasons why an imaginative reader required somebody more enterprising than Inspector Brace or Reginald Du Kink. He required a skillful story told in reverse by a skillful storyteller. He required (need it be repeated?) the quality of fair play, the quality of sound construction, and the quality of ingenuity. And already, at the beginning of the 1920s, this decade saw new writers who possessed just such qualities.

It saw the debut of Agatha Christie in *The Mysterious Affair at Styles,* based on the (then) startling novelty that the person first suspected turns out to be the murderer after all; he has wanted to get himself tried and acquitted so that he can't be tried again—a device later used by so many other writers. It saw Freeman Wills Crofts, with *The Cask* and its grisly contents, inaugurating the new fashion of the Unbreakable Alibi.

It saw John Rhode, in *The Paddington Mystery,* present a victim dead from no apparent cause—while telling us for the first time (and almost the last time) that Dr. Priestley's Christian name is Lancelot. It saw Anthony Berkeley's initial effort take the form of a "locked room" in *The Layton Court Mystery.* It saw Dorothy L. Sayers—with *Whose Body?*—setting an unfledged Lord Peter Wimsey to solve the puzzle of a strange corpse, clad only in a pair of pince-nez, found stabbed in a dry bath.

These 1920s, whatever may be said against them, thronged with sheer brains. What would be one of the best possible settings for violent death? J. J. Connington found the answer, with *Murder in the Maze.* Has anybody ever used the camera obscura, that eerie periscope device, for witnessing sinister events at a distance? Mr. Connington again, with *The Eye in the Museum.* In the 1920s, too, Philip MacDonald made his notable advent with *The Rasp.* R. A. J. Walling, in *Murder at the Keyhole,* demonstrated how you can force a reader to look literally in the wrong direction. And always with us during those days, cherubic, dependable and moaning like an animated cream bun, was H. C. Bailey's Mr. Fortune.

Now look towards the other side of the Atlantic. It must be acknowledged that America, during the same period, produced only two detective-story writers of the first class.

Regarding those who were not first class or anywhere near it, there is no need to mention names. Most of them were women, one or two of whom are still writing today. These ladies waltzed gracefully, waltzed well; but they waltzed always in the arms of Inspector Brace or Reginald Du Kink. We have pleasant memories of them all; theirs is the scent of arsenic and old lace. They call to mind colored frontispieces from their own books: the yellow gowns sweeping the floor, the padded rooms cozy with crime.

But there is one name which must be mentioned, because it belongs to a man who came dangerously near being first rate and who had more influence on his medium than anyone seems to have realized. That is the name of Arthur B. Reeve.

Arthur B. Reeve, who began in an earlier era—as, indeed, did most of the lady waltzers—entered the 20s with his once immense popularity fading away. Nevertheless his tales of Craig Kennedy had been read by hundreds of thousands, praised by Theodore Roosevelt, and turned into early film serials which held us petrified.

Craig Kennedy was Professor Kennedy of, presumably, Columbia University. Like Dr. Thorndyke, he was the scientific detective. His laboratory flashed with stranger sparks, and bubbled with more weird beakers and test tubes, than the laboratory of the late Dr. Frankenstein. For each occasion he had some new gadget, guaranteed sensational, to clap on somebody's wrist or wire underneath the chair. Square-jawed Kennedy in his high collar, whom we remember so well from the illustrations in the Harper editions, has marched into limbo with all his gadgets loaded on him. Much of his scientific knowledge, I believe, has been discredited. Nobody reads about him now. And yet . . .

He was first in the field of fiction with the lie detector, with murder by electrolysis, with radium poisoning, with death from liquid air. He taught writers the use of the Maxim silencer, and neither tears nor prayers nor curses can induce them to give it up. As a final achievement among many, in a story called "The Dream Detective" and later in a novel called *The Soul Scar,* it was he who introduced the profession to psychoanalysis.

This, in its way, is a solemn thought. For the humble annals of the detective story, it is like Watt studying the boiling kettle or Franklin flying the kite in the thunderstorm. In these days when every other mystery novel depends on a neurosis or a phobia or a fixation or whatnot, we can see now what wild vegetation has grown from that small seed. Psychoanalysis has been the most widely used contribution to the detective story since the days of Poe and Conan Doyle; and we might do worse than remember who planted the jungle in which our contemporaries lose themselves.

Well, never mind. We were discussing the American situation in the 20s.

Shortly past the middle of the decade, S. S. Van Dine published *The Benson Murder Case,* in which Alvin Benson was shot to death under circumstances which suggested the fate of Joseph Elwell the bridge expert. It was not a reconstruction of the Elwell case, as we can see for ourselves if we read the real-life account of the police officer in charge of that affair. But it brought forward a new writer who juggled suspects with such dexterity, like whirling Indian clubs, that we could only stare in admiration; and a new detective, Philo Vance, who said his method was psychology and scorned the cigarette ends found near Benson's body. Three years later, when a crooked lawyer was poisoned with some villainous new stuff called tetra ethyl lead in *The Roman Hat Mystery,* we saluted Ellery Queen.

Though these were the only practitioners of the front rank, both were so good that they held the scales almost level against their British confreres. It looked, in those far-off days, as though the golden age of the detective story had come. It now played strictly fair. It was adult. It had lost its clumsiness and grown to maturity.

Then came the 1930s. Then came the cleavage. The hard-boiled detective story, which for some years had been lurking in the magazines without anybody suspecting its inherent genius, suddenly blossomed out until it shadowed the whole field. Few writers, even experienced ones who had been dealing with a different type of story, were completely untouched by its influence. Novices rushed to get aboard the bandwagon. And there began, between the school of Sherlock Holmes and the school of Sam Spade, a difference which has been widening for more than thirty years.

Let us consider the hard-boiled type of story.

Whether you prefer this kind of writing is a matter of personal taste. Whether you acclaim it as good, on the other hand, depends on how it is done. If anybody wants to see how "economical, astringent, muscular prose" should really be handled, let him reread the best stories of Melville Davisson Post. Post was a great master of prose style, whereas most of the moderns are fairly answerable to some other description.

But we are not here concerned with literary quality. We are concerned with the detective story, and what goes into it. Dashiell Hammett has been praised as "a creator of the first rank," belonging among "the small handful of others who brought something really new to their chosen field of effort," and as one whose "lean, dynamic, unsentimental narratives created a definitely *American style,* quite separate and distinct from the accepted English pattern."

These are the words of Howard Haycraft, a sound critic, an admirable critic whose opinions we are bound to respect, and whom we can accuse of eccentric or unbalanced literary judgment only when he praises an undeserving hound named Carter Dickson.

But this originality, this glory of breaking fresh ground, again depends on what you do. You could get a finely original effect, for instance, by sending a whole procession of kangaroos across the stage during a performance of *Lohengrin* at Covent Garden or the Metropolitan Opera. You would be, definitely, a creator. You would have brought something really new to your chosen field of work. Or, to be more restrained about it, you could decide that the trouble with musical shows was the use of music, and the thing to do was have the musical show without any music at all; just as you can decide to have the detective story without any clues to follow or any rules to observe.

As we earlier discussed the saga of Brace and Du Kink, let's take a typical American detective novel of the later 30s. Its plot runs something like this:

The hero, Chip Hardstone, is a wisecracking private detective with an attractive blond stenographer. To Chip's office, in violent agitation, comes the lean, elderly, aristocratic J. T. Witherspoon, a millionaire with a country house in Sundown Hills.

Mr. Witherspoon's daughter, it appears, has got herself involved with a notorious character called Smooth Ed Spumoni. A priceless crystal flask, with goldwork by Benvenuto Cellini, has been stolen from the millionaire's collection. Matters at home are tense, since —in addition to his ne'er-do-well son, his rebellious daughter and his neurotic young wife—Mr. Witherspoon has further grounds for suspicion in that the butler is a blackmailer, the chauffeur an ex-convict, and the housekeeper a hophead. What he wants, he says, is to recover the Cellini crystal and free his daughter from the clutches of Smooth Ed Spumoni.

"But no scandal, Mr. Hardstone!" pleads the millionaire. "Above all things, no scandal!"

Already, before going to the country house, Chip has accumulated a lot of information. Practically every character in the story calls on him and tries to retain him. These he first bluffs and then insults —all except the representative of an insurance company, whom he merely insults.

Arrived at the house in Sundown Hills, Chip finds the "mad family" of earlier fiction now so completely nuts as to require a psychiatrist rather than a detective. The daughter removes her clothes; the wife intimates that she is willing to do so; the son tries to knock Chip's head off on sight. Other friends swing punches at the son, at Chip, or at each other; and Chip, who replies by insulting everybody he has previously missed, is interrupted with the discovery that one of the guests has been found dead—his throat mangled—in the swimming pool.

(Observe the departure of originality here. The millionaire himself is seldom murdered. He must be kept alive to pay Chip's fee.)

But one of the guests is murdered. No less than eight persons, it appears, know some vital secret about the murder. All of them have disappeared. It being Chip's job to find them, in a roulette-ball spin round the city, he concentrates first on a mysterious red-haired girl who has been traced to an apartment house at the corner of Pineapple and Banana.

Racing to the apartment house, Chip finds the girl gone but a corpse on the floor. He flies to a second apartment house, only to find the girl gone again and another corpse on the floor. By the time he has reached the third apartment house and the fourth corpse, he is in a spot. The police are after him, the reporters are after him, Smooth Ed Spumoni is after him, even the millionaire is after him to call him off. Chip won't be called off. He intimates, with something very like blackmail, that the old s.o.b. can't get out of it after bringing *him* in.

"All the same," says Chip, "this setup is hopeless!"

And again we agree, since the vital secrets turn out to be innocent side games in which everybody is chiseling everybody else, and have nothing to do with the murders. Chip, on the point of being arrested by Captain Hooligan of the Homicide Bureau, suddenly gets an inspiration—it is never very clear how—that the murderer is J. T. Witherspoon's wife. He confronts her; there is a gun fight all over the house; and the wife, waiting only long enough to scream out a confession, falls dead at his feet.

This is the end of the story, leaving the reader in some doubt as to just what did happen after all.

Now why, at the outset, are the adventures of Chip Hardstone so vaguely familiar? What strikes a reminiscent note? Despite the original kind of hero, despite the spit-in-your-eye style of writing, despite the chases and sluggings and kidnappings, we seem to have met this motiveless and clueless method somewhere before.

Don't we see that it's Inspector Brace and Reginald Du Kink all over again?

Instead of cuff links, bus tickets and lace handkerchiefs which bear no relation to the problem, we have "secrets" which bear no relation to the problem, either. Instead of the suspects doing their ring-around-the-rosebush outside the library, they now rush away from capture in cars and aircraft; but they still act either for no reasons at all, or for no reasons that are ever explained.

As for the fairness of the evidence, or the quality of the solution, the same test can be applied.

The American wheel, in these hard-boiled stories of the 30s, had turned full circle. We were back again among the whiskers and mothballs of an earlier era. Those very detective-story features of which the reader complained most bitterly in 1920, the features which were its essential faults, the features which craftsmen had worked so hard to eliminate ever since, were triumphantly hailed as a daring new departure from convention.

This period in America, it is true, produced its own first-raters. In 1934, with a story called *Fer-de-Lance,* Rex Stout by sheer power of characterization and plot construction at once joined the company of Ellery Queen and S. S. Van Dine. There was Anthony Abbot, whose grim first novel, *About the Murder of Geraldine Foster*—based on a legend of Courvoisier and Lizzie Borden—never seems to have achieved the full critical acclaim it deserves. In the front rank, or very close to it, were Clayton Rawson and C. Daly King.

But these were all practitioners in the great tradition, the clue-serpents and trap-baiters. Their narratives moved as fast as you could wish for; yet they ranged beside their British confreres of the same period, Margery Allingham and Ngaio Marsh and Nicholas Blake, in the vital business of presenting new ideas. In Nicholas Blake's first novel, *A Question of Proof,* you will find one instance of what is meant by the great tradition. The murder knife unaccountably vanishes; and the investigators can't find it because it has been hidden, in front of their eyes, by being used as a tent peg.

Yes; but what about the weaknesses in the English type of novel?

The fault here is just the same, though expressed in a different way. The "literary" type, like the hard-boiled, is too often apt to mistake style for substance. It imagines that with good writing, which sometimes becomes merely pretentious writing, you can disguise the lack of an original plot.

"Come, now!" the author seems to be saying. "I'm really a straight novelist, you know, indulging in this funny little medium of the detective story because nowadays it's become respectable. It's true I haven't got much of a mystery, or any very clear idea of how to handle it; but if I give you strong characterizations and much talk-in-a-mist, you won't mind that."

To which the answer is: Sir or madam, we do mind. Either you neglect the plot, which is bad; or else you fall off those stilts with a crash, which is worse.

The present anthology has been called *The Ten Best Detective Novels*—a title for whose arbitrariness you must blame the publishers. I myself should have preferred to call it ten "of the" best, assigning to this introduction a task less responsible than that of the recording angel.

Nevertheless—if we postulate our necessary qualities as fair play, sound construction, and ingenuity—there will be many to ask why this anthology does not begin with Wilkie Collins's *The Moonstone.*

The Moonstone, published in 1868, has been put at the top of the list by both G. K. Chesterton and Dorothy L. Sayers. And with reason. The problem of who stole the moonstone, that baleful yellow diamond, is only one feature of a story so skillfully woven that it remains a lesson in technique even today. It is also a greenhouse of Victorian charm, with its flower-painted door and its rose-growing detective and its amiable whiskered hero, who gives up smoking to please the heroine and by this small gesture partly brings about the whole catastrophe.

A too-enthusiastic reader, however, must be warned that the first chapters are tolerably heavy going. Old Gabriel Betteredge, the first of several narrators, requires no less than fifty-seven closely printed pages to set his stage, and encourages you with, "Cheer up!" at the end of the fifty-seventh (in the edition from which I quote: Chatto & Windus, 1905). The reasons against including it are mainly those of space: *The Moonstone* runs to more than a quarter of a million words, and would overweight even a formidable volume like this.

There are very different reasons for excluding another story which has been handed down from generation to generation as a classic: Anna Katharine Green's *The Leavenworth Case.*

This American landmark, which appeared in 1878, must be treated with reverence as being the first novel in history where our unfortunate millionaire (in this case the retired tea-merchant Mr. Leavenworth) is found shot through the back of the head in his library. Listen, now, to a description of the beautiful Mary Leavenworth, one of the dead man's nieces:

> Seated in an easy-chair of embroidered satin, but rousing from her half-recumbent position, like one who was in the act of launching a powerful invective, I beheld a glorious woman. Fair, pale, proud, delicate; looking like a lily in the thick creamy-tinted wrapper that alternately clung to and swayed from her richly-moulded figure; with her Grecian front—

Don't laugh; Miss Leavenworth's Grecian front isn't what you think it is. And, in any case, young Raymond was really impressed.

> —her Grecian front, crowned with the palest of pale tresses, lifted and flashing with power . . . her whole appearance was so splendid, so startling, so extraordinary, that I held my breath in surprise, actually for a moment doubting if it were a living woman I beheld, or some famous pythoness conjured up from ancient story.

It would be unjust to make evil-minded comments on this picture, merely because the author wrote in the popular style of her day. In the best detective stories we shall find antiquated writing, which doesn't matter when there is a dexterous story to tell. What does matter is that we plod for hundreds of pages beside a detective who never unearths a single clue against the right person, and refrains from arresting the wrong person only because of his notion that no woman would think of cleaning a revolver after firing it.

Anna Katharine Green at her best could devise brilliant plot-tricks, like the ice-bullet of *Initials Only*, or the unearthly penance of *Dark Hollow*, or the "portrait" in *The Filigree Ball*, which is not a portrait but a face drawn in microscopic lines of handwriting. All excellent; yet something more is required than this. It is a real pleasure when we go on to Sir Arthur Conan Doyle and Sherlock Holmes.

The position occupied by Sherlock Holmes among present-day detectives is a trifle curious. He still towers over the rest of them, huge and ageless, with those piercing eyes fixed on a would-be critic.

"Yes?" he seems to be saying. And then again: "Yes?"

It is no good for his enemies to attack him as a character; he exists. He is as real as the pavement of Baker Street and as unmistakable a personality as Mr. Churchill. So his detractors (as the fashion is) will acknowledge he is a great man but deny he is a good detective. Even his admirers, while praising Holmes and Watson as living people, sometimes intimate that the stories themselves are rather thin stuff. "Holmes," we read on more than one occasion, "is always picking up some small object, which he conceals from Watson and from the reader."

The operative word is "always;" it has become customary to say this, and the only objection is that it simply isn't true.

Our difficulty is that we have been, most of us, so familiar with these stories from early years as to forget their essential cleverness. They are a part of life, a part of youth, as entwined with boyhood as our first long trousers or our first girl friend. A happy light mists everything. We are too close to the stories, too hypnotized by Holmes; we can't see the plot for the personality.

It is true that with *A Study in Scarlet* (1887) Conan Doyle had not yet found his method. But then he had not found Sherlock Holmes either. In the brilliant study, published in 1945, by Adrian Conan Doyle, son of Sir Arthur, you will read of a first draft of *A Study in Scarlet* in which Holmes did not appear at all.* The great man was an addendum, an afterthought; in *A Study in Scarlet* Conan Doyle was concerned far less with detection than with the Mormons and Jefferson Hope's vengeance. Even in *The Sign of Four* (1890) he was still searching. Conan Doyle found his true method only when he had leisure to sit down and write the short tales of *The Adventures* (1892) and in his best stories he never lost it again.

Taste may cause debate here. But it can be suggested that, in any list of the dozen best short stories, six of most people's choices would be "The Red-Headed League," "The Man with the Twisted Lip," "The Speckled Band," "Silver Blaze," "The Naval Treaty," and "The Reigate Squires."** And in each of those stories you will find every vital clue fairly and honorably set forth.

You doubt it?

You say that in "The Red-Headed League," for example, we are not told what Holmes sees when he looks at the knees of Vincent Spaulding's trousers?

But we have already heard that Holmes recognizes "Spaulding;" we know Spaulding's trick of diving into the cellar; we see Holmes hammering on the pavement with his stick; we are carefully informed that one of the buildings in line with Wilson's pawnshop is the Capital and Counties Bank. In this story of a tunnel dug for a bank robbery, we must realize that the stains on the trouser-knees are not a clue at all; they are proof, clinching proof, which Holmes legitimately keeps back until the solution.

Again, in "The Speckled Band," it is putting the cart before the horse to maintain we should have been told about the snake's fang-marks on the victim. The whole problem was to find those marks, to discover *what* could have killed Julia Stoner. We are given the ventilator—note how deftly to begin with, by the scent of cigar smoke—the clamped bedstead, the dummy bell-rope, the locked safe, the saucer of milk near the looped dog-leash, the carefully repeated insistence on Dr. Roylott's fondness for Indian pets. If few readers of *The Strand Magazine* in 1892

* Adrian Conan Doyle, *The True Conan Doyle* (John Murray, 1945), p. 17.

**A poll taken in the London *Observer* to determine the most popular Sherlock Holmes tales, and including the novels as well as the short stories, listed four of these titles out of eight. See H. Douglas Thomson, *Masters of Mystery* (Collins, 1931), p. 140.

thought of a snake, it was not for want of evidence. It was because young Dr. Conan Doyle had been the first to use one.

Now take a scene which contains perhaps the most famous words in the saga. The scene occurs in "Silver Blaze," a puzzle honorably displaying every card from the curried mutton to the dressmaker's bill; and its famous words, even at risk of over-repetition, must be quoted again here.

"Is there any other point to which you would wish to call my attention?"
"To the curious incident of the dog in the night-time."
"The dog did nothing in the night-time."
"That was the curious incident."

This is generally quoted as an instance of Sherlockismus, or some other fancy name. But it isn't a character-twist; it is a clue, and one of the cleverest clues in fiction at that. It is the trick by which the detective, while making you wonder what in the name of sanity he is talking about, nevertheless gives you fair opportunity to think for yourself: the sort of clue which Conan Doyle invented, and which nobody has ever managed so well since.

Of the two remaining novels, choice for this anthology lay between *The Hound of the Baskervilles* and *The Valley of Fear*. The latter has been chosen for two reasons: first, because its opening chapters contain perhaps the best Holmes-Watson dialogue in the whole series; second and more important, because its main problem turns on a clue which ought to be as celebrated as the dog in the night-time, or (if we include the *Hound*) both dogs in the night-time.

"The dumb-bell!" exclaims Sherlock Holmes, this time without reference to any official policeman. "All my lines of thought," he declares, "lead me back invariably to one basic question—why should an athletic man develop his frame on so unnatural an instrument as a single dumb-bell?"

It is a legitimate question, a puzzle to set the police biting their nails. Do you remember our discussion a while ago, about clues repeatedly dangled in front of the reader? And the story in which, afterwards, you can tell what each character was thinking at a given time?

In the investigation of the murder at Birlstone Manor, observe the happy significance which attaches to Dr. Watson's umbrella. (No, I am giving nothing away.) Re-read afterwards the interviews with Barker and Mrs. Douglas; consider the testimony of the half-deaf housekeeper. In the second part, which so shocks moderns and pleases your obedient servant, consider each double-innuendo. And let detractors claim, if they can, that Conan Doyle does not play fair.

The Yellow Room! A Supernatural Crime!

With some such exclamatory terms were the good feuilleton-readers of Paris set buzzing and chattering when there appeared, in the supplement to *L'Illustration* for September 7th, 1907, the first installment of Gaston Leroux's new serial, *The Mystery of the Yellow Room.*

This noble enigma was first published in England in the same year through the medium, it is a little disconcerting to find, of the Daily Mail Sixpenny Novels; perhaps it was inevitable that the *Yellow Room* should get into the Yellow Press. But it is still the best novel in the fashion it made so deservedly popular—the apparently supernatural crime revolving round a "hermetically sealed room."

True, there had been locked rooms before Leroux's time. Edgar Allan Poe, prodigal of invention as always, had included one in "The Murders in the Rue Morgue" as he included nearly everything else. But his sealed room was not really sealed; we discover that one of its windows was fastened only with dummy nails; and no present-day artificer (I hope) would cheat his readers with any such unspeakable swindle.

This is not said in deprecation of Poe; the father of the detective story must not be called off-side in a game he invented himself. The interesting thing, here, is why Poe introduced this situation at all. For the problem of the locked room—which some may suppose to be a fantasy of fiction writers—actually has happened more than once in real life. A curious reader may be referred to the strangling of the Prince de Conde behind a bolted door, and the stabbing of Rose Delacourt in a locked attic: both *causes celebres,* both occurring in France, and both in the first three decades of the nineteenth century. Students might speculate as to whether Poe, who published "The Murders in the Rue Morgue" in 1841, had ever seen any account of them.*

---

*Louis Andre, *The Mysterious Baronne de Feucheres* (Hutchinson, 1925); C. L. McCluer Stevens, *From Clue to Dock* (Stanley Paul, 1927), pp. 213–216. In the first case, contemporary opinion seems to have decided that the trick was managed by a door bolted from outside by manipulating a piece of ribbon after a fashion used in several detective stories. In the second case, no solution has ever been found; though one suggestion was that of an ourang-outang or large monkey—just as in Poe's story later. Gross's *Criminal Investigation* (Sweet & Maxwell, 1934) lists several locked-room problems. It is noteworthy also that many of the details of a real-life case quoted by Gross (p. 392) parallel those of the attack on Mlle. Stangerson in the *Yellow Room.*

Again, in the field of fiction, there was Israel Zangwill with a novelette called *The Big Bow Mystery*. It contains an adroit dodge, first use of the victim who is presumed to be dead before he (or, in this case, she) really is. But each step of the story grows progressively more cumbersome and confusing, becoming somehow entangled with politics and allowing the villain at last to commit suicide on the steps of Number Ten Downing Street.

It remained for Gaston Leroux, a Parisian journalist, to produce a masterpiece with *The Mystery of the Yellow Room.*

The great quality of this book, for all its stifled emotionalism, is that it comes alive. Events march and move with real breathlessness and diabolism. We are snared by its very imaginative conception—the lonely pavilion, the cry of the cat called the Good Lord's Beast, Professor Stangerson and his daughter with their scientific experiments on "the instantaneous disassociation of matter"—when the instantaneous disassociation of matter, apparently, is just what we get. For the criminal, here, does more than escape from a locked room. In a later chapter, as Sainclair writes:

> I was utterly bewildered. Indeed, the phenomena of that still unknown science called hypnotism, for example, are not more inexplicable than the disappearance of the body of the assassin at the very moment when four persons touched him!

Its effects land with a crash of impact, just like that. They take you off balance; they startle you into belief. Yet each has a logical explanation. And Leroux, unlike the bloatedly over-rated Simenon of present days, plays scrupulously fair with the evidence. We note with pleasure that Joseph Rouletabille, the young reporter-detective, has picked up Sherlock Holmes's trick of the enigmatic clue. "Oh, if only she had had her hair arranged in bandeaux!" cries Rouletabille, in a frenzy of despair. And again:

> "How do you know the handkerchief was blue, with red stripes?"
> "Because, if it had not been blue with red stripes, it would not have been found at all."

But Gaston Leroux's greatest contribution was in widening the field of the locked room to include the general "impossible situation": the thing that can't happen but does happen. He developed it with the dissolution-act of the *Yellow Room,* and the incredible murder of the Green Man in a later chapter. He opened up possibilities which the Carnacki stories of William Hope Hodgson, or the scientific conjuring tricks of L. T. Meade and Robert Eustace, had as yet only touched. It would be difficult to underestimate the immense influence these two elements—the enigmatic clue of Conan Doyle, the impossible murder of Leroux—exercised over writers who followed them.*

The enigmatic clue, for instance, looms up again in the work of A. E. W. Mason. But here the whole approach is different, adding still another quality to the growth of the detective story. Here it is character, character, and character all the way.

"Your idioms, I know him!"

That is the triumphant cry, accompanied by a posturing attitude, as Inspector Hanaud of the Surete airs his knowledge of the English language. Never has a French writer managed a French detective so entertainingly as English writers have done. We know Hanaud. We know his burly figure, his blue chin and blue Maryland cigarettes, the deep-throated chuckle when he tramples all over his prim friend Mr. Ricardo, or complacently indulges in the English spikking.

> "Ten thousand pounds on the table, and he had not one sliver!"
> "Stiver," Ricardo corrected.
> "As I said, one sliver," Hanaud agreed equably. "Mrs. Hubbard, she was naked. You understand?"

But, paradoxically, the greater Hanaud grows as a character the less impressive he is in the story. In the later novels, especially, we are always waiting for him to fire off a string of gags like a radio comedian. It is significant that in Hanaud's first appearance—*At the Villa Rose* (1910)—he shows no trace whatever of the buffoon. He is sinister, satiric; no more. Even with *The House of the Arrow* (1924) this tendency is only foreshadowed. Which is exactly as it should be.

For Mr. Mason strikes straight at the emotions. The strength of his writing gives us, with almost intolerable vividness, the heat of bricks baking in the sun at Aix-les-Bains or the clash of bells from a Dijon steeple. Against this background we are caught into a whirlwind of emotion, of human beings in peril. There is no detachment; hardly even time to breathe; and, except at odd times, very little opportunity for laughter.

*Notably G. K. Chesterton, who unfortunately cannot be included here because he did not write a full-length detective-novel. From the references to it scattered through his essays and stories, we know how deeply G.K.C. was impressed by the *Yellow Room*. and his fondness for the enigmatic clue needs no emphasis. Of the fifty Father Brown stories, no less than seventeen deal with a seemingly supernatural crime.

"I tell you," says Hanaud, as the police stand in Madame Dauvray's bedroom after that evil night at the Villa Rose, "this is human! Yes, it is interesting just because it is so human."

We begin, as a rule, with some beautiful girl menaced by doubt or danger. Popularly speaking, this situation is sure-fire. It never fails. But it must be handled by an expert. The human mind recoils, for instance, from what some lady-novelists of the Had-I-But-Known school would have done with Celia Harland in *At the Villa Rose* or Betty Harlowe in *The House of the Arrow* or Joyce Whipple in *The Prisoner in the Opal*. The formula of the Had-I-But-Known school is not to attempt a detective story but endlessly to re-write *Jane Eyre,* with Rochesters more roaring and gibberings more pronounced than any dreamed of by Charlotte Bronte.

Mr. Mason's triumph is in arranging matters so that, instead of an arbitrary plot creating the characters, the characters shall create the plot. He starts with his people. He dwells on visual detail from every expression of a face down to the smallest trifle of hat or shoe-button. Everything, including the unexpected ending, arises from the murderer's own twisted motives. The criminal—though you may never notice this until afterwards—is always alert, always tense, responding on every page to some stimulus of suggested guilt.

This is what the detective novel had not hitherto fully explored, a purely psychological quality in which a turn of an eye, a gripping of a window-ledge, could become as legitimate a clue as any footprint. It remained for this new technique only to find new ways—always new ways!—in How to Conceal the Identity of the Murderer. And, on How to Conceal the Identity of the Murderer, a whole chapter of tips for the beginner might be compiled from the works of Agatha Christie and Ellery Queen.

Agatha Christie is the female Sixteen-String Jack, the original Artful Dodger: you must never take your eye off her for a second. It has already been indicated how she upset the apple-cart with her first novel, *The Mysterious Affair at Styles,* in 1920. She even upset it with her choice of a detective.

It is nonsense to maintain, as some have done, that Poirot was modelled after Hanaud. A comparison of dates and books will show that Hanaud did not begin to display any exotic mannerisms until four years after Poirot's first appearance. What Mrs. Christie did was to take the comic little foreigner of the music halls—always with us, twirling waxed moustaches and shrugging his shoulders amid a firework splutter of "Zut, alors!" or "Mais oui!"—and transform him into the keen-eyed avenger with the little grey cells. As Hercule Poirot, he is a joy for evermore.

"I'm sick of the little blighter!" his creatrix once complained at a Detection Club dinner where a number of us were airing our grievances. But this, we felt sure, was merely a mood: like the startling mood of Mr. Bentley when he announced that any love-interest in detective stories should be confined to an appendix at the back of the book. For nobody else has ever tired of Hercule Poirot, and nobody else ever will.

Poirot is a symbol of Mrs. Christie's method. Everybody now knows that in *The Murder of Roger Ackroyd* it is the narrator who turns out to be the criminal. What seems not so generally known is that with *The Man in the Brown Suit,* an inferior novel but a better hoax, Mrs. Christie anticipated her own device by several years.

The Man in the Brown Suit is told from two aspects: straight narration in the third person, intermingled with chapters from the diary of a bluff and likeable old baronet. It is the bluff and likeable old baronet (you now guess) who proves to be the murderer. But Sir Eustace—note this difference—has carefully warned the reader that he will write in his diary only what he is willing to have everybody see: a stroke which *Roger Ackroyd,* for all its oblique fairness, does not contain.

Nevertheless, even this is a tour-de-force, like the superb juggling in *Cards on the Table* or the island strewn with stiffs in *Ten Little Niggers,* which may not be repeated.* Where Mrs. Christie scores, over and over again, is in the use of a trick which we will call the Implied Alibi.

Now the implied alibi is a very different thing from one of those elaborate police-nightmares— "Well, Joe Manders is out of it; he's got an alibi"—which Inspector French so painstakingly breaks down. On the contrary, the whole trick consists in *not* stressing the fact that Joe

* Or should not be repeated. We also find the Roger-Ackroyd formula used in Brian Flynn's *The Billiard Room Mystery,* Anthony Berkeley's *The Second Shot,* and Anthony Gilbert's *The Clock in the Hat-Box.* Though in these instances it is quite legitimate, each author giving a different reason for employing it, the practice at one time became so common that you could never begin a story told in the first person without wondering uneasily whether it might not be That Man Again.

Manders has an alibi; in scarcely even mentioning it; in accepting Joe Manders's innocence as so radiantly obvious, under the circumstances, that it has never even occurred to the author (bless her heart) to suspect him herself.

At the time the murder was apparently committed, Joe has been sitting on the beach with the detective. Why even consider the possibility?

Once you have lured the reader into this trap, you have got him fast. It is a form of hypnotism. Whole brass-bands of clues can march past without making him blink an eye to notice them. But once let your own eye stray for a second in the direction of Joe Manders—once intimate by the slightest twitch that you, the author, are thinking of him—and the spell is broken. The reader is after that suspect like a dog after a cat. You might as well concede defeat from the page where it occurs.

How many times Mrs. Christie has rung the changes on this form of alibi it would be spoiling too many stories to reveal. The alibi itself usually consists of somebody dressing up as somebody else, either to establish the wrong time of death *(Evil Under the Sun)* or to show the real murderer never went near his victim *(Appointment with Death)*.

Yet this is far from being her only dodge. Another good card, which we might call Misdirection As To The Source of Danger, is played well in *Peril at End House* and comes down as a veritable ace of trumps with *Murder in Mesopotamia*. Even to the mania theme in multiple murders—where some ostensible lunatic seems to be polishing off victims for no reason, though we realize quite well that the right corpse is hidden in a pile of wrong ones—even to this theme she brings some fresh twist which is more than sanity disguised as madness.

Through such cases struts Poirot, undisturbed by flying red-herrings. His mannerisms never jar the story, which is light and swift and filled with thumb-nail characterizations. You will find him at the top of his form in *Death on the Nile,* which I venture to think the best of what Torquemada called "the little grey sells." Poirot, perhaps, might have told us about the bullet-hole in the table. But if you spot the murderer you deserve a medal.

The same statement, with equal fervor of emphasis, can be made about any of the earlier novels of Ellery Queen.

Though this writer belongs to the end of Mrs. Christie's decade, his first story appearing in 1929, he is bracketed with her at this point because both are specialists in the dazzle of the thunderbolt ending. He can hocus and flummox the most experienced. Let's see how he does it.

When any character first steps out on the stage of a detective novel, steps out and speaks his first lines, that character is subjected at once to the reader's pitiless scrutiny. A fierce spotlight beats on him. "Well, now!" says the reader, unmoved by any distracting gestures on the part of the author, "what's that fellow *doing* there? Is he part of the action? Is he needed to work the machinery? Because, if he isn't, that character's likely to be the murderer."

Where Agatha Christie is the Artful Dodger, Ellery Queen is the Confidence Man. He preys on human nature. His trick consists in smoothly getting you to accept some character—in reality the criminal—as a necessary, if humble, part of the mechanism. This character must not be dragged in; he must have a right to be where he is. Suppose he appears in some minor official capacity: a coroner, say, or the house-physician of a hotel where the murder occurs? He can then talk his head off, and have a right to. Nobody will suspect him. Or, extending this principle but still keeping it for the sake of argument to the medical profession, he may be the docile assistant to some doctor who *is* under suspicion; put there by the author, apparently, only to confirm or deny certain vital facts. Instead of this character butting into the story, it is rather as though the author had tried to keep him out.

Here is the secret behind the shattering denouement of *The Greek Coffin Mystery,* or *French Powder,* or *Dutch Shoe.* Like the implied alibi, it is a form of hypnosis; once you have slipped your murderer past the reader's glazed eye, long strings of clues can follow him. Ellery Queen presents his evidence fully and fairly, by telling us what is seen. But he does more than this, with a device peculiarly his own. In addition to describing the clue that is there, he makes great capital out of the clue that isn't there.

Let us suppose that Xavier Claverton, a New York playboy, collapses of cyanide poisoning on Fifth Avenue and is carted off to the morgue. At the morgue appear Inspector Queen, Sergeant Velie, and Ellery himself, to examine the dead man's clothes and the contents of his pockets. They are shown a raincoat, a soft black hat, grey coat and vest, blue shirt and dark-blue tie, underwear, black socks and shoes, fifty-four dollars and eighteen cents in money, a billfold, a wrist-watch, a fountain-pen, some letters and a bunch of keys.

Whereupon Ellery gives a long, low whistle, whose meaning is not elucidated until the end of the story.

"Don't you see, Dad," he explains then, "that Claverton's belongings did not include a pair of trousers?"

"By jing, son!" mutters Inspector Queen. "You mean the poor fellow wasn't wearing any britches?"

"Exactly, Dad. You grasp the point at once. Therefore I asked myself: why should Claverton, a man of impeccable taste in other respects, have been walking down Fifth Avenue without his pants?"

This dialogue (I admit) does not actually occur anywhere in the saga. But you can find the principle operating in novels like *The Chinese Orange Mystery* and short stories like "The African Traveller." In addition to its fiendish ingenuity, it is also perfectly fair. If the missing item is not spotted by the reader who himself will be wearing a shirt or tie and not improbably a pair of trousers as well, then he has only himself to blame.

Ellery (the detective) grows in stature through the later novels, as the early Van-Dine influence lessens. He is no longer a bouncing young man; he is genuine; he convinces. The startling solutions remain, with more adroit evidence—as in the arrowhead clue of *The Devil to Pay,* or the concealment of the murderer in *The Door Between*—and a compactness of story necessitating fewer characters. That is why any critic complaining of too many characters in the earlier stories, an obscuring of the criminal behind mere numbers, is here offered a later novelette called *The Lamp of God.* The field is narrow; but you will be misdirected. Artifice has become art.

If there is any writer more passionately addicted to upsetting the apple-cart than Agatha Christie or Ellery Queen, that person is Anthony Berkeley.

Mr. Berkeley himself will take no offence, it is to be hoped, if I say that few people seem to have understood him; certainly many have misunderstood what he has been trying to do. His famous preface to *The Second Shot,* in which he argues that the old crime-puzzle should become a puzzle of character, has often been interpreted to mean that it should grow less and less like a detective story. This pronouncement has been hailed with delight, especially by those who can't write detective stories for beans.

But look more closely at what the creator of Roger Sheringham really ly says.

It will become (he writes) a puzzle of character rather than of time, place, motive, and opportunity. The question will be not, "Who killed the old man in the bathroom?" but, "What on earth induced X, of all people, to kill the old man in the bathroom?"

Now this is not very revolutionary. In fact, with those key words *of all people,* it is not revolutionary at all. Its thesis is that we should stick to the formula of the least-likely person, while demonstrating at the end that the least-likely person should have been recognized as the most-likely person after all. Which is, and always has been, the definition of a good detective story. Assuredly it is a definition of Mr. Berkeley's own method. That is how *he* kills the old man in the bathroom. And we seldom get out of that bathroom without falling with a crash on its slippery floor.

No; the question that arises here is a question of evidence.

Mr. Berkeley's contention has always been that purely material evidence in detective stories—a cuff-link or a bus-ticket or a bottle of ink—is unconvincing because it can point two ways, or three ways, or all ways at once. By selecting what you want, you can make it prove anything you like. This is the theme of *The Poisoned Chocolates Case,* a masterpiece of wit which rises to Gilbert-and-Sullivan grandeur as each wild-eyed sleuth convicts a different person on the same set of facts.

Most of the problems Mr. Berkeley sets are deceptively ordinary-looking to start with. His people and circumstances are the people and circumstances of everyday life. When he introduced Roger Sheringham with *The Layton Court Mystery* in 1925, he was careful to point out that his detective is "very far removed from being a Sphinx, and does make a mistake or two occasionally." Against this background of reality—the popular-price hotel of *The Piccadilly Murder,* the newly-weds' suburban home in *Murder in the Basement*—move characters drawn with effortless skill, as though the author were merely reminding you of somebody you knew.*

* The death of John Bentley, in *The Wychford Poisoning Case,* is based on the death of James Maybrick at Liverpool in 1889. In *Poisoned Chocolates* you will find parallel cases cited from the "book" which figures so prominently in the later evidence; and the book itself is not imaginary: it is Edward H. Smith's *Famous American Poison Mysteries* (Hurst & Blackett, 1926).

But this is the trap. This is how he gets his effects. An unwary reader, lured into thinking this is all routine stuff, does not see the crafty Apache lurking in ambush to wallop out with a tomahawk.

For Mr. Berkeley must always twist or double-twist something. If he is not doing it with facts, he is doing it with character. Whenever a hint of the grotesque does peep out of his comfortable atmosphere, as in the sinister invitation of *Panic Party,* or the murderers' charade of *Jumping Jenny,* it is a flash of somebody's character; and it is the disclosure of somebody's real character which comes with such a shock at the end. Herein lies the strength of the detective story as a "puzzle of character," and also its danger. After pouring scorn on the ease with which material clues can be twisted in *The Poisoned Chocolates Case,* Mr. Berkeley then twists the dead woman's character—not very convincingly, perhaps—to provide his final surprises. It is magnificent; but it is six of one and half a dozen of the other. For psychology must play fair too.

It is in this realism of detail, this preference for a clue in human nature rather than in the dropped cigarette-end, that Anthony Berkeley is akin to the late S. S. Van Dine.

I do not, of course, suggest any similarity between Roger Sheringham and Philo Vance. Nobody, not even Chief Inspector Moresby, has ever wished Mr. Sheringham a kick in the pance; whereas this has been suggested, often vociferously, for the aristocratic detective who looked like John Barrymore, talked like a Dictionary of Familiar Quotations, and dressed ("Is it warm enough for a silk suit? And a lavender tie, by all means.") like God knows what.

But let's be honest about Philo Vance. Despite his mannerisms, despite an "English" style of speech which has caused some hilarity in England, he is a triumph of his creator's method. Few detective-writers of the front rank can ever have possessed less *ingenuity* than S. S. Van Dine. He had small skill at misdirection; his phonograph alibi of *The Canary Murder Case,* even when it was published in 1927, could not have deceived a little golden-haired child. His best dodge in *The Greene Murder Case* is a variant of a real-life incident used with greater effect by Conan Doyle in "The Problem of Thor Bridge."

S. S. Van Dine's real success came from taking pains; taking pains, and still again taking pains. You may not be deeply moved to hear that:

Once when Vance was suffering from sinusitis, he had an X-ray photograph of his head made; and the accompanying chart described him as a "marked dolichocephalic" and a "disharmonious Nordic."

Yet it goes into the picture, small detail built upon small detail, until the reader is battered into submission. Philo Vance's reality cannot be doubted. You would recognize him in your sitting-room even if you only threw him out. If S. S. Van Dine had ever murdered the old man in the bathroom, we should have been given every aspect of that bathroom from the name of the maker stamped on the plumbing down to a footnote describing the quality of the soap.

Inside this framework, Vance has three-dimensional existence. Once he steps out of it (as in later novels) the whole thing collapses. Its strength lies in being a framework, as rigid as a cage; the author merely destroyed his effectiveness by trying to break the bars. When Philo Vance turns into a man of action and pursues gangsters, we regretfully decline to believe. And when he is permitted to fall in love, as in *The Garden Murder Case,* the author himself was so dubious that the whole plot is based on mystifying us as to which girl Vance is in love with.

But in *The Bishop Murder Case,* and still more strikingly in the *Greene,* his story has deadly impact. Imagination has been added to the accumulation of detail; it is the commonplace made startling by the abnormal. So painstaking has been the description that we could find our way blindfolded through Professor Dillard's house in West 76th Street. We know every nook and cranny of the old Greene mansion overhanging the East River. It might be a neighbor's house; and yet into it has come a prowling mass-murderer.

"That book scared me," a friend of mine once declared, about the slaughterings in the Greene household. "I can't tell you why, because it's not a ghost story. But that book scared me."

A follower of detection fiction could have told him why.

In addition to the careful detail, Van Dine never allows you to forget the *presence* of this evil force. Not by the number of corpses; any writer can scatter dead bodies all over the house and have little to show for it; but in many ways far more subtle and more disquieting.

There's somebody here, and yet we can't see him. He touches us on the shoulder; we hear him breathing outside a door; there's a faint creak at the end of the passage; but we can't see him. Chester Greene talked to him—look at the expression on Chester's dead face!—yet there's nothing but a black bullet-hole, a sly step, the smell of burnt candle-grease where somebody's been reading in the library. It is the mere hint, the half-suggestion (as in a ghost story) which builds up this sense of suffocating evil. And it might be under the bed now. And the goblins will get you if you don't look out. That is how a fine craftsman weaves the spell in *The Greene Murder Case;* and those who nowadays labor hopelessly to get such effects are recommended to study his methods. S. S. Van Dine, who professed to regard the detective story as a matter of mechanics, could succeed with horror where he so very often failed with plot.

Atmosphere? For that we must look also to the works of Philip MacDonald.

Mr. MacDonald, so often justly praised for his humorous touches and his sound construction, seems to have escaped too-frequent recognition for another quality he manages even better: the atmosphere of sheer human evil which has breathed out of those country houses and wet woods and darkling landscapes since he published *The Rasp* in 1924.

G. K. Chesterton, as preface to a not-very-satisfactory novel by Mr. Masterman,* once wrote a brief essay in which he enumerates the virtues of a good practitioner by listing the things which the good practitioner does *not* do. The essay is heart-warming; twenty years have not dimmed its vitality or its truth. As it rises to a crescendo in the list of things the good detective-writer does not do, there is one point at which we can all give a special round of applause.

"He does not," thunders G.K.C. "he does not say it was all a mistake, and that nobody ever intended to murder anybody at all, to the serious disappointment of all humane and sympathetic readers."

Now this is a mistake which Philip MacDonald very seldom makes either. His, in general, is a fight-to-the-death contest against a malignant enemy. Atmosphere is heavy in *The Noose;* it becomes a poisonous fog in *The White Crow.* There is a reason for that wiry staccato prose, which raps like knuckles on a table, and for the tensity which sweeps along Anthony Gethryn as it sweeps along the narrative. Colonel Gethryn, C.M.G., D.S.O., is not fooling. And neither is the criminal.

On the technical side, Mr. MacDonald is master of every trick from the implied alibi— "It was, of course, never recognized as being an ali-

* Walter S. Masterman, *The Wrong Letter* (Methuen, 1926).

bi," says Gethryn at the conclusion of *The Rasp*—to the Chestertonian reversed-identities of *The Nursemaid Who Disappeared*. He is not free from faults; on two occasions he makes an apparent murder turn out to be a suicide, which seems (to me, at least) the single unforgiveable sin. But there are clues to spare, clues both material and psychological. And through everything runs this driving intensity: it kindles a blaze of emotion even when, as in *The Maze*, we read only the bare evidence at a coroner's inquest.

Murder Gone Mad, though it does not contain Anthony Gethryn, is presented here because there are some who consider it the best detective novel written by Mr. MacDonald or any other author. Like *The Greene Murder Case*, it deals with multiple killing; but observe the differences. The theme of *Murder Gone Mad* is Jack the Ripper in a modern garden suburb, where Gethryn's talents would be useless and only police organization can succeed. You are warned that this is no sham mania; it is the true blood-seeking; and even Superintendent Pike walks warily at the heels of "The Butcher." Its climax, after a miasma of terror, should raise your hair. The reader must walk warily too.

Walking warily, in the physical sense at least, is a necessity which nature has imposed on the person of Rex Stout's Nero Wolfe.

We would not have it otherwise. Wolfe looms vast and Buddha-like among the beer-bottle caps, with wiggling forefinger and inscrutable face. He was spry enough to kill a snake in *Fer de Lance*; he survived even the train-journey of *Too Many Cooks*. But in general we prefer to find him sitting behind his desk, while people rave at him, or absorbed with orchids on the top floor. In recent years there seems a conspiracy to say that his strength as a character is a little eclipsed by that of his assistant. I admire Nero Wolfe too much as an investigator, and like him too much as a person, tamely to hear him slighted in favor of the insufferable Archie Goodwin. Archie Goodwin has been described admiringly by Mr. Haycraft as "paint-fresh." Another quality of fresh paint, you may have noticed, is that it is wet.

But this again is a matter of personal taste. Even if a critic's dislike of Archie's type should be greater than my dislike (which is considerable), he would be compelled to admit that this latter-day Buster Brown is a character. Mr. Stout's literary skill could turn anybody into a character, just as he fashions clues from the most unlikely materials. During

Nero Wolfe's absences, he is no less nimble with the yellow cleaning-tissue which traps the muderer in *Red Threads,* or the gloves in the watermelon of *Crime on Her Hands.* All the same, we prefer the Gargantuan trickster to be on the scene.

"All we can do," Wolfe announces on one occasion, "is to try our luck on the possibilities until we find a fact that will allow only one interpretation. I detest alternatives."

The massive and sublime self-confidence of this remark would make Roger Sheringham stare. It would draw a goggle-eyed murmur of "Mais quel homme!" even from Hercule Poirot. As a general rule, the detective who seeks after facts with only one interpretation is chasing marsh-lights with a butterfly-net. Yet from Wolfe we accept it; he is like that. In the powerful story called *The League of Frightened Men,* with its tortured figure of Paul Chapin, you will find Wolfe the psychologist drawing a moral which might well be heeded by many writers of the too-hard-boiled school.

If any criticism may be made, it is an obvious one. There are some of us, maddened, who have occasionally wished Wolfe would stop arguing about who is going to pay his fee, and get on with the business in hand. True, this is an integral part of his nature. He would not be Nero Wolfe without it. He himself has met the objection, with icy and crushing dignity, by saying he is not in business for fun. We find the Neronian philosophy summed up during the investigation of Clyde Osgood's murder in *Some Buried Caesar.*

> "If all this is true—you knew it last night, didn't you? Why the hell didn't you spill it when the sheriff was there? When the cops were there on the spot?"
> "I represented no interest last night, sir."

But he ought to be doing these things for fun. Every really great detective does. This deplorable commercialism will ruin our sense of sport. "I play the game for the game's own sake," said Sherlock Holmes, who himself had a living to earn; yet there is only one instance (that matter of the Duke of Holdernesse's cheque) when the greatest of them all ever stepped out of character. Nor can Wolfe's attitude be attributed to modern American business methods. It is not recorded that Ellery Queen ever took a fee; and we can imagine the acid remarks that would have ensued if Markham had attempted to slip Philo Vance a retainer. In England, excluding Scotland Yard professionals like French and Alleyn and Bobby Owen, the total amount paid out to detectives cannot have exceeded twenty-five shillings in the past quarter of a century. It would be dangerous even to mention the subject to Gethryn or Dr. Priestley. As for Lord Peter Wimsey. . . .

Enough! That's enough. It brings us, finally on this list, to Lord Peter Wimsey and Dorothy L. Sayers.

However much the hero's love-affair has messed up the plot in other careers, it can scarcely be denied that his meeting with Harriet Vane was the making of Lord Peter Wimsey. Allowing a detective-hero violent emotion is either kill or cure. He emerges as a character, and emerges triumphantly, if he has always been more than a rack of neckties and a polished top-hat. Between the vapid-looking young man of *Whose Body?* in 1923, and the figure on the stage of the Comedy Theatre when the play-version of *Busman's Honeymoon* was produced in 1937, there is a world of difference.*

In *Strong Poison,* midway between those two dates, Wimsey met the dark-haired Harriet. With *Have His Carcase, Murder Must Advertise, The Nine Tailors* and *Gaudy Night* he became as a character progressively stronger, solider, less in need of mannerisms or eyeglass. It would be possible to maintain that the quality of the plots matured as well.

This implies no deep criticism of the earlier stories. Miss Sayers could not have written an undistinguished novel if she had tried. But the "murder" in *Clouds of Witness* (forgive this return to the subject) is proved to be suicide—amid elaborate incidents including a trans-Atlantic flight, a full-dress trial before the House of Lords, and a finale in which Wimsey, Parker, and the Duke of Denver are seen reeling tight as ticks through Parliament Square. The idea of committing murder with an empty hypodermic, though neatly handled in *Unnatural Death,* was not a new idea. There are times, in the short stories of *Lord Peter Views the Body,* when Wimsey becomes a jumping-jack figure flopping all over the place among secret societies and triple impersonations.

Most of all there was occasionally a wavering: a sense of brilliant talents employed at a job which had begun to bore the author, and half persuaded her to drop Wimsey altogether. Then the author wrote a story

* The play, by Miss Sayers and Miss M. St. Clair Byrne, antedated the novel. Those who say *Busman's Honeymoon* is no true detective story should have watched its fine construction when emphasized by the limitations of stage technique. The shattering of the lamp is the best sensation-denouement you will ever see.

in which Philip Boyes, the lover of Harriet Vane, was poisoned with arsenic in what looked like a squalid case. Harriet stood on trial at the Old Bailey; Wimsey saw Harriet; Miss Sayers seemed for the first time really to see Wimsey; and there ensued the series of fine novels we know so well.

If *Strong Poison* is chosen for this anthology, it is not necessarily as the best achievement. There will be many to maintain the superiority of *Have His Carcase,* with its last twist on how to establish the wrong time of death. Or of *The Nine Tailors,* where the chill of the fen-country, the boom of bells amid drifting snow, become so vital a part of the plot. Or of *Gaudy Night,* in which an overpowering sense of menace takes the place of a murder.

Will carpers kindly note, by the way, that this sense of menace—of the goblin that might get you—can be just as effective as any corpse? Have bodies, by all means. But they won't necessarily startle anyone. Whereas the writer of anonymous letters, the wrecker of rooms, the person who hangs up evil dummies as a symbol, can be magnified to terrifying proportions: just as, in *The Greene Murder Case* and *Murder Gone Mad,* it is the malignant mind that counts. This is the secret of *Gaudy Night.* All the characterizations, the working out of the love-affair between Wimsey and Harriet, must not blind us to the fact that it is plot, plot, and plot all the way.

Strong Poison, however, appears here because of its effectiveness in the more purely traditional style. Who killed Philip Boyes? And, if Harriet is innocent, how was it done? Because Harriet's fate depends on it, because Wimsey's peace of mind depends on it, everything is whittled down to the sharp urgency of the main questions. Each event, from the callous detachment of the spectators at the beginning— "Everybody looks like a murderer in a wax-works; have a choc?" —to the eating of a more sinister kind of confection when Wimsey confronts the murderer, rests on the eternal basis of who, how, and why. To answer those three questions of who, how, and why, to answer them in some novel and yet legitimate way, will always be the function of the detective story.

So we come to the end of a survey which has covered many years and no inconsiderable number of books. And now (I confess it) I am seized by a horrible temptation. My Better Nature, seraphic with up-turned eyes and halo, pleads and whispers, "No!" But the devil won't be denied; gleefully he beckons. I have enjoyed writing this introduction so much—in contrast, it is to be feared, to the labors of the weary reader—that I want to end it with a list of rules on What to Do and What Not to Do.

Admittedly, this has been done in full tabular style by Carolyn Wells, by S. S. Van Dine, by H. Douglas Thomson, by Basil Hogarth, by Howard Haycraft, and others. More cautious lines have been taken by Monsignor Knox and by Miss Sayers herself. And I think these two latter writers were wise.

Once the evidence has been fairly presented, there are very few things which are not permissible. The oath of the Detection Club, stern though it may sound, does not forbid the employment of conspiracies, gangs, death rays, ghosts, trap doors, mysterious Chinese or homicidal lunatics. It is not so harsh as that. It merely enjoins the writer to preserve "a seemly moderation" in the use of them. The only thing it rules out, and rightly rules out, is the use of mysterious poisons unknown to science.

Those who nail a manifesto to the wall, saying, "The beginner will do this, and must under no circumstances do that," are in many cases quoting not rules but prejudices. That is the danger. It is a prejudice, like my own prejudice against having the murder turn out to be a suicide; and should freely be indicated as such. With all due respect and admiration for those who have compiled lists, it would not be difficult to show that they were often giving dubious advice and sometimes talking arrant nonsense.

"Disguise," declares one writer—to take a single instance— "disguise, of course, went out with the bustle."

To which the answer is: "My dear sir, that is a prejudice. Furthermore, it's not true. Have the goodness to read, among other stories with whose titles half a page could be filled, G. K. Chesterton's 'The Dagger with Wings,' R. Austin Freeman's *The Mystery of Angelina Frood*, Q. Patrick's *S.S. Murder*, Ellery Queen's *The Dutch Shoe Mystery*, Philip MacDonald's *The Wraith*, E. C. Bentley and H. W. Allen's *Trent's Own Case*, Anthony Berkeley's *Top-Story Murder*, or Agatha Christie's *Three-Act Tragedy*. Disguise is one of the best weapons in the armory. The test of a device is not whether it is new or old; there's nothing new under the sun; the test is what novel twist can be put on it."

Here, then, is my own list of Dos and Don'ts: compiled partly from those of the writers quoted above and partly from my own heart's blood.

1. The criminal shall never turn out to be the detective, or any servant, or any character whose thoughts we have been allowed to share.

2. The criminal shall never at any time be under serious suspicion until the unmasking. If you haven't the ingenuity to keep his identity a secret until the end, at least pretend you have. Even if the reader outguesses you, and your thunderbolt ending doesn't come off, the effect is far more satisfying than if you apologize for your murderer by "clearing" him in an early chapter.

3. The crime shall be the work of one person. While the murderer in some instances may be allowed to have a confederate, you will ruin your story if two or three or four people are dragged in as accomplices. The essence of a detective story is that the one guilty man shall fool the seven innocent; not that the one innocent shall be fooled by the seven guilty.

4. The crime shall be clean-cut. If a character disappears and is assumed to be murdered, state frankly what has happened to him. If he hasn't been murdered it's a pity; but the reader has a right to a clear stating of the problem.

Those are four golden maxims. In each one I believe. And each one you will find shattered—shattered admirably, shattered to bits, shattered by a mighty hammer—in the "best" detective novels, while the reader wishes to do nothing but applaud. Because they are not really rules; they are only prejudices.

The greatest trap into which a critic can fall is to maintain that something is being "done" in the current year, as though there were a style in shrouds as well as in hats, or to maintain that something else has gone out of fashion. When Carolyn Wells's *The Technique of the Mystery Story* was first published in 1913, the late Miss Wells was already talking about outworn devices. But nothing ever has gone out of fashion, and nothing ever will, provided only that the old trick can be worked in a new way. Yesterday's fashion may not be today's; but it may be none the worse for that. On the contrary, it may be a devil of a sight better.

So let them write their stories, the hopeful young men and women!

Let them not be frightened by that worst bogey of all, the feeling that they have got to be innovators. Let them remember that the real test of their mental skill is in the drive and nimbleness and strategy of their play; it does not consist in putting the goal posts in the middle of the field or dashing through half the game with a ball that isn't here. And you and I, serene in our armchairs as we read a new detective story, can continue blissfully in the old game, the great game, the grandest game in the world.

SECOND THOUGHTS – AFTER 17 YEARS

I well remember when and how the above outburst was written. It was written in London during the cold and gusty spring of 1946, and in my flat on Haverstock Hill. Despite an acute housing shortage, I had obtained that flat for reasons quite apart from my Scottish luck. When I moved into it in 1943, Adolf Hitler still walked the earth. He had yet to unleash the Little Blitz, the flying bombs, the rockets, and other drolleries from his inexhaustable sense of humor. But we were all expecting something of the sort. And nobody except your obedient servant was stupid enough to want a flat on the top floor.

If I were to write again of favorite detective novels, should I change anything above? Not one sentiment, not one author. The ensuing seventeen years have produced no writers who are better, nor any (tell it not in Gath) one-half so good. It may be that for four of the authors I should choose a different novel. A. E. W. Mason, for instance, might be better represented by *The House of the Arrow;* Philip MacDonald by *The Rasp;* Ellery Queen by *The Chinese Orange Mystery;* and Dorothy L. Sayers by *Strong Poison.*

But this is a minor matter; it is the author and his detective who count. "Then you still believe all that?" will be the whisper of kindly friends. "Haven't you learned anything in all these years?" Since I have learned wisdom in no other respect, it is useless to hope for it here. And a man should always be willing to defend his prejudices. As he gets on in years, those prejudices may constitute the most satisfactory sum total of all the things he has—or is.

Ellery Queen's Mystery Magazine, March 1963

READERS OF Carr's book reviews know that he enjoyed many varieties of crime fiction, including not only fair-play detective stories but also spy novels, police procedurals and suspense stories. A few years after he wrote "The Grandest Game in the World," he discovered that he also liked *some* hard-boiled private-eye stories: "Once upon a time, mind you, I didn't like these. I didn't like them, that is, until suddenly—amid a spinning of blood, brass knuckles and flying bodies—I discovered that the author was calmly inserting the evidence into the bureau drawer. His secret was his pace and his timing; and those, as a rule, mean a thundering good story." He objected, however, to writers who claimed that they were producing detective stories but neglected to devise a coherent plot. In 1950 Carr wrote that if Raymond Chandler "could add the fatigue of construction and clues . . . then one day he may write a good novel." Dashiell Hammett, on the other hand, "has never disdained clues and has always given them fairly." In short, a detective novel, whether probable or improbable, realistic or fantastic, hard-boiled or a chess problem, must be fundamentally a good story . . . the kind of story that John Dickson Carr wrote for almost fifty years.